LAUREN CHILD first introduced the character of
Ruby Redfort in her three award-winning, bestselling
CLARICE BEAN novels. Since then she has been inundated with
letters from fans asking for the RUBY REDFORT books.
And it must have worked, because this is
number three in the series.

Lauren is also the creator of the phenomenally successful
CHARLIE AND LOLA books, as well as Associate Producer on
the TV show of the same name. She has sold millions of books
around the world and won many prizes, including the
Smarties Prize (four times), the Kate Greenaway Medal
and the Red House Children's Book Award.

The RUBY REDFORT series features codes and puzzles created
with the help of super-geek consultant **Marcus du Sautoy**,
Simonyi Professor for the Public Understanding of Science at
Oxford University and all-round genius.

LAUREN CHILD

CATCH YOUR DEATH

HarperCollins *Children's Books*

First published in hardback in Great Britain by HarperCollins Children's Books 2013
HarperCollins Children's Books is a division of HarperCollins Publishers Ltd
77-85 Fulham Palace Road, Hammersmith, London W6 8JB

For Ruby Redfort games, puzzles, videos and more, visit:
www.rubyredfort.com

Visit Lauren Child at **www.milkmonitor.com**

1

Copyright © Lauren Child 2013

Series design and illustrations by David Mackintosh

ISBN: 978-0-00-733410-0

Printed and bound in Australia by Griffin Press

For **Peps**

'Smell is one of the most powerful triggers of the human memory.

An odour is a portal to the past, instantly transporting the smeller back to some long forgotten time. The conscious mind might be unaware of the memory, but, just as smelling salts can rouse a person from a dead faint, so smell rouses the subconscious and awakens the dormant memory.'

DR DAVIDSON WALTER F MACKINTOSH PHD CBE, *Ulwin University, co-writer of the highly regarded textbook,* Nasal Passages

The Abandoned One

THE GIRL OPENED HER EYES AND BLINKED UP AT THE
SKY. From where she lay, curled on the pine-needle floor, she
could see pure blue, vivid behind a latticework of black branches.
Sensing that she was alone, the girl sat up and looked around.
She listened for footsteps, voices, but heard no human sound
at all, just the hot lazy birds and insects buzzing and zithering.
The picnic things were still laid out and a chain of ants was busy
deconstructing the leftovers. She picked up the novel which lay
where her father had sat, *The Abandoned One – A Thriller*, and
she began to read.

But an hour later and almost halfway through, her parents
still had not returned. Had there been some emergency? Was her
father looking for help? Her mother waving at passing planes?
Had they both been devoured by bears or some other wild thing –
some terrible beast that lurked in the faraway forest? Or had they
simply forgotten her, left her here? Her four-year-old imagination

began to run wild, egged on by the pages of the book.

She calmed herself, took deep breaths, inhaling the forest aroma. The scent of the pine was a comfort, reassuring and familiar, and her common sense drifted back to her. She was aware that the most likely explanation was probably the actual one: her parents had gone to the river to fetch water and had got sidetracked.

She waited, stayed exactly where she was, remembering this was the advice given by the yellow survival manual that sat on top of her father's bureau. But time ticked on and night began to fall and no one came back. She stood up and pushed her feet into her boots, tying them carefully, doubling the knot so they would not come undone.

She pulled on her red waterproof mac with its sensible hood, just in case the weather broke – in the wilderness you could never be sure. She took the winding path down to where the river must certainly be, and as she walked she breathed deeply, filling her tiny lungs with pure forest air, and as she inhaled she smelled a smell so delicious, so like perfume, she couldn't help but follow where her nose wanted to lead her.

She left the path and twisted through the dark trees and the tangles of briars and fallen branches, and came to a place where the moon could reach if only the cloud would let it. Ahead of her was deathly dark, and so it was with great caution that she stepped into black. As she did so, she felt her coat snag on something sharp; she pulled, but it pulled back – the tiny girl now caged in thorns.

Trapped.

She sensed something ahead of her, quite near. Something alive, something dangerous, something bad. The cloud moved, the moon shone and the girl gasped. For barely three feet away, staring at her with the palest blue eyes and the sharpest glistening teeth, was a wolf.

The girl stood very still, watching the beast, its gaze fixed upon her. She waited; she closed her eyes to block it out. Her heart beating fast and her breathing shallow and unsteady. She listened to the creature and heard the same sound, the same panic, the child and the wolf both locked in fear.

Slowly, the girl began to unpick herself from the brambles, pulling the thorns one by one from her legs, twisting out of her little hooded coat until it was all the briars could claim. She stepped out of the thicket and saw what held the wolf; it was trapped in an ugly mouth of iron teeth. Her four-year-old instinct took hold: it told her to free the desperate wild thing and so, picking up a rock, she struck the trap over and over until it gave, and the bleeding paw of the wolf was released.

For a moment the beast looked at the girl, its eyes in hers, hers in its, and for just a second they knew each other's thoughts.

In the distance a voice called out, two voices. 'Ruby, Ruby! Where are you?'

The wolf held her gaze just a second longer. Its beautiful eyes, crystal blue and ringed with violet, gleamed; then it turned and melted into the darkness of the forest.

And the wolf, like a wisp of smoke, was gone.

An Ordinary Kid

WHEN RUBY WAS SIX, she was entered by the Junior Chess Club, known as The Pawns, in a local city tournament. Game one, she found herself drawn against Mr Karocovskey. Not the opponent anyone would wish to be sitting opposite for their very first public game, at least not unless that person wanted to get home early so they could watch *Tiny Toons*. Mr Karocovskey had been a big champion in his heyday and had played chess against many famous Russians. Now he was an old man with a sharp brain, not as sharp as it had been, but he was still a grandmaster and the best chess player in the state.

Ruby looked at him across the table. He had a nice face – his eyes, watery and grey, looked like they might have seen the woes of the world. This man knew what it was to yearn for something and struggle to get it.

She could see what he was going to do ten moves ahead. She lost the game skilfully. Mr Karocovskey was very generous about his win; he smiled kindly, shook her hand and thanked her for being such a challenging opponent. He was a gracious winner, a good sport.

Seventeen-year-old Kaspar Peterson smirked. He wasn't surprised she'd lost: he didn't see there was any way this squirt of a six-year-old girl was going to win against a champion – she wasn't going to win against anyone. Ruby Redfort challenged Kaspar to a game. He casually accepted.

She beat him in five easy moves. He was an ungracious loser, a bad sport.

Ruby had been reluctant to beat old Mr Karocovskey; she had no such qualms about thrashing Kaspar Peterson.

Some several years later...

Chapter 1.
A positive mental attitude

'THE ONLY THING TO FEAR IS THE BLUE ALASKAN WOLF, which by the way doesn't exist.'

These words were spoken by Samuel Colt, a former special agent turned environmentalist. Now he had taken up work as a Spectrum survival trainer. He was a tall, well-built man, getting on in years, but still in good shape, the kind of guy you wanted to have on side, the kind of guy you would be relieved to have show up, and the kind of guy you would hope to see standing on the horizon if you found yourself lost – unless, of course, he was the reason you had tried to get lost in the first place. If so, your heart might sink more than a little.

Colt had a large grey moustache and shoulder-length hair. He wore a wide-brimmed hat, and clothes that gave him the look of a trapper – he wouldn't have looked out of place had he travelled back in time a hundred years. He had seen it all and survived it all and he knew what he was talking about. There was nothing unfriendly about Sam Colt, a little straight talking perhaps, but never cruel.

'Cruelty has no place in the wilderness. You sometimes need to be single-minded, tough as an old lasso, but you don't gotta be cruel.' He believed in that. 'You don't kill unless you have to and if you have to you make it quick.'

'Blue wolves you don't gotta concern yourselves with,' he continued, 'but regular wolves? Be prepared for those fellas. My best advice: avoid them. You don't seek 'em out, you don't feed 'em, you don't pet 'em, you don't look 'em in the eye. That goes double for bears; bears are a whole lot more trouble than wolves and wolves are trouble enough.'

'Who's going to be dumb enough to feed a bear or a wolf?' whispered trainee Lowe.

'You'd be surprised,' said Colt.

Samuel Colt, among all his other fine attributes, had very acute hearing and trainee Lowe was somewhat taken aback.

'You don't clean up after a meal, that's feeding; you're leaving a trail from him to you and, I assure you, you don't want to do that.'

'But what if you do run into a pack of wolves?' asked trainee Dury. 'What then?'

Today was a theory day and the trainees were indoors, taking notes and asking questions. There was a lot of studying to do, though Colt's job was mainly to teach the practical stuff. He preferred that: being outdoors was natural – inside, not so good.

Sam Colt scratched his head and sighed. 'If you should find yourself in this predicament, then there are a few ways you might handle things.' He scanned the trainees to see who might know. 'Redfort? Give me two pieces of good advice.'

Ruby leaned back in her chair. 'If you're able to, you wanna get up a tree pretty darned fast, but don't count on the wolves leaving you to enjoy the view; they've been known to sit it out, waiting for people to come down. Crocodiles behave the same way, though if you have a wolf on your tail then you're unlikely to have a crocodile after you, so I guess you can tick that worry off your list.' She paused before adding, 'Only run for it if you're certain you're gonna reach that tree before the wolf reaches you. Running gets it all charged up – brings out the hunting instinct.'

Colt nodded. 'That's correct.'

Ruby knew all this from the many books she had read over the years. She had written up some of these survival tips, the ones she considered particularly useful, in a pea-green notebook. Most of them she now knew off by heart and, as Colt went through the various dos and don'ts of outdoor survival, Ruby found herself mentally replaying what she had learned.

SURVIVAL SUGGESTION #7:

Dealing with dangerous wildlife

1. WOLVES

SURVIVAL RULE 1:
Keep a clean camp. *Wolves have an exceptional sense of smell: they can smell prey from up to 1.75 miles.*

SURVIVAL RULE 2:
Keep a fire burning. *Wolves don't like fire.*

SURVIVAL RULE 3:
Do not run. *Unless you are sure you can run at over thirty miles an hour (no one has yet).*

SURVIVAL RULE 4:
Stick with the group. *Wolves are less likely to attack if you are in a large group than if you are alone, so don't wander off by yourself.*

'There are many theories about these creatures,' Colt continued. 'Some say, in places where they've been aggressively hunted, wolves remain wary of man, preferring to avoid any human interaction at all. Others say that the wolf is a ruthless predator and will attack if it gets any opportunity. Either way, it don't matter. My advice is the same: keep away from wolves and try to make sure they keep away from you.'

Ruby was thinking back to her own wolf encounter a long time ago on Wolf Paw Mountain: she had not followed any kind of advice, but had done the very worst thing as far as the textbooks were concerned, yet she had lived to tell the tale – how, she had no idea.

Unlike the other trainee agents, Ruby Redfort was not sleeping over at Mountain Ranch Camp. This was due to the fact that, unlike them, she was still attending Junior High. This made her task a little more complicated than anyone else's: she was still expected to make it to class each school day, get her homework in on time and show up every afternoon for survival school.

To make it more complicated still, no one, not the school, not her family or friends, was aware that she had been recruited by the secret agency known to only a few insiders (and a handful of evil geniuses) as Spectrum.

The division Ruby worked for, Spectrum 8, was run by LB, a woman who took no nonsense and no prisoners. She was not someone who tolerated mistakes or stupidity, and mistakes as far as LB was concerned were stupidity. For this reason it was credit to Ruby that, even though she had made more than one or two errors in her short Spectrum life, she was still an agent who had lived to tell the tale (had there been someone she was authorised to tell it to).

It wasn't easy, but Ruby Redfort wasn't going to complain about it – all she had ever wanted was to work for a secret agency, not just as a code breaker, but as a field agent, out there facing danger and experiencing adventure. She had a lot of tests to take before this dream would become a reality and she was determined not to blow it.

So, every day, Ruby left school, dropping by her home before heading to a secret location where she would get picked up by a Spectrum agency helicopter and dropped at the mountain camp. Every evening the helicopter would take her home again.

That night, after she had got home and changed back into her regular clothes, jeans and T-shirt (this one bearing the words *trust me, I'm a doctor*), Ruby went downstairs to the kitchen to grab some dinner.

Her mother frowned a little when she caught sight of the T-shirt, but decided to let it go. 'Your hair looks nice honey,' she said.

'How was school?' asked her father.

Ruby shrugged. 'Oh, you know, schooly.'

'Did the *Evening Bark* arrive yet?' asked Brant.

'I don't know, I didn't notice,' said Ruby.

'I'll go see,' he said. Brant Redfort went to the front step to pick up the evening newspaper, the *Twinford Hound* (the Redforts always *referred* to it as the *Evening Bark* because it tended to be full of loud and sensational news).

Brant walked into the kitchen, reading the paper, his brow a little furrowed.

'Bad news?' asked Sabina.

'Warning of forest fires,' sighed Brant. 'The mountains and canyons are tinder dry and unless we get some rain the chances of the forests going up in flames are high.'

'Oh dear,' said Sabina, 'I don't like the sound of that, not one little bit.'

Brant's face brightened. 'Hey honey, you're going to like the sound of this.'

'Oh yes?' said Sabina, sitting up in her chair as if she needed to really concentrate.

'Melrose Dorff are having a launch.'

'Oh fabulous!' exclaimed Sabina. 'What are they launching?'

'The Lost Perfume of Marie Antoinette 1770,' said Brant.

'It's French.'

'Oh, French, I like the sound of that!'

'Didn't I tell you that you would? Not that a whole gallon of perfume could smell better than you do,' he said, sniffing Sabina's neck.

'Oh brother!' muttered Ruby.

Brant continued reading: *"Madame Swann, perfumer to the rich and tasteful, famous for her discerning nose, has brought her recreation of Queen Marie Antoinette's exclusive perfume from Paris to the West Coast. Let Them Smell Roses, the Lost Perfume of Marie Antoinette 1770, will be launched at a fabulous soirée where attendees will also be able to view some of the ill-fated Queen's most precious jewellery. An exciting announcement will be made on the night – it will be strictly an invitation-only event."*

Sabina looked forlorn and then puzzled. 'But why haven't we been invited?' she said. 'I mean we usually are.'

This was an understatement: the Redforts always were.

'Don't worry sweetheart. I'm sure there'll be a logical explanation. Maybe they haven't mailed the invitations yet.'

'I hope you're right Brant. I don't know what I'd do if I didn't get invited to this particular launch party.'

Ruby rolled her eyes, but said nothing.

After she had wolfed down her supper, she went back up to

her room. She was keen to do more reading before she turned in for the night. She had been studying hard for the past weeks – reading everything she could, absorbing it, digesting it and living by it.

What she didn't know was that it was precisely this rigid adherence to the facts she had learned and the rules she had made that was going to lead to her downfall.

Chapter 2.
The whole foraging deal

ON DAY SEVEN SAM COLT BEGAN BY TALKING ABOUT
BASIC SURVIVAL SKILLS.

He hunkered down and motioned for them to gather round.

'Anyone want to tell me the two most important things needed
in order to survive out in the wild... other than water?'

They had spent the first week mastering the skill of locating
water, how to ensure the water was safe and how to make water
when there was none.

'Fire and shelter,' said Ruby.

'Correct again Redfort. Fire is your friend, except when it
gets out of control. You have a responsibility never to let your fire
get away from you. Forest fires you can't always prevent, but you
can ensure your campfire doesn't cause one.'

Ruby didn't need reminding about this warning.

It was:

SURVIVAL SUGGESTION #1:

Basic Skills

2. FIRE

SURVIVAL RULE 5:

Only build a fire in a place where you can keep it contained.

'Once you've found the right place to *build* your fire,' Colt went on, 'and once you've secured the surrounding area, tinder is what you'll be needing next. Basically, you wanna find stuff that burns real easy and real quick. Tree bark, dried grass, paper – even cotton from your clothing if you're desperate – all make good tinder. Or you could crush up pine cones or birds' nests. Next on the list is kindling, then slow-burning fuel, meaning logs. Once you have all your materials lined up ready, all you gotta do is set fire to 'em... easier said than done.'

He smiled and walked towards the door. 'Since making fire is just about the most important skill you need, you better get practising.'

The trainees all followed Sam Colt outside and spent the rest of that day trying to make a spark. As Colt had warned, it was 'easier said than done'. All in all, it took about a week to master fire.

Day fourteen, after school, and Ruby was sitting in the kitchen of Green-wood House, the Redforts' stylish, modern Twinford home, making herself a little snack. The toaster pinged and up popped her two slices of toast: both were the bearers of unhappy news. Unlike most people's toasters, Ruby Redfort's doubled as a fax machine and was capable of delivering important messages from Spectrum when you had just sat down to eat a delicious snack.

Ruby picked up the toast. The message was grilled into one side.

The first piece said:

'Foraging: one hour from now.'

The other said:

'Don't spoil your appetite.'

Ruby had been waiting for this day to arrive with a particular sort of dread. Having done some reading up on foraging, she couldn't say it really appealed to her. She looked at the clock: she still had forty minutes before she needed to head off, still time to ask Mrs Digby's expert advice on the subject.

Mrs Digby had been with the Redfort family since before Ruby was born and with Ruby's mother's family forever or thereabouts.

'I know all there is to know about mushrooms and toadstools, which ones will kill you and which won't,' Mrs Digby said.

'You know a whole lot about the wild Mrs Digby, that's for darn sure.'

'The Digbys have always lived off the land and have always had it hard. We had it hard when we sailed over with the Mayflower and we've had it hard ever since, years and years of hardship and years of living off the free stuff that nature provided, no matter how disgusting, which it's not unreasonable to say since it certainly can be at times.'

'Just how poor were you Mrs Digby?' Ruby asked this question not because she didn't know the answer, but because the housekeeper enjoyed telling her.

'Not a bean to rub against another bean. Which is why we had to forage. Mostly it was a cornucopia of goodness, but occasionally it was enough to turn a sailor's stomach.'

Mrs Digby was an excellent cook (though not a fashionable one) and she knew how to rustle up a supper fit for a president from 'a dried-up onion and a pile of leaves', if that's all the ingredients there were.

'Never turn your nose up at an edible mushroom. They might look like pixie furniture, but I've always told you Ruby: eat your mushrooms and you won't go far wrong – full of protein is what they are. That's why all these vegetarian types go cuckoo for 'em.'

Ruby checked her book. 'You're not wrong. It says here, mushrooms are rich in most vitamins, especially B and C, and they contain nearly all the major minerals, particularly potassium and phosphorus.'

Mrs Digby was a little surprised and, in her own words, tickled that Ruby was taking an interest in the theory of food and cookery, though she would have been more tickled if Ruby would take on the practical side too.

'Since you're so interested in cooking all of a sudden, how about you take over stirring this pot,' said Mrs Digby, 'while I read the funnies for five minutes?'

Ruby checked her watch. Still thirty-nine minutes before she had to be at the helipad. She rolled her eyes and got stirring.

Back at camp, some hours later, Ruby was busy trying to concoct a stew out of some unappealing roots and some ugly-looking fungi – Colt assured her none of it was poisonous; it was important to get this right since if you got it wrong you might wind up as extinct as the Blue Alaskan wolf.

'I hope you all have understood the need to be getting *au fait* with roots and berries and wild growing things,' said Colt. 'Things you might not ordinarily want to put under your nose, let alone on your tongue.'

Ruby wriggled slightly in her seat; for all her research, one of her least favourite things about survival training was the whole eating deal. She wasn't particularly crazy about chowing down on roots and foliage, nor did she like the idea of resorting to grubs when desperation struck. During the hours of training, she longed for her CheeseOs and her Slush-pops, but what she yearned for more than anything was her banana milk, hard to find in the wild.

Today she had spent several hours foraging and several more trying to work out what to do with this unappetising harvest. Now the meal was as cooked as it was ever going to be, she closed her eyes and raised her fork to her mouth.

'Redfort, I'm guessing you don't know the difference between a toadstool and a mushroom... or perhaps you're done with surviving?' The voice was one Ruby recognised from her dive training in Hawaii.

'Holbrook, if you're trying to get your hands on my chow, you're outta luck buster.'

'You call that supper Redfort? I'd sooner boil up my socks than chow down on what you've cooked up.'

'I'm sure they'd taste good 'n' cheesy,' said Ruby.

Despite the way they spoke to each other, they actually got on like a forest fire.

Ruby didn't poison herself with her stew, though she couldn't help feeling that Holbrook's socks indeed might have been less disgusting. Even the cube of Hubble-Yum she spent the next hour chewing on couldn't quite eradicate the taste of that stew.

She was relieved when the helicopter dropped her home late that night and she could raid Mrs Digby's larder. She found a tray of fresh-baked cookies with a note from the housekeeper that read: hands off kid.

The following day's challenge was to build a shelter. Colt spent the morning trying to impress upon his recruits just how important it was to keep warm and dry when out in the wilderness.

'You get yourself soaked to the skin, and cold as an iced-up river, and you're exposing yourself to all kinds of trouble. You need to build a shelter and get dry. The act of building the shelter will keep you warm. You don't get warm and dry and you're nigh on likely to get sick, and if you get sick in the wilds that makes you vulnerable and when you're vulnerable you have a pretty fair chance of dying.'

His manner was gruff, no frills, which didn't matter because survival didn't require frills.

'Knives, flashlights, matches, waterproofs, they're all frills,' was something Colt might say.

Holbrook and Ruby teamed up for the shelter building; they also worked together on the canoe hollowing: both disciplines took a lot of concentration, not just energy but skill. Once they were done, they took the new canoe out on the lake to see if it would float; it did.

'You know what Redfort? I take my hat off to you – you're not the sap I thought you were gonna be,' laughed Holbrook.

'I guess that's lucky Holbrook, because you're a deal more feeble than I'd expected and I hadn't expected much.'

This was when Holbrook decided to roll the canoe and dunk them both in the lake. It rolled without any trouble and though

Ruby was kind of mad at him for getting the better of her she couldn't help being sort of proud that this incredible boat had been created with her own two hands – with the help of Holbrook of course; she had to concede that.

Ruby Redfort had always been sure of her mental abilities, but had not realised she could turn her hand to other more practical skills. Right now, sitting soaked through in her hand-carved canoe, she felt like the world was her oyster.

It was a good feeling. But not one that was going to last.

Chapter 3.
The ways of the wild

RUBY HAD BEEN OUT AT MOUNTAIN RANCH CAMP on and off, travelling back and forth, for approximately a month and her survival skills were coming along. She and Holbrook passed all their practical tests without a hint of trouble.

Ruby was determined to excel and in a few short weeks had got as knowledgeable as Holbrook ever was, and Holbrook was no slouch. She felt satisfied that she knew the theory of survival, back to front and top to bottom; she was competitive and she was a hard worker, but no matter how much work she put in, Sam Colt would always say the same thing: *'Redfort, you're getting stuck on detail and it's making you miss the whole big picture.'*

Skills that involved patience were not a problem for Ruby Redfort: patience was a virtue she had been born with. She could contentedly sit and wait for single drips of rainwater to fill a drinking glass if this was what it took. She could build a shelter that was really pretty comfortable and light a fire within about ten minutes. With all these tasks, she understood the need for patience and perseverance. This determined attitude was of great benefit to her since patience and perseverance were pretty essential virtues when it came to the tasks of survival.

Strength wasn't a big problem either; sure, she wasn't as strong as some of her co-trainees – she was, after all, only thirteen – but what she might have lacked in sheer brute strength she made up for with her technique, learning how to move heavy logs and branches, rocks and earth by rolling, balancing, pivoting. All this theory she stored in her head, confident she had the information squirrelled away for that time when it might save her life.

However, as good as Ruby was at these practical tasks, and although she had read and stored about as much knowledge as any survivalist, she couldn't seem to convince Sam Colt that she was able to tune herself into the wild itself.

'There are some things that ain't in any book Redfort.' He paused. 'It's like my pal, Bradley Baker, used to say: "Sometimes the best way to think about a problem is not to think about it."'

Talking to any outsider about Spectrum was strictly forbidden, but despite this hard and fast rule there was one person who did know about Ruby's double life and his name was Clancy Crew.

Clancy was Ruby's closest friend and most loyal ally; he could sniff out a secret at a hundred paces and it had taken him no time at all to discover something was up and even less time to get Ruby to spill the beans.

Ruby had broken a pretty big Spectrum rule here, Spectrum rule number one being **keep it zipped**, but on the other hand, telling Clancy Crew she was an undercover agent was like confessing to a priest or a doctor: the information would go no further. Clancy Crew never, *ever* told: he was like a human vault. Dangle Clancy over a river full of piranha and he would never say a single word; every last finger would have disappeared before he even began to open his mouth.

Ruby wished she could talk to Clancy at length about what her trainer considered a gap in her ability, but Clancy was away with his father on some lengthy ambassadorial tour and so they had only managed a few snatched phone conversations. It wasn't enough time to go into any detail, to really explain to Clancy how she felt, how puzzled she was that her trainer thought she was in some way lacking in understanding. In any case, it wasn't easy to explain anything on the phone and they mainly ended up discussing how mad Clancy was at his ambassador dad for getting him all dressed up in stupid blazers and ridiculous polished loafers.

'What next?' Clancy would whine. 'Little tartan bow ties?'

On this, the final week of training, Ruby dialled Clancy's number and hoped he would be there to pick up. She had just got home from school and was expected to dine with her parents. and their friends the Humberts, before being helicoptered back out to the training camp: it made for a long day.

'So how's it going Rube?' Clancy asked from his hotel room in Washington.

'OK. I think I'm doing pretty well. I mean I know stuff, it's just I don't seem to know stuff,' she replied.

'I think I know what you mean,' said Clancy, who did know what she meant: he was sharp at picking up on things that weren't clear.

'I just don't know how to fix it,' she said. 'I mean my instructor says things to me like, "You need to throw away the handbook Redfort." But why? Why do I wanna throw away the handbook?'

'I think he's talking about instinct Rube. You gotta know the rules and then you gotta forget the rules, you know?'

'No,' said Ruby.

It didn't make any sense: she had spent thirteen years assembling a little book of life rules, a sort of guide to navigate her way through each and every day, so why would she ignore them now, just when her very survival was being put to the test?

Ruby thought about this as she travelled back to camp that evening.

It was true. She really didn't understand what Clancy was trying to explain or what Samuel Colt was trying to tell her. The previous day Colt had sat her down and tried again to make her understand.

'You gotta learn to use your instincts,' he said.

'I use my instincts,' countered Ruby.

'No you don't. You approach things like you're reading a book of rules, like there's one way, but out in the wild stuff changes a lot and everything can't always be fixed the way you wanna fix it.' Sam Colt looked at her, his eyes barely visible under the wide brim of his hat. 'I've been around a long time and, if there's one thing that nature's taught me, it's to never kid yourself that you're in charge.'

Again she stared at him like this made no sense at all.

'Don't meet nature head on, walk alongside. Don't try and control stuff, just go with what you got. It's all about adapting to circumstances. Circumstances change, you change with 'em.' He looked at her hard, trying to discern whether she had the faintest idea what he was talking about. 'You can have your plans B, C and D, but they ain't no good to you if nature decides otherwise.'

Colt wasn't wrong about this; in fact, just six months ago, two Spectrum agents had perished after their tent had blown away in a blizzard and Colt couldn't help wondering why two highly trained professionals had relied on something so flimsy out in such dangerous terrain where the elements ruled.

He lived day by day, hour to hour. 'You can try and predict what might happen next, but don't imagine it's gonna come out that way just because you thought you'd like it to.' *The only certainty is there is no certainty* was a sort of Samuel Colt mantra and his rule one, two and three: the rule he lived by.

The rule Ruby lived by was not unrelated. **RULE 1: YOU CAN NEVER BE COMPLETELY SURE WHAT MIGHT HAPPEN NEXT.** So why did she find this all so difficult? For the first time in her life, Ruby was failing. And she didn't like it one bit.

AFTER SEVERAL WEEKS OF INTENSIVE TRAINING, camp was finally at an end; next would come the test. Sam Colt spent the last day preparing the recruits.

'You'll all be on your own here and you'll have to navigate the terrain and take on the environmental challenges alone – that's alongside any challenges set by Spectrum. Base camp is in woodland, but where exactly is your problem. You reach there, you clock in, mission over. Your task is to make it by sun-up three days from now.'

He took a deep breath. 'I'm not looking to scare anyone here, quite the contrary, but the law of survival is pretty basic: you gotta believe in your ability to stay alive.' Samuel Colt had a pared-down approach to life and he was tough as winter earth. He firmly believed that all you need to survive is a positive mental attitude.

He looked at all their faces, some a little wary, even anxious, some confident, others like poker players, betraying nothing.

'Unpredictable encounters with wild animals aside, your chances are good so long as you hold onto this.' He tapped his head. 'And I don't mean physically, though course that helps. You gotta believe death ain't an option. Survival means getting out alive. And getting out alive means that on the most basic level you succeeded.'

Everyone went home that night and tried to get as much sleep as they could, aware that for the next few days sleep might not be found so easily.

The next day the trainees were each issued their mission briefing, handed their survival packs and offered a last chance to back out.

No one backed out.

A Spectrum agent, one Ruby didn't recognise, had appeared from nowhere and was now handing out brown envelopes containing their instructions. Ruby pulled the tag which ran down the side of the envelope and pulled out the brown paper contained inside.

On it was written a code.

Ú¥ÖLWÌ LÈßÐþR ÐþÈÖ¥ß ÖÌLHÈt RÇÈþñÌ KÖÚñWñ ñÄRtRñ
ÌÈ××××.

ñÖÈHtÖ ÈRHtÐş ÌÈ£ÖÈH ttÄMÌÒ ñÚñÖÚ¥ LÌWLÈÈ ŞÄñÇRÄ
H×××××.

KMÄÈ¥Ú RÖ¥ÄWÖ tÈHtñÇ RÄHÚÈŞ ñÈññÄÐ LRtŞÚÈ ÄRHÖŞÈ
ÖR£MÈH tÄRRÇÖ L×××××.

ÌŞWMÈH tRHÖŞÈ ŞÖÄŞÇR ÈHtVRÈ ÌRñÄÐÈ ÈtHtRt ÌÖtÄŞþ
Öt××××. *

KMÈÄÚ¥ ÖR¥ÄWÖ tÈHtÖñ ŞÈÐÇVR ÈÌRñÄÐ ŞÇRÖŞt Ì×××××.

LWKÄÐñ WÖÈÄŞM tRÌÚLñ tÚ¥ÖRÈ ÄñßÐÈ¥ ÖÈHtÄÈ ÄWLRtL
£×××××.

ñ£ÐÌÄÐ ÌÐHñÈñ ÄÇÈÖñÄ ÐþLÄÐÐ ÈtÌÌÚL ñtÚ¥ÖR ÇÄÈHÈH
tñÖLWÐ ÖÄÐGÈÈ Ð×××××.

ÖtñÇÈÌ ñÚñÖÖ£ tÖÖtŞß ÄÈMÇÄþ.

ÖÇÇKLñ Ì×××××; ÌÖMñÌŞ ŞÈLÇÐt MÖþÈ××.

ÄRWGÌñ ñ×××××: £ÌÚ¥ÖÈ ÄRþtŞÐ tÈÖÌÚR GLtñŞÈH tRHÖŞÈ
Ú¥ÖLWÌ LVHÄÈÄ £ÐÈÌLñ ÌÚ¥ÖRÌ ÖMñÌŞŞ

* ÈHtRHÖ ŞÈLWÌL ÈßRtRÐ ÈÈñÚÖt ÈHtñÇR ÄH¥ßtÈ ÄRÖHññ
ÄtÈG××.

Ruby looked at it, frowning, for a few seconds. Then she smiled. Whoever had created the code had divided the message into six-letter chunks to make it seem more complicated than it was, but she soon saw what she was dealing with.

The clue was the frequency of certain letters.

In English Es and Ts appear a great deal more often than most other letters and Zs and Qs are in comparison pretty rare. Ruby surmised this was a substitution cipher, therefore whatever symbol was taking the place of E would come up most often, followed by T, then O, then A. The clumps of Xs she figured were just there to confuse so she ignored them.

She began substituting the most common letters, and soon saw familiar groups, like E, H and T and U, Y and O. She paused for a moment; the substitution gave her the right letters, but no recognisable words:

UYOLWI LEBDPR DPEOYB OILHET RCEPNI KOUNWN NARTRN IEXXXX.

NOEHTO ERHTDS IEFOEH TTAMIO NUNOUY LIWLEE SANCRA HXXXXX.

KMAEYU ROYAWO TEHTNC RAHUES NENNAD LRTSUE ARHOSE ORFMEH TARRCO LXXXXX.

ISWMEH TRHOSE SOASCR EHTVRE IRNADE ETHTRT IOTASP
OTXXXX.*

KMEAUY ORYAWO TEHTON SEDCVR EIRNAD SCROST
IXXXXX.

LWKADN WOEASM TRIULN TUYORE ANBDEY OEHTAE
AWLRTL FXXXXX.

NFDIAD IDHNEN ACEONA DPLADD ETIIUL NTUYOR CAEHEH
TNOLWD OADGEE DXXXXX.

OTNCEI NUNOOF TOOTSB AEMCAP.

OCCKLN IXXXXX; IOMNIS SELCDT MOPEXX.

ARWGIN NXXXXX: FIUYOE ARPTSD TEOIUR GLTNSEH
TRHOSE UYOLWI LVHAEA FDEILN IUYORI OMNISS.

* EHTRHO SELWIL EBRTRD EENUOT EHTNCR AHYBTE AROHNN
ATEGXX.

Then she looked again. The clue now was the repeating
strings, like 'NCRAH', which had to mean 'RANCH', and
'RHOSE', which had to be 'HORSE'.

Conclusion:

What she had in front of her was an anagram.

Ruby smiled as she decoded the mission instructions in less than one easy minute.

You will be blindfolded and dropped by helicopter in unknown terrain.

On the other side of the mountain you will see a ranch.

Make your way to the ranch unseen and rustle a horse from the corral.

Swim the horse across the river and tether it to a post.*

Make your way to the second river and cross it.

Walk downstream until you are beyond the waterfall.

Find a hidden canoe and paddle it until you reach the woodland edge.

Continue on foot to base camp.

Clock in; mission completed.

Warning: if you are spotted rustling the horse, you will have failed in your mission.

* The horse will be returned to the ranch by another agent.

Ruby was the first to decode her message and as a result had gained time credit before she had even begun. Once everyone was ready to go, one hour and forty-five minutes later (Trainee Lowe sucked at codes), she lined up with the others and was handed her rucksack.

'Check your kit,' shouted the agent as a general instruction to the group, 'and make sure you take care of it. One: it's all you got and two: it contains some pretty costly Spectrum equipment.'

The rucksack contained:

```
Socks, one pair
Thermals
Gloves
Scarf
Waterproof overtrousers and coat
Penknife
Small cooking can
Energy bars x five
One canteen of water
Binoculars
Basic map
Home-made compass
A micro-parachute
```

Once she had checked through her kit and was all set, Ruby walked over to Sam Colt.

'Thanks,' she said. 'I'll remember everything you taught me. I got it all here in my head.'

Colt looked at her, his eyes full of concern.

'In your head is no good,' he said. 'Your gut is where you gotta keep it.'

Chapter 5.
Into the wild grey yonder

THE PLANE HAD BEEN FLYING FOR SOME TIME NOW and what with the blindfold, the noise of the engine and the overpowering smell of plane fuel, Ruby felt she had lost all sense of time and place. She had no idea how many other agents were in the plane with her, or at what point they had parachuted out. She just waited until it was her turn. She felt a hand press on her shoulder.

'You're up Redfort,' said a voice she didn't recognise. She got to her feet, a little wobbly from sitting so long and the plane's angle. With the help of the anonymous hand, she shuffled from the row of benches until she reached the place where the doors must be.

'You ready?'

She nodded.

'Sure you're sure?' said another voice she immediately recognised – it came from the cockpit.

Hitch's voice.

As far as secret agents went, Hitch was considered the best. He was Ruby's immediate boss, though some would doubt it to listen to her. If there was one thing that Hitch might want to change about Ruby Redfort, it was her mouth, or rather her inability to keep it shut when it might be a *good idea* to keep it shut. 'Kid, we have a rule here at Spectrum, rule number one in fact. Did anyone ever fill you in on it?'

When faced with this bothersome question, Ruby would widen her eyes and say, 'I'm not sure. Does it have something to do with not talking with your mouth full? Or is it no strappy sandals in the workplace?'

Hitch would mutter, '*Why me?*' and remind himself that she wouldn't always be thirteen and a total pain in the butt.

But, despite the banter and the occasional run-in, they got on very well and Ruby knew rule number one better than anyone.

SPECTRUM RULE 1: KEEP IT ZIPPED.

'Hitch?' she called from the back of the plane. 'What are you doing here?'

'Someone's got to fly this thing,' he replied. 'You OK kid?'

'Sure,' said Ruby. 'I'm looking forward to a little alone time.'

'Something goes wrong out there – you know I'll find you.' The merest hint of anxiety in his voice.

'What could possibly go wrong?' said Ruby. She felt the huge force of the wind as the doors were wrenched open.

'Any last wishes?' said the guy in charge of the jump.

'You gotta pair of earmuffs I could borrow?' she replied.

He removed the blindfold from her eyes and she looked down into the moonlit dark.

'Ah, stop whining Redfort and get outta here.'

And so she did.

As she tumbled through the night sky, thoughts unravelled and joined and twisted themselves together, and all the time she fell and fell until, with a jerk, her parachute shot open and now she was drifting jellyfish-like through the dark.

She strained to make out any part of the landscape. Then, all in a rush, she touched earth, a textbook landing. She detached herself from her micro-chute, folded it and neatly repacked it into the rucksack. It weighed very little.

She knew exactly what to do next.

SURVIVAL RULE 10:

STOP. *In other words:*
*S*tand still. *T*ake stock. *O*rientate. *P*lan.

STAND STILL.

Ruby had no idea where she was – it could be Canada,

Alaska or perhaps just some other state. That was the point of the exercise: drop you somewhere, in the middle of nowhere, where you knew neither terrain nor climate, and see if you survived. What Ruby was sure of was that she was not in Twinford any more. Far too cold. Twinford had been experiencing a heatwave, the hottest summer for fifty years, and the heat just seemed to keep on building.

This brief plunge in temperature should have come as a relief – might have been just what she was looking for if only she had been better prepared for it. Spectrum had dropped her with next to no information about where she was landing, but then that was the idea; could she get out of here alive? She instinctively gripped the small survival pack issued to her and walked to a small clump of trees out of the wind.

*T*AKE STOCK.

The night's icy fingers grabbed and prodded and made her bones ache. The first thing she did was to unpack her kit and put on everything that might keep her warm and dry. So far so good.

*O*RIENTATE.

She shone her mini-flashlight on the basic map she had been given. She had to make straight for the hill, or was it a small mountain? In the dark it was hard to tell. In any case, straight up and over was the only way to go.

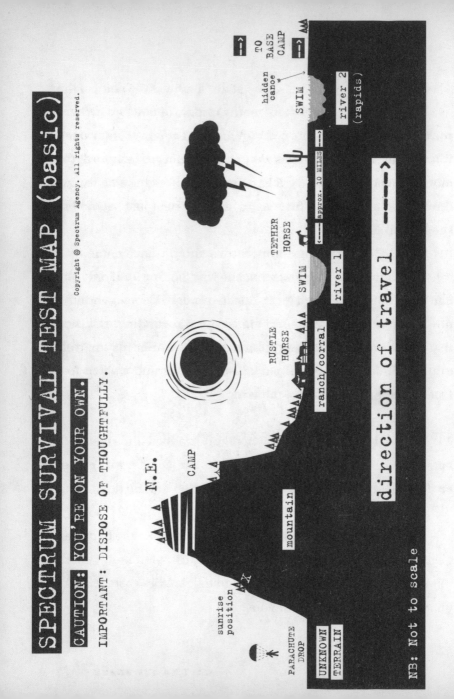

SPECTRUM SURVIVAL TEST MAP (basic)

CAUTION: YOU'RE ON YOUR OWN.

IMPORTANT: DISPOSE OF THOUGHTFULLY.

N.E.

sunrise position

PARACHUTE DROP

UNKNOWN TERRAIN

mountain

CAMP

ranch/corral

RUSTLE HORSE

river 1

SWIM

TETHER HORSE

approx. 10 MILES

hidden canoe

SWIM

river 2 (rapids)

TO BASE CAMP

direction of travel

NB: Not to scale

PLAN.

Ruby made the decision to keep moving. It was too dark to make a shelter and in any case the trek would serve to keep her warm. She judged that there was little of the night left, since the sky already appeared to be getting lighter, and navigating was no real problem since up was really the only way to go, plus, with the help of the moon, which every now and again slipped from behind the clouds, there was little chance of getting lost.

The dawn came when she was about halfway to the top and she was glad she had made the decision to climb – an hour later and the sun was already beginning to make the ascent hard work. She covered her head to prevent the chance of sunburn and drank the water contained in the survival pack. She needed to make sure she kept herself hydrated.

SURVIVAL SUGGESTION #13:

Keeping Healthy

SURVIVAL RULE 12:

Keep glugging water. *Staying hydrated helps you stay alert, control appetite, and maintain concentration and energy levels.*

Once she made it to the summit, which was really a ridge, Ruby rested in the shade of a large rock and ate one of her energy bars. From this mountaintop vantage point she could see the ranch below where she was expected to rustle a horse. She could even see the snaking ribbon of the first river twinkling in the distance, the same river she would need to cross on horseback. Far beyond that was a whole terrain she had no chart for: just markers, features of the landscape that would serve to guide her.

She called up the list of tasks in her mind.

Task one:

Make your way to the ranch unseen.

Once she had regained her strength, Ruby looked for a spot to camp out in, making sure it was on the north-east side of the mountain well out of view of the ranch; she didn't want them picking up the scent of a campfire.

The woodland was perfect, allowing for cover and plenty of materials from which to construct a shelter. There was a small creek and a clearing nearby and this was the area Ruby chose. She gathered slim fallen branches which she lashed together with creeper plants to create an A-frame, and then she clad the whole structure carefully with fir branches which she cut using her Spectrum-issue knife. She was pleased with the result. She then made a platform to sleep on, raised a little off the ground to prevent the cold getting into her bones – this she covered in dry pine needles and leaves.

SURVIVAL SUGGESTION #1:

Basic skills

1. SHELTER

SURVIVAL RULE 7:
Make your shelter as watertight and draught free as possible. *If you do not create a secure and stable shelter, you could end up in an unnecessarily dangerous situation, exposed to the elements.*

Once she felt happy with her shelter, Ruby began collecting fuel for a fire and got it going without any trouble. Then she spent some time searching for food and successfully gathered some edible plant life.

SURVIVAL RULE 13:
Don't forget to eat. *Without food, you are putting yourself at risk of fatigue and sickness.*

Everything went according to plan and Ruby soon had water boiling and a little while later a root tea stewing. Once she had cooked and eaten her gathered ingredients (not delicious though nourishing), she picked up her binoculars and headed up to the ridge again and down the south-west side of the mountain, keeping the ranch in her sights. When she felt she was near enough, but still at a safe distance not to be observed, she hunkered down.

Ruby spent the next few hours surveying the ranch, watching the ranch hands coming and going, working out when they were on duty and when they were off, and how often they stepped outside the building to check on the livestock or to have a smoke. When she was entirely satisfied that she knew all she needed to know, she went back to her shelter and turned in.

She slept well for several hours and woke at exactly the time she had planned to. It was good and dark, but with enough light to see what she needed to see. She gathered up her stuff and scratched camp so she would leave no trace.

Task two:

Rustle a horse from the corral.

Ruby Redfort was light on her feet and had no trouble moving without sound. As she approached the corral where the horses were held, she got down low and moved into the shadows.

If she had timed everything accurately and was correct with her observations, then there would be only one man patrolling the ranch and he would be walking round clockwise until the next guy's shift began. As far as she could judge, he must be on the far side of the ranch house by now. He would linger there and brew himself another pot of coffee in the tin pot that sat on the porch. Then he would pour a cup and slowly sip his coffee before reappearing perhaps eight minutes later. This meant Ruby had precisely seven minutes to select a horse, saddle up and get out of there without being spotted.

She took no time choosing a horse: she picked the one that seemed most trusting, most docile. Her choice of horse was a good deal better than her choice of saddle for, as it turned out, the one she had taken had a broken girth.

'Nice going buster,' Ruby muttered to herself. She registered this error in her head.

Mistake one: neglecting to check.

It was too risky to go back to the lean-to where the saddles were kept, select another and hope to make it out of there before the ranch hand reappeared. No, she would just have to ride bareback. Ruby led the horse by the reins, climbed onto the corral fence and mounted. It was agony to have the horse walk so slowly, but the sound of galloping hooves would no doubt alert the guard. Once she was into the trees and far enough away from the buildings, she picked up speed and flew through the night.

It was an exhilarating feeling, not just the ride, but the rustling itself: to get away unnoticed was the big deal. She felt like an agent – she was an agent – she was going to ace this test. Now for the next part of her assignment:

Task three:

Swim the horse across the river.

She gulped a little when she saw how wide it was, but there was no time for nerves; she needed to keep going if she was to make her deadline. The water was cold, but thankfully not fast-flowing and the horse did not object to what it was being asked to do. When they reached the far side, Ruby slid off the animal's back and felt the water squelching in her boots.

Mistake two: failing to remove one's footwear before crossing the river.

Bozo, she thought.

Part one of the mission was over and, as far she was concerned, this was the important part, the tough part.

Mistake three: failing to take equally seriously every part of the mission.

Chapter 6.
Hunker down

SHE TETHERED THE HORSE TO A POST AND PATTED IT GOODBYE. It would not be long before someone would arrive to deliver it home, no doubt drying it down and offering it a nosebag for its trouble.

If only Ruby had thought to give herself this same treatment, things might have worked out quite differently. But Ruby was ambitious; now all she cared about was arriving back at base camp early, really early. She was on a high, feeling pretty good about everything.

Mistake four: getting too confident.

Task four:

Make your way to the second river.

She decided to keep going, ignoring the natural shelter created by a small dip in the hillside, ignoring the perfect tree with its drooping branches that grew from this hollow, ignoring the fact it created a dry and comfortable place to camp out and get dry. Instead she trekked on in her sodden clothes, each step harder than it should have been because of the weight of the water in her boots and the rest of her garments.

Mistake five: failing to take care of one's physical self.

Ruby trekked for about two and three-quarter hours and the sun was now up and she was all but dry except for her poor feet which still squeaked in her boots. She stopped for a while and ate her last energy bar.

It wasn't enough.

She walked for another six miles before she heard a distant rumble. She looked up, but there was little to see except cold, dark nothing. A few minutes later, a lightning fork split the sky and the thunder rolled behind it and, as she ran, she heard the wind begin to shake the trees. It would not be long before the storm reached her.

SURVIVAL SUGGESTION #8:

The Elements

In times of crisis, storms, blizzards, hurricanes, it is always a good idea to seek sanctuary, get warm, get dry, conserve energy. Remember: get out of the deluge, hunker down, ride it out.

OK, said Ruby to the handbook imprinted in her mind, *that's all very easy for you to say, but where do you propose I hunker?*

It was a good question – there was very little in the way of hunkering-down landscape. As far as the eye could see, it was just flat, rocky terrain.

'Just keep thinking kid.' She could hear Hitch's voice in her head. *'The ones that keep thinking are the ones that survive.'*

She walked across the flat rock slab and searched for any part of it that might overhang the ground beneath. Twenty minutes later, she got lucky. A small overhang, positioned out of the wind, shielded the earth from the slicing rain. She used the micro-chute as a tent, securing it to the overhang and pulling it down in front to create a sort of cave shelter.

This isn't so bad, she thought. She was careful to remember to pin down all the flapping parts of the chute, aware that it might be torn away by a fierce gust of wind or simply allow cold to circulate inside the shelter. Fire was more difficult because of the gale blowing outside and it was hard to keep the flames alive and the smoke from billowing into her dwelling. She boiled up a root tea and, having drunk as much as she could endure, she worked on getting some shut-eye.

The night didn't pass without incident; the stones she had found to secure the material were not really heavy enough and as the gale picked up so did her tent. It was ripped from the rock and went spinning off into the night sky, just like Dorothy's little house. The dawn light took an age to come, but it was a huge relief to see it.

However, the day was about as pleasant as the night before: the only plus – it was light. Ruby trekked on, damp and demoralised, trudging through scrub and bushes. The weather was still terrible and getting worse. She didn't take shelter under the close-growing trees in the small woodland she glimpsed through the sheeting rain; she gave up checking in regularly with the home-made compass, it just didn't seem to work well, and then she dropped the needle and that was that. As for trying to read the stars when dark fell, forget it. They were nowhere to be seen.

*Mistake six: failing to **S**tand still, **T**ake stock, **O**rientate and **P**lan.*

She was alone and things had just not gone as she had expected. The words of Sam Colt came back to her. *'You can try and predict what might happen next, but don't imagine it's gonna come out that way just because you thought you'd like it to.'*

As the day arrived once more and became nothing but grey, uncompromising drizzle, Ruby began to feel the cruel pangs of hunger. Bypassing food had been a false economy: it had depleted her of energy and starved her brain of fuel. As a result, her thinking was off and things went from bad to seriously bad. She began to make dumb errors and soon lost her confidence completely.

As luck would have it (and few would call it *good* luck since it served only to make things worse), Ruby did finally stumble upon the second river.

The next task:

Cross it.

She realised she must be much further downstream than she had planned on being because she could hear the rapids. As she peered over the edge of the steep, rocky riverbank, she could see how she might get down to the water's edge, but could not immediately see how she was expected to cross the river. She felt exhausted; she hadn't eaten in a good while and didn't want to waste more time walking a mile upriver to find a better crossing place. Far too much time had been lost getting lost.

No, she would cross here. If she could make it down to the precarious-looking stepping-stone rocks, she would be OK – she would figure it out. It was a dangerous plan by anyone's reckoning: one slip and the rapids would grab her.

Mistake seven: taking an unnecessary risk.

Had she allowed her brain to hook up with her survival

instincts, she would have decided it might be wise to stop for a while. It had been raining continuously for five solid hours and the ground was sodden and the rock slippery. Thirty seconds into her descent, Ruby lost her balance, her arms flailed and she caught air as her boots slipped and her feet lost contact with the rock – a nasty collision and then Ruby found herself clinging to the branch of a near-dead tree. It was inevitable that either the tree or Ruby would finally have to let go – Ruby had no intention of losing her grip and so it was the tree that gave up first. She had lost count of the mistakes she had made and all she could think as she felt herself falling was, *What kind of duh brain are you Ruby Redfort?*

There was no time to answer this sad question before she plummeted down into the icy-cold water.

Chapter 7.
Great peril

FROM THAT POINT ON, Ruby's mind was no longer thinking: everything was beyond her control. Her body was wrenched this way and that, sucked under, spat out, dragged round rocks until she was finally tumbled down a short but furious waterfall.

The pressure was immense and exhausting, impossible to fight. She felt herself pushed to the very bottom of the stony river bed before several seconds later bobbing up into a pool of calm, clear water. She dragged herself onto the bank, spluttering water from her lungs and feeling both fortunate and unfortunate to be alive.

Unfortunate because she had now lost her entire kit, one boot and her glasses and, without her glasses, well, she couldn't really see a thing.

Mistake who-knows-what: losing a vital part of one's equipment.

Also unfortunate because Ruby was utterly lost and completely alone. She thought of Hitch's parting words:

'Something goes wrong out there – you know I'll find you.' But would he, could he? She certainly wasn't feeling optimistic. Would she ever see anyone again?

What was in some ways worst of all was the thought that if she did survive she would have to explain herself to Spectrum, to admit she had failed. Ruby knew she could never do that. She would have to keep the truth from them and instead fake an injury, an excuse for her failure to get back to base on time. She was busy contemplating what kind of injury it should be when she realised that there would be no need to fake one: her left foot was pouring blood.

It was the kind of wound that would be dealt with easily any place civilised, but in the wilds of nowhere was actually rather serious. A deep gash to her foot, painful and bothersome. How was she going to make it back now? She was just contemplating this troublesome predicament when she found herself losing consciousness.

When a person experiences tremendous pain or alarming injury, it is not unusual for the body to go into shock and shut down, resulting in heavy sleep. *This is the body's survival mechanism, there to conserve energy and deal with fear, stress, blood loss etc. In the right* *situation, this can be a useful state, there to protect against mental trauma, but in some circumstances, the wilds of nowhere, hostile environments and so on, it can put the victim in great peril.*

These words, which she had learned in the comfort of her Twinford home, echoed in Ruby's mind for a moment before she found herself drifting back in time to Wolf Paw Mountain. Very small and very alone, but for the creature with the pale blue, violet-circled eyes.

Then nothing.

**Meanwhile,
unlocking the large
carved oak door of the
apartment...**

...the elegant young woman stepped out of her heels and glanced down to see a pale blue envelope lying there on the black and white floor. It was addressed and stamped, but had been delivered by hand; there was no postmark and no name to indicate who it was for.

But Lorelei von Leyden knew that it was definitely intended for her.

Rather than pick it up, she fumbled in her purse and took from it a polythene bag containing a pair of white silk gloves; she shook them out and carefully pulled them on. Only then did she pluck the envelope from the cold marble. She reached for the paperknife that lay on the hall table and, piercing the paper, ran it along the top of the envelope.

She withdrew a completely blank sheet of white paper, held it between her fingers and wafted it in front of her nose, breathing deeply.

Then she staggered back as if she had had a terrible shock, as if she had just been given the most dreadful news.

Chapter 8.
A familiar face

WHEN RUBY WOKE, the first thing she smelled was woodsmoke. Someone had lit a campfire. She slowly sat up and peered around; it was all rather fuzzy and hard to make out, but then she heard a voice she knew well.

'You look in pretty bad shape Redfort.' Sam Colt was silhouetted against the light sky, a sky now clear of rain.

'How did you find me?' Ruby croaked.

'I'm a tracker, wasn't difficult,' he replied.

'How much time do I have?' asked Ruby.

'Depends how you look at it,' he said. 'You might consider time to be up or you might say you got all the time in the world.'

Ruby slumped back. 'What happened?'

'My guess?' said Colt in a slow drawl. 'You lost focus – set about trying to beat the elements. Sometimes you can be lucky with that approach.' He peered at her from under the brim of his hat. 'Sometimes not.'

'What do I do now?' said Ruby.

'Now we gotta stitch that wound on your foot, clean it up before it goes septic and then I'll get you to base camp.'

He made neat work of the stitching and although it wasn't exactly pain-free Ruby was grateful that he was able to take care of it without drama. He found her a spare pair of boots from his kit, a little too big but certainly better than no boots.

She drank a cup of something hot and sweet-tasting, but she was unable to eat – the pain had made her nauseous.

'You're gonna have to ride in back,' Samuel Colt said, saddling up. He helped Ruby onto the back of his horse and together they galloped across the plains.

When they reached the edge of a high bank on the edge of the woods, Sam pulled the horse up and helped Ruby down.

'I'll let you make your own way from here,' he said. 'That way it won't show on your test score.'

'I guess I flunked,' said Ruby.

'Depends how you define failure,' said Sam.

'Depends how Spectrum define failure,' said Ruby.

'Survival don't sound like failure to me,' he replied. He tipped his hat at her, turned and rode off, like he was the Lone Ranger himself.

Just below her, Ruby could make out a small wooden cabin

sitting in a clearing edged by pine trees. A figure was chopping logs and stacking them against the house. At least she thought that's what he must be doing, but it was the sound that told her so. The figure was a blur, her eyes unable to see any detail now she was parted from her glasses. If she *had* still had them, she would have been able to see how every once in a while the man looked at his wristwatch, then at the dimming sky, pausing before continuing on with his work.

She had no idea who this blurry figure was, but she was hopeful it might be Hitch.

Ruby limped into base camp by sundown, just. She punched in her time – she was about thirteen hours overdue. The man was sitting on a stool fashioned from an old tree stump and he was drinking a hot beverage, book in hand. He looked up.

'Better late than never Redfort.'

It wasn't Hitch.

Ruby slumped down on the grass. It was a nice enough night, not raining at least, but she was tired, really, really tired. She looked around her.

'Everyone else has been and gone,' said the Spectrum agent. It was the same agent who had doled out the mission briefing the day of the drop. His name was Emerson.

She sighed. *Did anyone else fail?* she wondered.

'Hungry?' asked Agent Emerson.

Ruby nodded.

'Didn't do so well finding food, huh?'

Ruby shook her head.

Emerson helped Ruby hobble to the tiny log cabin.

Inside was a fire and there were a couple of chairs set round a small wooden table. Two bowls, two plates, a couple of forks and a couple of spoons. A large metal pot dangled over the fire and a very good smell wafted out. Ruby suddenly felt a lot more awake. Emerson didn't seem like such a hard nut after all – he could cook at least.

For the first ten minutes she said nothing at all as she slurped the stew.

'Wow, you are wolfing that down Redfort. When did you last eat?'

She looked up. 'It's good,' was all she said.

Later, after Emerson had got her to the light aircraft and flown her back to the outskirts of Twinford, Ruby finally clapped eyes on Hitch. He was waiting there in the darkness like some kind of guardian angel.

The first thing Ruby did was to ease her left boot off. She had been dying to remove it, but she hadn't wanted Emerson to see the injury; she didn't need it to become some sort of big deal – not yet anyway.

'Sam bring you in?' Hitch asked.

'How dya know?'

'I recognise his bandage work,' said Hitch, glancing at Ruby's foot.

'How come he was tracking me?'

'I put in a request.'

They got into the car and drove into the night.

'So what happened out there kid, what took you?'

'I fell,' said Ruby. 'Hurt my foot.'

'That's a consequence,' said Hitch, 'not the reason.'

'I lost my glasses – they fell in the river.'

'So?' he said.

'What do you mean, so?'

'What I mean,' said Hitch, 'is why should that be a problem?'

'Are you kidding me?' said Ruby. 'I can't manage without them.'

'What I'm suggesting,' said Hitch, his voice calm and steady, 'is if you're saying your being thirteen hours late is really because you can't manage without eyewear then what are you doing trying to train as an agent?'

Ruby just looked at him. Then she said, 'You gonna tell LB?'

'No kid, I'm not going to tell LB, at least not if you tell me what's really the problem here.'

Hitch pulled the car over to the side of the road and let the engine quietly idle.

'I don't really get it myself,' said Ruby.

'Come on kid, give me a straight answer. You can flannel all of *them* – you can even get me to cover for you – but you can't pretend like I don't know something went wrong, something more than losing one geeky pair of glasses.'

'Colt didn't tell you?' asked Ruby.

'No, what Colt says to you is your business,' replied Hitch.

Ruby took a deep breath. 'If you really wanna know, Colt seems to think I rely on what I know instead of using my instincts. He says I gotta throw away the rules and react to what's happening out there.' She gestured to the darkness beyond them.

'So what's the problem?'

'I don't think I know how to do that,' said Ruby. 'So, when I go and lose my stupid glasses, I might as well throw in the towel.'

Hitch thought for a moment before saying, 'I think I might be able to help you there kid.'

'Yeah?' said Ruby hopefully.

'Might take a while; she's not the easiest person to track down.'

'Who?'

'I'll let you know if I find her.'

'So you're not gonna tell LB about my eye trouble?'

'Why would I tell her?'

'Why wouldn't you?' shrugged Ruby.

'Because kid, I can see that there's a whole lot more to you than your bad eyesight.'

She sighed, relieved. 'So you're not gonna tell LB I flunked?'

Hitch didn't answer immediately. He checked his mirror and made to swing back out onto the road and then he said, 'No need. LB already knows you flunked kid. She knew before you did.'

Chapter 9.
Activity normal

HITCH AND RUBY ARRIVED BACK HOME at Cedarwood Drive soon after midnight. They walked up the steps in silence and once in the front door Hitch whispered, 'Sleep like the dead kid,' before making his way down to his small stylish apartment at the bottom of the house.

Hitch had been with the Redforts for approximately four months and he had turned their lives around. He was there in the guise of household manager (or 'butler' as Sabina Redfort liked to brag) and he was good at it; no one would doubt his cover story.

But his real posting was as protector of Ruby; he was there both to keep an eye on her and work *with* her. If Hitch made a good butler, he made a whole lot better bodyguard and Ruby never once took it for granted. She had known him since March and already owed him her life twice over.

Now alone, she hobbled on up the two flights of stairs to her own private floor. Her room was much as she'd left it. A selection of her dirty mugs, cereal bowls and banana milk glasses had been collected up and removed, but generally her room was an unchanged scene of devastation. On the floor was a trail of clothes that led to or spread from the walk-in wardrobe. Record sleeves stacked one on top of the other next to the still turning turntable; piles of magazines and journals on all subjects fanned out across the rugs, and on top of these were pens, papers, telephones – all sculpted in various ridiculous shapes, some comical, some unlikely, a squirrel in a tux, a bar of soap, a corncob, a dog bone; and these four were not even the most eccentric.

The only place in any way orderly in her room was the bed; this was neatly made with the clean sheets pulled tight over the mattress and the quilt on top.

'Good old Mrs Digby,' sighed Ruby.

Because Mrs Digby had been the Redforts' housekeeper since always, she knew Ruby *as well as she knew every cooking pot in her kitchen* (as she was fond of saying). She might not interfere with the general appearance of Ruby's space, but she was insightful enough to know that just about anyone would rather come home to a clean, made bed.

Ruby for one was sincerely grateful. She eyed the bed longingly, then, before she lost all will to do anything but fall on top of it, she dragged herself to the bathroom and examined her face in the mirror. She was looking unusually pale; her complexion, normally olive-oil brown and healthy, seemed to have faded to a sickly grey. Her green eyes were a little bloodshot and her long dark hair was tangled and without shine. Ordinarily, Ruby was very particular about her appearance, styling her hair into a side-parting so one eye was almost obscured by a heavy curtain of glossy black-brown and fastened with a barrette; tonight she barely recognised herself.

Is this the face of failure? she wondered.

She set the shower running and had a good hot soak. Once just about all the mud and leaf was washed away, she got dry and dressed. She dabbed a little Wild Rose perfume on her neck and wrists. Boy, it was good to smell of something other than mulch and river sludge. She chose the warmest pyjamas she could find, long striped socks that stretched from her toes to her knee tops and – swamping her tiny frame – an outsized sweatshirt.

Even so she still felt cold.

Back in the bedroom she stood in front of the huge bookcase that extended from wall to wall, floor to ceiling. The bookshelves held Ruby's large assortment of written works: everything from spy thrillers and classic novels to encyclopedias, factual journals to comics, graphic novels and codebooks. All these books she treasured, reading them again and again, over and over.

She was standing there, wondering what book to pull from the shelves, when she heard the familiar squeak of her father's new and expensive Marco Perella deck shoes – the squeak was coming from outside, which surprised her since she was sure her father was tucked up in bed. She dimmed the light and peeped out of the window to check out what he was up to, but it was not her father she saw, but rather their neighbour, Niles Lemon, putting out the trash. He had on the exact same deck shoes as her dad and they made the exact same stupid squeak when he walked. They were, as far as Ruby was concerned, label before style, a whole lot of cash to look like a nerd. The only thing was Brant Redfort pretty much managed to look good in anything and Niles Lemon did not.

'What a bozo,' muttered Ruby.

Mr Lemon didn't have an original idea in his whole body. Last month he had purchased the same sunglasses her father wore and, two weeks ago, the same tennis racquet (it hadn't improved his game). Ruby reached for her yellow notebook, notebook 624 – the previous 623 were kept under the floorboards. She wrote:

```
Niles Lemon has bought the exact same deck
shoes as my dad. A total waste of several
hundred bucks.
```

These yellow notebooks of Ruby's were all filled with tiny and mundane incidents like this one. Every now and again an event of obvious importance would be added, but usually it was something pretty dull, funny or odd. Most of these happenings had taken place on Cedarwood Drive, plenty in Twinford and a few out of town. Ruby simply noted the things she saw, the everyday-ordinary and the once-in-a-blue-moon weird. This Niles Lemon incident certainly fell into the first category, but then one just never could be sure when something utterly banal was going to become significant. **RULE 16: EVEN THE MUNDANE CAN TELL A STORY.**

The pencil almost didn't make it to the end of the sentence before her eyes closed and the yellow notebook fell softly to the floor and Ruby was plunged into dream-filled sleep.

She was attempting to scale a cliff face; a pack of wolves was snapping at her feet: she could smell their fur, feel their claws. She felt a tug on her sleeve and hot breath on her cheek. She let out a squawk and snapped the light on.

'Jeez Bug, what are you doing creeping up on me like that?' Ruby sat up and scratched the husky's head and he licked her cheek again before lying down on the mat next to her bed.

Ruby sighed, shut her eyes for a second time and didn't open them until daylight crept into the room. The first thought that crossed her mind, the very first thought, was: *I failed.*

Chapter 10.
No place like home

STRANGELY FOR RUBY, she had found herself waking early. It was probably to do with having slept in damp undergrowth for three nights – her body had got used to the idea that it didn't want to lie down for longer than was totally necessary. Or maybe it was due to the lurking fear that gnawed at her dreams and caused her to stare up at the ceiling, wondering if this was the day when LB would kick her out for good; the Spectrum Field Agent Training Programme did not deal in failures.

She was shaken from her troubles by the marvellous smell which drifted up the stairs, reminding her that grubs and boiled-up bark weren't on the menu in the Redforts' architect-designed home.

Ruby pulled on jeans, a pair of Yellow Stripe sneakers and a T-shirt bearing the words *don't even ask*. She secured her hair neatly with a barrette and put on her spare glasses. Then she made her way downstairs and into the kitchen.

'Well, you could knock me over like a bowling alley skittle,' said Mrs Digby, her hands on her hips and lips sucking in air. The sight of Ruby up before the crows always made the housekeeper react this way. Ruby was no early bird and it was more usual to see her go to bed at five in the morning than arise at that time.

'How was camp?' asked Mrs Digby, who was under the illusion that Ruby was on some scouting type of a trip organised by Twinford Junior High – she had been training for it off and on for the past several weeks.

Hitch had taken over all the liaising with the school regarding trips, holidays and general arrangements so the Redford household was in the dark about Ruby's movements. It hadn't occurred to Mrs Digby to wonder why on earth the scouting training should take place during school hours, rather than in summer vacation; if Hitch said it was so, then she didn't question it.

'It was pretty terrible,' said Ruby.

Mrs Digby studied her face. 'You do look terrible, I can see that with my own two eyes, but *why* is the question I ask myself – don't you know how to have fun?'

'Ah, you know what it's like Mrs Digby, sleeping on bedrolls and eating oatmeal. What's fun about that?'

'You had bedrolls?' exclaimed the housekeeper. 'You young

people don't know you're born. When I was a child, we would have thought it was Christmas to sleep in leaves let alone bedrolls. And as for hot oatmeal...' She tutted and left the thought there.

Like Mrs Digby, Ruby also would have been grateful to have found some leaves to bed down in, but she knew if she mentioned how she had really slept and what she had really eaten, or rather *not eaten*, then the housekeeper would have by now been dialling the scout leader to give him a piece of her mind.

Ruby grabbed the pitcher of orange juice – she could use the vitamin C, her throat was bothering her and she was beginning to feel a bit feverish.

Hitch looked up from where he sat, reading the paper.

'Nice to see you again kid,' he said as if he hadn't seen Ruby for several days. 'Camp fun, was it? I'm guessing you kids spend your whole time singing and toasting marshmallows.' He winked at her and she gave him a sideways look as if to say, *You're some comedian.*

Mrs Digby tutted again at the mention of marshmallows and it set her off muttering about the privileged generation that was Ruby's.

Hitch pushed a mug of something hot in Ruby's direction. 'This might help, at least for a few hours,' he said.

Ruby gave it a sniff: it was the Hitch cure-all, his own familiar concoction and one that seemed to alleviate most ailments. He called it the *nine-hour rescue* because it would see you through for pretty much that time and then you would feel terrible again.

After Ruby had downed some pancakes and a quarter bottle of maple syrup (maple syrup being the reason for eating the pancakes), she headed off on her bike to the oak tree on Amster Green. She climbed it swiftly and was out of sight before anyone (if anyone had actually been around) could spot her.

She and Clancy had arranged via one of their long-distance telephone calls to meet early on Saturday morning, Clancy not wanting to wait a minute longer than necessary to hear about the survival training and, more importantly, to moan about his dad.

But Clancy wasn't there – she guessed it was too early even for him.

Ruby searched the hollow in the trunk to see if he had perhaps left a message – he had. As usual, it was folded into a complicated origami shape (this time a weasel) and written in code, a code to which only she and Clancy knew the key.

Tau bs grm pqxi ybbqd,

dg wifmsz Zmggc orraleq bh – EEIMVL.*

* AS USUAL, THIS IS A VIGENÈRE CIPHER. HERE'S YOUR CLUE TO THE KEYWORD: THIS ROYAL PERSONAGE'S SUGGESTION FOR SURVIVAL WAS TO LET THEM EAT CAKE.

Ruby sighed. 'Makes me glad I don't have a sister,' she muttered. She looked at her watch and thought she might wait it out. Hitch's nine-hour rescue had kicked in and she had stopped shivering. It was a nice day and she wouldn't mind the luxury of sitting still for an hour or two. Only thing was her mind kept circling round her failure, reminding her that all was not so rosy in Ruby world.

Chapter 11.
A beautiful thing

CLANCY, MEANWHILE,was wheeling his forlorn-looking, beat-up bike to the cycle store. He was furious with Minny; it was typical of her: first total her own bike then wreck his. *Can it even be fixed?* he wondered. He wasn't feeling too optimistic about the prognosis. When he was within a couple of yards of the store, he stopped.

He'd seen it in the magazines a few times, he'd heard it was coming to Twinford, the bike guy had told him about it, but he hadn't known that it was going to be in the store this weekend.

He stood there and looked up at the poster, just taking the thing in.

'Some beautiful machine,' he whispered. The poster, which showed the bike in fabulous colour with arrows pointing out all its good points, was displayed large in the bike store window. In huge print the poster warned: *The Windrush 2000. ONLY available while stocks last.*

Clancy gazed at it for some minutes before uprooting himself from the sidewalk and pushing his way into the store. He needed to get his old bike fixed (if indeed it could be fixed), but more than that he needed to know when the Windrush 2000 was coming and just how few were being delivered. I mean just how long did Abe the bike guy think stocks *would* last?

'Ah, around a few days,' said Abe. 'If this bike is all they say it is, then I imagine it's going to, you know, like whizz out the store.' He made a whizzing motion with his hand as he said this. 'I ordered what was available, but this baby's in demand.' He looked at Clancy with a serious expression. 'You know what I'm saying man? It ain't gonna stick around.'

Clancy did know what Abe was saying and he was beginning to panic inside. As a result, he was there a lot longer than he had meant to be and once he caught the time he ran like crazy all the way to Amster Green.

'Where've you been buster? I've been hanging around up here for about a day.' Ruby wasn't bothered by the *waiting*, the truth was she really didn't *mind waiting*, but she was irked that Clancy was late for *her*. Clancy Crew was rarely late for anyone.

'Ah, sorry Rube,' called Clancy, 'I got distracted.'

'Well, you missed some action that's for sure. Mrs Beesman

caused a collision when she let go of her shopping cart and it spun off into the street. This cheesy-looking guy in a big white Cadillac hit a fire hydrant and he got all hot and bothered and threatened to sue her and then Marla came out of the Double Donut and started hitting him on the head with a pancake flipper. Sheriff Bridges had to come and break it up. He had the siren on and everything.'

'I'm sorry to miss it,' said Clancy, with genuine disappointment.

'Yeah, well, Marla really let that guy have it. Said he deserved it for picking on a defenceless old woman.'

'I have quibbles about the "defenceless" part, but otherwise I'm with Marla,' said Clancy. 'Mrs Beesman might be a little strange, but I doubt she let go her cart on purpose; it's like her prized possession.'

'Yeah, she's not bothering anyone, and ever since we cleaned out her yard that time I've kinda had a soft spot for Mrs Beesman, you know what I mean?'

'No,' said Clancy, who didn't know why anyone would have a soft spot for Mrs Beesman; personally, she scared the life out of him, not that he would wish her any harm, but he wanted to avoid her at all costs.

Mrs Beesman was reputed to have at least seventy-four

cats which all lived in her small wonky house on the corner of Cedarwood Drive. She spent her days pushing a shopping cart full of cat food and listening to her transistor radio as she trundled to and from the SmartMart. She never spoke to another human soul. Mrs Beesman rarely seemed to purchase anything other than pet snacks and it was thought she too probably existed on a diet of cat food.

'Turns out she let go of her shopping cart because this mugger guy was trying to steal her cat, you know that big grey one she takes everywhere? I didn't see that part, just the aftermath.'

'Why would anyone try to steal that cat? It's only got one ear and I'm not sure it isn't a bit short of legs,' said Clancy.

'Who knows what motivates the criminal mind?' said Ruby.

'Well, we can be pretty sure it wasn't motivated by the desire to win best in show at Twinford Cat Club,' said Clancy.

'So,' asked Ruby, 'what was the big distraction?'

'Ah, nothin',' said Clancy, 'I'm too depressed to talk about it. Fill me in on your training?'

'I got lost,' replied Ruby.

'That doesn't sound good,' said Clancy.

'No, I was meant to be lost; the training was getting myself unlost.' She sighed.

'So did you?'

'I'm here, aren't I?'

'I guess you are. So you passed, that was good, huh?'

'No,' said Ruby. 'It wasn't and I didn't. There was a time factor and I didn't make it.'

'Oh, that's a drag,' said Clancy, looking at her. 'They gonna kick you out or what?'

'Your sensitivity is appreciated,' said Ruby.

'I'm just asking.'

It was a question Ruby didn't particularly want to answer. 'Well, it wasn't good. I was way too slow.' She let out a heavy sigh.

'So?' said Clancy, shrugging. 'You can fix that easy enough, just speed up.'

'It isn't that easy,' said Ruby. 'I seemed to royally suck.'

'You can't have flunked it all. So you got lost. I bet you were super good at everything else.'

'I sort of flunked on the whole foraging thing too,' said Ruby.

'Food foraging?' asked Clancy.

'What other kind is there?' said Ruby.

'Fuel?' suggested Clancy.

'No, fuel there was plenty of,' she replied. 'I'm just not so good at rootling around for things that look disgusting and then eating them.'

'I'm with you there,' said Clancy.

Neither of them said anything for a minute or two.

Clancy was thinking about this new side to Ruby, Ruby the flunker. It sort of made him feel better somehow, her not being good at something. He didn't *want* to feel good about something that made her feel bad, but it was a creeping satisfaction that he wasn't in charge of.

'So what you gonna do Rube?'

'I'm gonna order a big plate of French toast and forget about it.'

Clancy smiled. 'Sounds good to me.'

'Let's go to the Donut, get the skinny on what happened with Marla and the cops.'

Chapter 12.
Gilbert Gilbert

THEY CLIMBED BACK DOWN THE TREE and were sitting at the diner bar counter two minutes later. The place was full of talk; everyone was discussing Marla's heroic defence of the cat lady. No one had pressed charges and the cops were a lot more interested in the driver's untaxed Cadillac than they were in the damage a shopping cart and a fire hydrant might have done to it.

Ruby ate fast, barely saying a word.

'You skip breakfast or something?' asked Clancy.

'Nah, I had breakfast,' she replied, 'just can't stop feeling hungry I guess.'

'Maybe you got worms,' suggested Clancy.

'I doubt it,' said Ruby. 'I didn't eat anything that could give me worms.'

'There are other ways to get worms,' said Clancy.

'I don't wanna think about those other ways, thanks buster.'

'I was only saying,' he muttered.

Silence again and then he asked, 'So I'm guessing you did some fun stuff too. I mean you must have, right?'

'If you count parachuting from a great height, rustling a horse from a ranch and riding it bareback across a river and then making your way in pitch-black to a valley, finding a ditch and sleeping in it, then yes, I guess it was exciting.'

Clancy's eyes widened. 'I do count that as exciting, well, all but the part about your sleeping arrangements.'

'Yeah, I coulda done without the ditch myself, to tell you the truth, and the getting lost part wasn't so cool either, nor were the rapids and the having my foot stitched without anaesthetic.'

'I didn't know you could ride bareback,' said Clancy.

'Neither did I – it wasn't planned exactly – it was sorta necessary.'

'So what kinda things are they testing you on?' he asked.

'Survival more than anything, dealing with everyday wilderness conditions, extreme wilderness conditions and some incidental challenges, like forest fires, getting caught in rapids, attack by wild animals – any in-the-wilds emergency I guess.'

Clancy liked the sound of this; as a casual observer, he liked drama even if he didn't exactly like to be in the middle of it himself. The forest fire challenge was only rivalled by the fear of attack by wild animals. Both sounded to Clancy like things to be avoided.

'So what have I missed?' asked Ruby. 'I mean something must have happened these last three days.'

'Our neighbour Mrs Gilbert's spaniel, Gilbert, went missing.'

'Mrs Gilbert's spaniel is called Gilbert?' said Ruby.

'Yes, Gilbert Gilbert is what she calls him,' said Clancy.

Ruby pondered this information with an expression of puzzled pity.

'He was on his leash,' continued Clancy, 'tied to the fence, you know, so he could run round the backyard, but not actually get out of the yard – anyhow, he did.'

'Did what?' said Ruby.

'Get out the yard, and the weird thing is he musta slipped outta his collar somehow 'cause Mrs Gilbert found it down the street, but there was no sign of Gilbert Gilbert.'

'Quite the mystery,' said Ruby.

Clancy smiled. 'Isn't it?' he said. 'Maybe you should alert Spectrum.'

'Who's Spectrum?' said a voice.

They both jumped – Spectrum was not a word to be breathed in public and was not a word that Clancy was supposed to know, let alone utter.

Ruby looked up and saw the eager face of Elliot Finch.

'TV show,' she said.

'Never heard of it,' said Elliot.

Ruby shrugged.

'But then you guys watch a lotta TV,' said Elliot. He slid into the diner booth. 'Where've you been anyway?'

'Oh, here and there,' replied Ruby.

Elliot eyed her. 'You don't look so good, kinda scrawny – what've you been eating?'

Ruby shrugged. 'Just grubs and maggots, but I'm done with that diet.'

Elliot looked at her, unsure if she was joking.

'You want a donut?' said Ruby.

Elliot looked at his watch. 'Sure, I could eat.' He studied the menu. 'You seen Mouse? I'm meant to be meeting her here; we were gonna play table tennis in Harker Park.'

Harker Square, or Harker *Park* as kids and locals often referred to it, was *the* smart square in the centre of town. It had clipped hedges and ornamental apple trees as well as huge dappled plane trees, rose beds and several fountains – some traditional, some very modern and surprising (surprising in that they suddenly spouted water high into the air when people walked by – a lot of people had complained).

The square was surrounded by smart shops and office buildings, all built in the art deco style. Harker Square was popular: it was pretty, sunny with plenty of benches and shaded areas, and had just acquired a permanent outdoor table tennis table and Elliot was making the most of it. Mouse was a pretty good table tennis player, championship good actually, and Elliot was getting her to teach him some moves.

When Mouse eventually showed, she had come with news.

'Strangest thing – I got to Harker Park, but the ping-pong table is sort of gone, at least half of it's gone, I mean totally wrecked; looks like something actually took a bite out of it.'

'I bet it was that Flannagon kid,' said Elliot. 'I saw him and those boys he hangs out with hitting a baseball around the back alley behind the department store. I'll bet they wrecked the table tennis table and then went to find something else to destroy. They broke a window with their baseball too. That Flannagon kid is some hitter.'

'You saw them do that?' said Ruby.

'As good as,' said Elliot. 'I heard the sound of a ball hitting a bat and then I heard the sound of glass breaking, so it had to be them, right? I mean it's always them.'

'You gotta be careful accusing people without being a hundred per cent sure,' said Mouse. 'People end up in the big house every day, locked up for crimes they never even committed.'

Mouse's grandfather was a campaigner – he worked hard to protect 'John Q. Public's' civil rights and so Mouse had grown up with strong feelings about fairness and justice. She didn't much like Dillon Flannagon, but that didn't mean he was guilty of every act of vandalism in Twinford County, though he did seem to be responsible for most of them.

In any case, it didn't much matter if it was Dillon Flannagon or not: no one was going to be playing table tennis in Harker Park any time soon.

Elliot shrugged. 'So what now?'

'Beats me,' said Mouse.

'I'll think I'll order another waffle,' said Ruby.

'You have to be kidding,' said Clancy.

But she wasn't.

**The department store's
stylish restaurant was busy and
buzzing with fashionable
Twinfordites**

A young woman sat alone at a table, not concentrating on the menu she was supposed to be reading, but instead looking around her and glancing at the clock.

She took a small bottle from her purse and dabbed perfume onto her wrists; the smell of Turkish delight enveloped her and seemed to calm her. Her sharp blue eyes relaxed a little when she saw the young man zigzagging through the crowded room. He was casually dressed, unlike the other diners.

'I thought you weren't coming,' she said.

'I'm only two minutes late Lorelei,' said the man, checking his watch.

'Two minutes is two minutes,' she asserted.

Lorelei von Leyden was elegantly dressed in grey. Her spiked shoes tapped on the floor under the restaurant table: she was nervous.

'What's the problem?' he asked. 'I thought everything was going to plan.'

'I got a message,' she replied. 'I think... I think she knows.'

'How could she know?' he asked. 'She can't know; you're just paranoid.'

'You don't know her like I do Eduardo. I know she knows, she always knows, she knows everything.'

The man tried to catch the waiter's attention. 'So what are

you suggesting we do?' he said.

'Bring the plan forward; we need to get on with it – contact you know who, get him to deliver.'

She made to leave.

'You not eating?' said the man.

'I have to get back to the day job,' she said. 'Besides,' she sniffed the air, 'I don't think the food here smells so appetising.'

Chapter 13.
See you on the other side

IT WAS LATE THAT SAME AFTERNOON and Clancy was walking beside Ruby, pushing her bike for her along Amster towards home. Her foot was really aching and she was finding it uncomfortable to put pressure on it. The heat had eased off a bit and reached a pleasant temperature, and they were talking about the upcoming vacation and how they were going to spend it.

'My dad wants me to go on that camp out at Little Bear with the Wichitinos,' said Clancy.

Ruby nearly spat her bubblegum. 'You are kidding man? No way can you go!'

'Of course not,' said Clancy, a little offended that she might think he would willingly or even unwillingly attend Wichitino Camp. 'They'd have to hold me at gunpoint.'

'Jeez!' said Ruby. 'I'd never live it down.'

'What's it got to do with you?' said Clancy. 'It's me who'd be on dork camp rubbing sticks together.'

'Yeah,' said Ruby, 'and think how I'd feel as your friend, knowing you were toasting marshmallows and singing "Kumbaya" with a lot of bozos in short pants.'

'I'm sure they do more than toast marshmallows,' said Clancy.

'So now you're defending the Wichitinos?' said Ruby. 'You don't think it's totally dorky after all?'

'It's total dorkdom,' said Clancy, 'that goes without saying. I'm just *suggesting* that there must be more to it than heating up marshmallows.'

'Let's drop it,' said Ruby. 'Neither one of us is going on dork camp, period.'

They continued in semi-silence until they reached the fork in the road and Clancy peeled off up Rose and Ruby got on her bike and freewheeled down Lime. When she reached the bottom, she saw Hitch waiting for her. He was standing by the car, drinking in the sun's last rays.

'Hey, that's a coincidence!' called Ruby, skidding to a halt by the kerb.

'Not really,' said Hitch, pointing to the keyring clipped to a whole bunch of other keyrings that dangled from her satchel. She hadn't even noticed.

She was puzzled for a second and then it dawned on her.

'A mini locator?'

He winked. 'No flies on you kid.'

'You saying I can keep it?' asked Ruby.

'A replacement for the one you lost at the museum that time. You're lucky LB didn't take it out of your pay packet.'

Ruby hadn't exactly lost the original one; it had been sacrificed while assisting her escape, and the time Hitch referred to was an incident when Ruby very nearly lost more than a keyring.

The mini locator was a gadget dressed up as a kid's word puzzle with little sliding letter tiles that, once arranged correctly, spelled **HELP**. Once formed, this word **HELP** would set off a flashing light on the 'buddy' locator, which in this case was Hitch's watch. Then he would know not only that Ruby was in trouble, but also where she was. It had limited range, but when it worked it worked very effectively. It looked simple, and in a way was simple, but no one, not even the evil genius known to Spectrum as the Count, had spotted it.

'So you think LB has forgiven me for losing the great Bradley Baker's mini locator?' said Ruby, her tone sarcastic.

'She'll forgive you when you prove yourself to be half as good an agent as he was,' said Hitch. He seemed to enjoy winding her up on this subject. Bradley Baker was a Spectrum legend and although he had died in an accident many years ago his reputation for brilliance and bravery dogged Ruby every day of her Spectrum life.

'So why are you here?' she asked.

'To take you in to HQ,' he replied.

Ruby knew she was going to have to face the music sooner or later, but she had hoped for later. *Not today*, she thought. But all she said was, 'So where is it this time? The way in, I mean?'

This could seem like a strange question given that Ruby Redfort had been into Spectrum headquarters on many occasions and had spent hours and hours there working on cracking complex codes, but the unusual thing about Spectrum was that it never stayed in one place for long, or at least the *way in* never stayed anywhere for long. The first time Ruby had entered was via a manhole; last time it had been through a door in the boiler room of the municipal swimming pool.

Hitch pulled up in one of the bays by the iron railings that surrounded Twinford's Central City Park. He switched off the engine and opened the car door. 'Here,' he said.

Ruby slowly got out. 'Where is here?'

Hitch pointed to the path. 'You see where it bends and disappears?'

Ruby nodded.

'To the right of it, over by that huge tree, can you see those boulders?'

Ruby nodded again. There were some large rocks which had been used to landscape the park, to make it look more natural, sort of New York Central Park style.

'Behind them you'll find the toddler playground,' said Hitch. 'You'll work it out from there.'

Ruby looked at him, her mouth open.

'Man! You are surely kidding?'

Hitch shook his head.

'I'm thirteen – that playground is for babies; how's it gonna look if I start swinging around on the jungle gym?'

'That might look unusual for a kid of your age. But I'm not sure what that would have to do with finding the door into Spectrum.'

'So where is it by the way, the door?'

'You'll work it out kid, that's what we pay you for.'

'I'll bet it's inside the caterpillar pipes, isn't it? You guys really get your kicks making me do these dorkish things, don't you?'

'I don't think you should take it personally kid. Just think of it as another test – how well can you act?'

'Swell,' said Ruby. 'And I guess you'll be taking a different route? No monkey bars for you.'

'See you on the other side kid,' said Hitch. He winked at her and walked across the road.

Chapter 14.
Hanging by a thread

RUBY SHRUGGED AND WALKED ON DOWN THE PATH for all the world looking like a kid exploring Twinford Central City Park on a bright summer day.

She opened the gate to the toddler and children's playground and pretended she was looking for an imaginary little sister. There were plenty of mothers and nannies all occupied with babies, wiping faces and pushing little kids on swings. No one was there to relax exactly; no one was reading a novel or simply hanging out in the sun, so the only way to blend in was to look like you might be minding a young child.

Ruby was right: the one place where it was possible for a concealed door to be hidden was, just as she had thought, inside the caterpillar pipes. She thanked the stars that there was no Wendy house – that would have been a humiliation too far.

Ruby fed herself into the wide metal tube like it was the most normal thing in the world. It was about twelve feet long and had other pipes wiggling off in different directions. It wasn't at all dark because there were human-sized holes in the top of the tubes so the children could stick their heads out and call to mommy.

Right in the middle of the pipe's curved wall was a little sticker of a fly. A small child was gently picking at it, trying to peel it off and no doubt eat it. (Little kids were always eating things that didn't need to be eaten – *survival camp would be a breeze to them.*) Ruby surmised that access to Spectrum must be directly below the fly sticker and therefore directly beneath the sticker-eating kid.

The kid didn't look like it was going anywhere; it seemed perfectly content sitting on its behind, mumbling away to itself.

It had been a long time since Ruby was a toddler, but one thing she still remembered was that little kids are easily bribed.

She took the packet of Hubble-Yum bubblegum out of her pocket and carefully placed a square of it in the kid's view. The kid immediately began edging towards it, eyeing the gum greedily. It took a minute or so, but soon enough Ruby and the kid had switched places. Ruby felt around until she found the hidden latch; this she turned until a hole opened up big enough for her to fit through. She cautiously eased herself into it, half in half out, like a person getting into a cold pool, when suddenly she slipped, let go and fell down a long dark tube, the door clanking shut over her.

She felt like Alice in Wonderland must have felt as she tumbled and slid and finally fell out of the tunnel, landing in a pitch-black nowhere.

'Oh brother,' she whined.

'You made it,' said a voice through the dark.

Ruby shrieked.

'I didn't know you were afraid of the dark kid?'

'You shouldn't creep up on people like that man.'

Ruby was lucky that she couldn't see him smile; that would have put her nose out of joint worse than it was already. Hitch took her arm and led her along while she fumbled for her torch – she needn't have bothered. The corridor went from dark to light, from stone grey to vivid green in about five paces, and at the end was a door painted the exact same shade. Hitch punched in a code and the door swung gently open.

They stepped into the large Spectrum atrium with its spiralling black and white floor and its huge domed ceiling; on the far side was Buzz the telephone operator sitting within her circular desk, surrounded by a flock of coloured telephones.

'Hey Buzz!' shouted Ruby.

Buzz peered at her over her unfashionable spectacles,

spectacles that had not *become* unfashionable, but just never had been and never would be. Buzz responded with a feeble raise of her hand.

'Friendly as ever,' remarked Ruby.

'Ah, she's not really a kid-person,' said Hitch.

'Is she even a person-person?' said Ruby.

'No, I wouldn't call Buzz a *put people at their ease* type; that's kind of the point of her really,' said Hitch. 'LB doesn't want someone chatty; she wants someone efficient.'

They walked over to the desk and waited for Buzz to finish her conversation, if you could call it a conversation – it seemed to merely be a whole lot of yeses, noes and the occasional instruction.

Buzz replaced the receiver and looked up at Hitch. She almost seemed to smile, but it could have been an involuntary mouth twitch caused by the throat lozenge she was sucking.

'LB has requested you wait outside her office,' she said, picking up a red receiver. 'She can give you four minutes.' Buzz began speaking down the phone in Mandarin.

Hitch and Ruby made their way to the huge door beyond which lay LB's office. They sat down on the stylish chairs arranged nearby and waited and then waited some more.

The intercom symbol flashed on Hitch's watch.

He spoke into it, the voice came back in his ear and he winced, almost imperceptibly, but he *did* wince. He looked at her.

'LB,' he said. 'She wants a word.'

Ruby stood up and waited for Hitch to follow, but he stayed right where he was. 'You not coming?'

'No, you're on your own kid. She wants to see you alone.'

'Is that a good thing or a bad thing?' asked Ruby.

Hitch raised an eyebrow.

'Oh,' said Ruby. The eyebrow communicated a lot – it wasn't going to be good news. 'Does she want to congratulate me on my work in the training field?'

'That's what I like to hear, a good positive attitude,' said Hitch. 'Think happy thoughts.'

Ruby beamed him a big fake smile. She turned to go.

'Oh and kid, just remember: don't make it any worse than it has to be,' he warned. 'I.e. I would suggest you lose the limp.'

'Thanks for the advice,' said Ruby, meaning it. She needed all the help she could get. 'Wish me luck,' she sighed, walking over to the large black door.

'I wouldn't rely on luck,' said Hitch.

Ruby knocked, waited for the voice to call 'enter' and went in.

LB was sitting at her white desk, studying pieces of paper

covered in dense notes. The all-white office gleamed; there was no colour at all in that room other than the red nail polish on LB's bare feet, the red lipstick on her lips and the red perspex file on her desk.

The file related to Ruby – she had seen it before. It contained a lot of information, Ruby's past and present, her talents, her successes, her faults and her failures, and it was, Ruby feared, her faults and failures that LB wanted to discuss.

'So Redfort, I hear you screwed up.'

'I think you're putting a very negative spin on it,' said Ruby.

'Please feel free to convince me that there *is* a positive spin to your performance – based on the fact that you completed your task arriving thirteen hours late?'

'Twelve hours,' muttered Ruby.

LB checked the document again. 'Oh yes, let's be accurate: twelve hours, fifty-seven minutes and three seconds *late.*'

That sounded worse.

'I rustled the horse OK, I swam over the river, didn't drown – I was just a little tardy is all.'

LB looked down at her papers. 'Let me check that... no, here it would suggest, and I quote Agent Emerson's words: "*You completed your mission unnourished, ate nothing for almost two days and arrived bewildered and exhausted.*"' She gave the papers a second glance. 'Oh yes, and: *"You lost some valuable kit."*'

Ruby was about to speak, but LB held up her hand. 'One moment,' she said. 'I see you are a stickler for accuracy so let me check which items you actually lost.' LB read through the long list of missing kit before saying, 'That's right. Everything you were issued with.'

There was no mention of having been found injured, bleeding and unconscious by Sam Colt, no mention of him dropping her off just yards from base camp because she was barely able to walk. *So Sam bent the rules.* Ruby had suspected as much. She owed him one.

'But I arrived, didn't I?'

'If crawling into camp is arriving, then I guess you did,' said LB.

LB raised an eyebrow.

Ruby opened her mouth to speak, but LB clucked her tongue to indicate she hadn't finished.

'And, to cap it all, you got sick. How incredibly careless.'

'I appreciate your sympathy,' said Ruby.

'Cut it out Redfort, and by the way I should warn you that I have a chronic headache so if I were you I'd keep it short and stick to explaining what in the name of stupid was going on.'

'The thing is I wasn't really hungry,' said Ruby.

'I think we all know that had there been a donut tree out there it would have been quite a different story,' said LB. 'You failed to forage, failed to eat, failed to nourish your brain, you lost energy and you couldn't navigate your way back to base in the time allocated.'

'Look, I wasn't going to share this with you, but I sorta lost my glasses.' Ruby hadn't meant to bring this up, but she was getting desperate. Perhaps it would bring out LB's sympathetic side.

LB looked at her quizzically. 'Your judgement is way off Redfort, if you think that's going to put you back in a professional light.'

'Yeah, but the thing is, I've learned from my mistakes,' said Ruby.

'The point of the exercise is to prove that you don't make mistakes,' countered LB.

Ruby sneezed again. 'But I rustled the horse pretty well. So I caught the flu. I made it back, didn't I? Isn't that the whole point – surviving?'

'You nearly caught your death. What's the point of a dead agent?'

'But I didn't, I survived.'

'Only because Emerson waited around for twelve hours, fifty-seven minutes and three seconds to bring you in – in my book that's called getting rescued.'

'Sometimes people need rescuing. You're telling me you've never been rescued?' said Ruby.

'Not because I lost my glasses,' said LB.

'It doesn't have to mean everything,' argued Ruby.

LB looked at her hard. 'In Spectrum's book it means failure; maybe you're just not cut out for this.'

Ruby opened her mouth to protest, but LB raised her hand.

'You want me to make my decision now,' she said, 'or after I've had a cup of mint tea and swallowed two aspirin?'

Ruby kept her mouth shut.

'If you'd prefer me to spend time evaluating your rather desperate performance instead of making a judgement here and now, then I'd keep your mouth shut, firmly shut, as in clamped, closed, *zipped*.'

Ruby said not a word. LB looked down at her files.

'Oh and by the way,' she added, 'I wouldn't get all smug about the horse rustling. You abandoned a saddle right near the corral, it was spotted and the horse was then presumed stolen.' With that, she picked up the phone and dialled 8. 'Buzz, do you know where my Paris paperweight has got to? It seems to have vanished into thin air.'

Ruby left the room without getting so much as a *see you soon* from her superior. She couldn't believe what was happening. She had never failed at anything in her life, unless of course she'd meant to fail in order to get out of something.

How had everything suddenly gone so bad?

Chapter 15.
A bad odour

HITCH LOOKED UP WHEN THE DOOR OPENED.

'So you survived,' he said.

'Ah, it was a breeze,' said Ruby. 'I think she's considering giving me some type of a medal.'

'Always good to keep optimistic kid,' said Hitch, patting her on the back. 'I heard optimism is the number-one rule of survival.'

'No,' said Ruby. 'Apparently, that's punctuality.'

Ruby thought it was probably time to head on home, but it seemed Hitch had other ideas, as he set off down the corridor and beckoned for Ruby to follow.

RUBY: *'Where we going now?'*

HITCH: *'Just calling in on Harper.'*

RUBY: *'Who's Harper?'*

HITCH: *'Someone with a medical qualification.'*

RUBY: *'Why do you need someone with a medical*

qualification? You sick or something?'

HITCH: *'No. To check out those stitches of yours.'*

RUBY: *'They're fine.'*

HITCH: *'You a doctor?'*

RUBY: *'I'd just rather leave it, OK?'*

HITCH: *'You're squeamish?'*

RUBY: *'LB, she'll find out.'*

HITCH: *'No. She won't.'*

RUBY: *'She knows everything.'*

HITCH: *'What makes you think that?'*

RUBY: *'She told me she does.'*

HITCH: *'Don't believe everything she tells you; she wants you to believe that.'*

RUBY: *'I do believe that.'*

HITCH: *'Well, believe me, she doesn't.'*

RUBY: *'She's very persuasive.'*

HITCH: *'It would seem so.'*

They arrived at a Band-Aid-coloured door – Hitch knocked.

RUBY: *'So how can you be so sure this medically qualified person won't inform LB?'*

HITCH: *'Because Dr Harper owes me, and Dr Harper is pretty cool.'*

Dr Harper *was* pretty cool and she dealt with Ruby's leg almost without referring to it, like it wasn't actually there.

DR HARPER: *'Nice stitching – Colt, I presume?'*

RUBY: *'Good guess.'*

DR HARPER: *'Not a guess. It's obvious.'*

She inspected the stitches to make sure the wound was healing OK and then she rebandaged Ruby's foot.

DR HARPER: *'You have pretty small feet, huh?'*

RUBY: *'I guess.'*

Dr Harper went to her cupboard and rummaged around until she found a pair of rather small sneakers.

DR HARPER: *'These have been in here for years, ever since Bradley Baker was a boy – he barely used them by the way. I doubt they are too odorous.'*

Ruby eyed the sneakers suspiciously. They weren't as cool as her Yellow Stripes, far from it; they looked very like little kid sneakers.

RUBY: *'You expecting me to wear these?'*

DR HARPER: *'Well, I wasn't suggesting you put them on your mantlepiece.'*

RUBY: *'You know what? That's nice of you and all, but I don't think I need alternative footwear; my Yellow Stripes are super comfy.'*

DR HARPER: *'Ah, stop being so superficial. Put these on and you aren't ever going to want to wear another shoe again, plus they've got other benefits.'*

Ruby slipped her foot into the sneaker.

RUBY: *'You're not kidding. These are like air or cloud. I can barely feel them. What's the other benefit?'*

DR HARPER: *'I'll let you discover that.'*

RUBY: *'They're just comfy, right – there is no other benefit?'*

DR HARPER: *'You're good to go.'*

RUBY: *'Thanks...'*

Pause.

RUBY: *'I don't s'pose there's any chance of getting a...'*

Dr Harper reached for a piece of headed paper and scribbled a few words on it, signed it and handed it to Ruby.

'I'll leave you to fill the date,' said Harper. 'Nice to meet you. See you next injury.'

Ruby smiled and slipped the doctor's note into her satchel. It would no doubt come in very handy.

'So how come Dr Harper owes you?' she asked as she and Hitch walked back down the corridor.

'That's between her and me,' said Hitch, tapping his nose.

Ruby was a little late home and her parents were already sitting at the kitchen table and had got started on their supper – the Redforts were eating casual tonight.

Sabina was yawning uncontrollably and looked like she might actually fall asleep in her bolognaise.

'Sorry,' said Ruby, 'got held up.'

'No harm done honey, just good to see you,' said her father. 'How was scout camp?'

'Oh, you know, scouty,' said Ruby, peering into the saucepan on the stove.

Ruby served herself some bolognaise and slid into her seat. She looked at her mother. 'You OK Mom?'

As if on cue, Sabina yawned again. 'I couldn't sleep a wink last night. All the time I was hearing this strange sound, a kind of snorting.'

'Sure it wasn't Dad?' mumbled Ruby through a mouthful of spaghetti.

'Now Ruby, that's not nice. Your father doesn't snort, he snuffles cutely – it's his adenoids.'

Mrs Digby coughed meaningfully and started clearing the table. '*The man snores*,' she muttered under her breath. '*Call it adenoids if you like, but there ain't nothing cute about it.'*

Brant Redfort seemed pretty oblivious to this little discussion. He was wearing his tennis shorts and was in a chipper mood – he was pretty much always in a chipper mood, but he was particularly so this evening because he had made mincemeat of Niles Lemon on the tennis court (not actually difficult because Niles Lemon could barely swing a racquet).

'Funny thing,' he said. 'Niles told me he and Elaine received their invite to the Marie Antoinette perfume launch a couple of weeks back. Did ours ever show up?'

'No,' said Sabina, frowning. 'You don't think we've been blacklisted, do you?'

Mrs Digby pulled an invitation from the pile stacked on the shelf. 'This what you're missing?' she said, slapping it down on the table.

'You're a genius,' said Sabina, clasping her hands.

'If the definition of genius is to open one's God-given eyes and see what's under your own nose, then I guess I am.' Mrs Digby didn't understand the need for getting all dramatic about things that required no effort whatsoever.

'Smells like a fabulous evening,' said Brant, sniffing the invitation.

'Sounds like a total yawn,' said Ruby, yawning.

'I just hope that French pong has a better odour than the stink out in the yard,' said Mrs Digby, who was standing on the back steps, holding her nose.

'What kind of odour?' said Brant.

'Farmyard,' said Mrs Digby.

Ruby's parents both got up to take a sniff. Ruby could barely smell a thing, what with her bunged-up nose.

The telephone rang and Sabina answered it.

'If you're phoning about the smell, we can't help it,' she said.

'Mrs Redfort?' said Clancy.

'Oh, hi there Clancy. We're having some odour problems. I guess you're wanting Ruby.' She handed the phone to her daughter.

'Hey Clance, how's things?' said Ruby.

'Not so good,' said Clancy. 'In fact, bad, pretty bad.'

Ruby pulled up one of the stools at the kitchen bar. 'How bad?'

'I got a message from Abe at the bike shop; turns out my bike can't be fixed,' he said, 'it's kaput. Fixing it will cost more than it's worth. My dad says I can get a second-hand one, but I'm gonna have to pay for it myself because I didn't exactly look after the other one so well.'

'But didn't you tell him it was your sister who totalled it?'

'I couldn't; my dad's as mad as a coyote at her already. She shouldn't have been riding my bike 'cause she was grounded at the time so if I tell him *how it* happened she's gonna be dead meat – he'll probably ground her for the rest of her life and I don't want that on my conscience. Besides,' said Clancy with a heavy sigh, 'my sisters and I have a rule: never sell a fellow comrade out, i.e. *don't tell Ambassador Crew.*'

Ruby could see his dilemma all right; there was nothing Clancy could do but swallow it. Clancy happened to be about the most loyal person in the state and if he made a promise not to rat you out then he never would.

It was one of the qualities Ruby particularly valued him for.

If Clancy had a rule to never sell out a friend, then Ruby had her own **RULE 6: NEVER HAVE A FRIEND WHO WOULD SELL YOU OUT.**

**The phone rang,
a shrill ring in the dark of
the apartment**

Lorelei hurried over to the ornate desk and plucked up the receiver.

'Hello? Eduardo?' A pause. 'What do you mean he's gone?'

She listened, her fingers tapping anxiously on the desk top.

She took a breath. 'And what about the creature?' The question was almost whispered.

She sank down onto the chair. 'No...' she said. 'That can't be.'

She closed her eyes, a moment's pause. 'Find him,' she said, her voice clipped and certain.

'Just find him!'

Chapter 16.
If pigs could fly

RUBY WOKE WHEN THE SUNLIGHT TOUCHED HER FACE. She had been so tired the previous night that she had forgotten to close her blinds. She wasn't feeling so good. Despite both Hitch and Mrs Digby's efforts with their various flu remedies, nothing was really taking the edge off the joint-ache she felt, or the drilling headache, or the clammy sweating and shivering.

She stumbled to the bathroom and took a look at her still pale face with its dark panda eyes. She looked not quite as bad as she felt.

She picked up the conch phone and dialled Clancy's number.

'You wanna come over, watch some TV?' asked Ruby. It was only 10 am, but so what.

'Sure,' said Clancy. 'We could watch that crummy wilderness show... what's it called?'

'*A Long Time Lost*,' said Ruby.

'Oh yeah, that's it. Hey, kinda ironic, huh?' said Clancy.

Ruby didn't reply so Clancy explained. ''Cause you were a long time lost, I mean, and the show's called *A Lon—*'

'Yeah bozo, I get it. See you later.'

She hung up. Then she pulled on a second pair of socks followed by some sheepskin knee-high boots, wrapped herself in her dad's old zipped sweater and tottered downstairs to the kitchen.

Mrs Digby tutted when she saw her. 'You look ready for the grave. Sit down on the double.'

'Ah, it's not so bad Mrs Digby. I still have a pulse.'

'And not for long, if you ask me.'

Ruby's mother walked in and over to the large kitchen window.

'I knew it wasn't Brant,' she said. Sabina had her nose to the glass and was staring intently out of it.

'Knew what wasn't?' said Ruby, she by now had *her* nose in the fridge and was groping around for the banana milk.

'The snorting.'

'Oh, that – so what was it?' said Ruby, sneezing a violent sneeze.

'A pig, a pig in the backyard. I saw it, just a back view, but I saw it.'

'A pig?' spluttered Ruby.

Sabina nodded. 'It was a really big one too with very fat legs.'

Mrs Digby just rolled her eyes and muttered a small prayer to the saint of sanity.

'When did you see it?' asked Ruby.

'About four o'clock this morning, I think it was four o'clock because I'd just had a vivid dream about your father snoring and I woke up and saw a pig.'

Ruby resisted the temptation to say what she wanted to say and instead asked, 'How big was this pig?'

'About *yay*,' replied her mother, stretching her arms wide apart to suggest huge.

'Mom, you know that seems pretty unlikely, don't you?'

'I certainly do,' agreed her mother. 'Think how surprised I was when I caught it pottering around – or whatever it is they do.'

'Truffling around,' corrected Ruby. 'They truffle.'

'Well, no wonder the yard smells if that's what they do,' said her mother.

'How do you suppose a pig got into our yard Mom?'

'Well, that I *don't* know,' said Sabina, her brow furrowed. 'Who keeps pigs around here?'

'That would be nobody,' replied Ruby.

'That's what *I* thought,' said her mother. 'But I guess we're *both* wrong. I *would* call Mrs Attenburg...'

'Why would you do that?' said Ruby. 'She's a bird watcher.'

'That's what I'm saying,' said Sabina. '*I would call her* if this was a bird problem, but it's a pig problem so I don't suppose she can help.'

'Unless it's a flying pig,' said Ruby. 'I'm sure she knows all about *them*.'

Clancy arrived within twenty minutes, having bribed his little sister Olive to lend him her bike. It was tiny with a little pink basket at the front and he had to stand on the pedals the whole way. This really made his back ache; it also made him look ridiculous. Not that looking ridiculous was ever of big concern to Clancy Crew, but today, for the first time in his life, he felt he wouldn't mind being the cool kid. Just for once. The one riding the cool bike. Was it so much to ask?

'I hope you aren't thinking of taking Ruby out of this house,' said Mrs Digby sternly. 'She'll catch her death if you do.'

'Mrs Digby, it's about a hundred and five degrees outside,' said Ruby. 'How do you propose I'm gonna catch my death?'

'You're already halfway to it,' asserted Mrs Digby. 'You are not to go out on that roof of yours, not on my watch. I've taken the hatch key just to be sure.' She pulled the key from her pocket to make the point clear.

'Quite so,' agreed Sabina. 'She's not to step out of this front door Clancy, promise me that.'

'Oh, I do Mrs Redfort. We were going to hang out *here*, watch some tel... play some scrabble or maybe read an encyclopedia, you know, mind-expanding things.'

Ruby rolled her eyes, *read an encyclopedia?*

'Good idea,' said Sabina. 'Expand your minds! You might be sick, but you don't have to be stupid.'

Mrs Digby looked at Sabina Redfort rather pityingly, shook her head and muttered something that no one could quite catch, and Ruby and Clancy made their way up to Ruby's room.

The TV show was kind of interesting, in part at least, though the main character, Joe Little-Corn, should have been called Joe a-little-corny. He kept putting his ear to the ground and feeling the earth and leaves to get a sense of who might have passed that way. It was set in the past before the invention of the automatic washing machine and yet old Joe Little-Corn looked like he had his clothes laundered on a regular basis – as Clancy was keen to point out, along with all the show's other flaws.

'He doesn't have a beard, but just when did *you* see him shave?' Clancy asked.

'And just where does he plug in his hairdryer?' said Ruby, who found Joe Little-Corn's long tawny locks with their perfect glossy wave just a little too much to swallow.

Joe had finished his morning coffee and was now busy hollowing out a canoe. He was a quick worker and had finished it by lunchtime.

'Oh, come on man,' groaned Ruby. 'No one's gonna make a canoe in that sorta time.'

'How long does it take?' asked Clancy.

'I reckon my survival trainer can do it in a day,' said Ruby.

'Can *you* hollow out a canoe?' asked Clancy.

'Sure I can.'

'What about that?' said Clancy, pointing at the TV. Joe was lashing together a tree shelter now.

'Yep,' replied Ruby.

Once Joe had finished the shelter, a few minutes later, he took the canoe out on the lake and quickly caught a large sea bass for supper.

'Can you catch fish?' asked Clancy.

'I'm not sure I could catch a *sea bass* in a freshwater lake,' said Ruby. 'That's gotta take a lot of skill.'

It was true, Joe did seem to have the knack – not many people could catch an ocean fish in the middle of a North American landlocked state.

'So if you're so good,' ventured Clancy, 'I mean not as good as Joe Little-Corn of course, but still, if you're so good, then why can't you work out how to make it back home with or without your glasses?'

Ruby shrugged. 'I don't know. I guess I don't have that old "into the wild" instinct. I read all the books and did the training, but when it comes to it I sorta find myself... well, you know, lost.'

'So what about Spectrum and your training?' asked Clancy.

'I'm still waiting to hear. I could be in, I could be out,' said Ruby.

'They're just keeping you hanging?' said Clancy. 'That really sucks.'

'Yeah, it's the worst feeling,' said Ruby. 'Impending failure.'

Chapter 17.
Lick your nose and yawn

RUBY AND CLANCY SAT AROUND FOR THE WHOLE MORNING. Mrs Digby brought up restorative soup and insisted on Ruby drinking some rather pungent tea; by 3 pm Ruby was suffering from cabin fever and was desperate to get out. She had taken some more of the Hitch nine-hour rescue drink and was feeling not so bad.

'Mrs Digby's never gonna let you out in your condition,' said Clancy.

'I know that,' said Ruby.

'It's a pity,' said Clancy, 'it's a really nice day and we coulda called in on Red.'

'No pity about it,' said Ruby, pulling her jeans on over her pyjamas.

'Are you outta your mind?' said Clancy, flapping his arms. 'I promised your mom I wasn't gonna let you step out the front door. She'll be mad as a mad thing if she thinks I've lied to her.'

'Don't sweat it, I'm not gonna step out the front door,' Ruby assured him.

'So what are you doing?' said Clancy.

'Clance my friend, just do as I say and we'll be sitting in the sun before you can say *guacamole*.'

'Don't tell me you're gonna exit via the roof because I saw Mrs Digby pocket the hatch key,' said Clancy.

'Nah,' said Ruby, 'nothing so obvious.' She was now fully dressed in hat and scarf. Her T-shirt, which bore the words **no sweat**, was concealed by a fleece-lined jacket and she was busy pulling down the blinds and stuffing a large pillow under the comforter. In the gloom it made a convincing human-sized shape. She took a long black wig from her childhood dressing-up box and placed it in the bed, spreading the hair across the pillow. So long as no one came too near, they would never know that the pillow and wig combination wasn't Ruby.

'OK,' said Ruby, 'you go downstairs and explain that you're leaving 'cause I'm a total flake-out.'

'And what are you gonna do?' asked Clance.

'I'm gonna exit via the laundry chute. Just keep anyone from looking out across the driveway.'

While Ruby fed herself into the chute, Clancy tiptoed downstairs; he did a very good impression of a person who was trying not to wake a sleeping sick kid.

He gestured up to Ruby's room. 'If you go in Mrs Digby, don't get too near. She's sleeping super lightly and I had to practically crawl out on my hands and knees.' He whispered, 'You know how she gets if she's woken.' He made a face to indicate unpleasantness.

Mrs Digby gave him a silent nod and Clancy knew he was in the clear. She had swallowed the whole story.

He met Ruby down the alley that connected Cedarwood to Lime; Bug was at her side. Ruby looked kind of ridiculous dressed in a fur-hooded parka, hat, scarf and boots when every other Twinfordite was wearing shorts, sunglasses and flip-flops, but she wasn't bothered.

They set off towards Red's place in Silver Hills – taking the short cut across the canyon. Once you dipped down away from the tarmacked road, you might as well be anywhere: not a house, not a telegraph pole in view for a half-mile.

They were just about to climb up the other side when Bug froze.

'Did you hear that?' said Clancy.

'Yeah,' said Ruby, 'but what was it?'

Bug growled.

'Do you mind if we don't find out?'

'Probably just a wild dog or something Clance.'

'A wild dog? You say that like it's a good thing. Dya know what wild dogs *aren't* capable of?'

'Responding to the sit command?'

'They can't resist ripping a person limb from limb,' said Clancy.

'Not me,' said Ruby. 'I've read up on the whole wild dog deal. The thing you gotta do is stand still, don't run, don't look it in the eyes and keep licking your lips, your nose if you can. It's a good idea to yawn too – a tired dog is a passive dog – that's how they look at it, so the more you show them you're no threat, the more they're likely to leave you alone. Just lick your nose and yawn!'

'Well, if it's all the same to you, I think I might just head on back to planet earth,' said Clancy. He felt the urge to flap his arms, but he stopped himself because he didn't want to attract any unwanted attention from the wild thing.

'Look, we got Bug here, OK? No dog in its right mind is gonna mess with us.'

'Exactly,' said Clancy, 'no dog in its *right mind*. What if this dog isn't in its *right mind*?'

'Then we're gonna have to climb a tree pretty quick,' said Ruby, striding ahead. The nearest tree was about 300 yards away so Clancy broke into a bit of a run. Bug began to bark, his fur on end. He seemed to be urging Ruby to get a move on. The sound of the wild thing was getting nearer, or at least it seemed to be, though what with all the birds rising into the air at once and wild rabbits dashing to and fro, it was hard to keep track of what was going on. Ruby, sick as she was, picked up the pace and did her best to keep up with Clancy who was way out in front.

Behind her, the wild noises continued, getting closer and closer, and Ruby was mightily glad when she glimpsed the tarmac road ahead. They made it up and out of the canyon without being torn limb from limb, though Bug didn't relax until they made it back to where the houses began, his fur spiked up along his back.

**'I found him,' said
the voice down the end
of the telephone line**

'And the creature?' said Lorelei, pushing her pretty feet into her stiletto heels.

'No sign of it,' said the voice, 'and our friend here won't talk.'

'Well Eduardo, you are going to have to make him,' she replied.

'You better come over and see for yourself; it might be harder than you think. He doesn't trust you.'

'I'm not asking him to trust me, I'm asking him to give me what he owes me,' snapped Lorelei.

'He thinks you have a dark plan in mind,' said Eduardo, mischief in his voice.

'Well, of course I have a dark plan. Why does he think I paid him in unmarked notes?'

'He says he regrets his decision to do business with you,' said Eduardo.

'He's going to regret ever laying eyes on me,' said Lorelei as she slammed down the receiver.

Chapter 18.
105 degrees

CLANCY WAS PRETTY GRATEFUL TO GET TO RED'S PLACE;
he was all on edge about the wild dog or Hound of the Baskervilles
or whatever it may have been and he sort of slumped down on a
kitchen chair like he had just survived some terrible near-death
experience.

Red's mom, Sadie, was tense too, but this was because of the
forest fire that had been reported on the other side of Great Bear
Mountain. Nowhere near Twinford, and no reason at this stage to
believe that it would be heading their way, but Sadie was already
worrying about her mother, who lived north of Little Bear.

'It all depends on the wind,' she sighed. 'Who knows which
way it's going to blow?'

'Little Bear hasn't had a major forest fire in more than a
decade,' Ruby reassured her, 'at least not one that threatened a
town north of it.'

'I know you're right kiddo, but I can't help worrying,' said

Sadie. She looked closely at Ruby. 'You're pretty well dressed for a heatwave, aren't you?'

Ruby nodded. 'It's this flu thing I have. I just can't get warm.'

'I'm surprised Mrs Digby let you out,' said Sadie.

Clancy twitched in his seat and Sadie put her hands in the air. 'I'm not talking,' she declared. Sadie Monroe had a live-and-let-live attitude.

Red and Clancy and Ruby hung out in the backyard until the sun got low. The Monroes had a great view of the mountains from their little house high up on the north-west side of the city. There was no sign of smoke from any forest fire and nothing to suggest trouble on the horizon.

They decided to leave before Ruby was missed, and set off south down the steep canyon road with its pretty houses and wildflower gardens. The road, Vine Street, took them through Tripperdale, an attractive tree-lined walk with its vintage clothing outlets and record stores, a place where kids liked to hang out at weekends or after school. If you walked far enough down Vine, it would lead you to the beach.

Clancy Crew was walking down the middle of the street, kicking an old tin can. Ruby was sticking to the sidewalk and had Bug on a leash.

Clancy was telling her about the thing that had happened the night before at his dad's ambassadorial shindig. Mr and Mrs Vincento had not seen the funny side and Minny was now looking at six weeks of staying home weekends.

'That's a riot,' said Ruby. 'How come you didn't tell me last night?'

'I only just found out. Boy, is she ever in trouble now,' sighed Clancy. It was another scorching day; the heatwave had really set in.

'Pardon me Clancy, but your sister Minny is not exactly a portrait of the smartest kid in town.'

'Minny's smart,' said Clancy. 'She can speak three languages.'

'Sure, she's school smart, but she's not savvy smart. Fine, she wants to do bad things, but why does she get caught so much? Have you ever asked yourself that?'

'You know when the temperature reaches a hundred and five degrees people go crazy,' said Clancy. 'They just can't deal with the heat. I guess that's what's happened to Minny.'

'You're saying everyone goes crazy when the temperature hits a hundred and five degrees?' said Ruby.

'Not everyone obviously, but it is a temperature that people on the whole can't tolerate; it's a key one for sending folk off the rails,' he said.

'And where did you read that?' said Ruby.

'In one of my mom's magazines,' said Clancy. 'It said, "*Heat can really affect the brain.*"'

'What happens to all these heated-up brains?' asked Ruby.

'I don't know, but if we stand here long enough we might find out. I mean I wouldn't be surprised if some guy doesn't come running down the road, screaming his head off and chucking stuff all over the place.'

Ruby stopped walking and looked around.

'Seems pretty quiet to me,' she said.

Clancy shrugged. 'Maybe everyone in Twinford's got air con.'

When they peeled off Vine and rounded the corner of Breeze and Larch, Clancy stopped.

'There it is,' he said in a strange whisper. 'The thing I want more than anything on this whole planet, the only thing.'

'The only thing you want in this whole world is in that store?' said Ruby. All she could see were bikes and bike parts.

'Yeah,' said Clancy in the same weird whisper.

'I don't get it, what are we looking at?' asked Ruby, staring at the store window.

'The bike, the Windrush 2000,' sighed Clancy. 'Cool, huh?'

Ruby looked at him. 'For you, that bike comes before world peace or the discovery of intelligent life on Mars?'

'You know what I'm saying Rube,' said Clancy. 'This is the *"thing" thing* I want more than any*thing* else.'

'I guess it's a nice bike. *Yeah*, I can see that, but I can think of a whole lotta *things* I want a whole lot more than that bike.'

'That's what my dad keeps saying. *"Clancy, I can think of a thousand and one better ways to spend my money than on some blue bicycle."* I keep telling him it's not just *any bike,* it's *the only bike,* the only one worth having.' Clancy had studied the bike catalogues over and over; he had literally gone to bed with them, slept on them and woken up with his cheek squashed to the inky pages, and he knew for a fact that the Windrush 2000 was the best bike on the market for a kid of his age. 'Not only does it *look* cool, but it's got speed too.'

'Sounds OK,' said Ruby, checking out the price tag, 'but considering it costs a whole heap of dollars, I guess you oughta expect it to be cool and speedy.'

'Sure,' agreed Clancy. 'But there's more to it than that.'

'One would imagine,' said Ruby, blowing a large bubblegum bubble.

Clancy didn't say anything: he was just staring, almost hypnotised by the bike's perfection.

'What?' said Ruby. 'It's got a nice shiny bell?'

Clancy ignored that. 'I mean Rube, it's got these tyres, right, these tyres that are unpuncturable. You don't need to be weighed down with a bicycle pump or a repair kit. Never have the problem of a puncture, imagine that?'

'I'm trying,' said Ruby.

'You don't believe me?' said Clancy.

'I believe *you*,' said Ruby, 'I just don't believe *them*, the bike manufacturer guys. No one yet has come up with tyres that can't be punctured. If you get that bike, don't chuck away that puncture-repair kit man.'

Clancy frowned. 'Well, it's the coolest bike I've ever seen and look at it, it's that amazing blue. You can't miss it. I gotta get my hands on one somehow or I'm gonna lose my mind.'

'Talking of crazy,' said Ruby, 'my mom said she saw a huge sorta pig run across our yard.'

'What?' said Clancy.

'Some sorta huge pig-thing is what she said,' said Ruby.

'And where does she imagine this huge pig came from?'

'*Imagine* being the operative word,' replied Ruby. 'She seems to think someone musta got themselves a smallholding.'

'What did Mrs Digby say?'

'She said, "*Your ma's been sitting around in the sun too long and the heat's finally got to her.'"*

'I told you,' said Clancy. 'It's the temperature: it's making your mom hallucinate.'

'So maybe you'll get lucky and your dad'll start losing it too,' said Ruby. 'Hey, perhaps if you offer to smile extra hard in his publicity photos he'll get you that bike.'

Clancy came to a dead stop in the road. 'That's *it*,' he said. 'That's what I'm gonna ask him.'

'Clance, I was kidding.'

'I'm *not*,' said Clancy. 'It's a good deal for him and it's a good deal for me.'

When they reached the side alley next to Ruby's house, Clancy said, 'So how are you gonna get back inside?'

'Ah, it's a breeze,' said Ruby, pulling off her jeans and T-shirt to reveal her pyjamas. She stuffed the clothes through the open window of the laundry room and then walked up the front steps to the house.

'Mrs Digby will hear you,' hissed Clancy.

'No way,' said Ruby, 'she'll be watching *Crime Hour* by now – she won't hear a thing.'

Ruby, as usual, was right about this, and she easily made her way upstairs unnoticed. Bug followed noiselessly – he was a very well-trained dog.

**The door to the
warehouse groaned
its iron groan...**

...and spiked heels clicked on the stone floor.

Bound to a metal chair was a figure, small in the vastness of the space. Yet, despite the uncompromising situation, this figure was still defiant, not yet broken.

Not yet.

'You...' he uttered.

'Yes, it's me. Who were you expecting, the Girl Scouts?' Lorelei laughed. 'No, no one's coming to rescue you.'

'I don't care about myself,' he said.

'That makes two of us.' Her blue eyes twinkled.

'I will repay you your money. I tried to. I came to your apartment, but you weren't there.'

Lorelei's eyes narrowed. 'You have no business coming to my apartment. How did you even get ahold of my address?'

He tried to calm her by keeping his voice low and steady. 'I told that other guy when he brought me in, I *will* repay you.'

'And how do you propose to do that when it's clear that you have been spending my money on little luxuries? Your shoes, for instance, how much did they cost?' She tapped her foot like she was waiting for an answer.

'I will repay you,' repeated the man, 'everything – more than you gave me.'

'I didn't give you anything, I *paid* you for something and that something is now mine, only you released it. So where is it?' She was angry, very angry.

'The thing is,' he said, 'I've changed my mind. I don't like what you're planning. I let it go – the deal's off.'

Her face was very close to him now, her perfume quite intoxicating. 'A bit late for climbing up to the moral high ground, don't you think?'

'I never would have agreed to it if I'd known what you were up to,' he said. His eyes held hers and the hatred he felt was quite tangible.

The elegant woman laughed, a short, sharp, unamused laugh.

'Yet you didn't think to ask.'

'You should have told me,' snarled the man. 'How was I to know you had such foul plans?'

'All that money? And yet it didn't occur to you something unpleasant might be afoot?' Lorelei's shoes click-clacked on the hard floor. 'A stranger offers you a suitcase of cash and in exchange all you have to do is turn your head the other way, close your eyes, open a gate – and yet you gave the "why" no thought?'

The man was silent.

'I made a promise – *you* made a promise. Did no one ever

tell you a promise is for life?' She regained her composure, straightened her jacket. 'So tell me where I must look.'

'I'll never tell,' he said.

'You might want to have a little rethink, unless you really feel death is such a good option.'

'Too late, it's gone,' he said.

Lorelei walked towards the door. 'Like I said, you might want to think about that. Stew on it, why don't you?'

Chapter 19.
The thing

IT TOOK SOME PERSUADING FOR RUBY TO CONVINCE HER PARENTS AND MRS DIGBY that she was well enough to attend school, but, as had often been remarked, Ruby was a very talented actress and arguer so had the ability to convince most people of most things.

Mrs Drisco was less than overjoyed to see her brightest pupil and possible nemesis back in class again. Ruby had been away for a few days and Mrs Drisco had prayed she would be away for a few more. She had actually secretly hoped that perhaps Ruby would be off until next term with some nasty summer cold or an ankle sprain.

'Ruby Redfort, you're not late! What a nice surprise. I feel bad for feeling so sure you would be.' Mrs Drisco smiled a tight and uncomfortable smile.

'If it makes you feel better Mrs Drisco, I almost was; I had planned to grab a waffle before class, but the waffle stand was all shut up – so I guess my loss is your gain.' She gave her teacher the big eyes; she looked like an angel.

Mrs Drisco was racking her brain for a really sharp retort, one that would put Ruby Redfort right back in her box, but her sour train of thought was interrupted by a commotion in the corridor.

Gemma Melamare was screaming. Screaming was actually a polite word for what she was doing: it sounded more like a hyena being strangled.

'What in the world of uncivilised is occurring?' demanded Mrs Drisco, flinging the door open wide.

Gemma couldn't speak because she was too busy shrieking and when she finally did manage to utter words all she said was, 'I saw this thing slithering down the corridor!'

Mrs Drisco, who couldn't tolerate the sound of a shrieking child *or* teenager for that matter, shouted very loudly in order to drown out the sound of Gemma's hysterics. 'Well, no doubt this "thing" – like the rest of us – is partially deaf by now!'

Gemma was then sent off to the medical room to go and have a lie-down.

No one knew what she had seen or for that matter believed that she had seen anything at all; Gemma Melamare was just the kind of girl to shriek her head off in order to get out of class or to attract some boy's attention. She got a lot of attention from boys because she was perfectly pretty, as sweet-looking as her cohort, Vapona Begwell, was not. Like Vapona, Gemma was unpleasant, really unpleasant, but due to being such a perfect portrait of cute, people found this hard to take on-board. Beauty can throw a lot of people off the scent.

When the bell rang and everyone spilled out into the corridor, Ruby got a chance to chat to Clancy before the next class.

'So what did your dad say?' she asked. She was chewing on a piece of bubblegum, midway to blowing a bubble, and her voice was somewhat distorted, but Clancy knew exactly what she was talking about. He looked downcast.

'He said, *"No way, no day,"*' said Clancy, dragging his bag along the floor.

'Clancy Crew!' snapped the sharp voice of Mrs Drisco. 'We do not drag our backpacks along the ground; we are not apes.'

'I didn't know apes used backpacks,' said Ruby. 'I kinda thought the use of backpacks is what separated man *from* the apes?'

'Miss Redfort, you are this close to a detention. I mean it, this close,' said Mrs Drisco, holding her quivering hands very close together.

'Oh, that *is* close,' said Ruby.

Clancy yanked his friend round the corner before there was *no* space at all between Mrs Drisco's hands.

'So where were we?' said Ruby. 'Oh yeah, you were telling me about your father. He said, *"No way, no day"*?'

'Yeah,' said Clancy. 'He said, *"Smiling for the camera is all part of being the ambassador's son."*'

Ruby's bubblegum bubble popped and she fed the pink string back into her mouth. 'Well, there's a surprise. By the time your old man reaches for his wallet, you'll have grown a beard Clance.' She gave him a look and slung an arm across his shoulder. 'Don't let it get you down Clance my old pal. It's just a bike, right?'

Clancy sighed. 'I guess, if you can call the Windrush 2000 *just a bike*. By the way Rube, you might want to go easy on the perfume.'

'What dya mean?' asked Ruby. 'It's the same perfume I usually wear.'

'It's not the smell, it's how much smell you're smelling of – it's like you bathed in it or something.'

'Oh, must be my nose – it's all stuffed up – I can't smell a thing,' said Ruby. 'This morning I drank a whole glass of bad milk. I nearly puked.'

They peeled off towards their different classes – Clancy to French with the formidable Madame Loup, Ruby to biology with the Dread Mrs Greg.

Mrs Greg was called the Dread Mrs Greg because she was one of those people who was absolutely certain that she was right. Unlike Mr Singh or Mr Piper, both inspiring teachers, Mrs Greg was everything that made school a bore. For this reason Ruby generally used the classroom time to do a little of her own reading up on things.

Humans have lost a lot of their natural ability to easily distinguish one scent from another, though it is possible to tune up one's olfactory skills. *Perfumers and wine experts have to work on this sense to improve their understanding of what they are smelling and distinguish scents, one from another. However, although we may not have the ability some of our early ancestors had, we use this sense more than we think. Subconsciously, we are very aware of people's odours; we make judgements and decisions based on scent we are not conscious of.*

We react to chemicals both natural and engineered and a person's odour can be a reason for trusting or not trusting, feeling reassured or not. Sometimes a smell can mislead: we might be inclined to like a person because of the perfume they are wearing or the washing powder they launder their clothes with, even though this is a superficial and applied smell and nothing to do with the individual's biological scent.

The way a perfume reacts with the skin of the wearer changes from person to person, which is why we might like a perfume worn by one person and not another. We all have our own natural smells, smells our subconscious is aware of, smells animals can pick up on even when we humans can't. A shark for instance can smell a drop of blood in a hundred litres of water. A dog can pick up the scent of an escaped convict and track him across rocks, woodland and – despite what movies may have us believe – even rivers. The human nose is less attuned to subtleties of smell than the animal nose.

Ruby considered Bug, how he relied on smell to tell him most of what he needed to know. Sure, he used his eyes, his ears, but it was his sense of smell that was most important. She read on. The book also contained a chapter showing the chemical make-up of smells. It turned out that smelly substances contained 'aromatic compounds', circular structures of carbon and hydrogen such as benzene rings.

Benzene, C6H6, is a ring of six carbon atoms, connected by alternating single and double bonds:

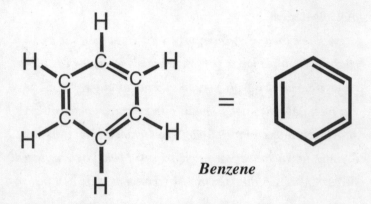

Benzene

*The **right image** shows standard chemical notation which omits carbons and most hydrogens for the sake of space. In this kind of diagram, there is a carbon atom at every corner. Hydrogen atoms are worked out according to how many bonds are shown leaving each carbon atom.*

This was all pretty fascinating, Ruby thought. The idea that the characteristic smell of an ordinary herb, for instance, was often the smell of just one or two chemicals, out of the hundreds which make up that plant – but the ones which we recognise and identify with it. The smell of vanilla is contained in a single chemical the molecular structure of which is a benzene ring with three hydrocarbon branches sticking off it:

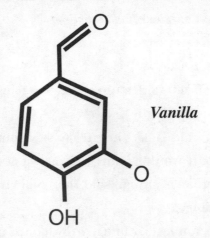

Vanilla

None of this was exactly relevant to what she was supposed to be learning about today in Mrs Greg's lesson but it was interesting information and forty minutes later Ruby had finished the book.

She met up with Clancy at lunch in the queue for the salad counter.

'So what dya think Melamare actually *saw*?' said Clancy.

'Her own reflection,' said Red. 'My guess is she forgot to put her make-up on this morning and her real naked face gave her a chilling fright.'

'Yeah,' mused Clancy, 'I wonder what she does look like without all that pancake.'

'Did I hear someone say pancakes?' Del Lasco sauntered into the canteen.

'Oh, hey Del,' said Ruby. 'We were just talking about Melamare's face.'

'Oh yeah,' said Del, 'I heard she saw something that gave her the chills. It wouldn't surprise me – *I* saw something *real* strange yesterday evening,' said Del, 'real strange, I'm telling you, crazy strange.'

'You're beginning to sound like my mom. I mean jeepers! She swears she saw a giant pig running across the yard.'

Del looked Ruby hard in the eye. 'She probably did, ever consider that?'

'A giant pig Del? You seen a whole lot of those lately?' said Ruby.

'No, but I've seen a giant cat, a tiger most probably.'

'A tiger?' repeated Red. 'You really saw a tiger?'

'I doubt it,' said Elliot.

Ruby took a slurp of her milkshake and said, 'Del, you might wanna start calling yourself the exaggerator.'

'Look who's talking – aren't you the one that said you saw an alien space craft hovering over the Crews' house?'

'It's true,' said Mouse, 'you did.'

Ruby sighed. 'You're never gonna let that go, are you Del?' What Ruby had actually seen was an unusually designed hot-air balloon land in the Crews' grounds, a mistake anyone with unusually poor eyesight and steamed-up glasses might make.

'Yeah, well, I'm just pointing out that as far as exaggeration goes you have your moments,' said Del.

'OK, well, let's drop my "moments" for twenty seconds and talk about yours. You see, all I'm saying is that when you say you saw this tiger walking around Twinford how do I know you aren't talking about some fat old tabby cat?'

'Yeah, right Ruby, tabby cats are likely to swallow Mrs Gilbert's spaniel – whole, all in one.'

'And who's saying that's ever happened?' said Ruby.

'Only all of everybody,' said Del.

'Oh and there you go again – I don't hear myself saying that there's a spaniel-swallowing tiger on the loose.'

'I think there is,' said Red.

'You see! Everyone but you is saying it.'

At precisely the moment where this argument looked like it might turn physical, the school bell went.

'OK, I better get changed for athletics practice,' said Del, heading off towards the locker rooms. 'By the way, anyone else here smelling rose bushes?'

'No,' said Ruby.

Ruby was going to be sitting out athletics training on account of her foot so she went and found a seat in the shade and watched.

Clancy was feeling pretty confident, and it wasn't *like* him to feel confident. There was only one more training session left before the interschool track and field event. Clancy had always been a good runner, but had never actually won a final because there had always been someone in between him and coming first.

His main adversary, however, was himself. He could talk himself out of winning very easily by talking himself out of competing, the little voice in his head telling him that he was likely to be humiliated, that he would trip, that he was useless anyway.

But this time Clancy wasn't to be defeated, not by himself, not by anyone. Marley Cassolet had got slower, or perhaps she had lost her hunger to win, or maybe Clancy had speeded up? Dean Brice had moved to senior school and Ruby, well, this time Ruby wasn't in the running.

**The warehouse
was hot**

It had a corrugated metal roof, glass skylights and not a single window, and the sun was beating down, and yet the woman looked as cool and collected as a catalogue model. The only concession she had made to the heat was to pluck off her jacket and hang it neatly on the hook on the back of the door. The man on the chair, however, looked a little more dishevelled, a little less defiant, a little broken even. He was not doing so well; the bruises to his eyes and nose told the whole story.

The woman called Lorelei was entirely focused on the job at hand and the job at hand was interrogation. 'You have put me in a very uncomfortable position, I owe *somebody* and I don't like to owe anyone any*thing*.'

The figure hunched on the metal chair didn't answer.

She circled him; not for one minute did she drop her gaze or interrupt it with a single blink.

'I am unable to settle my debt because you double-crossed me. Now all you need to do is tell me where it is.'

She was wearing him down, like a tiger circling its prey.

When he spoke, his voice cracked with despair. 'Lorelei...'

'You don't call me Lorelei,' snapped the woman, 'you don't call me Ms von Leyden, you don't get to breathe even a syllable of my name!'

'OK,' murmured the man, 'I'm just trying to explain that I

made the wrong choice here…'

'Too bad,' she said. She wasn't shedding any tears; why should she show mercy to a specimen so pathetic, so hopelessly stupid? He looked as pitiful as the pile of broken metal chairs and the twisted rusting ladder, tangled and hopeless, in the corner of this disused warehouse.

She changed tack, threw him a bone, her eyes piercingly blue as she said, 'Repay your debt to me by telling me where it is and then all of this, all of this, will just go away.' She gestured loosely as if there really was nothing to get upset about, as if with the uttering of a word this wretched creature's life could be restored to normality.

The man knew better; he could not be saved by simply *"telling"*. He knew how it would go, whether he told her or not. The outcome would be the same: he was a dead man.

'Let me repay you,' he whispered. 'Let me give you back your money. And then let me go.'

Lorelei laughed and her blue eyes flashed cold. 'Unless you tell me where it is,' she said, 'I doubt very much you'll be leaving this warehouse with a beating heart.'

Chapter 20.
The writing on the wall

SCHOOL WAS OVER FOR ANOTHER DAY and Ruby was on her way to hang out with Del at Elliot's place near the beach. In fact, the three of them had got as far as the bus stop when Ruby spotted something written on the wall: a chalk drawing of a fly and a trail line like it was buzzing off towards the centre of town, towards Central City Park. It didn't take her a whole deal of time to work out what that meant; she was obviously required at Spectrum.

She faked a pretty dramatic sneezing fit before she broke it to her friends.

'Ah, you know what, I'm not feeling so good. I think I'm gonna have to bail.'

'You what?' said Del. 'All of a sudden, in this last *thirty seconds*, you don't feel so good?'

'Come on Del, look at her,' reasoned Elliot. 'Her nose is all stuffed up she's sneezing her head off. She sounds like some kinda alien.' He paused to examine Ruby's face. 'She doesn't look great either, bloodshot eyes and puffy... And she's got a limp.'

'Thanks Elliot... well, sorta, I coulda done without the photo-fit description, but anyhow... So look, I'm not trying to ruin your life here Del, I just feel lousy.'

Del shrugged. 'Yeah Rube, I didn't mean to be a Grinch about it.'

'Don't sweat it,' said Ruby, giving Del a friendly punch on the arm.

She headed off up the road and, when she spotted a cab, whistled for it to stop, got in and directed it uptown, towards the park.

As she approached the toddler playground, Ruby thought she caught sight of Vapona Begwell; this was all she needed, a run-in with her least favourite schoolgirl. She ducked down as she entered the playground enclosure, but heard no jeering voice as she bolted marine-style into the caterpillar pipes. Maybe she was mistaken.

Hitch was waiting for her at Spectrum.

'Glad you recognised my work,' said Hitch.

'*You* actually chalked that fly?' said Ruby.

'Not exactly,' said Hitch. 'My idea – I got one of our technicians to execute it.'

'Figures,' said Ruby. 'You don't strike me as the chalk graffiti type.'

They set off towards a bank of elevators and stepped inside. Hitch pressed a yellow button and the doors closed.

'Where are we going now?' asked Ruby.

'Blacker has a job for you,' said Hitch.

When they stepped out, they were either several floors above or several floors below, Ruby wasn't sure. They walked a little way along the snaking corridor, passing doors of yellow, all different hues and tones. A minute or two later, they reached one that was the yellow of butter – they stopped in front of it and knocked.

Blacker was perched on a stool in the middle of the large room; papers surrounded him and the hanging lights which dangled from the ceiling illuminated the chaos, but in a friendly sort of way. On the walls behind him were plans to a building Ruby did not immediately recognise. Though, once she noticed the many staircases and banks of elevators, the mainly large open spaces, she surmised that it was either offices or a department store building.

Blacker up to shake hands with both Hitch and Ruby and in doing knocked the coffee cup he was drinking from on the floor. was a typical Blacker scene. He started to mop up the mess with something not cut out for mopping – was it his discarded tie? Ruby couldn't tell. He smiled and said, 'Good to see you Ruby.'

'Hey Blacker,' said Ruby, 'good to see you too.'

'I'll leave you both to it,' said Hitch.

'Where are you going?' asked Ruby.

'I have something to pick up,' said Hitch. 'Easier to do it on my own.'

He left the room.

'So what's up this time?' Ruby asked Blacker.

'Well, we have a little trouble at the store, Melrose Dorff being the *store*, the *trouble* being theft.'

'Shoplifting or robbery?' asked Ruby.

'More like disappearing into thin air,' said Blacker.

'Oh,' said Ruby, 'that sounds interesting.'

'Not to Melrose Dorff,' said Blacker.

RUBY: *'What are we talking? Watches?'*

BLACKER: *'Jewellery.'*

RUBY: *'What type of jewellery?'*

BLACKER: *'The most expensive kind. It's from an antique collection designed in the 1920s – Persian, upmarket, meaning no one I know could ever afford.'*

RUBY: *'What's the maker's name?'*

BLACKER: *'The makers are sisters, Katayoun and Anahita Hatami...'*

RUBY: *'Katayoun & Anahita... I know it.'*

BLACKER: *'You know some random things.'*

RUBY: *'My mom has a Katayoun & Anahita necklace; it comes from my dad's family – his father was in the jewellery business. It's seriously valuable – my mom keeps it in the City Bank.'*

BLACKER: *'And I'd advise her to keep it there.'*

RUBY: *'I'll let her know.'*

BLACKER: *'Actually, better not. Twinford City is set to host the biennial Gem Festival early next year. If rumour gets out about jewellery thefts at our most prestigious store, then I think that hope will fly right out the window. We're trying to keep this pretty hush-hush.'*

RUBY: *'What kinda things have been taken?'*

BLACKER: *'So far, a tiepin, a brooch, an earring, a pendant on a chain.'*

RUBY: *'An earring?'*

BLACKER: *'Yes, just one.'*

RUBY: *'OK, so what do you propose doing? Presumably you've staked the place out, right?'*

BLACKER: *'That's where you come in. We have Froghorn on* camera detail, behind the scenes; we thought it best to keep him out of public range.'

RUBY: 'So what dya want me to do, sit with him?'

Ruby wasn't crazy about that idea. She and Froghorn weren't exactly bosom pals.

BLACKER: 'I don't think that would be such a good idea, no. We were thinking you might like to stake out the store. Since your mom and dad have been invited to the Marie Antoinette perfume launch, it would be natural for you to go too.'

RUBY: 'Cool – you need me to get some kinda disguise?'

BLACKER: 'That won't be necessary, you are the disguise.'

RUBY: 'How dya mean?'

BLACKER: 'You're a school kid. Who expects a school kid to be staking out a store?'

RUBY: 'I guess. So what am I looking for?'

BLACKER: 'You're there to observe. Check out the guests, the people hosting the event, the staff, the waiters. Who they are, what they do, how they behave – no one's going to notice a kid, so keep your eyes peeled and report back anything you think might be of interest.'

They discussed the plan thoroughly and agreed on how they should proceed.

'OK,' said Ruby. She got up to go, meeting over.

'By the way,' called Blacker. 'Stop by the gadget room: your equipment is ready for you to pick up.'

Ruby walked along the long twisting corridors until she found the orange door. She punched in the time code and entered the gadget room.

She stood stock still when she saw the strange-looking figure standing at the far end of the room.

'Who's that?' she called.

A mumbling sound came back.

'That you in there Hitch?' she asked. 'No wonder you wanted to be alone.' Hitch was busy pulling on some weird kind of black cape-mackintosh-mask-hat thing.

'You got the Batmobile parked somewhere?' said Ruby.

'I've always got the Batmobile parked somewhere,' said Hitch flatly.

Ruby made a face. 'You're not seriously thinking of wearing that, are you man?'

'If I can work out which way round it goes, then yes,' replied Hitch. He looked at the label before realising his mistake. 'Ah, that's the problem: I've got it inside out.' He took it off, turned it the right way round before pulling it back on. He was now wearing a completely weird silver cape-mackintosh-mask-hat thing. 'That's better,' he said.

'Yeah, now you look completely normal,' said Ruby in a highly sarcastic tone. 'Just make sure you wear it a long way away from me, will ya? I don't wanna be seen dead with anyone dressed like that.'

'That's kind of the idea kid. It's a blaze coat, not a fashion statement. It's built to withstand extreme temperatures and get you through flaming buildings and undergrowth unscathed. What with that forest fire raging the other side of Great Bear, no one wants to take any chances – it could reach Twinford and Spectrum need to be prepared.'

Hitch picked up some boots and began pulling them on.

'Nice accessorising,' said Ruby.

'One day kid, you might be glad to see me dressed up in this.'

Ruby collected the three tiny pieces of technology that Blacker had requested for her and put them in her satchel.

They were about to exit Spectrum when Buzz called out across the atrium. 'LB wants to see you now Ruby Redfort. Make your way at once to her office.'

Ruby turned and headed towards LB's door, her satchel slightly dragging on the floor.

'Your bag is dragging,' said Buzz. 'It's annoying.'

'What is this – school?' muttered Ruby.

Hitch looked at her and said, 'Kid, if there's one thing I would advise you do, it's to keep that big mouth of yours shut. Why in the name of bozo did you tell LB about losing your glasses?'

'I don't know. I kinda panicked and it came out.'

Hitch nodded. 'LB has the knack of getting people to tell the truth.'

'What dya think she wants? You think this is bad news or something?'

'All I know is she said she'd made a decision,' said Hitch.

'Oh,' said Ruby. She took a deep breath.

'Good luck kid,' said Hitch.

**'But it's gone,
don't you see that?'**

His eyes pleaded with her. 'Long gone.'

Beads of sweat were running down his nose.

'But I don't think you understand,' said Lorelei. 'If it's gone, then I'm in a lot of trouble, and if I'm in trouble then you are in a whole lot more. You will pay with your life and just to make things perfectly clear: I don't bluff.'

She pulled out a heavy object from her purse and curled her finger round the trigger, her expensive shoes click-clacking as she moved carefully across the hard stone floor, her eyes sparkling and her Turkish delight fragrance suffocating the air.

'So are you going to tell me where it is now?'

He shook his head.

'Oh, have it your own way,' she snapped. 'You're boring me.'

She raised the gun.

'Wait!' cried the man, his face full of disbelief. 'You can't kill me! Without me, you'll never find what you want, let alone control it.'

'But you said it was gone,' said Lorelei, taking aim. She was enjoying herself with this fish caught on a line, wriggling for his life.

'If I found it for you, would you let me go? Really I mean?'

'But of course. We can be civilised about this.'

She lowered the gun.

Chapter 21.
The decision

WHEN RUBY ENTERED THE WHITE OFFICE, LB was, as usual, busy writing something on someone's file, glasses perched on the end of her nose, brow furrowed.

'Sit.'

Ruby sat.

LB didn't look up nor did she put her pen down; she continued to write as she spoke.

'Against all my better instincts I'm going to give you one more chance to prove yourself capable of becoming a field agent.'

Ruby opened her mouth to speak, but changed her mind when she remembered Hitch's words.

'If you fail,' continued LB, 'there will be no more discussion about your suitability; you will be taken off the active agent programme and instead will concentrate on your code-breaking work inside the Spectrum headquarters.'

Again Ruby resisted the urge to speak.

'I should inform you that this is not a decision I would have made had it not been for Hitch arguing your case. He assures me that you will not make me regret this decision, so can I point out that you will be letting *him* down should you fail this second stage of training?'

Ruby merely nodded.

'Someone will let you know when this second test will take place. For now your input is required on this jewellery theft case. I want it cleared up by the end of the week.'

Ruby looked at her like she was clearly insane, but happily LB did not see the face she was making and merely said, 'Go,' and that was how the 'conversation' ended.

Chapter 22.
The moral compass

THE NEXT DAY RUBY WAS NOT FEELING WELL ENOUGH TO DRAG HERSELF OUT OF BED, though somehow she did – just not in time to get to her homeroom before the school bell rang.

Mrs Drisco was on fighting form; she was holding her detention slips, all ready to issue.

'So Ruby, what excuse do you have for us today?'

'Let me think,' said Ruby. 'Oh yeah.' She reached into her satchel and pulled out a doctor's note.

There were no two ways about it, this was a genuine, bona fide doctor's note. The handwriting was scrawly and challenging to read, which only served to make it all the more authentic, but the message was clear enough.

Ruby Redfort was seen this morning by me, Dr Harper MD, and I am unhappy to report that she is experiencing a great deal of discomfort and a fair amount of pain in her left foot.

The medication I have prescribed may cause her to feel nausea, vomiting, acute stomach cramps, headaches, mouth ulcers, nasal congestion, sudden fainting spells and a need for regular trips to the bathroom.

Therefore, I would recommend that she be free to come and go as she pleases for at least the next week or so. Please see that she gets as much help and assistance as she requires and no unnecessary badgering.

Mrs Drisco looked drained – this was just not playing fair. There was nothing she could do but give in to Dr Harper's unreasonable recommendations.

Ruby sat down, satisfied that she had Mrs Drisco exactly where she wanted her.

Clancy's day was not going so well. Mr Piper the philosophy teacher had been discussing the moral compass all human beings are supposedly born with or without. As with all Mr Piper's lessons, everything was open for debate. Sometimes, Clancy found this maddening. There were some things Clancy Crew felt sure about and this was one of them.

'I mean can't he just take a view?' he asked Ruby when they met up. 'Just actually believe one thing over another? Why does everything have to be open to debate?'

'Because that's the point of his class Clancy. If he doesn't debate it, there's no point.'

'Yeah, but he asks me my opinion, and I tell him.'

'Tell him what?' said Ruby.

'Tell him that I think the human being is basically good, born with a moral compass, and then he starts debating that and saying, "*Just how many good Samaritans have you seen lately?*" and I say, "*OK Mr Piper, not a whole lot actually, but I think the human instinct to do good for fellow man is strong,*" and he says, "*And what about the human instinct to do bad, to cause pain to one's fellow man?*" and I say, "*I have given it more than a little thought Mr Piper, and I have made up my mind on this one, so can we please drop it?*"'

'He teaches philosophy class Clance, he never *will* drop it.'

'He goes on and on debating it for so long that I actually do want to do *him*, my fellow man, harm.'

'And maybe that's his point Clance,' said Ruby. 'Maybe he's trying to get you to see that you have the same instinct to do bad as you do to do good.'

'Well, he might just regret it,' said Clancy.

'If it makes you feel any better, I had chemistry class and I didn't do so well either.'

'How come?' asked Clancy.

'My nose.' Ruby pointed to it. 'Look at me, I can hardly breathe let alone smell.'

'So?' said Clancy.

'So the whole lousy class was about smell. We had to sniff things like solutions and compounds to see if we could identify anything that gave us a clue about their chemical structure. And me? – I couldn't smell a frankfurter if you stuck it up my nose.'

'You probably shoulda stayed at home Rube,' said Clancy, who really wouldn't have minded skipping school, today being the day he got his French exam results. Now he had them he would prefer not to go home. 'The bad news is Madame Loup says I have to resit my French exam,' he said. 'She says I've got one more chance, but what's the point? I'm never gonna pass.'

'Yeah, you are Clance, I swear you're gonna pass. You gotta convince yourself you can do it. And when you do maybe your dad might be feeling a little more generous; maybe he'll decide to help you out with buying a new bike.' She gave him a friendly slap on the back. 'I mean stranger things have happened; my mom saw a giant pig in the backyard.'

'You know you might just be right,' said Clancy, his face brightening. 'Maybe if I pass my French my dad will be so happy that he'll decide to buy me the Windrush 2000.'

'Well,' said Ruby, 'hope is a wonderful thing.'

**He heard the
familiar sound of
spiked heels on
hard floor**

...and waited for the door to open. He had a plan now: he would give her the information she wanted, lead her right to it, only he would surprise her at the last minute. She wouldn't know what had hit her. She had no idea what she was dealing with; she had no idea just how dangerous it was.

Chapter 23.
The scent of bubblegum

RUBY WENT ON HOME, keen to get her homework done and put a little practice into using the gadgets she'd been given for the Melrose Dorff stake-out. She hoped to get a little quiet time before dinner.

As she walked in the door, she heard her mother's voice.

'You'll never guess what Barbara, but I'm pretty sure that pig I saw is a hippo. A small one, but there's little doubt in my mind it was a hippo. If it wasn't, then it's a pig with awful fat legs.'

Ruby caught these words as she opened the front door; her mom was in her bedroom chatting on the phone. Ruby peeped round the door and saw her sitting at her dressing table, examining her face while talking to her great friend Barbara Bartholomew. She would no doubt be talking for a very long time.

Barbara had obviously cracked one of her Barbara jokes because Sabina was practically busting a gut: tears were rolling down her cheeks and she was incapable of speech. Ruby sprinted silently upstairs; now might be an excellent time to make what her mother would call *an unsuitable snack for a growing child*.

She tiptoed into the kitchen, not wanting to alert anyone who might be around to stop her, meaning Mrs Digby.

When Ruby came back downstairs a half-hour later, her mom was still talking on the phone, but this time to Marjorie Humbert. Ruby knew this because Sabina had her on speaker so she could at the same time paint her toes. Marjorie's rich voice squawked out of the tinny box.

'I just hope that forest fire doesn't head this way.'

'What forest fire?' said Sabina.

'Oh, you haven't heard? Clover Canyon has caught and people are worrying it's going to reach Great Bear, but it seems to be heading north-west so Twinford should be safe.'

'Well, that's a relief,' said Sabina. 'This house has been razed to the ground once already. I'm not sure I could go through that again.'

'No,' said Marjorie sympathetically, 'and it would be such a shame if the perfume launch was cancelled.'

Ruby went back upstairs to the living room and got comfortable. She liked to have the whole room to herself, and now if she was lucky she could settle into an hour of uninterrupted reading before Clancy stopped by. She was sure he would since he was probably dodging his father, not wanting to give him the bad news about his French test.

Ruby got her wish for peace and quiet and had had the living room all to herself for the past hour. She was happily lying on the couch, blowing bubblegum bubbles and reading several books all at the same time, and only looked up when she heard her father's shoes.

'Shucks Rube, you know how I feel about bubblegum.'

He had picked up the scent seconds after he crossed the threshold. Brant Redfort hated bubblegum; not only did he think it vulgar, both the chewing and the bubble-blowing, but he also hated it because of the memories the smell of it evoked, one in particular.

Once, when he was a ten-year-old kid, a boy called Mickey Durrant had cruelly rubbed Hubble-Yum into his scalp. The result was an ugly, close-cropped haircut, executed by Mrs Bell the school secretary – boy, should that woman never have been allowed to wield a pair of scissors. Just a whiff of that fake-strawberry smell and he was back there in that schoolyard, feeling frustrated and humiliated. For Brant Redfort, bubblegum represented all that was wrong with childhood.

'Jeez, sorry dad, it's Clancy's. He left it the other evening and I just got kinda hungry studying,' said Ruby. 'You know, too busy to grab a snack... and what with Mrs Digby being out and all.'

She handed her dad the pack like she couldn't care less about bubblegum.

None of this was actually true: Clancy Crew wasn't even a small fan of the stuff – sure he chewed gum, but not bubblegum; he always found it went sort of dry after about ten minutes of chewing – no, he preferred straight chewing gum, the mintier the better.

The *reason* Ruby tiptoed around the issue of bubblegum was because Brant Redfort was very determined about it and when he was determined about something he couldn't be budged. Perhaps this was because he felt *truly* strongly about very little – good manners being top of his list, which was a fair enough thing to feel strongly about. The importance of saying *Gesundheit* when a person sneezed? Not so sensible.

The bubblegum thing fell somewhere in between – nothing odd about not being keen on it, but slightly odd to not even allow it in the house. Ruby Redfort was a person who knew her own mind and didn't like being pushed around; however, she was also blessed with common sense. She had a rule – **RULE 42: DON'T WASTE TIME ARGUING WITH SOMEONE WHO WON'T IN A**

MILLION YEARS CHANGE THEIR MIND.

Ruby took the balled-up pink out of her mouth.

'So how are you planning to enjoy the vacation honey? You got ideas?'

'Not really,' said Ruby, only telling half the truth. 'Nothing firm anyhow.'

'Well, if you're looking for adventure, you could always join Camp Wichitino. I don't want my girl getting bored. Remember, you're only a kid once in your life.' He sighed. 'Might as well have fun – live a little.'

'I'll keep that in mind Dad.'

'That's my girl,' said Brant, mussing his daughter's hair, an affectionate gesture that Ruby always found irksome.

He left the room and she heard his expensive shoes squeak as he made his way down the stairs. Ruby turned back to her books and as she did so popped the bubblegum back into her mouth.

What she was reading was pretty interesting: it related to what she had been learning in class, concerning smell and memory. Many scientific studies had been carried out into just why smell is such a strong link to past events. Her dad's problem with bubblegum totally fitted with the theory. The studies seemed to agree that it was to do with the fact that:

Olfaction is different from the other senses. It is extremely old in evolutionary terms, and has more than one pathway into the brain.

Like the other senses – taste, touch, sight and sound – it reaches the cerebral cortex via the thalamus, which regulates unconscious processes.

*But **unlike** the other senses, smell also has a direct projection into the limbic system, a part of the brain surrounding the thalamus and so closely associated with feelings that it is often called the 'emotional brain'. Specifically, smell has a pathway that runs into the amygdala and the hippocampus. The amygdala is implicated in emotion and instinct. The hippocampus deals with memory and learning by association.*

In other words: smell signals directly enter parts of the brain that deal with emotion and memory. This means that they can easily arouse strong recollections of the past, along with accompanying feelings.

The reason her father reacted so badly to the odour of bubblegum had nothing to do with the actual smell of fake strawberries, but the fact that he *associated* the smell of fake strawberries with something bad that had happened to him long

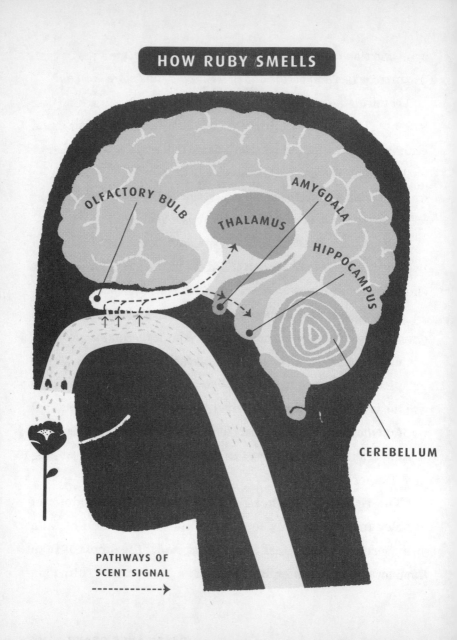

HOW RUBY SMELLS

OLFACTORY BULB

THALAMUS

AMYGDALA

HIPPOCAMPUS

CEREBELLUM

PATHWAYS OF
SCENT SIGNAL

ago, and the way it made him feel. Just a whiff of that smell triggered a memory and set him on edge.

It was a remarkable thing when you thought about it. That Ruby, who wasn't even on the planet when her father had endured this schoolboy mishap, could so easily take her father back in time, conjuring the same emotions he had felt when he was just ten, was kind of remarkable, and all this just by chewing bubblegum.

Ruby didn't hear the doorbell; she had moved up to her room so she could concentrate better on what she was studying.

Clancy was surprised when Brant Redfort opened the front door and handed him a not quite full pack of bubblegum.

'I don't approve of this Clancy, but it's yours to use off the premises. I hope you'll forgive me for pointing out that it will do you no good at all, I'm sure it's bad for the gut. Anyway, if that's understood, then we'll say no more about it.' He patted him on the shoulder. 'It's swell to see you Clancy. I hope you'll be joining us for supper.'

'O... K...' said Clancy a little uncertainly. 'Is Ruby in?'

'She sure is, go on up.'

Clancy scooted upstairs as fast as he was able, knocked on the door and entered the room.

'Your dad's acting weird,' he said.

'Must be the temperature,' said Ruby. 'Now take a look at this.' She took out the miniature camera Spectrum had issued her with. It was a tiny device set into a decorative fly, which was attached to a ring to be worn on the middle or ring finger of a small hand. The lens was in the fly's eye and photographs were taken by pressing the ring band at the back of the ring with the thumb of either hand. It was very discreet and simple to use. One could point it pretty accurately at what one wanted to photograph and take pictures without arousing suspicion.

Clancy was impressed. 'That's a nice piece of kit,' he said appreciatively. 'What are you expected to do with it?'

'It's for a stake-out at the *Let Them Smell Roses* launch.'

'Huh?'

'Spectrum has me on stake-out duty at the Melrose Dorff perfume launch. I'm gonna be there with my folks so it makes sense for me to tag along.'

'So what's the stake-out in aid of?' asked Clancy.

'Some pretty pricey jewellery has been disappearing from the store. I'll be nosing around while everyone's drinking cocktails and doing the whole socialising thing.'

'So what does this thief guy do?' asked Clancy. 'Climb up the drainpipe and in the window?'

'No one has seen him and no one has worked out how he could be getting into the building,' said Ruby.

'Perhaps it's an inside job,' said Clancy. 'You thought of that?'

'Yeah, we have, but you see at night this kinda grille thing comes down surrounding the Katayoun & Anahita cabinets – it's like a super huge cage, so there's no way anyone's gonna get inside that.'

'But what's to stop them raising it during the night? If it's someone who works in the store, then they'd know how to raise it back up.' Clancy was pretty sure this was how it was managed. 'It has to be a disgruntled shop worker,' he said.

'Can't be done,' said Ruby. 'It's all automatic; as soon as the shop closes, the grille comes down; as soon as it opens, it goes up no involvement from the store security or anyone who *works* in the store.'

'So...' said Clancy. 'With this stake-out deal, you're trying to catch the jewel thieves in the act?'

'That's the idea, but I don't think it's very likely.'

'And what's that?' asked Clancy, pointing at what looked like a bracelet lying next to Ruby on the floor.

'Very small binoculars,' said Ruby, picking up the teeny gadget.

'Cool,' said Clancy. 'What's it meant to be?'

'You know, a bangle,' said Ruby, slipping it on her wrist. 'You wear it like so,' she demonstrated, 'and when you want to take a closer look at something you flip this piece up' – she was referring to the hinged gold figure of eight with its circles of decorative glass – 'then you can rest your chin on your hand like you're just sorta thinking when really you're looking through a pair of binoculars.'

'I didn't think you were into jewellery,' said Clancy.

'This isn't jewellery buster, it's state of the art. By the way, what happened with your French exam?' asked Ruby.

'One last chance,' said Clancy. 'So what happened with your LB meeting?' he asked.

'One last chance,' said Ruby, 'maybe not even that – I wouldn't trust LB not to change her mind, that's why I've gotta do well with this whole Melrose Dorff case, otherwise I reckon I'm gonna get kicked out for sure.'

Clancy had never seen Ruby look so worried about anything: all that confidence was gone, all that Ruby Redfort cool had melted away, and suddenly she was just like him, fallible.

**He smiled as he
smelled the fragrance
of Turkish delight...**

...and he knew who had entered the room before he had even lifted his eyes to meet hers. 'I'm ready,' he said. 'Shall we go?'

She cocked her head to one side and said, 'Slight change of plan.'

He searched her face, puzzled. 'What do you mean?'

'The thing is, I've been doing some research of my own; you know the City Library is full of useful information, books on every subject, every subject under the stars, amazing how much one can learn.'

His face fell.

'Who would have thought it was going to be so simple.' She smiled. 'Yes,' continued Lorelei, 'I know how to find your creature and I know how you control it too.'

She reached into her purse and pulled out the gun. 'Time to say *búcsú*, is that what you Hungarians say? I'm a little rusty I'm afraid. Anyway, no matter, however you say it, it's goodbye and this time it's final.'

She extended her arm and pulled the trigger.

Click.

Nothing.

She frowned and then laughed. 'You know I really can't be bothered to kill you tonight, I have somewhere to be and my dress isn't ironed and goodness knows where I stored those spare bullets – no time to look.'

She left the room, clanking the door shut behind her, her stiletto heels echoing down the corridor.

Relief did not register on the man's face; death was inevitable now that his secret was discovered; he had no plan B and was beyond hope, so it didn't matter when it came.

He gazed up at the broken skylight and then in a blink of an eye all that changed. He turned to look at the pile of metal debris in the corner of the room.

Plan B, he thought.

Chapter 24.
All that glitters

'WHAT'S GOING ON WITH YOU CREW? I saw you loitering around the bike shop last night. Is it that new sales girl – you fallen in love or something?'

'Cut it out Del,' said Clancy. 'I don't even know what girl you're talking about.'

'It's not the girl,' said Mouse, 'it's the bike. He goes there every day, don't you Clance?'

'How do you know?' asked Clancy.

'I've seen you lots of times,' said Mouse.

Ruby and her friends were making their way to school from the bus stop, and they had stopped by the waffle stand to grab a bite before class.

'Well, it must be some bike,' said Elliot. 'Because that salesgirl sure is pretty.'

'Too pretty for you Finch,' said Del.

'What? You saying she wouldn't go out with me?'

'Not in a million,' said Del.

'So you're saying she'd date Clancy?'

'I'm saying she wouldn't date either of you.'

'That's what you think,' said Elliot.

Clancy wasn't interested in this debate; he was busy thinking about the bike and how it would never be his unless his dad grew an actual heart or he himself robbed a bank.

'Never gonna happen,' muttered Clancy.

'What?' said Ruby. 'You still down about that blue bike?'

'It's a Windrush 2000,' said Clancy.

'Clance, you either gotta stop feeling sorry for yourself and make it happen or...'

'Or what?' asked Clancy.

'Or... get over it. I mean I'll loan you my bike if you'd lighten up for twenty minutes. I'm not really riding much now my foot is all sewn up – feel free to ride it until you get a new one.' She looked at him, his face a picture of dejection.

'No offence Ruby, and that's a real nice offer and all, but it doesn't really compare,' said Clancy.

Ruby couldn't agree with him. 'You're getting your head turned by looks Clance; appearances can be deceptive my friend. Take that girl at the bike store. She's pretty, yes, but Elliot can do better.'

'I don't think so,' spluttered Del.

'She'd be *lucky* to date Elliot: she clearly has no brain at all,' said Ruby.

'She went out with Max Cunningham for a year,' said Elliot.

'My point exactly,' said Ruby, gurgling down the remainder of her shake. 'A total duh.'

The afternoon was taken up with sport – not that Ruby would be doing much. She could walk OK now she had the Bradley Baker sneakers, but the way her foot was, stitches and all, naturally she'd had to pull out of the Twinford interschool athletics. Clancy wasn't exactly broken up about missing the chance to compete against Ruby; he couldn't be sure that if she was running he would actually beat her, but now he didn't have to worry about that.

Gemma Melamare was the one real threat; sure there was Dillon Flannagon and Cassius Knole, perhaps even Ronda Lewis, but to lose to any of them would be deemed OK. They were all fast, all contenders, but Gemma was nasty. She had always looked down on Clancy and Clancy was sick of it; he had had enough of being treated like some dorky bozo. He was going to win.

And he *did* win.

He beat Gemma by a hair's breadth, but it was enough.

'Way to go Clance,' shouted Ruby from the bleachers. He glanced over at her and saw that she was genuinely happy for him, no faking. As he looked at her smiling face, he began to wonder if he really would have beaten her had she been running. She looked so easy about it, maybe she knew she could do it, could take this small victory, his win, away from him and it didn't matter to her because she was faster than him, better than him.

And suddenly somehow this race won felt not quite a win.

When Ruby returned home, she walked into the middle of an interesting conversation. The Redforts were all attending the Melrose Dorff launch and Mrs Digby had the night off. Hitch was busy shaking martinis for Brant and Sabina who were sitting on the curved sofa in the living room. They were both dressed in their finest and all ready to go.

'That Mrs Beesman must have really lived a life once,' said Brant, spearing an olive with a cocktail stick.

'You think?' said Sabina.

He nodded as he popped the olive into his mouth. 'Judging by the expensive jewellery she was carting around when I stepped into the office this morning.'

'What *are* you talking about Brant? Mrs Beesman doesn't have a cent! Well, she has a *cent*, but she couldn't have anything much more than a cent and, if she has anything *worth* anything, she would surely sell it to get some *dollars*,' said Sabina. 'Have you seen her coat? It's all holes. I left one of my winter wraps on her stoop in January, but I've never seen her wear it – Barbara suspects Mrs Beesman made it into a cat blanket.'

'Well, I'm telling you, her *cat* looked like it was wearing a pretty pricey-looking rock around its neck,' said Brant, 'and I know more than a little about jewellery, my old man having been in the business and all.'

'I can't argue with you there honey; if you say it was top dollar, I believe you.'

'It has to be quality costume jewellery,' conceded Brant, 'but still, good antique costume jewellery can fetch a buck or two.'

This was a strange conversation in light of everything that had been going on recently, and when Ruby made it up to her room to change she wrote it down in her yellow notebook number 624.

```
Wednesday morning: Mrs Beesman's one-eared
cat spotted somewhere near Dad's office
wearing quality costume jewellery.
```

She flicked back a few pages to where she had written:

`Stranger tries to grab Mrs Beesman's cat.`

She then drew a red line across the pages to connect the two Beesman notes.

`Is there a link?`

She had no idea, of course, if there could possibly be any kind of connection between the sighting of a cat wearing a jewel on its collar and a man trying to grab the cat – for one thing, Ruby had no way of knowing if the cat had been wearing the collar at the time of the attempted cat snatch, nor did she think it was likely anyone would imagine Mrs Beesman would own anything worth stealing. But it was interesting that her father thought so.

**It had been a
difficult climb...**

...the ladder was unstable and rusty, but he had made it and now he was free and looking down through the broken skylight at the deserted warehouse room.

If he could just make it from the high roof, he would be OK. He could see the canal, he could see the road, the quiet suburban houses and he was going to have to take a chance. His mouth was dry; it was a long way to fall, unlikely that he would survive it.

He took a deep breath.

He must not fall.

Chapter 25.
1770

RUBY WAS TO ARRIVE WITH HER PARENTS, just like she was one of the invited guests, which indeed she was. Despite declaring that the event sounded like a total yawn, Ruby was kind of eager to go, stake-out or no stake-out – the thing was she had always been into perfume and scents. She had a sizeable collection of fragrances and those who knew her well could identify her by the perfume that lingered after she had left a room, usually a wake of wild rose and bubblegum.

Ruby had made sure the fly surveillance ring was firmly jammed on her finger before getting ready. Ruby didn't wear a lot of jewellery, it wasn't really her thing, but the fly ring was different. For a start, it wasn't purely decorative, and for seconds, well, it was a little bit unexpected, edgy and dark.

She had made an effort with her appearance and had ditched her jeans and T-shirt (emblazoned with the words *you're so dull I have a headache*) for a vintage red and black A-line dress with a round collar and deep pockets. Her mother was pleased even though the garment smelled strongly of mothballs.

'You really clean up well, you know that Ruby?' Then she caught sight of the Bradley Baker sneakers.

'Honey, are sneakers really the best footwear with that ensemble?'

'I think it works,' said Ruby.

Her mother just looked at her, her hands on her hips – she meant business. Brant made a face at Ruby which suggested he was not going to back his daughter up and it was unlikely to be a fight she was going to win. So reluctantly she dragged herself upstairs to find some alternative shoes.

She chose the sparkly red clogs her mother had bought for her back in April, the same red clogs that she had used as a weapon at the museum launch; the throwing of them had preventing an important statue from being stolen by an undesirable man (this explained why a chunk of wood was missing from the sole of one shoe). The undesirable man was criminal mastermind and murderer Count von Viscount.* The main thing tonight was that the clogs looked good and Sabina was content and off Ruby's case.

Finally, Ruby picked up the last gadget Spectrum had given her. It was a tiny earpiece, which would allow them to record her conversations and speak to her if they needed to give her instructions.

She placed it in her ear and walked downstairs.

Hitch drove the Redforts to the department store, newly restored to its former 1920s glory. It was an elegant art deco building with carved stone detail and impressive gilt and glass doors. The Italian marble floor gleamed and the huge chandeliers sparkled and all the guests looked kind of delighted with themselves as they floated round the shop, peering into the fabulous curved glass counters, sipping cocktails of all varieties.

The Lost Perfume of Marie Antoinette 1770 was displayed on a Louis XVI table, ornate and a tad vulgar. The perfume bottle was neither ornate nor vulgar, however: it was an object of simple beauty, like the fragrance it contained – at least this was what the label claimed.

All the guests oohed and aahed when they caught a drift of the scent: jasmine and rose petals, and several other unspecified ingredients *'playfully tumbling together to create in fragrance form a portrait of a young Austrian woman picking up her skirts and running through a French flower garden'*. Or so the label said.

Ruby thought the perfume was OK. Despite her cold, she could actually smell it, so that was something. She helped herself to a squirt and dabbed it onto her neck. OK, it was nice, but it really wasn't worth all this fuss.

Next to the perfume table in a large glass display cabinet were Marie Antoinette's jewels.

'Remarkable,' uttered Brant. 'What my pa would give to put these jewels under the hammer.'

The security man eyed him suspiciously.

'Auctioneer's hammer,' explained Brant hastily. 'My pa was an expert in fine antique jewellery.'

'Talking of which, aren't those gorgeous!' Sabina was pointing at the Katayoun & Anahita collection, antique Persian art deco jewellery designed especially for the launch of Melrose Dorff in 1927. Ruby glanced at them; no one seemed aware that any of the jewellery had mysteriously gone missing.

Like most of the guests, Sabina found herself drifting towards them, mouth open and eyes wide with wonder.

Ruby tagged along with her parents and while they talked she listened to the murmurings of the crowd, followed their enchanted gazes and watched their excited gestures.

She saw nothing suspicious at all.

Finally, the announcement came: the mayor's wife stood on the department store grand staircase and revealed Twinford's plans to host the Gem Festival in February. It was very much an open secret since the planning had been going on for at least a year and a half, but this didn't stop everyone congratulating themselves for living in the city that hosted the mostest.

And then it was the turn of Madame Swann, the creator of *Let Them Smell Roses*: The Lost Perfume of Marie Antoinette 1770, to speak. She took to the floor with great aplomb, her heavy French accent stealing the show from the mayor's wife, who was no speechmaker.

Madame Swann was tiny, dramatically so. The drama was mainly generated by a dead thing, a mink possibly, which crept round her neck and trailed down her tiny back so its lifeless claws almost tiptoed on the floor. On her head was a bird of some kind, again dead and attached to a perky hat. The shoes she wore were blue silk and encrusted with gems, the soles perched on precariously high heels, but still she was smaller than all the other guests, except perhaps for Ruby. Ruby was unusually small for her age – though she had every intention of growing taller than Madame Swann.

On Madame Swann's left hand was a ring that coiled round one of her small sturdy fingers, a golden dragon with piercing blue eyes. Ruby noticed that when Madame Swann caressed its head it puffed a cloud of fragrant smoke from its nostrils.

'Musk,' she declared when she passed the Redforts after

her brief speech. 'I am a slave to that scent.' Her voice – a raspy French cliché – added to her theatricality.

'That's some ring,' said Brant. 'My wife would get a big kick out of that; where did you buy it?'

'Oh, this ring cannot be bought,' replied Madame Swann, smiling to reveal slightly greying teeth. 'This ring was designed by the Hatami sisters many years ago and it is one of a kind: no other ring exists like this one.'

'Isn't that always the way?' said Brant. 'The best things always *are* one of a kind.' Brant turned to see Sabina now at his side. 'Just like my beautiful wife,' he said. 'She's an original. When they made her, they broke the mould.'

'Thank you honey,' cooed Sabina. She kissed him on the nose.

Madame Swann smiled hard – she was trying to convey a charmed delight in these rich-looking people with their fat wallets, but frankly she was struggling.

'My wife and I adore your perfumes,' said Brant, picking up one of the elegant *Let Them Smell Roses* bottles and giving it a long sniff.

Madame Swann battled to retain her distorted grin.

'I'm forgetting my manners,' said Brant, extending his hand. 'Brant and Sabina Redfort.'

Madame Swann's smile perked up considerably.

'*Oh là là* Monsieur and Madame Redfort, what a great pleasure to meet you!' And of course she meant it. Monsieur and Madame Redfort were, after all, two of the most influential socialites in town.

'You must come and visit me in my hideaway. I am renting the most beautiful little *maison* in the middle of the pine forest on the edge of the lake. I have to be in nature – my nose cannot manage the pollution of the big city.'

Further conversation revealed that the 'little *maison*' of which she spoke was in fact Still Water, Arno Fredricksonn's most famous private building. Designed just before he built the Redforts' home, Green-wood House, Still Water was a triumph of modern architecture; a house suspended over a lake so it *'fused effortlessly with the tranquil landscape'*, or so the journals claimed.

Ruby couldn't see anything particularly unusual about the evening. It was the standard meet and greet and mingle deal. Lots of influential Twinford folk, the press of course, and a few lucky hangers-on who had managed to somehow get their hands on an invitation.

If one was being entirely truthful, Madame Swann's elegantly bottled fragrance was somewhat outdone by the staggering blue of the Katayoun & Anahita jewels artistically displayed on disembodied velvet hands and slender velvet necks. Every mirror in the store seemed to reflect back these dazzling blue gems and it was impossible for the guests not to be lured away from the *lost perfume of Marie Antoinette* and gape in awe at the Persian collection.

However, though there was much interest in these stunning pieces, no one seemed 'suspiciously' interested and nothing happened to cause any of the security team any sleepless nights.

The stake-out was fun up to a point, but, as the evening wore on, the time began to drag a little. Ruby had taken as many furtive photographs as it seemed worth taking and was by now a little weary from both flu and foot-ache, so sat down on an overstuffed velvet stool. She idly picked up a feather that had no doubt fluttered off some lady's expensive blue boa and started stroking her face with it. She had almost sent herself off into a trance-like state when she heard a loud hiss in her ear.

'Little girl! Will you get with the programme!'

The shock of the voice in her ear caused her to topple from the plump purple seat and land in a slightly undignified sprawl on the marble floor.

'Jeepers Redfort, you're acting like you're about thirteen years

old... oh, my mistake, you're just acting your age.'

The voice was Agent Froghorn's, often referred to as the Silent G because the G in his name was not pronounced, making the sound Fro instead of Frog. Ruby rarely bothered herself with this detail. Ruby's mispronunciation of his name was *one* of the reasons the Silent G disliked her so much – there were many others.

Not that Ruby cared one little bit: she considered Froghorn a potato head and, though he might have scored high on the Spectrum test and though they regarded him as a highly intelligent agent, to Ruby he would *always* be a dummy, and she really couldn't see that changing; once a potato head, always a potato head. As far as she was concerned, Froghorn was one of the stupidest clever people she had ever met and if she never heard his voice again it would be too soon.

So of course it had to be him at the other end of the earpiece.

'What's that you have in your hand and why are you rubbing it on your face?'

Ruby stuffed the feather into her pocket – she didn't need him to see that, it would make his day. By the time she had got to her feet, it was a little late for a smart reply. She was pretty mad at herself. *Nice going Ruby.*

One thing of interest did occur. The evening had a surprise ending when, just as Madame Swann took to the floor to thank everyone for coming to her 'little soirée', she turned white as a ghost, uttered a shrill '*Non!*' and suddenly and quite unexpectedly collapsed.

Ruby, little camera clicking away, scanned the faces of the guests and checked the display counters to see what could have caused such a reaction. No explanation was given by Madame Swann, and the guests left in a muddle of uneasy chatter.

So a Frenchwoman had fainted – big deal. Nothing of any importance had been uncovered so it was hardly going to convince LB that Ruby Redfort was some kind of crack Spectrum agent.

**Lorelei
unlocked the door
to the warehouse…**

...and her eyes immediately fell on the vacant chair. She stepped in a circle around it as if she expected the man to magically reappear. But the words abracadabra would not suffice to bring him back.

She called out and Eduardo came running. 'What is it?' he shouted.

'He's gone,' she said, her voice steady and hushed, not betraying the panic she felt. But her heels *tip-tapped* and Lorelei reached for her bottle of perfume, wafting Turkish delight into the air to calm her nerves.

Chapter 26.
Outshone

RUBY'S MOTHER WAS ALREADY ON THE TELEPHONE by
the time Ruby walked in to grab some breakfast. It was evidently
not her first phone call of the day.

'*As I was just saying to Grace, it was quite an evening
what with Madame Swann hitting the deck and all... The
fragrance was divine of course, but rather old school if you
know what I'm saying. I guess very 1770s...*' **She laughed**.
'*For my money, I prefer the Scent Lab counter, you know
where they mix all the perfumes for you there and then, so
much fresher, more you know, pure... modern yet traditional,
yet sort of now.*' **She nodded.** '*I agree... I agree Barbara...*'
She began to laugh. '*You just keep on spraying yourself
with room freshener...*' *she could barely catch her breath* '*...I
agree, who's to know the difference! Uh huh, uh huh, well, the
Katayoun & Anahita jewels really stole the night... I know,*

*I know, I'm telling you Barbara, you should get Ed to buy
you a pair of those earrings... well, tell him to sell the car!'*
She doubled up laughing again. *'Well, the house then!'*

Ruby poured herself some Choco Puffles and did the quiz
on the back of the packet.

TIME bomb SHELL   **MOVIE ___ SIGN**
NOSE ring FENCE   **TRASH ___ OPENER**
CHEESE straw POLL   **LIP ___ INSECT**

She had figured all the answers out by the time her mom
put down the phone and called out:

'Ruby, you know that pig I saw? I'm ninety-nine per cent
certain it was a hippo.'

RUBY: *'I'm not sure what to say.'*

SABINA: *'It was running pretty fast.'*

RUBY: *'Maybe it's in training.'*

SABINA: *'Mock me all you want Ruby, but you won't laugh
so much when you find it in the lap pool, possibly doing its
business.'*

RUBY: *'So long as it brings its own beach towel I'm not
judging.'*

Brant Redfort walked in.

RUBY: *'So Dad, did you hear the news? We're gonna be sharing the pool with a hippo.'*

BRANT: *'Ruby, I don't much care for it when you describe people that way.'*

RUBY: *'No, an actual hippo, as in potamus.'*

Brant looked confused. *'I think I missed a part of this conversation.'*

RUBY: *'Mom, do you wanna fill him in?'*

BRANT: *'Interesting as that surely would be, I need to get to the office.'*

RUBY: *'Me too.'*

She grabbed her satchel and headed out into the heat of the morning. As she caught the school bus, she thought about the Madame Swann swoon: was it caused by the heat or a few too many cocktails or was it simply Madame Swann getting all melodramatic? When she arrived at school, she told Red about it.

'Could it have been, you know, for publicity or something like that?' said Red. 'My mom says a lotta celebrity types do a lotta dumb things to get their names in the papers.'

Red's mother was a costume designer for the movies and so had 'seen it all' – as Mrs Digby would say. It wasn't such a dumb idea. Madame Swann did seem like a person who would be happy to grab the attention any way she could, especially if it looked like the eyes of her guests were wandering in the direction of the famous Persian jewels.

Ruby went to find Clancy who was standing by his locker, trying to close the door before everything he had stuffed in there pushed its way back out.

'You look like you gotta lot on your mind; anything exciting going on?' he asked.

'Ah, you know, just the usual,' said Ruby, yawning. 'Staking out the city department store, trying to spot a cat burglar, and chatting to my mom about how to pin down a hippo.'

'What?' Clancy's face was all scrunched up; he had skipped breakfast and he felt his brain wasn't working so well. Clancy was one of those kids who burned energy really fast; without food, he sort of stopped functioning. He didn't push through and stagger on, he simply conked out. Mouse could go hours without food, days even, she lived on air, but Clancy, well, Clancy was a different kid.

'How did the stake-out go?' he asked.

'Uneventful,' said Ruby.

'Oh,' said Clancy. 'Shame.'

He stood for a moment, looking a little glazed.

'So,' he said finally, 'what's with the hippo?'

Ruby had an unfortunate biology lesson; she had forgotten to do her homework assignment and, without even having read what the assignment was about, she was hard pressed to convince anyone that she *had* done it, but unfortunately left it at home.

Ruby was rarely in trouble for this sort of thing and it was somehow humiliating to be taking a detention for what she would consider a situation easily avoided. To rub salt into the wound this run-in with Mrs Greg was followed by a run-in with Vapona Begwell who obviously *had* witnessed Ruby going into the toddler park play area the other day.

'So what is it with you Little Redridingfort, you regressing or something?'

'What's your problem Bugwart?'

'I saw you crawling inside the caterpillar tubes and don't pretend you got a little squirt sister or something because I know you don't.'

'I didn't know you took such an interest in my family situation.'

'So you were just crawling about in there like a duh brain,' sneered Vapona. 'It doesn't surprise me.'

'Ever heard of snakes Bugwart? The boa constrictor kind?

Ever seen what a python can do to a toddler?'

'Don't make me puke laughing Redfort, there's no way you're gonna get me to believe you saw a python go into the caterpillar tubes and there's even less of a chance you're gonna convince me you went in there after it.'

'I got no interest whether you believe it or not,' said Ruby. 'All I'm asking is that you get your big nose outta my business.'

'Redfort, you're full of it!' jeered Vapona.

Ruby was a little late home since she had the after-school task of writing a 5000-word essay on the importance of Mrs Greg's biology assignments; she'd had a tough time trying to think what to write.

Back in her bedroom Ruby printed out every one of the little photographs taken at the 1770 launch the previous night. They were the size of small Polaroid prints, about two inches by three inches. She looked at them all very closely, but could see nothing to get suspicious about. She looked especially carefully at the pictures she had taken of the Madame Swann collapse, but again she drew a blank. All she saw were men and women dressed up to the nines, smiling and clapping, having a good time, people turning, people looking shocked, people moving in to help: in other words, nothing out of the ordinary.

Ruby's examination of the photographs was interrupted by a piece of toast which was left outside her door. She read it, then gathered the pictures into her satchel and pulled on her boots and headed back to the city toddler park.

Oh brother! she thought. *I hope Bugwart isn't around.*

She didn't feel the day could get much worse, but, as it turned out, the night was young and there was plenty of time for things to hit a lower low.

Chapter 27.
Drawing a blank

'SO REDFORT, WHAT DID YOU LEARN FROM LAST NIGHT'S SURVEILLANCE?' LB was looking at her intently like she needed an answer that would tie everything up and allow her to close the file and move on.

'I found out that Mrs Gruemeister is allergic to shrimp and so is her cousin Sybil. Jeff, the pianist, really wished he'd learned to play the flute and a few of the guests thought Madame Swann shouldn't have worn mink with that outfit and several thought she shouldn't have worn a dead bird on her head,' replied Ruby. 'Including me actually.'

LB picked up the red perspex file – Ruby's file. 'If you're trying to tell me something of interest, then might I ask you to get to the point?'

'What I'm trying to say,' said Ruby earnestly, 'is that I saw nothing. At least *nothing* that adds up as any interest to you, and I'm good at looking for details: dull conversations at boring parties are a specialty of mine. But I could make no connection between what I *saw and heard* and what we're looking out for.'

'So you didn't notice the host collapse to the floor,' said LB.

'Well, I was coming to that,' said Ruby. 'I think there's something a little off about Madame Swann.'

'What do you mean by "off"?' said LB.

'I guess fake is what I mean. I wouldn't put it past her to fake a faint to get people talking about her,' said Ruby. 'I mean she made all the papers, didn't she? They barely mentioned the whole deal about the Gem Festival.'

'So you think there's nothing more to it?'

'I'm not saying nothing for sure, I'm saying nothing I could see, but I need to keep looking,' said Ruby.

LB placed the file back on her desk.

'So,' she said, 'where next?'

'The footage, the close-circuit TV, there must be something that could tell us what's been going on with the thefts,' said Ruby.

'Froghorn has been over that with a fine toothcomb,' said LB, looking over at Blacker. 'At least that's what I understand?'

Blacker gave a nod. 'I set him up with a ton of tapes and he's been looking through them all day every day, but there's no sign of anyone robbing the place.'

'Yeah, but is he *actually* looking?' said Ruby. 'I mean really looking? I hate to criticise anyone's reputation here, especially someone with such white teeth and shiny hair, but I have noticed that he kinda lacks patience.'

LB gave Ruby a look. 'Yes, I'm aware of how you feel about each other.'

Ruby gave a mock shocked look. 'Well, I knew I didn't like him, but I always thought he was very fond of *me*?'

'Redfort, cut the baloney and tell me what you want,' said LB.

'I'd like to take a look at the tapes myself,' replied Ruby.

LB turned to Hitch who had just arrived.

Hitch, without more than a second's pause, said, 'Let the kid take a look; if there's something to see, she'll spot it.'

'OK,' said LB, 'I'll let Froghorn know – by the way, have you seen my Paris paperweight? It appears to have gone missing.'

In response to this Hitch merely raised an eyebrow.

When they were out of earshot, Ruby asked, 'So what's the whole deal with this paperweight?'

'Sentimental,' said Hitch. 'It was the first thing Bradley Baker ever gave her.'

'Oh,' said Ruby.

After a short walk down the lower-floor corridor, Hitch and Ruby arrived at the tape room. In the glass sound booth was

Agent Miles Froghorn, watching the small screen in front of him as he sipped a wheatgrass shot.

'Two of my favourite things combined,' muttered Ruby. 'An unpleasant person drinking an unpleasant drink.'

'Play nice Ruby, you know LB likes her agents to be the best of friends.'

'So why doesn't she keep him outta my way, in another part of the building... or planet?'

'Because this is his detail and, if you wanna get involved here, you're gonna have to do things his way.'

But Froghorn was perhaps even less pleased to see Ruby than Ruby was to see him. He didn't want this upstart in his office, making comments about the way he was conducting his work. What LB saw in her, he did not know. He observed that she had another of her vulgar T-shirts on: ***make mine a donut***.

It was so disrespectful.

After more than three hours of watching, something finally happened. The screen seemed to flicker.

'What was that?' said Ruby.

'What do you mean "what was that?" The screen flickered; it happens on these store cameras – someone jolts it and it moves.'

'Who would jolt it?' asked Ruby.

He gave her a pitying look. 'How would *I* know little girl? But I'll take a wild guess and say a *store assistant*?'

Ruby looked at the plan of the shop floor: each security camera was marked on it and this camera, camera 12G, was placed up high, about twenty feet above the floor.

'Must be some tall store assistant,' she said.

'So it's not a store assistant,' said Froghorn.

'So then what is it?' said Ruby. ''Cause it doesn't look like interference to me.'

'Now you believe you're an expert on surveillance-camera footage?' said Froghorn.

'No, I don't think I'm an expert at sitting in front of a TV screen and watching footage of shoppers shopping; that's what *you* do.'

The insult didn't pass Froghorn unnoticed. 'Great to know you think you might be good at *something* Redfort, because I hear the whole survival training didn't go so well.'

'I'm glad you care enough to take an interest in my training.'

'I heard you failed,' said Froghorn.

'And who did you hear that from, the Twinford Knitting Circle?'

'It's all around Spectrum,' said Froghorn, 'the talk of HQ: *"Will little Ruby Redfort get canned?"'*

Ruby imagined clonking Froghorn on the head and, by conjuring this picture, managed to keep her composure.

'All I was suggesting,' she said calmly, 'is that this could be a flicker caused by something moving very close to the camera lens.'

'All right, so let me put it this way little girl,' said Froghorn, 'what could it possibly have to do with the robberies?'

'I don't know,' replied Ruby, trying her very hardest not to call the potato head sitting next to her a potato head.

'So why don't we continue with the job in hand and not waste time.' Froghorn said this in such a patronising tone that Ruby found it hard to keep from calling the potato head beside her something a whole lot worse than a potato head.

They watched for another hour and Ruby couldn't help circling back to the flicker.

'Froghorn' – she remembered the silent G this time – 'would you mind just at least replaying that tape again?' She hoped that the correct pronunciation of his name might make him more compliant.

'Just to remind you, because you seem a little out of your depth here, we're looking for a thief, not evaluating the camera quality of Melrose Dorff's security system.'

'What's wrong Froghorn, having a bad hair day?'

Instinctively, Froghorn neatened his hair.

'You're so busy telling me,' said Ruby, 'that you're the expert here, the expert at sitting on your smug butt watching a little screen, that it hasn't occurred to you that you might be missing something, yet I don't hear you coming up with one possible suggestion that might help us solve this case. And by the way, sure, I might have flunked survival training, but at least I got to go out and try for it. I don't see anyone trusting you to survive in the great outdoors buster, no doubt because you wouldn't be able to manage three minutes without your skincare regime, let alone three days without food, shelter and clean undershorts. You don't know squat about squat and I don't care how big your IQ is, you're still the biggest duh brain I ever had the misfortune to meet, so I would suggest you ram your—'

Just before Ruby could finish making this suggestion, Hitch entered the room.

He looked from one to the other. 'Do I sense an atmosphere?' Neither of them spoke. 'I think I do... perhaps we should all take a little break.'

He led Ruby out of the room and along the corridor. 'Come with me kid before you say something stupid on top of all the stupid things you've no doubt already said.'

**'So how is the
perfume trade?**

I see you have a new fragrance out and I was curious about the name – 1770? Are you sure that shouldn't be 1970?'

Madame Swann gasped. How did Lorelei know?'

'Oh dear, poor Madame Swann, you thought I wouldn't find out. Tut tut, never kid a kidder.'

'What do you want Lorelei?'

Lorelei von Leyden toyed with her drink. 'Nothing much really, I just need you to teach me something is all.'

'And what could I possibly teach you? I taught you everything I know and you treated me like dirt.'

Lorelei shrugged. 'Not quite everything; there was something you neglected to share.'

'And what would that be?'

'It concerns a certain process, an extraction of smell.'

Madame Swann's face hardened.

'You tell me how to do that,' said Lorelei, 'and I'll keep your little secret safe.'

Chapter 28.
For the good of all

RUBY SENSED THAT HITCH WAS UNUSUALLY ON EDGE as they walked down the corridors. Something was on his mind, bugging him. Ruby was aware that he had had a meeting with LB and she wondered if LB had said something to unsettle him – whatever it was, he wasn't sharing.

When they got to the orange door of the gadget room, Hitch said, 'Now kid, I need to step in here, for just five minutes. Do you think you can stay out of trouble for three hundred seconds?'

'What are you saying?' said Ruby. 'You suggesting that I might touch something?'

'No,' said Hitch, 'I'm suggesting that you might *steal* something like all those times before. Just try and keep your hands in your pockets until we get out.'

They made their way through the corridors and punched in the code and entered. There was no sign of anyone, just a note on the workbench at the far end of the room. Hitch picked it up, frowned and said, 'OK, so I need to go into the back room and search through some boxes until I find what I'm looking for – you sit tight.'

'What *are* you looking for?' asked Ruby.

'Not that it's any of your business, but I'm picking up the Bradley Baker watch,' said Hitch.

'I should say it's totally my business,' said Ruby. 'LB gave that watch to me.'

'No,' said Hitch, 'LB requested that you keep that watch; it's yours to use in the field until she says otherwise.'

'Now you're nit-picking,' said Ruby.

'Now you're getting on my nerves kid,' said Hitch.

'I was only saying,' said Ruby.

'And I'm saying two words: zip it.'

Ruby snapped her mouth shut and gave him a cross-eyed look.

'Better,' he said. '*Your* watch, aka Bradley Baker's watch, has been fixed up and should be somewhere in the back room, but I'm not sure exactly where, so while I go look, you stand still.'

Hitch disappeared and Ruby walked up and down, peering into the cabinets, most containing what appeared to be mundanely ordinary objects.

She was just taking a look at the parachute cape again when

she noticed something gleaming on the floor just under one of the cases. She walked over and picked it up – it was a silver cufflink, one of Hitch's, though she hadn't noticed it drop. She stood up and banged her head as she did so. It was then that she discovered that displayed in the case next to the lost cufflink was a whole series of objects that related to being lost and getting found.

One of the very dullest was simply a small white and green striped canister. It looked a lot like a tube of mints – in fact, very much like an old-fashioned-style packet of Fresh Breath Mints. The label next to it said:

GROUND GLOWS [Taken out of commission in 1962]
To be used when trekking at night in uncertain
terrain. Help the trekker retrace his/her steps,
or a specified ally to follow the same route.
Made up of two parts: flat glow lights and
discreet shoe fix activator. **Instructions**: attach
activator to footwear and dispense glow discs as
you walk. Discs will only light up when in range
of the activator. Multiple activators can be
issued, for example to a fellow agent wishing to
follow the same trail.

There was a warning, but the ink was smudged and Ruby couldn't make out all that it said, just:

```
WARNING! after heavy rainfall they
    can    ra  c an  nr   ia e
```

These seemed like clever little illuminators because they had the advantage of only being useful to the user. They were very discreet and very handy if you happened to want an agent to follow your trail at a later time without tipping off an enemy tracker. No doubt they had aided the rescue of more than a few Spectrum agents over the years. Ruby wondered why they weren't issued as general survival kit; it would save a whole lot of bother – at least to her.

She looked at them for the longest time, well, actually, only about 3.5 minutes, but it seemed a long time as she stood there, thinking about what the right thing to do might be.

It turned out the right thing to do was to borrow them without telling anyone. She didn't want to involve Hitch because he shouldn't be implicated, just in case trouble was caused and also (and perhaps more importantly) because he might stop her. Ground glows were just the thing she needed and therefore they seemed to be a very sensible thing to take with her. *I mean how dumb would it be if I got lost and some whole mission got blown when, if only I'd been carrying ground glows, everything woulda been fine?*

There was also the small matter of LB, who would no doubt be firing Agent Redfort if she slipped up again during basic training. That decided it: Ruby put the ground glows in her pocket; after all, they had been taken out of service so who was really going to care?

'What are you up to kid?'

Ruby, caught off guard, jumped.

'I found your cufflink!' she said.

'I haven't lost a cufflink,' said Hitch. He took it from her. 'That's Bradley Baker's cufflink.' He looked puzzled. 'How did that wind up in here?'

It wasn't until much later that Ruby got back to watching the store security tapes. She had snuck back to the room where she and Froghorn had been working.

She got in easy enough: she remembered the sound each numeral made when pushed. The trickier part was finding the microtapes themselves: she had no idea where Froghorn had put them. After a little rummaging, she began to realise that they must still be loaded into the microtape reader. Of course

Froghorn had activated the security code on the number pad and of course this was known only to Froghorn. *What could it be?*

She looked at the pad for a moment, and noticed that four of the numbers were a little more worn than the others: they had a sort of sheen from being repeatedly pressed. Naturally Froghorn would be too arrogant to change his code.

1, 2, 7 and 9, thought Ruby. *But in what order?*

Then she smiled. It had to be **1729**. The smallest number expressible as the sum of two cubes in two different ways. Just the kind of number a geeky desk agent like Froghorn would choose.

Of course, because Froghorn was Froghorn, she couldn't ask him which tape the flickering thing had shown up on. He was never going to help her out like that.

She got lucky after approximately two hours and fifty-five minutes. She slowed the tape down and enhanced the image as much as she could; it was pretty blurry, but was clear enough for her to be sure.

'Well, I'll be darned,' said Ruby, 'it's a bird.'

She called Blacker and filled him in.

'I'm on my way,' he said.

The thing Ruby most liked about Blacker was that he

was just not interested in giving her a hard time about minor misdemeanours. For instance: gaining entrance to a locked office without permission; sitting at someone else's desk and breaking into their password-protected computer.

'Thought you might need one of these,' said Blacker, passing her a jelly donut wrapped in a serviette. He pulled up a chair next to hers.

'There it is,' said Ruby, freezing on the distorted image of a bird.

'So we have an intruder,' said Blacker.

'But it doesn't help us a whole deal,' said Ruby, 'I mean not as far as the robberies go.'

'Maybe not,' said Blacker, 'but it does mean that there's a lapse in security. I mean somehow that bird got into Melrose Dorff and I would doubt it was through the revolving doors, so we're probably looking at a window or a roof.'

'I guess,' said Ruby.

'Either way,' said Blacker, 'we should get down there tomorrow and tell them they've got something flapping around in store.'

Chapter 29.
Good and bad

CLANCY HAD GONE TO THE BIKE SHOP EARLY so he could gaze at the Windrush 2000 before meeting Ruby at the tree. But she never showed and by the time he realised that she never would it was too late to grab a bite at the diner. He was pretty hungry and found himself resorting to chewing on a piece of the bubblegum from the pack Mr Redfort had inexplicably handed him. But it just made things worse: his gut started rumbling and he felt hungrier than ever.

He was working himself up into a pretty bad mood: he was now both starving *and* late for class, and if his dad found out about it that meant another reason for him to get on his case. Maybe he just shouldn't care so much, become more like Ruby. She wouldn't worry about all these details; she didn't even care enough to show up at Amster Green. He needed something he could rely on and the Windrush was that something: he had to get his hands on that bike.

It was when Clancy was walking across Main and down Riverdale on his way from Amster Green, that he saw something kind of odd; it looked like a bundle or a slumped sack. He crossed the street and began to see that this bundle had shoes – well, feet and legs actually. Clancy guessed it must be a homeless guy sleeping in the early morning sun. He slipped off his backpack and let it fall to the grass, then cautiously walked towards the man.

He took a closer look at the guy's shoes and realised that they were pretty expensive as footwear went, not the footwear of vagrants. He knew this because Ruby's dad had the very same ones, made by Marco Perella. Blue and white deck shoes or, as Ruby would call them, 'dork shoes' – she had been complaining about the noise they made. Clancy could also see a price sticker on the bottom of the left sole. These shoes were not only expensive but newly purchased.

The man seemed to be unconscious, possibly drunk. Clancy took a cautious sniff. No, the guy wasn't drunk, there was no whiff of alcohol, but he did smell strongly of something, a mix of *one* really nice smell, probably some expensive cologne, and one very unpleasant smell that Clancy didn't like to imagine, but it was definitely on the scale of *poor bathing regime*.

He took the man's hand in his and squeezed. Did the

man respond? He wasn't sure. The hand clutched a cotton handkerchief neatly folded as if he had recently taken it from his pocket. Clancy took it from him and considered mopping the sick guy's brow – was that the type of action a person took in this sort of situation? The thing was, Clancy wasn't quite sure, but he felt he should do *something* if only to prove his point that the human being was basically a compassionate mammal, something he was beginning to doubt.

He ran to where he had dumped his backpack and looked to see if there was anything in it that could be of use. However, before he could employ his Boy Scout first-aid training, a car drove up and both doors were flung open. Two people, a tall young man and a slim young woman, ran towards the tree. Clancy was kind of relieved; his scouting days seemed a long way in the past and he wasn't certain that he was capable of saving a person's life if that was what was required.

'Oh, thank goodness,' said the woman, her face ashen. 'It's him.'

The tall guy looked concerned; he bent down to feel the man's neck, searching for a pulse.

The woman looked at him. The guy nodded. Her face relaxed a little. She sniffed the air, following the scent, and turned to see a boy chewing on some bubblegum, the sun behind him.

'Shall I call the paramedics?' Clancy asked. 'There's a phone booth just up the street, I can be there in a *minute*.'

'There's no need,' she said. 'I mean that's really kind of you,' she paused before continuing, 'but you see this happens a lot.' She stopped. 'That sounds bad, I'm sorry. What I mean is, he lives next door, has done for years, a really nice man, a good friend, but he has troubles, troubles the hospital can't fix. He's been missing for days and we have been so worried, but the cops, they said they couldn't help.'

'Really?' said Clancy. 'You're sure he's gonna be OK? 'Cause he seems in bad shape.'

'It looks worse than it is,' said the woman softly. 'He forgets to take his medication and then gets sick; we know what to do, been doing it a long time,' she said. She bit her lip. She looked so sad.

The woman was pretty, beautiful actually, and the kindness in her eyes made her more so. She smelled of something sweet, something good, a smell that suited her.

Clancy nodded sympathetically; her face was pale, like she had been up all night. Tears glinted, making her eyes shine bluer, and Clancy felt sorry for her, really sorry.

He watched as the couple eased their friend with great care into the passenger seat; he still had his eyes closed, but looked comfortable, his head resting on the kind woman's shoulder.

'Good luck,' called Clancy as they drove off. Suddenly he felt better about life – not everyone was mean-spirited; not everyone was out for themselves. It was too bad it didn't happen more often. Too bad his debate teacher, Mr Piper, couldn't witness this, an example of the good neighbour. Then he remembered how sick the man had looked and Clancy felt bad again. Boy, did life suck sometimes.

Chapter 30.
Nice detergent

RUBY HAD NOT MANAGED TO SEE CLANCY BEFORE CLASS; he was late arriving which was most unusual and then she realised why: she had forgotten to meet him on Amster Green.

Oh brother, she thought, *that won't make him any happier.*

She was keen to tell him about her latest findings, tame as they were; discovering a bird had flapped in through an open window or door was hardly like coming face to face with Nine Lives Capaldi or having Baby Face Marshall try to strangle you, but it was something. She couldn't help but feel satisfied that she had once again proved Miles Froghorn totally wrong and she thought Clancy might get a kick out of that.

Ruby went to wait for him to come out of philosophy class. The pupils spilled out of the room, chatting excitedly about what they had discussed; Mr Piper was a popular teacher and his class was considered interesting. Clancy might argue otherwise; he was last out and looked demoralised.

'Are you OK Clance? You look kinda shattered.'

'Don't even ask,' said Clancy as they made their way along the long corridor, down the stairs into the bright light of the schoolyard.

'By the way, where were you? I waited and waited, but you never showed.'

'I totally flaked,' said Ruby. 'I was up real late working on this whole Melrose thing and I just forgot. I owe you – you need a doctor's note or something to explain why you were late? I got one from the dentist too if you prefer that?'

'No, too late, Mrs Drisco already marked me down for an essay on the importance of punctuality,' said Clancy.

'I'll do that,' said Ruby, 'no sweat. When do you need it for?'

It was hard to be mad at Ruby Redfort. Clancy had always found that to be the case, which somehow, right at this moment, made him feel madder still, like she had this power over him.

They sat down at a lunch bench and Clancy swallowed down a sandwich as fast as he could, followed by potato chips; they helped. He forgot about being crabby at Ruby and instead grumbled on about his run-ins with his philosophy teacher.

'So I told Mr Piper about what happened this morning and all he could say was, *"This is just one example and how do you know that these people are good-spirited, what does it actually tell us? What did you actually see?"'*

Clancy was going on about the sad but yet somehow happy incident he had witnessed before school, but Ruby's mind had wandered off and was on other things.

'I wouldn't have spotted him at all if it hadn't been for his dork shoes,' said Clancy.

Ruby was thinking about the CCTV footage.

'At first I thought he was just some hobo, sleeping it off,' continued Clancy, 'but then I saw his footwear and realised he must have a few bucks. They were just like your dad's – same brand and all, you know, the squeakers?' It wasn't like Clancy to notice the brand of a pair of shoes, but Ruby had been going on and on about them so much that he had become very familiar with the shoemaker.

Ruby was sort of half listening to her friend, but mainly she was thinking about the bird, how had it got there and maybe she should go and check it out. She could take that tiny camera and catch the bird in action – really rub Froghorn's nose in it.

'So the guy gets picked up by these really nice neighbours of his and I guess it was kinda heart-warming. I feel bad though 'cause I took the guy's handkerchief, not on purpose or anything.' He pulled it out of his pocket. 'It smells nice.'

Clancy waited for Ruby to say something, but she didn't.

'Rube?'

'Uh?'

'Are you even listening?'

'Sure I am, this sick guy is out of it on the sidewalk in his expensive Marco Perella shoes and you try to help, but before you can these nice folks stop by and help the guy – who turns out to be their sick neighbour – into the car. It was heart-warming and if I might say so it has cheered you up about a thousand per cent.' Ruby had a talent for hearing things while she was actually thinking other thoughts. It drove Clancy crazy because although he could tell when she wasn't really paying attention he rarely if ever managed to catch her out.

'Is that handkerchief clean by the way?' she asked.

Clancy shrugged. 'I guess, looks clean to me. Why?'

'Hand it over, I need to blow my nose,' said Ruby.

'You can't blow your nose on some other person's handkerchief,' said Clancy.

'You said it was clean,' said Ruby.

'That's not the point,' said Clancy. 'It's not yours.'

'It's not like you're ever gonna see the owner again,' said Ruby.

'I know, but I should try and get it back to him.'

'What? Are you gonna take an ad out in the personals? *Green striped handkerchief, believed to be clean'* – she looked at it more closely – *'monogrammed with the initials SS, I think, or is it FF? Smells of'* – Ruby sniffed it – *'some really, really nice detergent...'* her voice trailed off for a second – *'call Clancy Crew for its safe return?'* She breathed in the scent again. 'Boy, is that some nice detergent – I can smell it even with a stuffed-up nose – it makes me think of a forest.'

Clancy took it and sniffed. 'It doesn't smell anything like a forest.'

'I didn't say it did. I said it made me think of a forest, the moon too.'

'The moon doesn't smell of anything,' said Clancy.

'How would you know? You ever been to the moon?'

'Here, have it,' sighed Clancy. 'I was trying to be a good citizen, but you take it if it reminds you of the moon so much.'

'Thanks, I appreciate your goodness,' said Ruby, sniffing it again. 'Smells too good to use, I'll just keep it in my satchel. I can sniff it when I need to breathe something other than Melamare's tacky hairspray – why does she have to sit in front of me? It gives me the worst headache.'

Chapter 31.
The uncatchable thought

AFTER SCHOOL WAS OVER, Ruby went to meet Blacker at a diner not far from the store.

'Well?' said Ruby. 'What did you find?'

'Turns out there is a hole in a small pane of glass in the maintenance team's restroom window. It's to the back of the store, behind the jewellery department. The bird must have flown in through there and out into the store.'

'Dillon Flannagon,' said Ruby.

'Pardon me?' said Blacker.

'Dillon Flannagon, he's some hitter. My friend Elliot said he thought he saw him hit a baseball through one of the department store's windows. I guess he was right.'

'So that explains how a baseball wound up in the toilet. The maintenance guy was puzzled about that,' said Blacker.

'How come he didn't notice the broken window?'

'It's high up and really small – he just didn't see it – and even if he had no one would think much of it; there's no way anyone could use it to break in. Those windows don't have any way of opening and only a pixie is going to make it in that way.'

'Do you believe in pixies?' asked Ruby.

'As it happens, no,' confirmed Blacker, his face deadpan.

'So if we're ruling out pixies,' said Ruby, 'then I guess we have zero in the way of suspects.'

'I'm afraid it looks that way,' agreed Blacker. 'It explains how the bird got into the building, but not a whole lot else.'

'I guess not,' said Ruby. There was a little thought flitting round and round her head, but she couldn't quite catch it.

They said goodbye and Blacker headed on back to Spectrum, but Ruby decided to go and take another look around Melrose Dorff.

Ruby stepped into the rotating door and let it spin her from the oven-hot day into the cool luxury of the shop. She looked around at the shoppers: the place was abuzz with activity; people browsing, trying on, holding up, smelling, applying and tipping faces at countertop mirrors.

She walked to a place where it was possible to view the jewellery counter without making it obvious that she was watching. She studied people as they came and went. Shoppers moved like coral fish nibbling their way through the reef. They were drawn to each counter in turn: trying on sunglasses, jewellery and hats, applying make-up, creams and perfume before drifting towards doorways, darting into elevators out of sight.

She waited to see if the bird might appear, but it did not; perhaps it had gone for good. She had been in the store for some time and found her eyes constantly flitting to the perfume counters: there was something interesting about the way people picked up the decorative bottles and sniffed the odours they contained. Their facial expressions as they breathed in the perfumes belied their thoughts – happy memories, lifted spirits, revulsion, indifference. Her eyes drifted from one perfume concession to another, but it was the Scent Lab counter that particularly interested Ruby; here the fragrances were mixed freshly whenever a customer made a purchase.

Ruby peered through the bangle binoculars so she could see more clearly; she was fascinated to watch the woman work. All the ingredients were bottled and displayed on the shelves behind or kept in refrigerators in the back. People came and went, nothing unusual about any of them, until a businessman walked by, perfectly dressed, not a button out of line, his hair greying at the temples, thinning a little on top. His expression was that of someone who had time on his hands before an appointment – a lot of people used the store this way, a place to kill time until they had to get to their next meeting or lunch engagement.

When he passed the Scent Lab counter, he almost didn't stop, but lingered just for half a minute as he took a cloth from his glasses case and began to clean his spectacles – it was just a very slight pause – before moving off to mingle in with the other drifting shoppers. There was nothing odd about the businessman's behaviour, it was only that Ruby was sure that there was now something on the countertop that hadn't been there before, a blue envelope.

Dusk was falling by the time Ruby reached home and, though she had had little in the way of lunch and no dinner, she wasn't particularly hungry. She made herself a mug of Flu-Sip and piled some cookies on a plate – she also took an orange for good measure: she could use the vitamins.

She took out her list and looked again at what had been stolen:

```
A tiepin
A brooch
An earring
A pendant on a chain
```

All the pieces were small and all were created with blue gems. One was a very rare blue diamond. It was true the jewellers Katayoun & Anahita were famous for using blue gems, but there *were* other equally valuable pieces on display. If the thief was only interested in the *blue* jewels, then this meant the culprit had not picked the pieces at random, but had some sort of a plan for them.

```
But why only one earring?
Is it the stones themselves the thief is
interested in rather than the jewellery they
are part of?

Why not take all the pieces on the same day
Is this thief a thrill-seeker?
Or does this thief enjoy outwitting the store
security system?
```

Most importantly, how had the culprit made him or herself invisible? There was not one witness to the robberies and none of the door or window alarms had gone off, nor had the floor sensors picked up any movement – which meant the store security cameras had not been triggered by the intruder. Therefore, the only night footage recorded was when the security guard did his rounds. This happened once an hour. Ruby had been over the night footage so many times that she knew it by heart. The daytime footage was another matter; that played all day and she had not spent so long examining this, so she decided to look again.

She plugged in the microtape player and watched the store tapes, starting at the beginning when the jewels first arrived. Due to the arrangement of the counters, jewellery being next to perfume, it was possible to see the Scent Lab in most of the footage.

As she watched each boring tape, one after another, hour after hour, she began to notice something – it was becoming interesting. Ruby was seeing patterns; comings and goings. She began to see the same familiar silhouettes and faces, regular customers and passers-by.

There was that same businessman for instance; he clearly passed through the perfume department regularly. Sometimes he would take a perfume sample handed to him as a scented stick. He never, ever smelled them; he would just slip it into his pocket; perhaps he was just being polite, not wanting to offend the woman who worked there. He never did more than smile at her and he only so much as glanced at the jewellery next to the counter and appeared interested in neither perfume nor jewellery.

On one of the tapes Ruby noticed him drop a letter. It landed address side down and on the back it was stamped with a decorative seal that maybe looked like an eye, Ruby couldn't quite tell. The assistant did not see the man drop the letter, but when she spotted it lying there on the floor she picked it up and put it behind the counter. Ruby wondered if it was still there waiting for someone to claim it, or had she perhaps mailed it on?

The other regular who showed up on the tapes was a tall young man, much younger than the businessman, who occasionally walked through the store, perhaps on his way to the coffee house, always dressed in jeans and a casual-looking shirt. He did not look like a Melrose Dorff customer; perhaps he worked there in the maintenance department. When he passed by the counter, the Scent Lab assistant would usually speak to him, sometimes even giving him a small sample of scent – perhaps, Ruby mused, she had a crush on him.

There was a knock.

'Yuh huh,' called Ruby.

Her father stuck his head round the door.

'Ruby, you've been up here for hours. Do you maybe want to say hello to your old dad?'

'Hello Dad,' said Ruby, not shifting her gaze from the screen.

'How was your day?'

'Ah, hot,' he said. He peered at the grey image. 'What is it with you kids?' said Brant. 'Seems like you could watch just about anything. I mean what kind of show is this Rube?'

'It's interesting once you get into it,' replied Ruby.

'By the way, if you're planning a dip, do be careful,' said her father. 'I think your mother might just be right about that hippo; most of the water seems to have ended up slopped over the patio.'

When Ruby called Clancy for a late-night chat, she mentioned what her father had said.

'So you're saying there *is a hippo*?' said Clancy.

'No bozo, I'm saying no one saw a hippo. I think they're both hallucinating.'

'So I'm right,' asserted Clancy, 'a simple case of double heatstroke!'

'But that doesn't explain why there was a whole lot of water slopped around the pool,' said Ruby. 'Something was in there, but what?'

'Maybe it was the pig?' said Clancy.

'The pig *is* the hippo,' snapped Ruby.

'I'm hanging up,' said Clancy.

Chapter 32.
Beggars can't be choosers

RUBY'S COLD WAS MOVING INTO A NEW PHASE: was it worse or better? She couldn't say. She felt like her head was stuffed with sponge and her nose was so blocked now that she couldn't even smell Bug and he really needed a bath. She reached for the garment on top of the pile of clothes on the chair in the bathroom. It was the red and black dress she had worn to the perfume launch. She could no longer smell the residue of 1770 fragrance nor the underlying smell of mothballs.

One of the things she liked about this dress was that it had deep pockets, big enough to take useful things. She took the yellow notebook from the doorjamb and slipped it into the left pocket and then went to her desk, opened the drawer and took out the tube of ground glows. She hadn't had a chance to try them out yet and she was itching to see how they worked. She dropped them into her right pocket.

The squirrel phone rang and she answered.

'Hippo control. We will lasso any hippo, no matter how small.'

'Huh?' came the voice.

'Go ahead caller.'

'Ruby? It's Red, what's going on?'

'Not much,' said Ruby, 'slightly bored.'

'No kidding,' said Red.

'What's going on with you?' asked Ruby.

'Same really, my mom's all jumpy because that forest fire west of Great Bear is blowing this way and my grandma's been evacuated,' said Red.

'That's too bad,' said Ruby. 'Sounds kinda serious.'

'Yeah, well, my mom thinks so. She wants me to wait by the phone so I just wondered if you wanted to come over?' said Red. 'Any time is fine.'

'I would,' said Ruby, 'but I'm not feeling so super. I might try and lay low. I mean I oughta if I wanna shake this thing.'

'Yeah, you're probably right. Take it easy,' said Red, 'feel better.' She hung up.

Ruby was fully intending to, but the world had other plans for her.

When she at last made her way downstairs, she went to find

the housekeeper. She was sitting in her apartment watching a morning horror flick, *The Cave of Forgotten Terror*. Ruby had seen this particular movie many times; so had Mrs Digby and she was easily able to follow the plot while she worked on one of her sewing projects.

Ruby looked over Mrs Digby's shoulder to see what she was doing. 'What's it gonna be?' asked Ruby.

'A feather brooch,' said Mrs Digby. 'I'm going to attach it to my good hat.'

'Did you buy those feathers,' said Ruby, 'or pull them off some smart lady's wrap?'

Mrs Digby sniffed. 'I found them, fair and square, in a park, practically tore my dress to shreds on a rose bush trying to reach them and then that fountain got me. I've a mind to call the mayor. Soaked through to the undergarments I was.' She carried on with her task.

Mrs Digby could turn her hand to most things and creating jewellery from discarded feathers seemed to be yet another of her talents.

Mrs Digby looked up. 'What are you doing wearing broken glasses?'

'I can't find my unbroken pair. Have you stumbled across them?'

'I have as a matter of fact and you were lucky they didn't end their short life sucked up the vacuum,' said the housekeeper, pouring some more tea from the large silver teapot.

Ruby looked at her more closely. 'You know you look kinda stylish today.'

The housekeeper squinted and put down her teacup. 'What are you after, child? Puts me off my lapsang souchong when you pay compliments.'

'Nothing, Girl Scouts' honour and all.'

'You're no Girl Scout,' said Mrs Digby.

'You just look kinda smartened up,' said Ruby.

'That's because I'm going out.'

Ruby peered a bit closer.

'You aware your earrings don't match?'

'I know,' said the housekeeper.

'They don't match *a lot*,' said Ruby, getting even closer. 'And one looks kinda, well, cheap.' This was true. While both earrings were blue, one of them looked like an expensive gemstone and the other was scratched plastic.

'That's because it's from out of a cereal packet,' said Mrs Digby. 'At least I imagine it was, but beggars can't be choosers.'

'You begged for them?' asked Ruby.

'I found them in the hedge,' said the housekeeper.

'So they belong to someone?'

'Who leaves their valuables in the hedge?' said Mrs Digby.

'No one I know,' replied Ruby.

'So there you are,' said Mrs Digby firmly. 'Finders keepers, losers regretters.'

Ruby had a few more questions on this topic, but she was interrupted by the sound of the doorbell.

'You go,' said Mrs Digby, turning back to the TV screen. 'The cave creature is about to devour the explorer and it's my favourite part of the movie.'

'Ah, come on Mrs Digby, it's bound to be for you.'

'I'm lying low.'

'So am I,' said Ruby.

'You go and I'll guarantee you'll find your other glasses,' said the housekeeper.

'You may be elderly, but you drive a nasty bargain, you know that?'

'It's not because I'm elderly, it's because I'm experienced,' said Mrs Digby. She turned the volume right up so she could properly hear the screams of the explorer.

Ruby went up the stairs to answer the door and found her glasses there on the letter table and Mrs Lemon on the stoop.

'Oh, hi Elaine.'

Bumping into Elaine Lemon on the front step wasn't worth the recovery of a pair of good glasses. Mrs Lemon was no doubt requiring emergency babysitting. Ruby could tell by the way she was smiling and frowning at the same time. A sort of pleading, desperate, hopeful look.

'Ruby! Just the teenager I was hoping to speak to.' Mrs Lemon always sounded slightly patronising when she was talking to what she would term 'a young person'.

'Nice to see you Elaine, and ordinarily I would love to chat, but I am just scooting from the family home to get my lenses fixed.'

'Can I hear screaming?' asked Mrs Lemon anxiously.

'That'll be Mrs Digby,' said Ruby. 'She's in a weird mood, probably something to do with the temperature.' Ruby ran down the front steps before Mrs Lemon could manage to squeak another word.

Chapter 33.
Hansel and Gretel

SINCE SHE WAS NOW OUT AND ABOUT, and unable to return until the coast was totally clear, Ruby decided she might just as well go call in on Clancy. She was feeling a little revived, but not nimble enough to make it all the way there on foot so she waited for the bus.

When she arrived at the Crews' place, she found Clancy sitting on his bed, reading.

'Good morning Ruby, what an unexpected pleasure. What brings you this way?'

'I had to get outta the house quick.'

'Do enlighten me,' said Clancy. 'I am, as you see, all ears.'

'Why are you speaking like that?' said Ruby.

'Like what?' asked Clancy.

'Like you're about a hundred and sixty-five years old?'

'Must be the book,' said Clancy, putting it down. 'It's set in the eighteen hundreds and I think I'm taking on the personality of the main character.'

'Well, try not to,' said Ruby, 'it's already beginning to irritate.'

'So why did you have to flee the Redfort abode?'

'Elaine Lemon,' said Ruby, slumping onto the bed.

'She required you to mind her offspring?' asked Clancy.

'I didn't wait to find out. Any chance of a beverage?' asked Ruby.

'I'll call for my house servant,' said Clancy, picking up the phone. 'Olive,' he said dramatically, 'do you want to know how it feels to have twenty cents in your pocket...? Very good, well, bring up two iced Coca-colas and the money will be yours.' He replaced the receiver.

'Nice going,' said Ruby, nodding.

Five-year-old Olive tottered into the room twenty minutes later with two less than full glasses of Coca-cola. It was clear that she had been sampling the drinks during the long journey to the third floor. Still, it was better than having to get up and make the drinks themselves, so they paid her the meagre wage and she left them, smiling and skipping all the way back to the kitchen.

'So what's going on at your place? Any big news?' asked Clancy. The Coca-cola seemed to have magically cleared up his nineteenth-century speak.

'Mrs Digby's got all dolled up for her poker game,' said Ruby, 'my dad's playing tennis again, my mom's at the gallery and Mrs Lemon's on the loose.'

'Sounds boring,' said Clancy.

'Yeah,' agreed Ruby before sneezing at least seven times.

'Man, you need to take some vitamins or something,' said Clancy. 'If you got lost in the wilderness now, you'd perish for sure.'

These words made Ruby remember something and she patted her pockets and pulled out a tube of mints or, on closer inspection, ground glows.

'What's that?' said Clancy, peering at the tube.

'Something I wanted to show you!' said Ruby, sneezing again.

'Mints?'

'You may think they're mints, but let me demonstrate.' Ruby rummaged for the shoe activator attachments and with not too much difficulty fastened one to the sole of her Bradley Baker sneaker. It was small and pretty much invisible.

'Here, give me yours,' she said to Clancy. He handed her his shoe and she attached the other activator to its sole.

'Now wait, give me around ten minutes and then see if you can find me.'

Ruby left the room and made her way down the long winding corridors of the Crew home. She went up the main staircase and down the back staircase; she went from floor to floor, right to the top of the house. As she went, she dispensed the flat discs that were the ground glows – they took on the colour of the floor they fell onto and became perfectly camouflaged and impossible to see. Once Ruby reached the roof, she pushed open the attic window, pulled off her sneakers and went and sat on the sloping tile roof. It was beautifully warm and the heat from the tiles soothed her healing foot.

The ten minutes were up and Clancy went to find her. He was amazed to see small buttons of light appearing as he walked. He turned around and saw that the light disappeared once he was more than a foot or two from the glow. It was easy to track her.

'Pretty cool,' he said as he pushed his way through the open window.

'Cool is not the word,' said Ruby. 'Lifesavers is what they are. I hadn't tried them before now, but yeah, I think they might just change old Ruby Redfort's fortunes.'

'But only if you have to retrace your steps,' said Clancy. 'If you have to get from A to B and back again, then fine, but what if you have to get from A to B to C?'

'That's another story,' said Ruby. 'I'm just enjoying the fact that I'll be able to find my way home if I really need to.'

'Just like those two kids, what were they called, you know, in that old book?'

'Hansel and Gretel?' Ruby suggested.

'That's it,' said Clancy. 'What happened to them again?'

'They couldn't find their way home because their ground glows got eaten,' said Ruby.

'Oh yeah,' said Clancy. 'They messed up with their breadcrumbs. Didn't the squirrels munch them?'

'Yeah, bad things can happen when you come up with a defective insurance plan like that – at least no one's gonna eat these babies,' said Ruby.

Clancy still had his mind in the fairy tale. 'And they got lured into a house made of candy, I remember,' he said. 'It belonged to a mean old witch.'

'She was only mean because those kids started eating her house.'

The sun was getting high by now and the light shining in her eyes seemed to set Ruby off sneezing again.

She fumbled for something to blow her nose with, but all she could find was an old scrumpled tissue still in her pocket from the perfume launch.

'You don't look like someone who's getting over the flu, you actually look kinda worse,' said Clancy.

'I know,' agreed Ruby, 'I can't seem to shake it.'

'So when are they sending you back out to retake your survival test?' asked Clancy. ''Cause you're gonna be in trouble if it's soon.'

'They haven't told me yet,' replied Ruby, 'but I sure as eggs is eggs am gonna be taking these little suckers with me. So long as I don't get lost it'll all be OK.'

'What about the robbery case? You come close to solving it?' asked Clancy.

'Not exactly,' said Ruby. 'I mean not; that's to say the trail has gone sorta dead on the whole jewellery theft thing.'

'You haven't found anything? No leads at all?'

'All I've achieved so far is to alert Melrose Dorff to a bird that flapped in through a restroom window. Turns out Elliot was right: Dillon Flannagon broke a window, hitting a baseball.' She shook out the tissue preparing to blow her nose again and as if on cue a blue feather floated from it.

'Is that one of the bird's feathers?' Clancy was pointing at it as it floated off towards the edge of the roof and down into the Crews' garden.

Ruby looked puzzled and then remembered where it came from: the perfume launch at Melrose Dorff, the feather which had detached itself from some smart lady's feather boa. Unless it hadn't...

'Maybe,' said Ruby slowly. 'I guess it could be, it would sorta make sense.'

'What are you doing?' said a small voice.

Ruby and Clancy turned to see Olive's face sticking out of the open window.

'You're not allowed up here, *Dad said.*' Her face was deadpan and annoying. 'Dad said, "*If you walk on the roof, you will break the tiles.*" That's what he said,' said Olive firmly.

'Get lost, would you Olive?' said Clancy.

'I'm just saying what he said,' she repeated.

'Well, quit bugging me about it,' said Clancy.

'I will if you give me one of those mints,' said Olive, pointing to the tube of ground glows which were lying next to Ruby.

'They're not mints,' said Clancy.

'They *are* mints, I can see they are,' said Olive.

'They're really not Olive,' said Clancy, picking them up and stuffing them into his pocket.

'They look just like mints to me,' said Olive.

Clancy looked at Ruby.

'The thing is Olive, they are sort of mints, but not *exactly*,' explained Ruby. 'They're mints for people with, you know, a need to go to the bathroom but can't.'

'You mean for people who can't poop?' asked Olive, with five-year-old directness.

'Yeah Olive, if you want to put it like that, then yes, that is what I mean,' said Ruby. 'Therefore, can I offer you a piece of bubblegum instead?'

'No,' said Olive. 'I heard that it can get all tangled up in your guts and strangle you from the inside.'

'First of all,' said Clancy, 'that's only if you swallow bubblegum – which you shouldn't – and second of all that's horse manure.'

'I'm going to tell Dad that you said horse manure and that you were sitting on the roof eating bubblegum,' said Olive.

'First of all, *you* just said horse manure, so you better tell on yourself; second of all, I'm not eating bubblegum because I don't actually like bubblegum, it belongs to Ruby; and third of all, get lost Olive.'

The five-year-old disappeared from view. The whole conversation was getting confusing and she had lost track a bit of whom she was now telling on.

'Boy, am I glad I don't have sisters,' said Ruby. 'She gonna go tell your dad? Because you really don't need the attention.'

'I doubt it,' said Clancy. 'He's away this week and she'll have forgotten about it by the time he returns.'

'I hope you're right my friend; you know how your dad hates horse manure.'

The two of them sat out there a little while longer before Ruby decided it might be safe to return to the family abode. Elaine Lemon had surely found a replacement babysitter by now.

She climbed through the window, scooped up her shoes and ran barefoot down the stairs; the carpet felt good under her sore foot. She walked out the back way, through the garden and there on the path spotted the little blue feather. She picked it up, wondering to herself if Clancy's thought might be right – was this the feather of the department store intruder? It was pretty exotic, shimmering lapis blue with small pink markings like little Os running along the length of it. Maybe she would look it up in one of her bird books at home and then she had a better idea.

Chapter 34.
A flight of fancy

MRS ATTENBURG LIVED A FEW STREETS AWAY FROM THE
REDFORTS. Her unpainted natural wood clapboard house had a
wraparound porch which was covered in bird feeders and potted
flowers. The house was set right in the middle of a large plot of
land planted with roses, shrubs and low-branched trees. It was
hard to tell where the garden ended and the house began, which
was the way Mrs Attenburg liked it since she was all about the
birds.

Ruby knocked on the screen door, waited, called and then
wandered off to see if Mrs Attenburg might be outside. She
was.

She was actually standing, binoculars in hand, staring at a
small bird with a green back, a yellow front and face and a black
patch on its crown like a little dark toupee.

She handed the binoculars to Ruby who immediately
identified the bird as a Wilson's Warbler.

'It certainly is,' said Mrs Attenburg. Ruby had spent so much time staring out of the window that she had a pretty good knowledge of all things ornithological.

'Nice little fellow,' said Mrs Attenburg, taking back the binoculars. 'What can I do for you dear?'

'I wondered if you might be able to identify this?' said Ruby, producing the feather.

Mrs Attenburg squinted at it.

'That's going to require my strong glasses,' she said. 'Come on inside.'

Ruby followed her up the wooden steps and into the house.

Without asking, Mrs Attenburg started some water boiling and set about making two cups of tea. Ruby was not fond of tea, but like most children had long ago discovered a method of drinking without tasting – it required a modicum of nose-holding which had to be carried out discreetly. Mrs Attenburg found her glasses and peered long and hard at the feather; she looked puzzled and then a little thrilled.

'Oh my Ruby, this is exciting; that bird's been dead for forty years.'

'Do you mean this exact one or just generally?' asked Ruby.

'I mean the species – extinct,' said Mrs Attenburg.

'But then how did one of its feathers end up on the marble

floor of Melrose Dorff?' said Ruby.

Mrs Attenburg scratched her head. 'Well, I don't have an answer to that. My guess is it came in as a decoration on someone's hat because I can't see how it could possibly have flown in under its own steam.' She sighed. 'Even if it wasn't an extinct species these birds aren't even *visitors* to America and, as far as I am aware, they haven't been seen in the wilds of their native Australia for the best part of seventy years. I've only ever heard of them being kept in captivity.'

'So what kind of bird do you think it is?' asked Ruby.

'I think it's one of these...'

Mrs Attenburg stood looking at her bookcase – it ran across the whole back wall of the house from the living room through the doorway into the kitchen. All the books had some connection to birds and nature. 'Now where is it?' she muttered. Her eyes finally alighted on the one she was after; a book called *The Lure of the Bowerbird*.

The book was old, but not wildly out of date, though the writing had an old-fashioned tone. It was cloth-bound and illustrated with delicate watercolours.

The bowerbird in general *There are twenty species of bowerbird currently on this planet of ours, though until* *approximately thirty years ago there was a twenty-first bird. This unusually small bowerbird was called the Lapis bowerbird on account of its stunning blue wings and interest in bright blue objects, collecting them to adorn its bower. {See page 234}.*

Mrs Attenburg thumbed through the pages until she came to a picture of a tiny bird.

The Lapis Bowerbird *Unusually small at about four inches long (most other bowerbirds averaging between nine and sixteen inches) the Lapis bowerbird has satin blue-black feathers, though when courting reveals vivid blue wings with bright pink circles and blue plumage. Like the Satin bowerbird, it is particularly interested in collecting blue objects.*

It lures female bowerbirds to it by creating a bower and decorating it with found blue objects – from flowers, to plastic bottle tops, candy wrappers and blueberries, anything which might attract the eye of a suitable mate.

'So you've never seen one yourself?' asked Ruby.
Mrs Attenburg shook her head. 'No, but I would pay good

money to. Unfortunately, I have never been so lucky, but my mother told me she once had. She saw it up at the Fengrove place. Flemming Fengrove used to have these big parties in that crazy house he built – it looked like a French chateau. He liked to show off, invite starlets and celebrities and famous folk; he had this sort of menagerie and my mother claimed he actually owned a Lapis bowerbird.' Mrs Attenburg's eyes had gone a bit glazed over with the memory.

'She said that Lapis bowerbird was the most beautiful thing she had ever seen.'

'I've heard about that place,' said Ruby. 'What happened to the old man?'

'Mr Fengrove?' pondered Mrs Attenburg, 'I heard he died – folks said he went mad as a hatter after the animals were sold, wouldn't let anyone up there after that, he was grief-stricken you see.'

'Why were the animals sold?' asked Ruby.

'The authorities demanded that he return all the rarest ones to the state zoo where they could be properly looked after so he sold the lot. In any case, no one wanted to work up there after the incident with the bear.'

'What incident with the... never mind,' said Ruby, interrupting herself. The phrase *mad as a hatter* had made a link with Mrs

Digby's best hat and the image of it was now circling around in Ruby's mind. She felt a strong need to take a look at it – maybe she could catch the housekeeper before she left for her poker game. The bear story could wait.

Ruby thanked Mrs Attenburg and hurried back to Cedarwood Drive, half hopping half hobbling.

Chapter 35.
Too big a coincidence

MRS DIGBY WAS LONG GONE – but she must have changed her mind about her outfit because the hat was still sitting on top of the bureau and newly attached to it was the feather brooch she had been fashioning. Ruby took out the bowerbird feather and held it against the brooch feathers; they matched precisely.

Ruby's head filled with possibilities; one after another they piled in.

She tried to focus on one thought at a time.

QUESTIONS

1. Exactly where did Mrs Digby find these feathers?
2. She mentioned a park that has roses and a violent fountain. There are several of these, so which was it?

3. Maybe Mrs Attenburg was wrong about the
bird. Maybe it wasn't so dead and gone after
all — is it actually alive and well?

What was that other thing niggling her?
Ruby fished out the yellow notebook from her dress pocket:

Wednesday morning: Mrs Beesman's one-eared
cat spotted somewhere near Dad's office
wearing quality costume jewellery.

But *where* near her father's office had he spotted the cat?
Ruby searched her memory: he hadn't exactly said, but
he had mentioned that he had passed by Mrs Beesman in the
morning as he walked into the office. What Ruby knew about
the cat lady (from her years of yellow notebook observations)
was that Mrs Beesman followed a very strict routine. She left the
house early around 7.20 and trundled up to Chatterbird Square
to feed the starlings and pigeons; she would trundle on to Harker
Square afterwards and usually had a sit-down on the bench on
the west side of the park at 8.05 am. Mr Redfort usually arrived
at work at ten minutes past eight on Wednesdays and would pass
by Mrs Beesman's bench as he cut through Harker Square.

Mrs Digby found earrings in a hedge.
Perhaps Mrs Beesman also got lucky finding
jewellery in a hedge?
So, if the bowerbird feathers were found in
a park with a fountain and rose bushes, then
this could be Fountain Square, Central City
Park or Harker Square.
Fountain Square is never referred to as a
park.

Ruby put a cross next to Fountain Square.

Central City Park has rose bushes, hedges and
a fountain, but the fountain is nowhere near
the roses.

Ruby put a cross next to Central City Park.

Harker Square is often described as a park.
It has rose bushes, hedges and a fountain,
and the fountain is next to the roses.

Bingo.

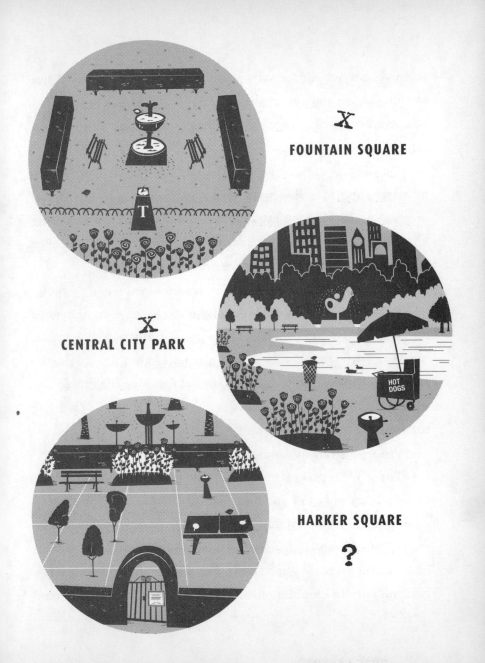

X

FOUNTAIN SQUARE

X

CENTRAL CITY PARK

HARKER SQUARE

?

Ruby found herself actually running to the bus stop as if her wounded foot gave her no pain and her flu fever had evaporated. She ran because she wanted to be right, as if any delay might make it not so.

On the one hand, it seemed like an absurd idea, as absurd as suggesting Mrs Beesman was a cat burglar, as absurd as suggesting Mrs Beesman's *cat* was a cat burglar, but having spoken to Mrs Attenburg it really didn't seem such a long shot. Magpies and bowerbirds, thieves and collectors both.

The park in front of the department store wasn't exactly small, but it wasn't huge like the city park. It had formal hedges and trees clipped into shapes and a great many flowerbeds and benches. Mrs Digby had claimed she had found the earring in the hedge, but which hedge was uncertain, Mrs Digby had not said... but then again maybe she *had*. Ruby remembered her mentioning that the roses snagged her dress.

Practically tore my dress to shreds.

There were several rose beds that were located in front of a hedge, but only one near enough to the fountain that could cause one to get *soaked through to the undergarments*. The hedge itself was wide and dense, perhaps a couple of feet deep. A satin black feather was caught on one of the rose stems. Ruby used her penknife to clip a small hole in the hedge, somewhere where no one would notice it. It took a while as there was a lot of hedge to snip through. Then she took off her watch, unfastened the back where the mirror was contained and flipped out the extendible zigzag of metal that it was secured to. She pushed her arm through the hedge as far as it would go and angled the mirror so it might reflect back what was on the other side where she could not see.

Suddenly a flash of blue. Shiny things, all dazzling blue, reflected back to her.

There was the Lapis bowerbird's bower, all adorned with its beautiful treasures, all neatly arranged between the hedge and the park's retaining wall, where no person ever went. A perfect place for a feathered thief to store his valuables.

Chapter 36.
Lost and found

RUBY AND BLACKER WERE STANDING BEHIND THE BIG
HEDGE IN HARKER SQUARE, staring at the bowerbird's
creation.

The bower was constructed as a delicate circle of twigs, a
perfectly round tunnel adorned with found things, all of them
blue.

And right in the middle sat a brooch, as if the bird was aware
that this was a great deal more valuable than the candy foil and
plastic bottle tops. The tiepin was clipped neatly to the entrance
like it was a 100,000-dollar doorbell.

There was no sign of the bird.

'That's some unusual cat burglar.'

'It explains the thefts,' said Ruby, 'but not where the thief
came from.'

'That is kind of a mystery,' agreed Blacker. He radioed LB
from his watch. She in turn called Sheriff Bridges who notified

the department store. The director of Melrose Dorff, relieved that the jewel thief was just an opportunistic bird and that the only lapse in security had been a small hole in a bathroom window, made the story public. She figured they would get a nice front-page piece in the *Twinford Mirror* which would no doubt bring people flocking to the store. Since all the jewels could be and would be recovered, it would not jeopardise Twinford's chances of holding the Gem Festival next year.

They could probably get an advertising campaign out of it: *Visit Melrose Dorff, our jewellery literally flies out of the store.*

Mrs Digby was at first a little disappointed to learn that her newly acquired earring, which went so well with her polka-dot poker dress, was in fact stolen goods. That said, once she realised that this meant she had recovered something highly valuable, she perked right up, enjoying all the attention and the trip to the police station. By way of a thank you, Sheriff Bridges had someone take her mugshot so she could keep it for a souvenir. However, two hours later, and not a single cop had mentioned the word 'reward', and Mrs Digby was beginning to feel unappreciated.

Her mood had certainly turned sour by the time she was dropped back home, and the bouquet from Melrose Dorff arrived not a moment too soon. A huge bunch of fragrant blue flowers and a note: *Please accept our enormous gratitude and this voucher to be spent in our store and redeemable against all Melrose Dorff merchandise*.*

Everyone at Spectrum was very happy about the recovery of the Katayoun & Anahita jewels, everyone that is except for Agent Froghorn. He got zero credit for his hours of effort watching all that dull security footage and he was greatly resenting the attention Ruby Redfort was garnering from solving the case.

'Boy, do you ever think you're the cat's pyjamas,' said Froghorn as they filed out of the debriefing.

'The cat's pyjamas? Are you for real Froghorn?' said Ruby.

'You muscle in on my case little girl so you can pick up all my hard work and make yourself look good. I know what you're up to, trying to become the new Bradley Baker, but here's the news: everyone knows you don't stand a chance, you're never going to make it as an agent so do us all a favour and give up.'

'Froghorn, did anyone ever tell you being a sore loser is a very unattractive trait?'

Ruby herself wasn't feeling as satisfied or as smug as Froghorn was imagining. She was concerned that they still had no idea where this rare and thought to be extinct bird had escaped from – she also had no idea where the bird was now.

✹ ✹ ✹

Meanwhile, back at the Crew home, something else had gone missing. Clancy had no idea what had happened to the forgotten tube of ground glows though he was pretty sure he knew who the culprit was. He had collected up all the glows and hidden the tube in his desk drawer, but now it was gone.

'Olive, have you been in my room?'

'No.'

'I know you have so you might as well tell me,' said Clancy.

'So why are you asking?' said Olive.

'To give you a chance to stop acting like a little kid.'

'I am a little kid,' said Olive.

This was true: Olive was only five.

'Olive, when you were in my room, did you take something?'

'I haven't been in your room,' said Olive.

Clancy rephrased the question. 'Olive, when you weren't in my room, did you take something?'

'No.'

'I know you did,' said Clancy.

'So why are you asking?' said Olive.

'Olive, can you just give whatever it is that you didn't take back to me.'

'I can't remember,' said Olive.

'Can't remember what you did with it?' he asked.

'What I didn't take,' said Olive.

'It was a little tube – looked like Fresh Breath Mints,' said Clancy.

'Oh yes,' said Olive. 'I ate one, but it didn't taste of mint and it was hard to swallow.'

'Olive! You're not supposed to eat them.'

'Why not? They say mints on the packet, I asked Drusilla.'

Pause.

'My friend Leah ate one too,' said Olive.

Clancy tried to keep calm.

'So are there any left or did you eat them all?'

'We just ate one, two, three,' said Olive. 'We were saving the rest for when we were really hungry.'

'So where are the rest of them?' asked Clancy.

'Don't know,' said Olive, skipping off. 'I never took them.'

Chapter 37.
From the jaws of death

CLANCY PHONED RUBY THE NEXT MORNING to explain about the missing ground glows.

'I'm really sorry Rube. I know that they're super valuable and irreplaceable and all, but Olive just won't tell me what she did with them.'

'It's not your fault Clance; it's just a downer is what it is. Now I have no backup plan for getting unlost.'

'Yeah, it totally sucks. I'll see if I can trick her into telling me.'

'Boy, are your sisters some trouble,' said Ruby.

'Yeah, Olive's sending me crazy; she keeps following me around.'

'By the way, I've done that punctuality essay of yours and it's a good one; the handwriting looks perfect,' said Ruby. 'It's here if you want to come and collect it?'

'Yeah, why not,' said Clancy, 'at least it'll get me away from Olive for a few hours.'

❀ ❀ ❀

He showed up a half-hour later and he wasn't looking one bit relaxed.

'You seem sorta edgy Clance, something going on?'

'I don't know,' said Clancy, 'maybe.'

'What do you mean, maybe?' said Ruby. She was sitting on the roof wrapped in a blanket.

'Rube, have you ever felt like you were being followed?'

'Yeah, plenty times,' said Ruby. 'More than once by you.'

'Well, I could swear someone's on my tail,' said Clancy.

'Who? I mean who would follow you apart from Olive.'

'No one I can think of,' said Clancy.

'Could be a hippo, ever thought of that?'

'No Ruby, I hadn't as a matter of fact, but thanks for taking this concern of mine so seriously.'

'I am taking it seriously. I mean my mom's seen a hippo, my dad thinks he's seen a hippo, who's to say you're not being followed by a hippo?'

'I guess *I am*,' said Clancy bluntly. 'I mean how much sunning do you Redforts do every day? 'Cause I hate to break it to you this way, but you're all sounding a teensy bit insane.'

'I'm just trying to be open-minded, that's all. I'm the totally last one to think it's likely that a hippo is roaming free in Twinford, but I'm beginning to think I've been too dismissive. You know Melamare thought she saw some *thing* which sounded from her description a little like a python and hey, think about it, Del thought Mrs Gilbert's spaniel Gilbert was eaten by a tiger and, let's face it, he *is* missing, and now *you* think you're being followed so we have to agree something's up, right?'

'OK,' said Clancy, 'so what now?'

Ruby pushed her sunglasses back on top of her head and looked at him hard.

'You have a hunch that something is following you, so when did all this start?' asked Ruby, like she was Detective Despo and the world of *Crazy Cops* was not a fiction.

Clancy sat back in his deckchair and looked up at the cloudless sky.

'A couple of nights ago, I just had a weird feeling like I was being watched. Then last night, when I was walking back from the park, I had a really strange feeling like I was being followed.'

'What kind of weird feeling? A weird bad, a weird creepy or a weird unusual?'

'A weird weird,' said Clancy, 'and then just now on my way here it happened again.'

'The same weird?' asked Ruby.

'No,' said Clancy, 'sorta differently weird. I mean last night I smelled this smell, a smell I think I smelled before, but I can't place it.'

'Where did you sense the weirdness today?'

'It was by Cedar Pond. I just sensed someone was watching me.'

Ruby was concentrating; she sat silently for a few minutes, contemplating what should be done, then she got to her feet and hopped down the open-tread staircase which led from the roof to her bedroom. She came back less than thirty seconds later with her pair of special agent issue binoculars.

'OK,' she said, 'so you leave and I'm gonna watch what happens. I can see pretty far from here, so long as you take the Cedar Street route and make a turn on Faber Drive, I can track you.'

'But what if someone *is* after me?' said Clancy. 'I mean what if they're waiting to make a move and suddenly pounce while you're looking through those magnifiers? I'll be long gone before you can reach me.'

Ruby went down the stairs again, rummaged around in various drawers and came hobbling back with a pair of walkie-talkies; she handed him one of the receivers.

'I can warn you if I see anything, OK?'

'OK,' said Clancy uncertainly.

'And if anything does happen and you get grabbed then you can tell me your whereabouts, and Hitch and me will find you. So go,' said Ruby, pushing him towards the stairs.

Clancy paused. 'I was going to climb down the tree and slip out the back gate, less chance of being followed.'

Ruby rolled her eyes. 'Being followed is the whole point bozo; you need to leave by the front.'

Clancy sighed. 'OK, but if I get snatched and murdered by a psychopath it will be down to you.'

'I'll plant a tree or something in your memory, OK? Now split.'

Ruby got into position; she had a great view from up on the roof and could see all the way to the ocean.

She watched as Clancy made his way down the street. He was walking fairly fast and she could tell he was resisting the urge to run. There was no sign of anyone, not a car, not a bike, not one single psychopath. She followed him round the winding streets as he made his way towards home. Nothing and then... something.

Clancy froze. It was so quick Ruby couldn't make out what it was. 'Keep walking buster,' Ruby muttered. As if he had heard her, Clancy began to put one foot in front of the other; he was acting really nervous and whoever was trailing him was going to sense it for sure.

Something moved in the bushes, then slowly, very slowly, walked out onto the sidewalk; it was a hundred yards away. Clancy didn't see, but Ruby did. She thumbed the switch on the walkie-talkie to send him a message in Morse code.

-.-. . .-.. .. -- -... / .- / - .-. . . . .

He didn't seem to register or maybe was too panic-stricken to decode the message so she buzzed him and watched as he fumbled for the walkie-talkie.

'What is it?' he hissed into the radio.

'Get up a tree now bozo!'

'What?'

'Climb, darn it!'

Clancy dropped the receiver and lunged towards the nearest climbable thing. He hoisted himself up onto a road sign and continued to climb right to the top, not looking back. Once he had got as far as he could possibly go, he looked down. What he saw was a Sumatran tiger, though he didn't realise this at the time, he wasn't counting the stripes or working out how close together they were, he just saw a very large cat with a lot of teeth looking hungrily up at him.

Clancy watched as the creature crunched down the walkie-talkie.

Ruby watched from her vantage point. 'Oh jeez.'

The authorities were there in no time at all; they had just come from a similar incident involving an entirely different species on the other side of town.

It was a great coincidence that it happened to be another boy Ruby knew.

Quent Humbert had been doing some bird watching down by Twinford River when he had spotted a large prehistoric reptile, actually a Siamese crocodile of a very good size.

Luckily for Quent, he had managed to squeeze himself into a concrete pipe, a drain too small for the Siamese croc which was over thirteen feet long. He was there for some hours because the reptile had decided to wait it out, sure that at some point Quent would make a false move and when he did he would be ready for it. Luckily, a fisherman on the opposite bank spotted the crocodile and called the Sheriff's Office. Quent Humbert unsurprisingly went into shock and was found to be incapable of verbalising what had happened.

Clancy was not exactly over the moon about his wildlife experience either.

'Why the Sam Hill did you tell me to climb a tree?' he exclaimed. 'Tigers *can climb* trees you know!'

'Yeah, but they prefer not to because they find it hard to get down,' said Ruby.

'Hard to get down?' spluttered Clancy. 'By the time it started worrying about getting down, I'd already have been devoured.'

'What I'm saying,' said Ruby, 'is it probably *wouldn't* have chosen to follow you up in the first place – anyway, you didn't climb a tree, you climbed a road traffic sign, so you were way out of trouble.'

'Yeah, no thanks to you! Why didn't you tell me to play dead – that's what you're meant to do if you encounter a tiger.'

'Because I thought the chances of you pulling that stunt off were next to zero; you'd have been flapping around like a flounder.'

They bickered on like this all the way back from the police station.

When she got home, Ruby went directly to her room and pulled out her notebook. Things had got pretty strange. She added the animals recently sighted: most were rounded up and their

THE SIAMESE CROCODILE — native to Thailand,
Laos, Cambodia — spotted by the unfortunate
Quent Humbert at Twinford River.

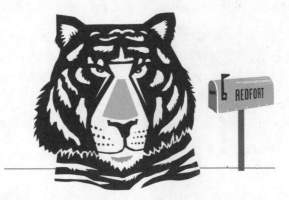

THE TIGER — native to Sumatra —
chased Clancy on the street outside my house.

THE PYGMY HIPPO — native to West Africa —
swimming in our pool.

BLACK—TAILED PYTHON — native to South—east Asia
— seen by Gemma in the school corridor.

LAPIS BOWERBIRD — native to Australia —
nesting in Harker Square.

A POLICEMAN CRITICALLY
ILL IN HOSPITAL HAVING
BEEN ATTACKED BY SOME WILD
ANIMAL (thought to be a
wild dog). Animal yet to be
identified as no witness to
the attack and the officer
still in coma.

species correctly identified.

Ruby looked up each animal in turn and discovered that every one of them was either rare, endangered or thought to be extinct.

**Lorelei von Leyden
hurried to answer
the phone...**

...and switched it to speaker; she had been busy sorting papers on her desk, papers that were giving her a headache.

'Tell me some good news,' she demanded.

'We found it,' said the voice of the young man. 'It was pretty easy once we knew how; we trapped it and took it up to the mountain hideaway. No one's going to discover it there.'

'Not even her?' asked Lorelei.

'Not even her,' said Eduardo 'Quit being so paranoid, you don't even know if she's in town.'

'If she's not in town, then why the messages? She's getting nearer and she wants me to know it.'

'She's trying to scare you by getting her flunkies to pass you these threats – it doesn't mean a thing. The important thing is we have the creature.'

'But what if it does mean something? What if she is here?'

'Look, how about I keep an eye out for her, track her down? What does she look like?'

'That's just it, I don't know. I've never met her, never even seen so much as a grainy photograph. She could be sitting right next to you for all I know.'

The man instinctively looked around him, but the square was empty, but for a friendly-looking middle-aged woman in a flowered dress reading and eating an ice-cream.

Chapter 38.
Alive

THE THEORY THE NEWSPAPERS HAD COME UP WITH was that the animals had been smuggled into the country illegally and were to be sold to a private collector or dodgy circus troupe – somehow the plan had gone wrong, the deal had collapsed and the animals had escaped or been set free.

Ruby checked in with Hitch; he was drinking his seventh coffee of the day and looked like he had a lot on his mind.

'So what's new?' said Ruby.

'Sheriff Bridges and his team have done a pretty good job contacting all the zoos and animal sanctuaries in the Twinford County area.'

'And?' said Ruby.

'And nothing. They followed up with door-to-door enquiries and led investigations into the many sightings (both real and bogus) of animals seen roaming around the city streets and municipal parks.'

'No leads?'

'Zip,' said Hitch. 'No zoo has been broken into and no zoo has accidentally left the gate open – so to speak.'

'So now what?' asked Ruby.

'It's not our case,' said Hitch. 'We haven't been assigned to look into it because it's got nothing to do with the kind of thing we do.'

'But what if there's more to it than we think?' said Ruby. 'Something more sinister than all these theories; maybe it's *not* about collectors or animal rights activists or someone who left the gate open.'

'If something comes up that falls into Spectrum's remit, then we'll be asked to step in.' Hitch put down his mug. 'But for now, I gotta go. LB wants me to head into HQ. I'll see you later kid.'

Ruby walked back up to the kitchen where Mrs Digby seemed to be preparing a ton of vegetables.

Ruby stared at the old lady for a while; a thought had been going round and round, ever since she spoke to Mrs Attenburg: *what if he's alive?*

The housekeeper looked up. 'What is it child, what's in that head of yours?'

'Have you ever heard of Flemming Fengrove?' she asked.

Mrs Digby stopped chopping. 'Now what put that name in your head child?'

'Someone mentioned him the other day,' said Ruby, 'so I wondered if you might have heard of him.'

'I've more than heard of him,' said Mrs Digby, 'I used to work for him.'

'You *worked* for him?' said Ruby. 'I thought you'd always worked for Mom's folks?'

'Always have, but now and again – when I was younger – I'd take on extra jobs, sometimes at the Fengrove place. The parties were something to see,' said Mrs Digby, 'but it was no easy ticket, I can promise you that; all those guests who needed feeding and all those animals wanting to eat you. Crazy times,' she added, returning to her carrots.

'Where is his place?' asked Ruby as if she was merely curious to imagine rather than about to make a mental note.

'North out of town,' said Mrs Digby, pointing with her carrot, 'all the way along until you reach the canyon road and then you just drive and drive until you get to a sharp fork to the left and then you head steep up in the direction of Wolf Paw Mountain. Easy to miss if you don't know where you're headed.'

Mrs Digby was getting unusually misty-eyed at this memory of a bygone time; she even went downstairs and took a black and white photograph out of her album to show Ruby. It was of the young Mrs Digby (before she became Mrs Digby) dressed up in a maid's uniform along with a whole lot of other young women. Behind them and around them and at their feet were a variety of exotic animals. The maids were all laughing, seemingly unaware of the possible danger they might be in.

Ruby handed it back to the housekeeper who propped it up on the shelf behind her and went back to her chopping.

'So he's dead now?' said Ruby.

'Dead?' said Mrs Digby. 'I'm sure I wouldn't know, but dead or alive I would doubt he's smiling.' She tutted. 'Strangest man I ever met and I doubt if he ever got less so.'

Ruby said goodbye to Mrs Digby and set off as if she was heading to school, though she had no intention of making it there. Instead she took the bus to the centre of town – she needed to spend some time checking out a few things and the City Library was a good place to start.

It was pleasantly cool inside and that, combined with the dimly lit interior, made it feel like a sanctuary, a long way from the sweat and hustle of the city outside.

She chose a spot at the long library table and slung her satchel over one of the green leather upholstered chairs.

She looked at the section containing the newspaper archive.

If the reclusive Flemming Fengrove was still alive, then he would be a very old man by now, but many years ago he had been one of the most celebrated and sought-after individuals on the celebrity circuit. For a small window of time he had been famous for throwing lavish parties at his home dubbed the Mountain Chateau, and for organising ambitious public events and spectacles, but these were all but forgotten now.

The public library remembered him in black and white, printed in the pages of heavy bound books; photographs of actors, starlets, politicians and renowned public faces. Old Twinfordites thought of him from time to time, but mostly he was long forgotten, dead and buried in the local history books.

But Ruby wondered:

```
Is this man actually dead and buried?
```

She looked at the public records, the answer came back:

```
No.
Is there a record of the endangered animals
Fengrove had been required to return to the
```

state zoo?

Answer: yes.

Is there a record of the animals Fengrove had gone on to sell?

Answer: yes.

Does either list mention the Sumatran tigers, pygmy hippos, the Siamese crocodile and the Lapis bowerbird?

Answer: no.

Was there ever a list of every animal Flemming Fengrove had actually owned?

Answer: not here.

Even if there was there was no one who could verify the truth of it.

Could it be that Flemming Fengrove, unbeknownst to the authorities, kept some of the animals secretly on his estate? Possibly bred them even?

Answer: possibly.

What if some of the animals were still up at Mountain Chateau? And what if someone had known about Fengrove's secret and had decided to release the animals, knowing that the old man could hardly get the police involved without incriminating himself? Perhaps this person or persons had planned to rescue the creatures and relocate them, but something had gone wrong and they had escaped.

It was a theory anyway.

It seemed like the only way to know the truth was to go up there and Ruby thought she might like a bit of company; it was a long journey after all and it might get boring without someone to chat to. The problem was that Clancy was right now taking his French test.

So just how was she going to get in touch with him?

Chapter 39.
Driving Miss Lazy

CLANCY WAS SITTING IN A HOT CLASSROOM, trying to remember the French word for elephant. He had opted to write an essay on the circus, having rejected the essay on vacations (because he didn't know the French word for vacation) and the essay on hobbies because at that moment he couldn't think of any actual hobbies that he had.

Now he found himself a good way through the circus essay and he realised that not only was he having trouble bringing to mind the word elephant, he also was having a problem with the word lion, clown and acrobat. It was hard to write an essay on the circus when you didn't know the word for elephant, lion, trapeze and acrobat. He had wisely decided that he should just get going, leave blanks and come back to them later – he was bound to remember before the time was up.

Forty-five minutes later, he looked back at his essay to see rather a lot of blanks; he needed to fill them with something, but he wasn't sure what. He had about fifteen minutes to go when there was a knock on the door. Mrs Bexenheath stuck her head round and said, 'Clancy Crew, your mother called and she requires you to return home immediately. She's sent a cab for you, it's out front.'

'My mother?' said Clancy.

'That's what I said,' said Mrs Bexenheath. 'It behoves me to inform you that you will not be allowed to retake this exam. Madame Loup expressed herself quite forcefully on this point.'

'Are you sure it was my mother?'

'Of course I'm sure. I've spoken to your mother often enough to know her voice when I hear it.'

'But my mother is in... oh jeez.' *Ruby Redfort*, thought Clancy. 'If it's all right with you Mrs Bexenheath, I'll just finish my test.'

'No, it is not all right with me,' said Mrs Bexenheath. 'I don't want to be on the wrong end of a telephone call from an angry mother.'

Reluctantly, Clancy gathered up his things and Mrs Bexenheath stood by the door, hands on hips. As he passed by, he handed her his unfinished test – another failure, another run-in with his father, but no more second chances; he would be held down a year for sure. He would be the laughing stock of the school. Boy, would Vapona Bugwart and Gemma Melamare have a field day. He was beginning to think Mr Piper the philosophy teacher was right: man was not born good, he was just out for himself, and when he got the chance he would laugh at those less fortunate, those unlucky ones who kept on flunking French.

As Clancy made his way out into the bright sunshine, he saw the cab.

The driver wound down the window. 'You Clancy Crew?'

'Yes...' said Clancy cautiously.

'OK, get in.'

Clancy climbed into the back seat and the driver started the engine. As he moved off into the traffic, he reached back and handed Clancy an envelope.

'What's this?' asked Clancy.

'How should I know?' said the cab driver. 'I'm just the guy driving the car.'

Clancy peeled open the envelope and read the message. It was printed neatly in code which translated as:

The cab is going to drop you home. Change into something that makes you look older. We're going to pay an elderly man a visit so try to look respectable. If you have any questions, call me.

'Oh brother,' he muttered. *Ruby Redfort is ruining my life.*

Clancy snuck into the house the back way and went up to

his room. He picked up the phone and dialled.

'Why are you calling?' said Ruby.

'I'm calling because you told me to call if I had any questions and I do have questions, a lot actually.'

'Have you changed into something older-looking?' she asked.

'No.'

'Well, get on with it buster, we've got to be somewhere.'

'Where?'

'I'll tell you when we get there.'

'Tell me now Ruby.'

'Can't, this is an unsecured line.'

'Are we about to do something illegal?'

'No.'

'Dangerous?'

'Probably not.'

'What?'

'OK, not. Now can I please put the phone down? I gotta hire a car.'

'But I can't drive,' said Clancy, 'and the last time I looked, neither could you.'

'I'll hire a car *and* a driver,' said Ruby. 'My mom uses this car service when Hitch is out of town and she can't be bothered to drive. They're called *Driving Miss Lazy* and they specialise in longish distance rides.'

'You have to be kidding me.'

'I am. They're called *We Drive You Round the Bend*.'

'That can't be true.'

'There's only one way for you to find out. Be there or you never will.'

'I'm just busting to know,' said Clancy in a sarcastic tone. 'By the way, won't they think it's a little unusual if a thirteen-year-old kid phones up and books a car to take them outta town?' It was a reasonable question.

'I doubt it. Mom says they spend their whole time driving rich kids around. They're used to being booked by teenagers. Anyway, I can sound older than I look,' said Ruby, 'and I can look older than I look.'

'OK, so you hire this car with a driver, what then? We go meet this guy – isn't he gonna think something weird's going on?'

'It'll be fine,' said Ruby, 'trust me.'

'I always hate when you say that because it always means you're about to get me into some big heap of trouble which you hope you can just bluff your way out of.'

'I did your detention essay, didn't I?' said Ruby. 'Got you out of that trouble?'

'It was you that got me into it. Besides, Mrs Drisco is trouble I can handle, my dad is trouble I can handle; an elderly man calling the cops about harassment is not trouble I can handle.'

Two minutes later and Clancy had agreed.

When Clancy met Ruby at the rendezvous, she looked quite different from the Ruby Redfort he knew. She was all dolled up (as Mrs Digby would say) and looked very strange in a wide-brimmed hat, sunglasses, rouge, hoop earrings and high-heeled boots, and carrying a large purse; she *did* look older though.

Clancy had done less well with his costume and merely appeared odd.

Ruby looked Clancy up and down.

'That the best you could do? I'm gonna have to pretend you're my weird nephew, Dusty, from the mountains.'

'What! How is it my fault? I was sitting my French test a half-hour ago and now I have to get into some insane disguise so I can be most probably murdered by an *insane* elderly man.'

'Just get in the car Dusty,' ordered Ruby.

Clancy got in the car. The driver wasn't even a little bit interested in them, but still a lot of what they said was said in code.

'So why are we going to see this old guy?' asked Clancy.

'I'm not sure exactly, it's just a theory' said Ruby. 'But a long time ago he used to keep all these exotic animals up on his estate. People said he sold them off years back, but I'm not so sure. I mean where else would all of these strange animals have come from?'

'Oh,' said Clancy, 'so we're gonna see some man about his escaped crocodile, that about it?'

'I guess you could put it that way,' said Ruby.

'Right,' sighed Clancy. 'There's *no* chance my dad's gonna get me that bike now.'

'Why not?' said Ruby.

'Because now I'm gonna flunk my French. I doubt very much that he's gonna buy me a bike as a reward for trying.'

'Clance, he was never gonna buy you a bike as a reward, get real – he hardly *ever* remembers your birthday. What did he give you last time? Oh yeah, an alarm clock.'

'That was one awful gift,' said Clancy, remembering the event like it had just happened.

'Anyway, what makes you think you'll flunk French?' said Ruby.

'Perhaps the fact that I didn't have time to finish the test,' said Clancy, 'because my "mom" pulled me outta school.' He sat back in the seat, dejected. 'Ah, who am I kidding? I was never going to pass. I couldn't remember the word for elephant.'

'*Éléphant,*' said Ruby.

'Yes,' said Clancy.

'No, elephant is *éléphant,*' said Ruby.

'Really?' said Clancy.

'Yeah,' said Ruby.

'Exactly the same as in English?'

'Basically, yeah, except for there's accents on the Es.'

'Well, I couldn't remember the word for lion either.'

'*Lion,*' said Ruby.

'Or cage,' said Clancy.

'*Cage,*' said Ruby.

'Oh brother,' said Clancy. 'Don't tell me trapeze is...'

'*Trapèze,*' said Ruby.

Chapter 40.
Selling insurance

THE DRIVER HAD NO IDEA WHERE THE FLEMMING FENGROVE RESIDENCE WAS; he wasn't nearly old enough to have heard of the eccentric millionaire, but luckily Ruby had listened carefully to Mrs Digby's description.

They had travelled a fair way out of town, several miles along the canyon road, before reaching the sharp fork to the left and on up to Mountain Chateau; Wolf Paw Mountain looming dark above it.

The long winding drive which led up to the house was shaded by trees, the branches so long unclipped that they formed a living cage around the snaking road. The mansion that appeared at the end of it gave the impression of having seen one too many winters, its stonework crumbling, its windows dark and sad like they had lost their spirit.

'I'm going to go discuss insurance with Mr Fengrove.' Ruby rummaged in her handbag. 'Too bad I forgot to wear my perfume. Darn it.'

'Why?' said Clancy. 'You got a body odour problem?'

'Course not buster, it's just perfume makes you seem older, more sophisticated.'

'Makes you smell like a rose bush,' said Clancy.

'Anyway,' said Ruby, 'I'll go knock on old Fengrove's door while you jump on over that wall and see if he has any wild animals in the back garden.'

'What!' Clancy's arms were flapping. 'Are you crazy? Have you actually lost your mind for two minutes?'

'Stop wasting time and get over that wall buster!'

'Why do *I* have to climb the wall?'

'Have you seen what you're wearing?' said Ruby. 'You look like a total nutjob; you can't knock on some guy's door, he's never gonna let *you* in.'

'And I suppose you think you look totally normal?' said Clancy.

'More normal than you,' argued Ruby.

'I'm not climbing any wall,' said Clancy, shaking his head. 'Uh uh. No way, no day.'

'I'd like to remind you that the meter is ticking, the car service charges by the minute and I only have fifty bucks.'

'I don't care,' said Clancy. 'I'll walk back if I have to.'

'*All right*,' sighed Ruby, 'have it your way. *I'll* go check out the animals while you go pretend to sell Mr Fengrove insurance.' She hitched up her skirt in preparation for climbing the wall. 'Let's hope he doesn't call the cops.'

To Clancy's mind this was not a good trade. He groaned.

'OK, OK, I'll go throw myself to the wild things, but if I die I hope you feel real bad about it.'

'I promise I'll never get over it,' said Ruby.

The heavy oak door was answered by an elderly man in a frayed cardigan and sagging trousers, both of which looked like they had been purchased many years ago for a lot of money. Once these garments must have lent him dignity and status, but now they made him look wretched and vulnerable.

Ruby was worried that the old man might smell a rat when he saw a thirteen-year-old girl dressed up as an insurance saleswoman, but she needn't have been concerned. Flemming Fengrove wasn't exactly at the top of his game. He seemed confused and disorientated, a shadow of a man. It was hard to imagine that this broken person had been a key player back in the 1920s when Twinford was regarded as a party town and Flemming Fengrove had danced and whirled the city's citizens into crazy abandon. Now he looked like a kid's toy bear that had lost most of its stuffing.

Ruby had thought it was going to be difficult to get this reclusive man to talk, but she was wrong. He seemed to *want* to talk. Perhaps now, after all these years of being alone, he needed to have someone hear him again.

Ruby introduced herself as Miss Grover, a junior insurance rep.

'Not interested,' said Fengrove.

'But you might be interested if I gave you a quote; we have very favourable rates.'

'I have no money to spend on such things,' said the old man.

'It's a lovely house,' said Ruby. 'You have style sir, that's for sure.'

The man mumbled a bit. 'Well, I don't know, maybe. I used to have.'

'So you live in this place all by yourself sir?' asked Ruby, looking around.

'Not by myself,' he replied. 'I still have some of my companions.'

'Companions?' asked Ruby.

'Animals,' said Fengrove sadly.

'*Some* you say?'

'Most have gone,' said Fengrove. 'I lost the first of them back in the 1930s. I managed to hang onto a few, but the man I trusted to watch over them, he stole them from me.' Fengrove looked like he might collapse and so Ruby led him to a chair and sat him down.

'This man, he was the zookeeper?' Ruby enquired.

Fengrove nodded.

'Has he been with you a long time sir?'

'Too long probably,' replied Fengrove. 'Ivan got greedy, wanted more and more from me. I told him I couldn't afford to pay him a penny more, I have no money. Not a nickel.'

Ruby doubted this statement since, even if this reputed millionaire had no cash, the house was clearly stuffed with antiques and fine art. The large painting in the hall looked like it might be worth a lifetime of salaries and he certainly wasn't spending money on the house upkeep.

'So Ivan left with no warning? Just like that?' said Ruby.

'First he let the animals go and then he disappeared. I went to find him, but he wasn't in his cabin; he just never returned.'

Ruby looked at him, so sad, so diminished. Everything he had worked for had gone; his talents wasted, he had wound up some embittered failure. With his dreams gone, it was as if he had completely lost his way. Ruby shuddered. How easy was it for success to become failure?

Chapter 41.
Toronto, Canada

WHILE RUBY WAS SEEKING ANSWERS, Clancy was climbing up and over a twelve foot stone wall which encircled the estate. It was a little harder than he had anticipated, but he dropped to the other side with no more than a grazed arm and a ripped sleeve, and began to search the grounds.

What he found first was an ancient turtle still puttering about in an ornamental pond spanned by a little fairy-tale bridge. The turtle looked happy enough, or at least too aged to mind. Some of the birds were still flapping around the aviary, content with the remaining birdseed and partial security, though the door was ajar and they were free to fly the coop.

Apart from the odd butterfly, all the other animals were gone. It wasn't a depressing place, it was like a lost land in a way and certainly well kept; compared to the house, it was in good order, but there was no doubt Mountain Chateau was a place time had well and truly ticked on past.

Clancy was just preparing to get out of there when he felt someone grab his shoulder. He shrieked a high-pitched shriek and turned very slowly to face what could only be a member of Mr Flemming Fengrove's security team.

This security guard turned out to be an elderly ostrich, but Clancy didn't want to tussle with him much either and so scrambled up the wall at great speed.

Ruby was waiting for him on the other side.

'You OK?' she said.

'Fine,' said Clancy.

'I thought I heard a scream.'

'That might have been the ostrich,' he replied. 'So what did you discover? You think the old man lost his marbles and let his animals go or what?'

'I don't think so,' said Ruby. 'In fact, I'm sure not. The guy's all broken up about it; he's been alone a long time and these animals were the only reason he had any marbles left at all.'

'You're telling me that he looked after all these creatures alone?' said Clancy.

'No, that's the thing, until recently he had a keeper, someone called Ivan. He managed the animals, looked after them pretty well too from what Fengrove says.'

'So where is Ivan now?' asked Clancy, looking around as if the zookeeper might spring out from behind a tree.

'Not in his cabin, at least that's what Mr FF says, but we might as well go take a look for ourselves,' said Ruby, moving towards the car.

'I don't think I want to,' said Clancy.

'What? You're afraid?' said Ruby.

'Sure I am,' said Clancy. 'What if we find his dead body?'

'Then he'll be dead and that's that.' Ruby shrugged.

'But what if he's all strangled on the floor, murdered? I don't want to end up in the same position.'

'So you think the murderer will be hanging out in the house waiting for some nosy parker to come on by?' said Ruby.

'It might be Mr Fengrove who's the murderer, ever think of that?'

'Have you seen Mr Fengrove? He's eighty-eight years old and looks more like he's a hundred and eighty-eight; he couldn't punch a fly if it was lying down.'

They arrived at the little house not ten minutes later. It was nothing much to look at, a simple, one-storey building constructed from clapboard. As Ruby had predicted, no one was there to answer the door and so she let herself in by way of a tiny device she pulled from the Bradley Baker escape watch; it took less than a second. The inside of the house was as modest as the outside; the owner had few possessions and his main interest seemed to be framed drawings of exotic creatures. He had some books on the same subject and there were old albums containing pictures of the keeper holding or standing next to animals both large and small.

Ruby discovered a ticket underneath some papers, stuffed at the back of a kitchen drawer. It was a train ticket to Toronto, Canada, unused and out of date by three weeks and there was a brand-new suitcase sitting in the wardrobe.

'Looks like he was planning to split,' called Ruby.

'But you said that *Flemming Fengrove* said that he'd already gone,' replied Clancy.

'Exactly, so what made him change his mind about train travel?' said Ruby to herself.

'You should see this!' called Clancy from the bathroom. A pretty expensive-looking watch dangled from his hand. 'I found it in that washbag by the sink.' He took it over to Ruby who was busy searching the bedroom. She looked up.

'Ivan doesn't look like the kinda guy who could have afforded that kind of timepiece,' said Ruby.

'Coulda been given to him,' suggested Clancy, 'a gift from Mr FF, for services to animals.'

'I doubt it very much,' said Ruby. 'Mr FF struck me as a person who keeps his wallet pretty close to his heart.' She inspected the back. 'There's no engraving, and in any case who gives a gift like this *with* the till receipt?' She picked up a piece of paper which had drifted under Ivan's bed. It was a receipt for a sizeable chunk of change. The watch had been purchased at Melrose Dorff. 'So now I'm thinking, why skip town without your new gold watch?'

'Or your suitcase,' said Clancy.

There were a lot of new and expensive things in the modest two-room home. It didn't add up. It was looking more and more likely that the guy had taken off in some kind of hurry since he hadn't even had time to gather his things – maybe he had got to Canada by some other means. Or maybe something had happened to him, which had made it impossible for him to get back to his home? Impossible to get to Canada. Perhaps he hadn't actually left Twinford County.

Clancy was pretty quiet on the journey home. He felt sort of down, depressed even – how had this nice man Fengrove, who used to be so popular and sociable, ended up so alone and lonely? Ivan the zookeeper had abandoned him, possibly even released his animals – how spiteful was that? Mr Piper was definitely right:

man was only interested in his own survival, born bad and good luck to anyone else.

The car took them back to town, travelling in from the north-east down Upper East Avenue, through the city centre and on westward. The plan to first drop Clancy back at his house on Ambassador Row and then head on to Cedarwood Drive. As soon as Clancy was out of the car, Ruby told the driver to turn around and head back the way they had just come, back towards the upper east side. There was something else she wanted to check out; something she didn't want Clancy to get involved with. She had a creeping feeling it might turn out to be dangerous.

Chapter 42.
Leaving a trace

THE ONLY THING RUBY HAD TAKEN FROM IVAN'S CABIN was the receipt for the watch and the only reason she had taken this was because she wanted to check out something that was written on the back.

She hadn't told Clancy what she was thinking of doing because she knew he would make a big old fuss and she didn't have time for it.

She got the cab to drop her at East 23rd Street, a smart neighbourhood not far from the city centre. She paid the driver and watched as he moved off into the heavy Twinford traffic.

She looked again at the faint pencilled scrawl on the back of the receipt. Apartment 9, East 23rd Street. No name, just this address. She buzzed apartment 9: no answer; she waited and tried again: still no answer. She would risk it; it didn't seem like anyone was there. It was easy to get in the building, the doorman was on a break, so she just pressed one buzzer after another until someone clicked the apartment block's front door open. Apartment 9 was on the fourth floor. Ruby took the stairs; she didn't want to risk the lift in case she bumped into one of the residents.

The building's corridors were well maintained if old-fashioned; they were also quiet: she couldn't hear a sound from anywhere. She knocked on the door, ready to run if she heard footsteps. For the second time that day she utilised the tiny lock-breaking tool. It wasn't as easy as breaking into Ivan's place, this door was pretty secure, but after a few minutes she figured out the trick to it and was in.

She stood listening, utterly still, but got no sense of another person in the apartment. She looked around. She was standing in a generous lobby area where there was a small round table, on top of which sat a vase of fresh cut flowers. Ruby walked carefully across the hall to the nearest door and gently pushed it open. The room was shrouded in darkness; it had heavy drapes that were pulled not quite all the way across the windows. As her eyes adjusted, she began to make out the shape of a couch, an armchair, a fireplace and a desk.

On the desk sat a phone, nothing more. She looked in the drawer, but that was also empty, then she bent down under the desk and saw the wastepaper basket – it was pretty full with newspapers, magazines and, right at the bottom, envelopes. Most were addressed with the same looped black ink handwriting and all were delivered by hand, but none of them bore the recipient's name.

As she searched through them, smells wafted out. Some still contained their letter, but, as Ruby pulled each from its container, she discovered every single one to be blank. Every piece of paper came from a different hotel. Each was branded with the hotel's name or logo.

Ruby carefully replaced the newspapers and other trash, and placed the writing paper in her purse, hoping that they would not be missed. She was about to move on when she saw another envelope which had fallen beneath the chair. She turned it over and realised this was the same envelope dropped by the businessman in the department store; she knew this because it was printed with the same decorative seal. The eye gazed up at her and Ruby wondered whose faces it had seen. How had it got here, whose apartment was this? She left the drawing and wandered to the kitchen, a tidy room, no clutter, no mess, but on the table she found a small bottle, clear and almost full of some kind of liquid. She unscrewed the top and the smell that wafted out took her straight back to her chemistry lessons: it was ether.

Diethyl Ether *a dense, gasoline-smelling liquid used as a solvent, or for anaesthetising people and knocking them out.*

Now why would someone have a chemical like that on their kitchen table?

She didn't have time to find out.

Ruby heard the sound of the elevator and heels stepping out into the passageway. She didn't wait for the key in the door; without hesitation, she tiptoed to the window, pushed it open and climbed onto the fire escape, only pausing to gently close it behind her.

Lorelei Von Leyden
opened the door to
her apartment

She put down her bags and walked to the study; she needed to make a call. On entering the room she paused and sniffed the air. What was it she could smell?

'Bubblegum?' she said.

Chapter 43.
Drawing a blank

THE NEXT MORNING, RUBY WOKE UP EARLY. She was still cursing her carelessness – she'd only just got out in time, before the occupant caught her.

And just who *was* the occupant? She didn't know. All she had now were some pieces of scented paper. *Bozo*, she thought.

She was about to close her eyes and have another twenty or maybe thirty minutes' dozing time when she remembered something very important that she had to do. She was going to need to enlist the help of Red Monroe. She stumbled out of bed and looked at her own weary face in the mirror; she still wasn't looking the picture of health. She scrabbled around in her bathroom cabinet for some vitamins – she looked like she might be missing a few important ones. She swallowed a couple and picked up the soap bar phone and dialled Red's number. Red answered it as her mom had already set off for work.

'Hey Red, could you do me a favour?'

'Sure, what dya need me to do?' Red always said yes; she was a nice kid that way.

'When you get to school, could you go to the secretary's office and distract Mrs B so she comes out into the hall? I need to get something from behind her desk.'

'No problem,' said Red, 'I'll be there at 8.15. Just let me know how long you need her out of the way.'

Red made a great decoy: she had such an innocent face that no one, not even the suspicious Mrs Bexenheath, could ever quite believe she could do anything even mildly bad. Second best at this was Mouse, but she was a little more nervy than Red, and if she was being totally honest with you she preferred to stay out of trouble's way, choosing to keep a low profile. It wasn't that she didn't want to help, it was just that she didn't need the heat.

By the time Ruby arrived at the secretary's office, Red was already speaking to Mrs Bexenheath. She was complaining about something she had seen in one of the lockers.

'I think it's a raccoon,' Red was saying, 'but you see it could be a marmot, to be honest Mrs Bexenheath. What with all these weird animals showing up all over the place, I'm just not sure.'

Mrs Bexenheath was looking worried until Red said, 'I heard there's a reward if the animal is exotic, I mean if it's something like a chinchilla, which it could be. I didn't get a good enough of a look.'

Mrs Bexenheath looked a little more animated; she even got up off her chair. Mrs Bexenheath liked sitting down and only stood up if her duties demanded it.

'I heard that you even get your picture taken and put in the *Twinford Mirror*,' continued Red.

Mrs Bexenheath put down her coffee cup.

'I'd better come and look,' she said. 'Someone is going to have to take charge.'

Ruby signalled seven minutes with her fingers and Red nodded, no problem.

Once the secretary had vacated her room, Ruby was in.

She knew where Mrs Bexenheath was likely to keep the test paper: she kept anything of any importance in her locked cupboard. She kept the keys to this on a keyring which she wore around her neck and it seriously weighed her down; the secretary had a lot of keys.

The Bradley Baker watch tool made easy work of the lock and Ruby was in in no time. Finding the test wasn't difficult either since Mrs Bexenheath was a very organised woman. Ruby removed the original Clancy essay and placed it in the shredder. Then she opened her satchel and pulled out an essay written in not too perfect French: it was all about the circus. The handwriting was Clancy Crew's, at least it looked like Clancy Crew's, and no one, not even his mother, would think to argue otherwise. It was neatly written, but not too neatly. There were a few crossings-out, but not a lot.

It was a brilliant forgery: not too good, but good enough.

Satisfied, Ruby left the room, pulling the door closed behind her. The whole thing had taken just under six minutes and having fixed Clancy's essay she thought she might take advantage of Dr Harper's sick note and take the day off.

She decided to go and hang out in Central City Park, do some thinking, which was just as well because a couple of hours later she got a buzz on her watch and was unsurprised to see Hitch's light had flashed on. She radioed him.

'Harper says she should take another look at your foot; those stitches should be about ready to snip.'

'Really?' moaned Ruby. She had hoped to get the chance to study the writing papers she had lifted from the East Avenue apartment; she had packed them in her satchel and been intending to call in at the library where it was cool and quiet. But instead she reluctantly headed off towards the toddler playground.

**Lorelei took her
jewelled telephone dialler
and dialled...**

...the young man answered. 'Lorelei?'

'Yes, it's me, where have you been? I've been trying to get hold of you all night.'

'What is it?' he said. 'Something happened?'

'You were right to be concerned; it turns out the little snoop knows more than we thought.'

'You want to do something about it?' said Eduardo.

'You bet I do. I'll use a lure, it shouldn't be difficult, think Hansel and Gretel.'

'You're going to use candy?' he asked, a little puzzled.

'Not exactly,' said Lorelei, 'but sort of.'

Chapter 44.
SJ

'IT'S HEALING OK,' was Dr Harper's first remark, 'but *you* don't look so good.'

Ruby wasn't *feeling* so good either; this was the worst cold she had had in a while and nothing she did made it any better.

Dr Harper reached to open one of her desk drawers – as she rummaged around for the tablets she was looking for, Ruby noticed a curve of broken glass wrapped in paper. It looked a little like a crystal ball, like a fortune teller might use, though this crystal ball seemed to contain not fortunes, but the Eiffel Tower.

Dr Harper handed Ruby a card of tablets and said, 'Take two in the morning; they might help.'

Ruby thanked her and got up to leave.

'Take it easy kid,' was Harper's parting advice, 'and come back if you start to feel like you might be dying.'

❋ ❋ ❋

'That's good advice,' said Hitch when Ruby reported back the doctor's words. He looked at her more closely. 'Actually, you really *don't* look so good. I'll drive you back after my meeting with LB.'

So Ruby sat in the Spectrum canteen, took out the envelopes and sat there wondering what they might mean.

Maybe, just maybe, someone here at Spectrum might be able to take a look at them. Hitch's meeting seemed to be going on a long while so what was the harm in doing a little investigating? After all, she had time on her hands.

Ruby knew the Spectrum lab was somewhere in the lower level complex, she wasn't sure where as she had never actually been taken there.

Spectrum was arranged without a directory: you either knew where departments were or you didn't. If you didn't, then you probably had no business going there. However, if you could work out where a department was simply by using your brain and your knowledge of Spectrum, then you probably deserved to find it. Each door in Spectrum was a different colour and each corridor was made up of shades and hues of reds, oranges and yellows, then greens, blues and indigos on through the colour spectrum.

Ruby thought about labs and what they meant to her, what was the first thing she thought of? There were Bunsen burners and gas flames – gas burned blue. There were metals in golds, silver, copper and browns, various chemical liquids and compounds and these came in a whole series of colours and there were tests one did which involved colour, like the litmus test. Red was for acidic and blue for alkaline; purple was neutral. Neutral seemed right for a lab so this was the colour of the door she went in search of.

A good choice as it turned out.

Ruby knocked and found a woman in goggles working at a long white bench covered in a lot of neatly arranged bottles and beakers and glass dishes. She sort of looked up when Ruby entered.

'Hello,' she said, 'I'm just trying to work out if this substance is corrosive or not. I'll be with you in a mo.'

Several minutes passed and then the woman said, 'Thought so,' and put down her tongs and pulled off her lab gloves.

'How can I help?' She looked at Ruby through her goggles and said, 'Gosh, you look young.'

Ruby was slightly thrown off guard by the lab technician's easiness – she didn't seem to mind some school kid walking in unannounced, like protocol at Spectrum was no big thing. Ruby looked at the badge clipped to the white coat the woman wore.

'Your name SJ?' she asked.

'I'd be pretty weird if I was wearing a badge which said SJ if I wasn't SJ, don't you think?' Then she thought about it. 'But actually you're right to ask because I could have borrowed SJ's lab coat and I could really be called Beryl or Anastasia, I wouldn't mind that – being called Anastasia – not Beryl, I'd mind that quite a lot.'

'My name's Ruby,' said Ruby.

'As in Redfort?' asked SJ. 'If so, then I think I've heard of you. Who sent you?'

Ruby thought it might be best to come clean and see where it took her; some people liked this approach and the lab technician seemed like she might be someone who would.

'No one,' said Ruby. 'I'm not really supposed to be here.'

'Nor am I,' said SJ, 'it's my lunch break. What do you want to ask me?'

'I've got some things I'd like you to look at.'

'Come on, hand them over.' SJ pulled on a fresh pair of gloves. 'You can't be too careful.'

Ruby opened her satchel and took out the plastic folders containing the papers. SJ, having wiped the bench clean, carefully spread them out across the worktop. She looked carefully at the letterheads then she looked at them again through a magnifying glass and then through a microscope. She held them up to the light and then she switched on an infrared light and an ultraviolet light. She did a flame test, a water test, dipped the corner of one into a solution and tried gently baking another in an oven but nothing happened. The papers seemed to be utterly blank; the letterheads were just letterheads.

'That's a surprise,' said SJ. 'I was expecting to find a microdot or some sophisticated invisible writing, something super clever – but nothing.'

'Oh well,' said Ruby, 'they aren't what I thought they were.'

'They pong a bit, don't they?' said SJ, blowing her nose. 'I'm not good on perfume, makes my nose run.' She blew hard. 'You know, they might simply be perfumed notepaper. People use it, don't ask me why.'

'But isn't it a bit weird to send people pieces of perfumed notepaper unmarked?' said Ruby.

'Not if you happen to be a perfumer,' said SJ. 'Then I would think it very reasonable. Now I really do need to grab a sandwich before I positively faint.'

Much to Ruby's disappointment, this all made sense; the person all these letters were addressed to might very well be a perfumer, in which case what was the big mystery? The only thing that didn't quite make sense was why a zookeeper might have had the address of a perfumer scribbled on the back of a receipt for an expensive watch.

And what was the ether for? She returned to the canteen and waited for Hitch. When he appeared, he looked kind of stressed, not his normal cool and collected self. When Ruby asked him if something was bothering him, he just shook his head and said, 'LB just keeps on about that darned paperweight.'

But Ruby didn't think Hitch's mood had anything to do with some old paperweight.

**'I hope you don't mind
Miss von Leyden...**

...but I let your mother into your apartment.'

Lorelei stopped dead. 'I'm sorry?'

'Your mother, she said you wanted me to let her in.'

'And what did my mother look like?' asked Lorelei carefully.

'Hard to tell, she was wearing a hat with a veil.' The doorman looked confused. 'Did I do something wrong, is she not your mother?' He was already reaching for the phone, fearful that he had made a terrible mistake.

'No, no, she's my mother,' she reassured him. 'I just wondered how she was looking. She's had a long flight and of course I worry about her so.'

The doorman looked relieved. 'Tell her, if there's anything she needs, I'd be happy to get it for her.'

'Oh, I will,' nodded Lorelei as she slowly turned, stepped into the elevator and pressed the button to the fourth floor.

The woman sitting at Lorelei's desk was perhaps fifty, fifty-five, maybe even a little older, it was hard to tell. The veiled hat sat on the chair next to her and she had taken off the smart navy coat to reveal a cheery-looking floral tea dress.

She had a brightness to her eyes, curiosity lurked there, like she wanted to know everything. Her features were delicate, she had no doubt been a beauty once, but hard times and cruel words had faded that to a cosy prettiness and her good looks only really came alive when she smiled and her blue eyes twinkled.

'You know my mother died when I was born,' said Lorelei. Her spiked shoes on the polished parquet gave the illusion of confidence, though Lorelei felt anything but.

'That must have been very sad for you sweetie,' said the woman.

'I've never given it a moment's thought,' replied Lorelei.

'Yes, I hear you're good at moving on. It's a useful quality sweetie, but you have to be careful not to move on so quickly that you don't leave things behind, telltale things that might give you away. I'm talking about loose ends: they can unravel so easily if you don't tie them up.' She winked. 'I hate loose ends, don't you? I mean, for example, take this one about your mother; can you be so sure that she isn't still alive? Maybe she didn't die when you were born. I mean if I told you that you're looking at her now, could you be sure I was lying?' She laughed. 'Your doorman seemed convinced.'

She shrugged before continuing. 'But, coming back to the point as we must, I have a sneaking feeling that perhaps you haven't been as tidy as you should have been. Perhaps you have left a few loose ends sweetie.'

Lorelei tried hard to swallow, but her throat was tight and

her mouth dry.

'You're a sweet girl Lorelei, your fragrance suits you, but you seem a bit out of your depth here, is that true?'

Lorelei bristled a little at this, but said nothing.

'If I hadn't heard such good things about you, I might let my imagination run away with me, let myself think that you were trying to double-cross me, but I guess that would be silly, you being such a good girl and everything. So reliable, so professional.'

Lorelei felt her heart beating twice as fast as it should.

'You see, I've come to collect what I paid you to deliver, but I get the impression that you don't have it, is that right?'

Lorelei struggled to come up with a good answer. 'It's true there have been a few obstacles and things haven't run smoothly, but your delivery will be made.'

'OK sweetheart, I'm going to allow you to see this thing through because I think you're capable of getting results, but if, and I say this merely to inform you, to warn you should I say...' Suddenly her appearance changed from someone kind and sympathetic to someone whose face was tough like iron.

"If you fail, then it'll be over for you, not in a wishy-washy-you'll-never-work-in-this-town-again way, but in a final kind of way. Does that make sense? I need you to deliver – double-cross me and... well, let's leave it at that, shall we?'

She smiled kindly like a mother might smile at her baby.

'Now, I've kept you long enough. I'm sure you want to get on; we can have a cuppa and a catch-up when you get back... if you get back.'

She got up and walked to the door, then turned back. 'I'd close that window if I were you sweetie; you could catch your death if the weather breaks.'

Chapter 45.
Turkish delight

CLANCY HAD BEEN LOOKING ROUND THE STORE for what seemed like the whole morning, but had actually been about forty minutes. He wasn't a very interested shopper and he was only there because it was his mom's birthday and he had to get her something. He was prepared to use all his savings since what he had been saving up for was now an impossible dream.

Clancy Crew had never been particularly interested in money or acquiring stuff, occasionally there might be an invisible-ink pen, or pair of running shoes or *bike,* but these came along once in a blue moon, that was all. Now he couldn't buy the Windrush 2000, what was the point of stuffing all this money into his piggy bank? But the gift he knew his mom wanted he couldn't begin to afford: a bottle of 1770 was way out of his price range.

He walked out of Melrose Dorff into the searing heat, dejected. He felt worse than ever, since he had just failed in the simple mission of buying a gift for someone he had known all his life. As he made his way along the sidewalk into the park, he noticed a woman sitting on a bench, the sun on her face, the store behind her. She looked kind of familiar, but at the same time not, and it was only when he got near that he realised why. She smelled of Turkish delight.

Clancy looked at the name badge pinned to her blouse. 'Lyla,' he read.

The woman looked puzzled and shaded her eyes with her hand as she tried hard to recognise his face. Then she smiled a beautiful smile, like she was very pleased to see him.

'Hey,' said Clancy, 'how's your neighbour doing?'

'That's sweet of you to ask,' she said. 'He's doing much better, thank you.'

'He looked pretty sick,' said Clancy. 'I guess he must be back at home taking it easy?'

'No,' said the woman, 'no, he's out of Twinford for good now. He finally saw that city life doesn't agree with him; he needed to grab hold of his dream.'

'Yeah, this city can get to you sometimes,' said Clancy. 'I wouldn't mind getting out of town myself, just for a while.'

'So why don't you?' she said. 'Aren't you on summer vacation by now?'

'Almost,' said Clancy 'but still I'm a long way from grabbing hold of my dream, I can tell you that for nothing, and without that there's no chance of me going anywhere.'

'So what is it?' asked Lyla. 'This thing you want so badly.'

Clancy sighed. 'It's a Windrush 2000,' he replied as if that was enough information for anyone. He saw that it wasn't and added, 'Oh, it's this really great bike. It handles well over any terrain, the tyres won't puncture, the steering is super good and the speed is something else, and also...' he smiled, 'it's this amazing blue. I would do anything just to have one good ride on it.'

The woman looked at him like she was really thinking; her face was sympathetic as if she understood just how it feels not to be able to get what you want.

'So what were you looking for inside the store, surely not a bicycle?' said Lyla.

'Oh, my mom's been yakking on about that perfume, you know, 1770,' said Clancy. 'I was going to buy her a bottle, but there's no way I can afford it, even with my bike savings. She's got a big birthday coming up and I wanted to get her something she actually wants.'

Lyla's pretty eyes sparkled. 'Maybe...' she said, 'maybe I can help you out with that – you were so kind to *me* and my friend, I'd like to do *you* a good turn. Come back the day after tomorrow.

I think I can get you a great deal on that perfume.'

Clancy smiled. 'Really?' he said. 'You'd do that?'

Lyla stood up. 'It would be my pleasure.' She turned to leave. 'I never asked you what your name was.'

'Clancy, Clancy Crew.'

'Sounds like a detective.' She laughed.

'You should meet my sister Nancy,' he said.

'Your sister's called Nancy Crew?' said Lyla.*

'Yeah, well, my parents weren't thinking too hard when they came up with it. My dad was probably too busy thinking about becoming an ambassador.'

'Oh, so your father is Ambassador Crew. How interesting.'

'That's one word for it,' said Clancy.

She looked at her watch. 'I'd better be getting back,' she said. 'I don't suppose you could do me a small favour, could you?'

'Probably,' said Clancy.

'I don't suppose you have any gum, do you? I have the most strange taste in my mouth – must be all that perfume I've been mixing, it's hard not to breathe it in... *Bubblegum* would do just fine.'

'You're in luck,' said Clancy, 'I have both.' He handed her his chewing gum and Ruby's pack of Hubble-Yum.

Lyla held the bubblegum to her nose and breathed in the

fake-strawberry smell.

'Oh, I remember this brand.' She took another long sniff. 'It takes me right back... like I smelled it yesterday.'

'Keep it,' said Clancy.

'Thanks,' said Lyla and she began to walk off down the path back towards the store.

'Hey,' called Clancy, 'so you never said– what do *you* want?'

Lyla laughed. 'Nothing much, but I wouldn't mind being impossibly rich; it could be fun, all that money, all that power, or maybe just world domination.'

'I don't think I can help you with that,' shouted Clancy, smiling.

'You never know,' said Lyla.

Chapter 46.
Gut instinct

RUBY HAD GONE TO BED UNUSUALLY EARLY and so was wide awake when Hitch called up at 6 am the next morning. She was lying on her bed reading one of her comics and lazily reached out a hand to answer the donut phone.

'Twinford animal wranglers.'

'Hey kid, I thought you might want to go talk to a friend of mine.'

'Sure,' said Ruby, 'but is this really a good time for a social call? Aren't we a little busy here?'

'Why? What are you doing?' asked Hitch.

'Broadening my horizons,' said Ruby, still flipping through her *Garbage Girl* comic.

'Glad to hear it, but this isn't really a social call. In fact, to be entirely frank with you, this friend of mine could never be accused of sociability. She's more likely to tell you to get off her porch than shake your hand.'

'So why do I want to put down my comic?' asked Ruby.

'Because this friend might be able to help you with your navigation problems,' he replied.

'How's that?'

'You'll see – Connie Slowfoot has helped more than a few agents in her time,' said Hitch, 'but as far as liking her goes – don't expect to.'

'So what address does this unlikeable woman reside at?' said Ruby.

Hitch might have sniggered at this, she couldn't quite tell over the phone, but if he did then Ruby understood why when he dropped her at the end of a rough overgrown path and pointed her in the direction of a wood-patched cabin that clung to the mountainside.

As Ruby climbed, she saw outside it a hunched and bent-up figure, a strange, gnarled-looking creature puffing out smoke.

The old woman looked up long before Ruby would have expected her to spot her.

'Who are you girl?' Miss Slowfoot shouted.

'Hitch sent me,' said Ruby.

'I don't recall asking who sent you. I asked you who you was.'

'Ruby Redfort,' said Ruby, 'my name's Ruby Redfort.'

The woman sat down then, right back in her rickety chair,

and rocked a bit while she sucked on her pipe.

'Hitch thought you could help me out,' called Ruby. She was still walking towards the shack even though she wasn't sure the old lady might tell her to get lost.

Connie Slowfoot nodded. 'Help you find your way I suppose; you got no-good eyes.'

'He told you?' asked Ruby.

'No,' said Connie, 'but I can tell.' She laughed her old crone laugh and rocked some more. Her accent was thick and strong like a character from history; no one spoke like that now, not in Twinford at least. 'I never heard your name before, but I can tell you blind as a bat in daylight without those glasses of yours.'

Jeepers! thought Ruby. The whole wild woman of the woods thing was kind of rankling.

'So,' said Ruby, 'what's your advice?'

The woman closed her eyes. 'You gotta see with your nose girl, ears too; you gotta feel your way through these woods, use your homing instinct.' She tapped her head and her hand disappeared into her wild, unruly hair. 'I know where my hand is because I can feel it. I don't need to see it.'

Ruby wasn't going to argue with the logic of that. She would listen for a while and then get out of there: this Connie was clearly one crazy old buzzard.

'You thinking I'm crazy girl, but you need to listen beyond your thoughts, you need to let your senses tell you what's true and what ain't. Don't rely on those eyes of yours, they no good.'

Connie was right about that. Ruby's eyes were not her strong point.

'You got brains girl, you just gotta stop relying on them, use your gut like nature intended.'

'How dya mean?' asked Ruby, waking up to the idea that this woman had something to say after all. She might be crazy, but she was sharp as a shard of broken glass.

'You see more with your eyes closed,' said Connie Slowfoot. 'You feel what's underfoot, what brush against your arm, your leg; you smell the air and hear the birds and the insects crawling up the trees, you taste the wind, feel the way it blowing, smell if rain coming; you make yourself blend and be part of it so you are the outdoors.'

Ruby said nothing. She just stared at the old lady while she rocked back and forth in her ancient chair.

'You know what I'm saying, you gotta think like a creature thinks girl, like people used to think afore they got too clever for their own socks. You gotta think like Mr Wolf think.'

'Mr Wolf?' repeated Ruby. 'You mean I gotta think like I'm a wolf?'

Connie snorted at this. 'You think you so well read, but you don't know about Mr Wolf. What books you been reading girl? Not the right ones that's for darn sure. Mr Wolf, he this man lived in the forest and tracked down that king of the woods, just about wiped him out.'

Connie stared into the middle distance as if she was seeing the whole thing played movie-like in front of her eyes.

'Many died afore him at the mercy of that big bad creature, it drew 'em to itself, and they met their end, torn to pieces, but Mr Wolf he knew better: he knew how to trap that wolf with its ownself's trap. He tricked him good, and that poor big bad wolf was no more.'

The old woman cackled. 'That was hundreds of years ago when we had Cyan wolves in these parts.'

'Cyan wolves?' said Ruby.

'The most dangerous kind,' said the woman, the laughter gone. 'They're man's enemy and man is the Cyan's enemy; neither wolf nor man does the other any good, no good, not at all.'

'What do you mean by *that*?' said Ruby.

'Can't get near 'em, can't stay away.' The woman leaned back in her chair and took another drag on her pipe.

Ruby furrowed her brow. 'You're talking about the Blue Alaskan, right?'

'Same difference,' chuckled the woman. 'All killers, all killed. Same wolf by another name.'

'Sounds like some old story to me,' said Ruby.

The woman laughed. 'You think as you please, but if you should smell it you'll change your mind swift enough, that's if you're able to think at all.'

'You're saying that there's some wolf no one seems to have ever heard of, at least not nowadays, that has a special power which can control folks?' Ruby was interested, but unsure whether to believe such a far-fetched tale.

The woman nodded her head as she rocked back and forth. 'That's right, a creature that can make you remember and forget all at the same time, that's what folks said anyways.'

'What do you mean by that?' said Ruby.

'A smell so good that if you smelled enough of it, it took you back to all the best times of your life, a smell so good it made you forget all the bad – so good it gave you that amnesia condition. That's what they said.'

She set about laughing again; the woman laughed a lot and it was setting Ruby on edge. She was fascinating in her own way, a bit too much mountain air perhaps, or maybe she had eaten one too many grubs, but still she was one interesting lady.

Connie stared back out into the middle distance and rocked

back and forth in the creaking chair, her lips pressed tightly closed. Ruby got the feeling that their conversation was at an end and she turned to leave.

'Thank you for your time Connie Slowfoot. I won't take up any more.'

'Time is for free,' said Connie. 'Time don't belong to no one; no one owns me and no one owns time.'

'I guess that's true,' agreed Ruby, 'but if it's all the same to you, I gotta get back.'

Connie Slowfoot shrugged. 'You do as you please girl.'

Ruby nodded and began walking away from the cabin. She hadn't made it ten paces when she heard Connie call, 'Girl, you mind my words, that blue wolf will rip you apart as soon as sniff you.'

'I'm not afraid of wolves,' said Ruby.

'I'm not talking about "wolves",' said Connie, 'I'm talking about *the wolf.*'

Ruby turned around. 'There aren't any Blue Alaskans, not for years.'

'That's what folks say and I thought they was right, but now I'm feeling something in my skin, telling me different.'

'I read they went extinct at least a hundred years back.'

'You can believe that if you want to,' said the old woman,

'I choose to play it safe. I shut my door tight at night just like my grandma did and her grandma afore her.'

'The Cyan wolf?' said Ruby.

'I don't know, I'm just a *lunatic* old woman,' said Connie, 'but I do know that wolf will rip you to shreds soon as sniff you... Unless, of course, you got the scent.'

'What is that supposed to mean?' Ruby called.

'What I say,' shouted the old woman. 'You meet that wolf, you better be sure you got the scent.'

These words curled through the air, carried on the breeze – they followed Ruby down the path and worked their way inside her head and echoed on as she walked down the mountainside, all the way to the road where Hitch was parked.

He opened the door for her. 'So did Connie give you any useful advice?'

'I'm not sure,' said Ruby. 'Maybe she told me everything I need to know and maybe she told me nothing.'

'Sounds like Connie,' said Hitch.

'So how come you didn't introduce me to her before,' asked Ruby, 'if it would have saved me a whole lot of trouble?'

'I didn't know where she was,' replied Hitch. 'She moves around a lot. I catch up with her when I catch up with her.'

'I thought you were a secret agent,' said Ruby, 'good at

tracking people down.'

'I'm pretty good at it when I want to be, but Connie, she's better. If she doesn't want to be found, she's not going to be found.'

'She sure can see a lot from a long way away,' said Ruby.

'Yes,' said Hitch, 'she sees pretty well for someone who's blind.'

Ruby looked at him hard. 'Connie Slowfoot is *blind*?'

'Blind as a bat in daylight,' said Hitch.

Chapter 47.
Around the next corner

CLANCY WAS IN A GOOD MOOD: things were working out. Maybe that Windrush 2000 wasn't such a distant dream; maybe it would arrive on his very doorstep. Lyla was going to help him out with that expensive French perfume so who knew what was just around the corner?

As it turned out, it was his *father* who was just around the corner and he did not look like he was about to give Clancy an expensive bicycle.

Ambassador Crew was unhappy about a lot of things, a whole list in fact – starting with:

Clancy's lack of punctuality resulting in detention.

Clancy having to retake his French test.

Learning of Clancy skipping school while retaking his French test.

Sitting on the roof when he had expressly been told not to.

And telling Olive that she was talking horse manure.

None of these things was he pleased about.

'But you don't even know what my test mark is yet,' argued Clancy. 'I might have actually finally passed. I could have done *well* even. I don't think it's fair to include this along with all that other stuff.'

But his father wasn't swayed by this argument.

'Why should I possibly think you could have passed, and why would I imagine that you could possibly have done "well"? You have never done well before; you have never put in the hard work to make it possible to do "well",' said his father. 'You are grounded until further notice and when I say grounded I mean no meeting Miss Redfort, no communicating with Miss Redfort and no socialising of any kind. You do not set foot off these grounds, do you hear me?'

It was impossible not to at that volume, thought Clancy. Anyone passing the ambassadorial home would have heard.

'What about school tomorrow?' asked Clancy. 'It's the last day.'

Ambassador Crew had forgotten about that. 'Obviously, I expect you to go to school,' said his father.

'So I *can* set foot off these grounds?' said Clancy.

'Well, clearly, yes, since you have one more day of school.' His father finally turned to leave. 'By the way, I have booked you on the Wichitino Camp in the hope it might drum into you some discipline. You won't thank me now, but in years to come I think you will be glad you learned a thing or two about hard work and team spirit, two qualities you are evidently lacking.'

It was bad enough to be grounded during the first week of the school break, but to be ordered to go on camp with the Wichitinos was an insult too far. Plus, how was he going to make it to the department store to pick up the 1770 for his mom? Clancy was going to have to do something so the first action he took was to call Ruby – another punishable offence, but at this stage what did he have to lose?

Ruby wasn't there so he left a message: 'Great, now my dad's enrolled me in dork camp and once he gets my test scores no doubt he'll leave me there. '

And then he hung up, no goodbye. Ruby Redfort was just like everyone else, only out for herself, and now she had got him in a whole heap of trouble, did she even care? He doubted it. Clancy headed off to school with appropriate dread – what were the odds that he had passed his French test? Zero? Less than zero? Was it possible to have odds that were less than zero? If it was, then he was bound to have them: it was just his dumb luck.

When Ruby returned home from the mountain and played her messages, she called Clancy right back, but unfortunately he was not picking up.

"Hey, this is Clance, leave a message if it's interesting. I'll call you back."

She used the number pad to leave a Morse code message:

—..- / —. / .-- / -..... / -.-..

Which would have made utter sense to Clancy if only he had had the capability to listen to it – for what Ruby didn't know was that Clancy's answerphone had just two minutes later been confiscated and was now sitting in his father's office.

Chapter 48.
A second chance

AS LUCK WOULD HAVE IT – or was it hard work? (he didn't think so) – Clancy Crew *did* pass his French. In fact, he returned home that afternoon, letter in hand, to find that he had passed well, better than he could have ever expected to, not absurdly well but believably well.

How had that happened? He didn't think he was anywhere near to getting a B–, especially since he hadn't even finished the test, especially since he hadn't even been able to remember the French word for elephant, lion, acrobat or trapeze.

Anyway, he had done it – it didn't matter how, he was home free.

Perhaps this would have a good impact on his dad's mood.

He left the letter on the hall table so his dad would see it as soon as he got up. This was the beginning of something good. Maybe things were finally looking up for old Clancy Crew.

Ruby had stopped in at the City Library to do some research on this Mr Wolf guy Connie had mentioned, but found not one single volume or pamphlet that so much as mentioned him.

Mr Latham had looked through the index cards, but there was no record of anyone taking out even one of the twenty-three books there should have been on the subject.

'What a mystery,' was all he could say. There were no books on the Cyan wolf either and so Ruby left the library empty-handed and none the wiser.

When Ruby got home that evening, Hitch was sitting in the back garden sipping a drink at the wooden table.

'Hey,' said Ruby, 'you been somewhere?' She was looking at the overnight bag on the ground next to him. Still attached was the flight label; it was marked Paris.

'Personal business,' Hitch said. He pointed to a chair. 'Sit down kid.'

Ruby sat, saying nothing; he obviously had something on his mind and from his expression she guessed it was important. He swirled the ice cubes in his drink, his elbow resting on the table, his chin resting on his hand. He looked like a man all out of ideas. After a short pause, he spoke.

'I'm going to level with you here kid: LB doesn't think you

can cut it.'

'That what your meeting was about?'

'Yes.'

'What did she say?'

'That maybe this isn't the right thing for you. Perhaps in ten years' time – maybe – but the thing you have to consider is, well, perhaps you were born to be a code breaker pure and simple.'

'She said she would give me a second chance,' said Ruby.

'LB's not sure that she made the right decision,' said Hitch.

'Why?'

'She doesn't think you've got what it takes to be a field agent.'

Ruby didn't shift her gaze or flinch or blink; instead she looked him in the eye and said, 'And what *does* it take?'

'Determination.'

'Determination I got,' said Ruby.

'You got to be tough kid, tougher than you can imagine.'

'Did I blub when my foot got all torn up? Did I lie down and die when the Count tried to bury me alive in sand? Did I stop work on this whole mission when my brain was like jello 'cause of contracting the flu?'

'No kid, you didn't,' agreed Hitch.

'So that proves I've got inner resources. Isn't that one of the important qualities an agent has to have?'

Hitch nodded. 'But LB's point is, why did you allow these things to happen? You should never have been captured in the first place – you were careless. You shouldn't have come down with the flu out in the field, that happened because you didn't pay attention. You lacked judgement. She doesn't know about your foot and she's not going to know, but I can't see her spilling any tears in your direction even if she did.'

'I'm not asking for sympathy, I'm asking for a second chance.'

'But maybe it's important for you to consider where your talents lie. Maybe you are more suited to four walls and a desk; maybe you need these constraints to work in so your mind can break out; maybe fieldwork causes you to lose focus.'

'You're the one who believed in me; you're the one who was sure I could cut it and I can prove you right. Let me go this one time, let me retake the survival test and *then* decide.' She looked at him, her eyes unblinking. No emotion, no little kid whining, just a clear-cut deal.

Finally, he nodded. 'All right,' he said, 'I'll stick to what was agreed. I'll back you, but this is on my head: you get into trouble it's down to me, so you make contact as soon as anything goes wrong. I mean anything.'

Ruby said nothing.

'That has to be the deal kid: you want to be a field agent you have to accept the ground rules; it's too dangerous to have an agent out there who isn't making the grade. You put everyone's life at risk that way.'

'I understand,' she said.

'I'll square it with Spectrum and LB, but you need to be ready, could be tonight tomorrow or next week, you won't know, but you gotta be there; you're not there, that's a fail.'

'I'll be ready,' she said.

'No going AWOL.'

'I'll be there.'

'Don't let me down kid.'

'I won't.'

'Oh, and I'll need the rescue watch – no gadgets on survival training and that includes everything. I don't want you blowing it by trying to sneak it.' He held out his hand.

'You think I'd do that?' said Ruby, doing her best to look offended while she handed him the rescue watch.

'Lose the halo kid, it doesn't suit you.'

There was a beep on his watch. He glanced at it and frowned.

Then he dialled in.

He didn't speak, just listened.

'What's happened?' asked Ruby once he had signed out of the call.

Hitch sighed. 'A body, it was found in the canal. Suspicious circumstances.'

'So what does it have to do with Spectrum?'

'I don't know yet, but Blacker seems to think there might be a link.'

'Who is it?'

'Some guy in expensive deck shoes. From the injuries looks like he might have fallen from a great height, injured himself badly and tried to drag himself to get help – his nice clothes were kinda torn up from the effort. No one knows how he ended up in the canal; he didn't drown, he was dead long before he hit the water.'

**Lorelei sat quite still;
she was thinking**

A plump velvet rose petal fell from the flower arrangement and landed like a drop of blood on the white marble of the floor.

She knew what she was going to have to do. One just couldn't have loose ends.

Chapter 49.
Try and you won't fail

WHEN CLANCY LOOKED OUT OF HIS BEDROOM WINDOW THE NEXT MORNING, he almost fainted because there standing just near the driveway was the Windrush 2000, brand-new and perfect in every way. His dad must have finally seen the light. This was something. This was his dad saying sorry, telling him he was right all along. This was the moment he had been waiting for all these years. He was right and his dad was finally telling him so.

He forgot about his bad feeling, and about wanting to leave Twinford, and instead he ran down the hall stairs two at a time. He ran out of the house and punched in the numbers to the electric gate and he hopped from one foot to the other as it very slowly juddered open. He slid through it and out onto the sidewalk.

But before he could make it to the bike, before he was in touching distance a terrible thing happened. A girl in a blue sweatshirt, jeans and flip-flops ran over to the bike, unlocked it, climbed on and cycled off up Ambassador Row.

Clancy had a hard time believing what had just happened. Why wasn't anyone doing anything about it? That girl had just stolen his bike! He looked around – had anyone even seen? What would his dad say? And then the truth dawned on him: *nothing*, his dad would say nothing because the girl had not stolen the bike; the girl had a key to a bicycle lock, a lock which *belonged* to the bike, her bike. He was suddenly weak, like he had been punched hard in the gut. There was no bike; the Windrush belonged to that girl in the flip-flops. Clancy turned back towards the house. 'Who wears flip-flops riding a Windrush 2000?' he muttered. 'She doesn't deserve that bike.'

Just to add insult to the whole bitter disappointment of the day, when Clancy stepped back inside the house, he saw a note from his father; it was written on one of his ambassadorial note cards and a metallic blue ballpoint pen lay on top of it.

Clancy,
In recognition of your struggle to finally complete basic French.
Best regards,
your father
PS Enjoy.

Clancy looked around; he couldn't see anything to enjoy. Maybe his father was going to present him with it later. He wondered what it could be. He picked up the pen; there was gold writing etched down one side. It said: *Try and you wont fail.*

There was something miserable about these words, as if to say, if only you would actually put in some effort, you might *actually* succeed. Also it was clearly untrue: plenty of people tried and failed and so trying was no insurance. Plus, it was disappointing to have a missing apostrophe when the pen guaranteed a perfect outcome.

All in all, it was shoddy.

Then, just to make matters worse, it dawned on him: *this* was the thing to be enjoyed; a cheap ballpoint pen was his gift.

'Oh brother,' he sighed. 'This even beats the alarm clock.'

Ruby was sitting up the tree in Amster Green, wondering where in tarnation was Clancy Crew. There was no message hidden in the branches and no missed call on her answer machine. She wanted to talk to him – she needed to talk to him, darn it. She was potentially facing one of the biggest disappointments of her life, the biggest failure, and he wasn't there.

She scribbled the coded words `fhrvos shf auspbrs bfhs` down on a piece of origami paper and folded it carefully.

The paper now resembled a rat. If she had had the time, she would have gone over there then and there if only to tell him what a lousy friend he was being, but she had bigger things on her mind, a whole lot bigger than Clancy Crew.

Chapter 50.
A highway to nowhere

CLANCY WENT TO SPEAK TO HIS SISTER MINNY. Minny, after all, was the one who never did anything she didn't want to do and, despite being caught numerous times, never seemed to buckle. If she had no good advice for Clancy, then at least she would be a sympathetic ear.

Clancy sat in Minny's room, giving her the low-down on everything that had happened and how their father had reacted to it. Minny sat on the edge of the window sill, arms folded; her mouth was set in a firm pinch like she was really considering all Clancy's options. Finally, she spoke.

'It would serve him right if you just ran away.'

Clancy didn't like the sound of that; it was the kind of thing people said they were going to do before they thought about exactly what they were running away to.

'I don't think that's a good idea,' said Lulu. 'I mean what are you gonna do out there?'

'Exactly,' agreed Clancy.

'That's not the point,' said Minny. 'It'll teach Dad a lesson; he grounds people way too much.'

'You're the only one who gets grounded,' said Lulu.

'Clancy's grounded,' Minny argued back.

'Yeah, now he is, but that's *once* and only because Olive ratted on him.'

'Did not,' said Olive from behind the door.

'Yeah you did,' said Clancy, 'and, by the way, this is a private conversation.'

'Well, I still think you should run away, just for a few days,' said Minny.

'What do you think?' said Clancy, turning to Lulu.

'Go on the dumb camp, save yourself the trouble.' Lulu found trouble boring; it interfered with her social life and brought more trouble.

'Are you kidding?' said Clancy. 'I wouldn't be seen dead in the Wichitino uniform.'

'All I'm saying is that if you hadn't trashed your bike then none of this woulda happened.' Lulu tended to see things for what they were.

'I didn't trash my bike, Minny did.' He was flapping his arms.

'Yeah and you covered for her which means you took the blame which means you have to suffer the consequences.' There was no arguing with Lulu's logic. 'You have a choice here: rat her out...'

'Hey!' said Minny.

'In which case you'll still be in trouble for lying,' continued Lulu.

'You will,' agreed Minny.

'Or,' said Lulu, 'run away, who knows where for who knows how long, and, when they send a search-and-rescue team for you, expect to be grounded for the rest of your life. My advice, go on the dorky camp.'

'Oh brother!' groaned Clancy.

'Like I told you,' said Minny, 'you gotta get outta here. I mean all you need to do is pack up a rucksack; you can take a tent and some food and stuff. You won't even need to go far, just to Boulder Valley.'

The idea was now growing on Clancy; he knew Boulder Valley really well, Ruby and he often hung out there, and he wasn't scared or anything. He knew where the underground creek was so he would have a good supply of fresh water and he could light a campfire, no problem.

'I'm telling,' said Olive from behind the door.

'If you do,' warned Minny, 'it's goodbye teddy.'

'I won't tell,' said Olive. Olive always took Minny's threats seriously because Minny usually meant what she said, at least when it came to things like this.

'You got to get out of here Clancy and you gotta go real early or it'll be Wichitino Camp for you.'

'Yeah, I know,' he said.

Still Clancy worried, even as he packed up his rucksack he worried, even as he set the alarm for 5 am he worried. Running away was a dramatic gesture, it could even sound heroic, romantic, escaping to freedom, but when the dust settled it was going to be him on his own in the middle of nowhere. It was going to get depressing.

Chapter 51.
A change of heart

CLANCY AWOKE EARLY THE NEXT MORNING to the sound of his alarm clock. The first thing he saw was his backpack; it was stuffed to bulging and sitting there next to his bed, like a fat little guard.

He groaned; he felt kind of stupid now in the bright light of day. What was he thinking of, running away? How far did he think he'd get? What a bozo. Lulu was right. Lulu was often right.

The room was stuffy, the sun slanting in from the east; he went to open the window and there he saw the bike. The dazzling blue of it. He stood just looking for a while and then the flip-flop girl appeared.

Boy, was she an early riser. She started busying herself, adjusting the handlebars and generally checking the thing over. He longed to go take a closer look; maybe she might even let him take it for a ride – just up the street and back.

It wouldn't hurt to talk to her.

And if he was quick no one would notice he had slipped out, no one meaning Olive, the only one likely to tell his father who was still fast asleep upstairs.

There was no one around, not even Drusilla. Yes, he would go and talk to the girl; after all, he was only stepping out of the gates for a few minutes.

Clancy stuffed his backpack on top of his closet out of sight. He didn't want anyone to see it and figure out what he had been planning. He tiptoed downstairs and quietly left the house. The heat of the sun hit him and he had to shield his eyes from its rays.

The girl was still tinkering with the bike, setting the saddle a little higher. He walked nearer to the gates and he thought she caught sight of him, but she didn't acknowledge him with a wave or smile, she just carried on doing what she was doing. He didn't want to bug her, but he wanted to see the Windrush up close, ride it round the block, just see how it felt.

He watched as she climbed on the bike and rode very slowly up the road. She called behind her to someone he couldn't see, her mom, Clancy guessed. 'I'm just gonna do a few circuits of the bike park up by Fir Forest Edge. I'll be back in an hour.' She clearly hadn't been living here long because no one from

Twinford called Fir Forest Edge, Fir Forest Edge, they all called it Fir Edge.

He wondered what school she attended, certainly not Twinford Junior High; she was older than him.

And as he thought these thoughts an idea came; he would cycle up there, introduce himself and get talking to her; she would probably be glad to make a new friend in the neighbourhood. He would ask her if he could take a turn on the Windrush. She wasn't going to say no; at least he hoped she wasn't.

He ran around to the garage where the bikes were kept. Nancy's bike had a flat, Lulu's bike wasn't there, Minny's bike was in the wrecking yard and so the only thing available to him was Olive's bike with its little pink basket.

'Oh brother!' he muttered. But it was that or a pogo stick and he wasn't going to get far jumping up and down like a bozo.

He grabbed the bike and there in the basket he saw a pack of bubblegum and a tube of mints – the ground glows, *that's where she put them!*

He slipped both items in his sweat-top pocket and wheeled the bike though the iron gates and off he set on the tiny bike like he was practising to become a circus clown.

Ruby was staring out of her bathroom window, watching the

neighbourhood toings and froings. Nothing much had happened. It was early and apart from Niles Lemon (who had already been out jogging), the dog walker and the grocery van no one was really doing much. This gave Ruby a lot of time to think and what she was busy thinking about right now was Clancy.

It didn't sit right with Ruby, being mad at Clancy. Sure, he could really be a major pain in the behind, but when all was said and done there was no friend like Clancy Crew. It was stupid feeling like this about someone she liked so much; it was a waste of time and wasting time was a foolish activity. If he wasn't going to pick up the phone to her, then she would go over there in person. She would climb in the window if necessary, though to be honest she would rather use the stairs.

By the time he arrived at the bike park, Clancy was sweating more than a little; it was quite a distance from the Crew house. The park was on the edge of things, where the road met the pines and the pines met the desert valley. Beyond it were the mountains.

When he skidded to a halt on Olive's tiny bike, Clancy thought perhaps the girl had changed her mind: she didn't seem to be there. Perhaps he had taken too long and she'd already gone, but as his eyes adjusted he saw her there sitting in the shadows under a large spreading tree, drinking a soda.

'Hey!' he called.

The girl looked up.

'I like your bike!'

'Yeah?' she said.

'I'm thinking of getting one myself,' said Clancy.

'Really,' said the girl.

'Probably,' said Clancy, 'I haven't made up my mind.'

'You wanna try it?' said the girl.

Yes! thought Clancy.

'Sure,' he said, like he wasn't bothered.

It sort of felt like he was flying, like *he* was flying, not the machine but *him*. The Windrush was as amazing as he had imagined, better in fact. How was he going to get one of these things? As he passed the girl for the fifth time, he caught her looking at her watch; she obviously had to get home, and so he reluctantly came to a stop.

'Thanks,' he said, 'I mean, really, that bike is something else.'

'You're welcome,' said the girl. 'Do another circuit if you want to.'

But he was staring at her now and thinking how she did look kind of familiar.

'Have we met someplace before?' asked Clancy.

The girl shrugged and smiled; she had a really nice face. 'If we have, I don't remember,' she laughed. 'Twinford's a big place.' She looked at her watch again.

She was twitchy – what was that about?

Ruby was greeted by Olive, who was idly swinging on the banister. Drusilla gave Olive a disapproving look as she crossed through the hall, but it didn't seem to bother Olive.

'Hello Ruby,' said Olive, 'do you like my shoes?'

'I wouldn't say *like*, but they are interesting,' said Ruby. They looked like tiny toadstools. 'Clance around?'

'Uh uh,' said the little girl.

'Where is he?'

'Gone,' said Olive.

'Gone where?' said Ruby.

Olive shrugged. 'He's run away from home.'

'I doubt that very much,' said Ruby, making for the stairs.

'I saw him packing,' said Olive, 'and now it's gone.'

'You're saying his backpack's gone?' said Ruby.

'Uh... huh,' said Olive, cleaning some dust off her shoes with her thumb.

Ruby raced up the stairs.

'You won't find him,' called Olive, 'because he's run away.'

Clancy's room was a mess; lots of drawers had been left open, their contents spewed out onto the floor. There was no sign of his backpack. It looked very much like the room of someone who had left in a hurry. Maybe Olive was right, or then again it could just be the untidy room of a thirteen-year-old boy.

RULE 17: ALWAYS CHECK THE EVIDENCE BEFORE JUMPING TO CONCLUSIONS.

She climbed up on a chair and looked on top of the closet; there was the backpack. She wrenched it down and it fell to the floor with a thump. Olive was right about the packing: it was full of lots of stuff one might take if one was running away. So, if he had run away, then why hadn't he taken it? There was no sign of a note in the room, no coded message for her.

Ruby walked slowly down the stairs and bumped into Minny coming the other way.

'Hey Ruby,' she said.

'Hey Minny, do you know where Clancy's gotten to?'

'Haven't you heard? Dad made him go on the Wichitino Camp. He left early this morning, I heard him go.'

Ruby was dumbfounded. 'What are you talking about?'

'I know,' said Minny, 'dorky, huh?'

'How come he left his stuff?' asked Ruby. 'I mean it's all

packed up like he was planning on taking it.'

'I guess he changed his mind about making a run for it.'

'So why not take it on camp?'

'He wouldn't need it on camp,' said Minny. 'Camp Wichitino provides everything, right down to your undershorts. Believe me, I know!' Minny had evidently done time at dork camp herself.

'Well, that explains where he's gone, but why didn't he tell me about it?' said Ruby.

'He's grounded,' said Minny. 'No phone calls, no nothing and then worst of all Dad told him it was either Camp Wichitino or he could say bye bye to his summer vacation. I guess he chose camp.'

'He's taken my bike with him,' said Olive.

'Why would he take your bike Olive?' said Minny.

'Because it's got a basket,' said Olive. 'It's really useful if you're running away.'

Chapter 52.
A long hard look

CLANCY KEPT HIS EYES TRAINED ON THE GIRL and noted how the smile was a little off, more fake than real. Her eyes didn't sparkle either: she wasn't interested in him, she wasn't interested in the bike, so why was she there? She was young, but she was no teenager, he was pretty sure of that now that he looked at her carefully.

For the first time in a long while Clancy started listening to the voice he usually relied on. His instincts were coming back to him, his warning system switched on – something was *not* just a *little* bit wrong, it was a whole lot wrong, that's what his gut was telling him. A breeze blew in from the desert, just enough to stir the air. It lifted the fragrance from the girl and carried it past Clancy. He breathed it in; the smell was Turkish delight.

He remembered the woman outside the department store. The woman who had been 'helping' her neighbour.

Get out of there! said the voice in his head.

Clancy let the thoughts race through his mind, one after another. Run? No way, no point, the girl would have backup, someone was bound to appear from somewhere and however good a runner he might be (and he *was good*) he wasn't going to get away from these guys; they would have a plan.

But the thing to consider was would they have banked on him having a bike? A bike like this?

He doubted it; they were probably far too certain, too sure of themselves to imagine Clancy might twig that he had been lured into a trap.

He was thinking: *I have a bike, there's a track, and if this machine is all it is cracked up to be then I have an escape route out of here.* The girl had no idea all these thoughts were lining up in his head. He was smiling (Clancy Crew was good at smiling when he didn't particularly feel like smiling, he'd had a lot of practice); he was sitting on the saddle, his fingers gripping the handlebars. The girl looked pleased: he was a fly trapped in her web.

He could hear a vehicle on the dirt road, a truck of some sort. His instincts told him that this vehicle was coming for him, that he had to get out of there before it got too close.

'I'll just take the Windrush round the track one more time. Is that OK?' he asked.

'Sure,' she said, 'enjoy.'

'Oh, I will,' called Clancy and as he gathered speed he suddenly veered off the bike circuit and took off, down the rock path towards the forest. He rode fast like every ogre in every book of fairy tales was on his tail.

He could vaguely hear the girl shouting; her voice sounded deeper, older suddenly. But then of course she was no girl, she was a woman: Lyla, the woman from the perfume counter, and he had a growing suspicion that Lyla, despite her beauty and her sweet fragrance, was anything but the nice woman she pretended to be. In fact, now he let his instinct take over, he was pretty sure that what she was, was a murderer. She had killed that man and Clancy was pretty sure she would murder him if she caught him. He could hear her shouting, screaming at him, but he didn't take it in; his only thought: to put as much distance between him and her and the truck full of murderers.

Two things were now bugging Ruby. One was Clancy's unClancy-like behaviour. Clancy was not the sort to run away; he was not an impulsive person, he always thought about the consequences; plus, he wasn't so keen on the dark.

Ruby also considered it very unlikely that he would go away with the Wichitinos without leaving a note to tell her he had gone on camp. Unless of course he was very mad at her, but if so why was he very mad at her?

Ruby paused to think about this and came up with more than a few reasons. For a start there was his detention, her fault because she had forgotten to meet him in the diner before school; that was pretty uncool. Then there was dragging him out of his French test and getting him to climb a wall and drop himself into a wild animal reserve. Well, that could be considered at the very least kind of thoughtless; she knew Clancy was stressed about being kept down a year if he failed his test, and then there was the whole dangerous animal thing – not good for someone who didn't exactly flirt with danger.

And to top that there was the whole tiger incident; she had actually set him up to be devoured by a wild creature. OK, so it wasn't intentional, but it would have been down to her if that cat had got his chops round Clancy's neck. These three examples alone were reason enough for Clancy not to want to talk to her. He was in big trouble with his dad and now he was off with the little Wichitinos; how much worse could it get for poor old Clancy Crew? It was all her fault and she needed to track him down and put things right; she would rescue Clancy from camp and bring him home.

Ruby really hadn't been on top of her game; she had missed a lot: she had not taken any notice of her mother's claims that a pig or possibly a hippo was loose in the backyard (it had seemed preposterous). Nor had she listened to her dad when he suggested her mom might just be right (the logical explanation: heatstroke). Del's report of a tiger she had dismissed as a Del Lasco exaggeration (fair enough), but there was other evidence, clues she should have picked up on. What had Gemma Melamare seen in the school corridor? (As it turned out, a python.)

What had taken a bite out of the Harker Square table tennis table? What had happened to Mrs Gilbert's dog? It seemed unlikely, highly improbable, that wild animals would be roaming the city of Twinford, but what kind of investigative agent was she if she didn't take the improbable seriously? To quote the great detective Sherlock Holmes:

'*When you have eliminated the impossible, whatever remains,* however improbable, *must be the truth.*'

Or, in other words, Ruby's **RULE 28: IT DOESN'T MATTER IF IT'S HARD TO BELIEVE: IF THERE'S NO OTHER EXPLANATION, IT'S GOTTA BE TRUE.**

So now she had woken up and what she was thinking about was Connie Slowfoot or more specifically what Connie had said. '*I'm not talking about "wolves", I'm talking about* the wolf.' These words had wormed their way under Ruby's skin, encircled her thoughts, resulting in a bad feeling in her gut, because what Connie Slowfoot was talking about was an extinct, possibly mythical wolf prowling the forests surrounding Twinford. Connie Slowfoot had said some pretty weird and far-fetched things and Ruby Redfort wouldn't have minded putting them to one side and ignoring them, but for the fact she believed her. Crazy as it all sounded, every word she had spoken rang true.

Ruby went downstairs to Mrs Digby's apartment to search out a book she had read many times as a young child. The book was precious to the housekeeper since it had been given to her by her father and, when younger, Ruby had never been permitted to look at it unsupervised for fear of it meeting some sticky end.

It was entitled *Improbable Truths and Believable Myths* and was more like a book of fairy tales than a useful encyclopedia. She remembered how much she had enjoyed being scared of some of the more gory illustrations and unpleasant descriptions. Ruby flicked through the pages, filled with all kinds of strange and exotic creatures; some had been erased from the planet and others had never existed in the first place. Eventually, she fell upon the page she was searching for.

The Cyan Wolf

Appearance: pale blue eyes ringed with violet. Dark tips to ears and fur that in moonlight can appear blue.

Like other wolves, the Cyan wolf had scent glands in its paws and these helped it to mark territory, warning rival wolves to steer clear and also to attract mates by telling them he or she was in the area. However, in addition to the above functions, the Cyan wolf also used its scent to lure its prey to it – the scent it created being so intoxicating that both animal and human alike would seek it out, losing all sense of fear in their quest to discover the source of this overpowering aroma.

This scent was of particular usefulness when food was scarce and the wolf needed to preserve its energy. By luring its prey right to its lair, it managed to survive in the most hostile of conditions.

The legendary scent of the Cyan Wolf was allegedly much sought after by perfumers. Unlike ambergris*, found in the intestines of sperm whales (also worth a small fortune to those lucky enough to find it), the 'Alaskan Cyan' (as it became known) needed no time to develop from a foul smell to a fragrant one.

Ruby looked up the footnote on ambergris.

* Ambergris is a waxy, flammable substance produced by the digestive systems of sperm whales. Having initially an unpleasant odour of decay, it gradually acquires a sweet, earthy scent. It has long been prized as a fixative in the making of perfume (allowing the scent to last much longer).

Alaskan Cyan, on the other hand, is not only a fixative but it is also the perfume itself, with an utterly intoxicating aroma. Consequently hunters, in particular one Jacob Holst, began to hunt Cyan wolves not for their skins but for their scent. By 1800 they were completely wiped out.

There was a drawing of a man being devoured horribly by the creature. The words underneath read: ***The wolf using its scent to lure a hunter into its trap and so to his death.*** There wasn't a whole lot of backup evidence to suggest this was true.

The final word on the subject read:

This savage creature was better known as the Blue Alaskan even though they were often regarded as two different breeds

of wolf, one fact, the other myth. Few now believe the reports
written about the wolf scent, and Jacob Holst (Mr Wolf as
he became known) was later discredited as a fantasist.

The book went no further.

Ruby picked up the black and white photograph of young
Mrs Digby and the other maids smiling broadly at the camera,
surrounded by rare creatures. The one to the left of Mrs Digby
looked very much like a wolf, a wolf with dark-tipped ears and
dark-ringed eyes. Could it be a Cyan wolf? But if so then why had
it not attacked the smiling people in the photograph? The answer
would have to wait until the housekeeper returned home – for
now one question was on Ruby's mind: was there more to the
scented papers than met the eye?

The only way to find out was to seek out an expert on the
subject of smell, someone with a remarkably good nose.

The bike was even better than Clancy had first thought; the
tyres, the suspension, the steering – he felt like he was part of
the machine, that he was the Windrush and nothing could catch
him. He had a good head start; he knew the truck would have
to drive back up the road and take the desert exit before it could
even begin to chase him. If he could just make it to the boulders,

he could hide out in the warren of caves, some of which he knew like the back of his hand. He would hide out until they gave up looking.

He turned to see how far they were behind him – nowhere as it turned out; they weren't even a speck on the horizon. All his fear evaporated as he travelled over the rocky terrain and headed towards the rock valley, the faraway forest of Wolf Paw looming in the distance.

He was going to outrun these guys. He might even get as far as the forest and, once there, he was going to lose them entirely, with or without the bike. He could hide out or he could walk on back to Twinford. His scouting days had trained him well and he had a good sense of direction. He even smiled at the thought; he felt fearless and in control, and that's when it all went wrong. He was so taken up with reaching the forest that he was not observing the large stones littering the route. It was merely a matter of time before he hit one.

Clancy felt the full force of the rock as his wheel came down hard on it.

He let go the handlebars and was flung off sideways. He got to his feet, a little shocked but unhurt, and stumbled towards the bike and climbed back on; instantly, he knew something was wrong.

The Windrush 2000, with its unpuncturable tyres, had a puncture.

Chapter 53.
Coming into focus

RUBY CYCLED OUT ALONG MOUNTAIN ROAD. It was the long
way round, but it was the way she knew and she didn't want to
risk getting lost on Little Bear Mountain. Once she reached the
track turn, she veered up Lake Road and cycled towards the
forest; the track took you round the three Little Bear lakes and
then on up the mountain.

As she passed the biggest lake, known as Emerald Lake, she
could hear the Wichitinos calling out to each other. Ruby stopped
for a moment and took a look at them through her binoculars:
they seemed to be having fun, unconcerned about their dorky
yellow uniforms, busy constructing rafts that they hoped would
float. She scanned the camp, hoping to catch a glimpse of Clancy
Crew, but she couldn't see him. *Probably on latrine-building duty,*
she thought.

The Wichitino Camp was a fairly long way from Autumn
Lake, which was where she needed to get to; she had gone way

too far west, but at least she knew where she was: better to be safe than sorry.

The Swann retreat, Still Water, was a house designed as shelves of stone jutting out across Autumn Lake, wide glass windows sandwiched between each layer so light could flood in. It was impossible to see the steel pillars that pinned it to the lakeshore so it appeared to be hovering magically over the water, several tons of rock deceiving the eye.

Ruby rode her bike up the wide raked wooden gangplank. The wind chimes turned slowly in the light breeze that blew in from the lake; there was no entry phone, no doorbell, no doorknocker, no door handle. She banged on the heavy wood with her small fist and just like that the door gave and Ruby stepped inside, Bug padding behind her. The floors were a mixture of smoothed rock and polished wood planks, the corridor a cool sanctuary leading to dappled, sunlit rooms which in turn opened out onto the glittering lake.

'Hello?' called Ruby. 'Sorry to walk in like this.'

No answer.

'But you know you have no doorbell?'

No answer.

'No lock either.'

She continued down the passage, Bug in front.

'Anyone home?'

Nothing, just the gentle lapping of water and sound of bird life and... a piano.

Ruby followed the music and found herself in a large room full of flickering light. A small woman wearing a simple black dress was playing a grand piano; the huge windows were all slid back into the walls and so the outside was inside and the inside, outside.

Madame Swann stopped playing.

'Who is it?' she said, but before an answer could be given she had figured it out for herself. 'Rose petals and bubblegum... Brant and Sabina's daughter,' and then she turned to look at Ruby.

'Hey, how dya know that?' said Ruby.

'I never forget a fragrance,' trilled Madame Swann.

'You're pretty good,' said Ruby. 'You know *everyone* by smell?'

'I have a good memory for scent,' she said, getting to her feet. 'My nose never forgets.' She held out her hand. 'A pleasure to see you again, but what has brought you to the edge of nowhere?'

'If you wouldn't mind, I need you to take a look at something for me,' said Ruby.

The perfumer nodded. 'If you think I can help.'

Ruby took the scented papers from her satchel and laid them on the table. Each was in its own plastic sleeve to prevent them from contaminating each other.

Madame Swann took one at random and shook it from its case and picked it up very carefully between her gloved fingers. The first thing she did, the very first, was to bring it up to her face and inhale.

'You sniff everything before you read it?'

'It is the way I look at things,' said Madame Swann. 'I see with my nose. Smell is the most important sense: it tells you all you need to know about a person or a place, even a piece of writing paper.' She looked at Ruby sideways. 'Besides, you surely came here for my nose?'

'I'm not going to lie to you Madame Swann, I *am* here for your nose. So what's the perfume? Where does it come from?'

'It's not perfume.'

Ruby was puzzled. 'What do you mean?'

Madame Swann shrugged. 'It's scents, lots of scents. There's pine and orange, sandalwood, vanilla...' She inhaled again. 'Thyme and anise.'

'But not a perfume?' said Ruby.

'No, just individual scents.'

One by one Madame Swann took the envelopes from the table and carefully now, with gloved hand, pulled out the slip of plain paper inside each envelope.

She wrote down the smells captured in each. 'Where did you get these?' she asked.

Ruby paused before answering. 'From someone's apartment. I'm not sure whose apartment exactly.'

'I don't understand,' said Madame Swann.

'I don't officially know the occupant. I just had an address and, well, these were there,' said Ruby. 'I wasn't exactly invited in – you know what I'm saying?'

Madame Swann nodded. 'I think so.' She smelled each one again, very carefully.

'I cannot understand why anyone would scent paper like this; it is not a good combination of smell. This one has vanilla, as does this and this, but this one is the only one to have sandalwood. It has something unpleasant too, something I would not put in perfume.'

Ruby was thinking of her biology class, the textbooks she had read on smell as communicator, how everything has smell and how everything communicates via smell.

'If I suggested these papers held a code, would you think I was crazy?' asked Ruby.

Madame Swann looked at her, a glint in her eye. 'Not at all,' she said. 'I think that is the only thing that makes any sense.'

Chapter 54.
Survival instinct

THE PROBLEM FOR CLANCY, among a whole *forest* of problems, was that he was utterly visible: he was a boy standing in the middle of a rocky desert terrain with not a shrub, not a tumbleweed to hide behind. He let the bike fall to the ground and began to run; he was a great runner, an even better long-distance runner than he was a sprinter; he had stamina and speed, but what use were stamina and speed when racing against a speeding car? Who can outrun a motor vehicle?

It was utterly pointless, but it wasn't in him to give up. Clancy Crew would run until they caught him and killed him because that was obviously what they had in mind. He'd seen too much, he knew that now. Why didn't they want him to call the paramedics? How could he have been so naive as to think that man was sick? It was clear to him now: the man had already been dead. Clancy could hear the roar of the truck growing louder and louder, coming closer and closer, but he would not stop, could not stop.

The truck slowed as it neared him; he could feel the engine vibrating through the rock and up into every single one of his bones, but still he ran. The sweat poured off his brow and traced down his cheeks; he stumbled on, determined, his eyes fixed on the horizon.

'Stop boy!' shouted a voice. But he couldn't; his legs were moving of their own accord and nothing could make them stop, nothing could make him stop, at least not until he heard the sound of a bullet ricocheting off the rock somewhere to the left of his head.

'You have a chance to live. I would take it if I were you. Unless you want to die. *Do you* want to die?' said the voice.

Clancy stood still; he didn't think he needed to answer. Who answered that kind of question?

'I take it the answer is no.'

Chapter 55.
Sniffing out a code

THEY CHOSE ONE OF THE SCENTED NOTES AND MADAME SWANN CAREFULLY DECIPHERED EVERY SMELL while Ruby wrote the perfumer's findings on separate sheets of paper.

Thyme.

Vanilla.

Anise.

Cinnamon.

Orange.

Ruby looked at the list. What were these scents telling them? How was this working? What was the key?

Thinking back to the survival test code, she played for a moment in her mind with anagrams, taking the letters of THYME and VANILLA and ANISE and so on and jumbling them up – but it didn't throw up anything meaningful.

Ruby stared ahead across the water and into the forest, her eyes unblinking, unfocused, letting the thoughts swim.

Molecules, names, types of smell, masculine, feminine, associations, what were the connecting factors?

Then she stopped. She was approaching this the wrong way round. She needed to remain logical.

The code was made up of smells.

But the *message* that the code masked would be made up of letters.

Conclusion: she needed to think of a way to get from smells to letters.

Smells to letters...

Letters...

She sat up straight.

She was remembering the book she'd read in Mrs Greg's class when she was supposed to be studying something else. She remembered the chapter that dealt with benzene rings.

Benzene, C_6H_6, is a ring of six carbon atoms, connected by alternating single and double bonds:

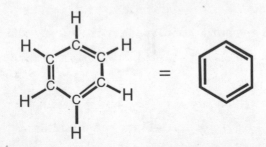

Carbon and hydrogen, she thought. *C and H.*

Letters.

She turned to Madame Swann. 'This is a long shot,' she said. 'But you wouldn't happen to know the chemical formulas for these smells?'

Madame Swann thought for a moment, clearly puzzled. 'I... Yes. I have a book which lists the formulas for most of the aromatic compounds.'

She went over to a bookshelf and came back with a heavy book. *Scents and their Basis in Organic Chemistry* was the title.

'Thyme...' said Madame Swann, flicking through the pages. 'That's Thymol, or 2-Isopropyl-5-methylphenol as they call it in the lab.'

She showed Ruby a diagram: as Ruby had expected, it was a benzene ring with twigs coming off it.

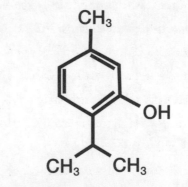

Thymol

'OK,' said Ruby. 'And the others?'

Soon Ruby had copied out, next to the name of each scent, its molecular structure. Her sheets of paper were now a mass of hexagons and little twig shapes and chemical formulas.

As Ruby studied more and more of the pictures she began to come up with a theory for how the smells could encode messages. What if each of the twigs coming off the hexagonal ring encoded a different letter? CH_3 might be Z, for example, and OH might be K.

Question: were there twenty-six of these twigs to allow one for each letter of the alphabet?

Answer: yes.

She began to feel that she might be on to something.

Each different twig shape corresponded to a different letter. Now she just needed to do a frequency analysis on the twig shapes like she'd done on the survival test code. Whichever twig came up most often would be E, then T, and so on.

Quickly she noted down the different twigs by order of most commonly occurring, and cross-referenced it with her mental crib sheet of English letter frequencies.

Thymol... that was a benzene ring with three twigs coming off it. If Ruby was right, the smell of thyme encoded three letters.

But which? She checked against her frequency crib and

came up with the most likely candidates: H, W and Y.

Mentally rearranging the letters, she got the word: **WHY**.

So, it's a substitution code and *an anagram.*

This was looking promising.

The next smell was vanilla, or 4-Hydroxy-3-methoxybenz-aldehyde. Ruby looked at the shape of the molecule on her sheet of paper. Again, that distinctive benzene ring with three more twigs. One was the same as last time and two were new. Referring to her crib she got the letter H again and then T and E.

THE.

Her confidence was growing as she decoded the other three smells and rearranged the letters. Finally, out came the last word: **DELAY**.

Ruby wrote down the message in full:

```
Why the delay
```

Deciphering the Chemical Codes

. . . .

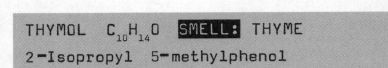

THYMOL $C_{10}H_{14}O$ **SMELL:** THYME
2-Isopropyl 5-methylphenol

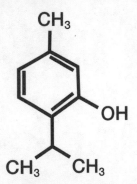

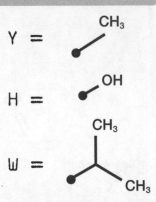

VANILLIN $C_8H_8O_3$ **SMELL:** VANILLA
4-Hydroxy 3-methoxybenzaldehyde

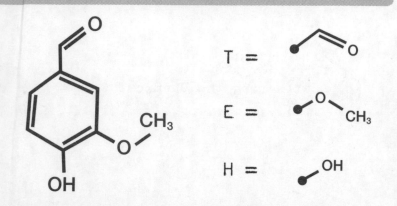

T =

E =

H =

ANETHOLE $C_{10}H_{12}O$ **SMELL:** ANISE
(E)-1-Methoxy-4-(1-propenyl) benzene

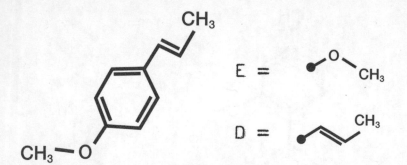

E =

D =

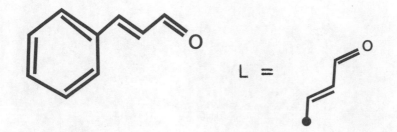

L =

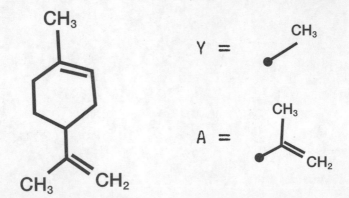

Y =

A =

Chemical Code Alphabet

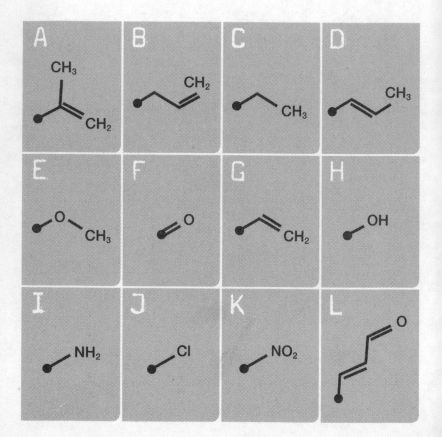

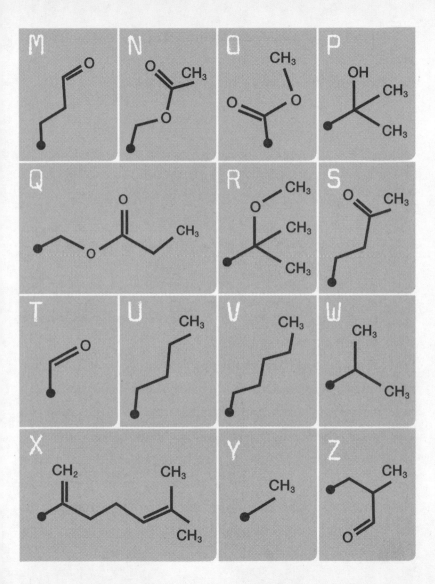

'*Mon dieu,*' said Madame Swann. 'They taught you this in school?'

'I sorta picked up along the way,' said Ruby.

Soon she had a list:

```
            Leave no loose ends
              Why the delay?
       Take the creature to Wolf Paw
    I trust you won't disappoint sweetie
 I will be arriving sooner than expected
               Make him talk
```

'There seems to be no order to them,' said Madame Swann. 'They could read many ways.'

'Not if you look at the writing paper.' Ruby pointed to the top of each piece of paper. On every one was a letterhead naming the hotel it came from: some of the letterheads were blind embossed and barely visible, some were just watermarks and only seen when held to the light, others printed very clearly, but the thing in common was that each paper held the name of a hotel and a place. The stationery would be in the drawer of each room for the use of the hotel guest. The person who had sent them was likely therefore to have been a guest in each of the hotels.

The Avenue Boutique Hotel: Upper East Twinford

The Conch: Suva, Fiji

The Grand Twin: Central Twinford

The Aloha: Honolulu Hawaii

The Dolphin: Perth Australia.

Surf Motel: West Twinford.

Ruby began to lay them out in the order she saw.

'The Australian hotel comes first,' she said.

'What makes you think that?' said Madame Swann.

'Because it's the furthest from Apartment 9, East Twinford.'

Rearranged in descending order of distance from East Twinford, the messages now read:

```
                Why the delay?
              Make him talk
           Leave no loose ends
        Take the creature to Wolf Paw
   I will be arriving sooner than expected
     I trust you won't disappoint sweetie
```

'The messages are more than instructions, they're also warnings: the sender is telling the recipient that he or she is getting nearer. i.e., "*Watch out, I am on my way.*" The sender wants her to feel fearful.'

'Why do you say *her*?' asked Madame Swann.

'The apartment seemed to be occupied by a woman and the sender doesn't trust her. I think he or she believes the resident at apartment 9 might be double-crossing.'

'We missed one,' said Madame Swann, pointing to an envelope which had slipped from the table.

They set about deciphering this one final message, sent from The 23rd Street Hotel, a mere stone's throw from apartment 9. It read:

```
Kill him
```

Chapter 56.
Think like Ruby

THE TRUCK PULLED UP ALONGSIDE, but Clancy didn't move; he didn't want to in any way confuse the person holding the gun.

He heard the truck door clunk open. Clancy turned, but he fixed his eyes on the ground – he did not look at the driver, the owner of the voice, the person holding the weapon. Ruby had told him that in a hostage-taking situation it was a good idea not to look at the hostage-taker; this way you couldn't identify them; this way they were less likely to shoot you.

'Get in,' said the voice.

Now what he needed to do was to focus on living, surviving this ordeal, and his immediate concern – other than trying to do as little as possible to aggravate them – was to work out where in all the world they were taking him since he was going to need to escape if he wanted to have a chance of living to a ripe old age.

OK, thought Clancy, *I'm in the back of a truck going who knows where, what's my next move?*

Clancy was thinking about Despo from *Crazy Cops*, a show he and Ruby loved to sit in front of every Saturday night. Despite the stupid name, *Crazy Cops* wasn't a stupid show and Despo, despite his failed relationships and dependency on black coffee, was a pretty good detective. Clancy was fairly sure that Despo would stay stock-still, cool as a cucumber, until the answer came to him. He knew *Ruby* would.

So that's what Clancy did.

All the time they drove, Clancy was thinking. The kind of thoughts he had were the following:

These guys were pretty confident and they were in one heck of a hurry. If they weren't, then they would have thought to tie his hands. Perhaps they didn't feel they needed to – what was this weedy kid going to do out here in the middle of nowhere if he *did* escape?

The fall from the moving car would probably kill him.

By the time they reached the forest's edge, Clancy was beginning to feel a little queasy, a combination of the bumpy track, travelling backwards and the fear of death. His mouth was so dry, he put his hand in his pocket to find a piece of gum, but instead he felt the ground glow dispenser, a neat, palm-sized tube. One click and a ground glow was released and dropped invisibly to the ground.

Clancy did exactly what he knew Detective Despo would do.

'I think I'm gonna throw up,' he moaned.

'Not in here you're not buster!' shouted the driver.

'We're not stopping,' said the one in charge. 'Wind the window down and stick your head out.'

'Can I at least face forward?' asked Clancy in such a pathetic-sounding voice that no one would imagine he had any kind of plan up his sweat top, other than puking.

'Go ahead,' said the man with the gun, 'but no funny stuff.'

'And no puke in my vehicle,' said the driver.

Clancy switched seats, wound down the window and stuck his head out, at the same time he pulled his hand from his pocket; the ground glow canister was concealed in his palm. From behind it simply looked as if he was using his arm to steady himself. No one saw him release the glows, one every several yards. They fell small and invisible onto the parched ground.

Ruby was staring at the broken code.

```
Kill him
```

'Who would be capable of creating these messages?' she said.

'Any skilled perfumer could create them; any skilled perfumer could decipher the scents,' replied Madame Swann. 'The question is not who *is capable*, but who would use fragrance to convey such dark desires, issue such dreadful orders?'

'And who would make perfume their code?' mused Ruby.

'I can think of one,' said Madame Swann slowly.

'You can?' said Ruby.

Madame Swann nodded. 'That night at the 1770 launch...' She twisted the dragon ring coiled round her finger before continuing. 'That night I smelled a fragrance I haven't smelled in a long, long time.'

'A perfume?' asked Ruby.

'A perfume I created many years ago.'

Ruby shrugged. 'So?'

'Only one person in the entire world has that perfume; it is very particular – and once it combines with the wearer's natural skin smell it becomes unique. I would know that fragrance anywhere.'

'Who does it belong to?' asked Ruby.

But it was as if the very utterance of the name would cause the poison odour to drift into the air and contaminate everything like a genie escaping from its bottle. Instead of answering this question, Madame Swann said, 'I gave it to her, as a gift for her work in my perfumery. She was a gifted student: so young, but with such an excellent nose, she became my apprentice. '

Ruby waited for her to continue.

'This girl, she turned out to have a very dark heart. In the end I banished her from my lab and when she left I hoped I had seen the last of her... but now she has come back to destroy me.'

'Destroy you? How?' asked Ruby.

'By killing my reputation.' She left a long pause before adding, 'She is blackmailing me you see.'

'With what?' asked Ruby.

'She knows a secret no one in this whole world knows, a secret that if spilled would mean no one would ever trust me again. It would stain my reputation and wash away the thing I love most.'

And suddenly Ruby saw everything. 'The Lost Perfume of Marie Antoinette...?'

'All fake,' said Madame Swann. 'The formula I paid so much for turned out to be a forgery.'

'How did your apprentice know?' asked Ruby.

'Because she was the one who forged it.'

The truck lurched and Clancy lost his grip on the ground glows and that was that. *Darn it,* he thought. *What was the point now? A big risk and for what?*

He would just need to remember everything he could see from this point on, look for every possible landmark, anything that could identify his path. Not easy when one is in a dense forest. One pine looked a whole lot like another. But he needn't have worried since the guy with the gun suddenly said, 'Maybe we should think about blindfolding the kid.' And seconds later he was plunged into darkness.

'What exactly did your apprentice want in return for keeping her mouth shut?' Ruby asked.

'She wanted me to tell her how to extract the scent from the Cyan wolf.' Madame Swann put her head in her hands. A single tear spilled from her eye, rolling down her check onto her ring so that the golden dragon appeared to be sharing her grief.

'You told her?' said Ruby.

Madame Swann barely nodded. 'She wanted one vial; enough to create a thousand bottles of the rarest of perfumes, she will become unimaginably rich. No one could resist such a fragrance.'

Suddenly it was all clear to Ruby. The messages, the wild

animals roaming the streets of Twinford, the Fengrove zoo. Someone had released all those creatures just as *cover*. As camouflage, for stealing the Cyan wolf and getting their hands on its scent.

What about the zookeeper? she wondered. *Ivan, what had happened to him?* Her best guess was that he'd been paid off, bribed to release the animals and hand the Cyan wolf over to Madame Swann's blackmailer. It would seem he had been paid well for this service if the gold watch was anything to go by, but had he double-crossed her, changed his mind?

'What will happen to the wolf?' asked Ruby, her eyes full of questions.

'One vial quickly taken is risky for the animal; if she extracts too much, it will die.'

'So you still haven't told me what her name is. Your assistant I mean.'

'Lorelei von Leyden,' said Madame Swann with a shiver.

'I've never heard of her,' said Ruby.

'That does not surprise me,' said Madame Swann. 'She goes by many names.'

'And you think Lorelei sent these messages?'

'Oh no,' said Madame Swann. 'It's not her voice. She would never use a term of endearment like sweetie, not even to be patronising or cruel. No, I think she was the recipient. It was her apartment you were in, but they were sent by someone more powerful than her.'

So someone else wants the scent of the Cyan wolf, thought Ruby.

'Find Lorelei,' said Madame Swann, 'and perhaps you will find the real threat to this beautiful creature.'

Ruby took the launch-night photograph from her satchel and handed it to Madame Swann. It was the picture Ruby had snapped just one second after Madame Swann's collapse. A jumble of colourful evening gowns and manicured hands holding glasses, perfect faces turned towards the steps as they watched their host fall to the floor.

'Do you see her here?' she asked.

'No,' said Madame Swann.

'But you barely even looked.'

'I don't need to, I won't see her there: disguise is her genius. You never see her unless she wants you to; her scent is what will betray her.'

'And what is her scent?' said Ruby.

Madame Swann glanced down at her dragon ring and hissed, 'The scent of Turkish delight.'

Chapter 57.
A dead man's shoes

THE WAY HOME WAS MUCH EASIER – Madame Swann pointed Ruby towards the woodland track – and much, much quicker. Even so, by the time Twinford was coming into view, the sun was beginning to sink in the sky and, as Ruby reached the bike park at Fir Edge, she was feeling pretty weary and certainly relieved that she was nearly home. She'd taken the short cut from the lake through the forest that skirted the mountain. It was quicker for sure, but it was hard work to cycle since there was no actual road.

When she got home, she would pass the deciphered codes onto Hitch. She knew he would be waiting for her at the house because he would want to brief her on the survival test. LB was such a hard case that she would doubtless expect Ruby to take the test regardless of the fact that she'd cracked a code and uncovered a plot to steal a creature on the very edge of extinction. A plot that no one, including Spectrum, was even aware of. Whether her discovery would actually prevent the criminals from succeeding was an unknown, but that was Spectrum's problem, not hers.

Poor Clance, she thought. He was going to have to endure Camp Wichitino after all.

As soon as she reached the bike park, Bug stopped still in his tracks and began to sniff the air.

'Come on Bug,' she moaned, 'we don't have time for chasing raccoons. We gotta go.'

But the husky wasn't listening. He zigzagged back and forth across the path, checking out every bench, letting the smell he had picked up lead him. He paused by a tree with branches that hung low, nosing around in the bushes behind it, and then barked and barked and wouldn't stop.

'What have you got there?' called Ruby. The dog didn't turn his head, he just continued to bark.

'You found something?' said Ruby, cautiously stepping towards the thick bushes, pushing aside the tangle of branches.

It looked like it had been thrown in because it was all caught up in the undergrowth, suspended in the twisting briars. It was a little kid's bike with a tiny pink basket.

The blood in Ruby's veins seemed suddenly very cold, for the bike was one she recognised well. It was Olive's and the last person seen riding it was Clancy Crew.

He could hear feet on the earth pacing round and round, like a horse might pace, but not so heavy. This animal didn't have hooves, it sounded more like a dog. He wondered to himself what kind of dog was it. He liked dogs, depending on the breed; he liked the small ones best, and the well-trained ones. He felt woozy, like he had been drugged, and he was disorientated. What had happened earlier? Was it last night or last week? He had no way of knowing.

He shut his eyes.

Ruby stood in the bike park, staring into the distance, but she wasn't looking, she was thinking and what she was thinking about were shoes.

Niles Lemon, her father, the man in the canal, the guy Clancy had seen collapsed under the tree. They all had shoes in common, expensive shoes. When he'd got the call, Hitch had specifically said *deck* shoes. If the guy he had seen pulled out of the canal was wearing *Marco Perella* deck shoes, then she would know almost for certain.

She would be as sure as she could be, without actually knowing, that the dead guy in the canal was the zookeeper, and that this same zookeeper was the guy who Clancy had seen slumped by a tree, and that Clancy had been a witness to his murder – or more accurately had witnessed his murderers moving his already dead or nearly dead body. The woman who had claimed to be the man's neighbour and friend was neither: she was Lorelei von Leyden, killer. And she would kill again; she would kill Clancy because he knew too much. There was no time to lose, there was no time to go back to find Hitch, there was no time to take a survival test.

'Which way did they go? Where did they take Clancy?' asked Ruby. She was talking to herself, to the dog, to birds, to the rocks and trees, but Bug seemed to understand. He headed off down the path into the trees and beyond to the desert.

As they raced across the valley, Ruby's hopes began to rise. She saw the bicycle tracks: had he got away? If he had, he would have tried to make it to the Boulder Valley caves, then she knew he would be safe. No one knew those caves like Clancy did. Up ahead she could see something shimmering in the desert heat, discarded, abandoned in the middle of nowhere. What was it? As she got nearer, it began to come into focus. She could see it was blue, she could see it was metal and she could see it was a bike: not any bike, a Windrush 2000.

**Clancy woke up to
the smell of Turkish
delight...**

...And, for just a moment, he forgot he was tied up and locked inside a stranger's outbuilding. The smell was so sweet, so restful, but then he heard the cut-glass voice of the perfume assistant and it all came back to him – he was glad of the blindfold. He didn't want to look into her cold blue eyes.

'So what were you doing in my apartment?' she demanded.

'I don't know what you mean,' stammered Clancy. 'How could I have been in your apartment? I don't even know where you live.'

'You were there, I smelled your bubblegum.'

'But I don't even like bubblegum.'

'Really?' she said.

'Yes, really, so tell me why would I be in your apartment when I have no idea where you live, chewing bubblegum which I don't like?' said Clancy. He was a little irritated by now; whatever they had drugged him with had robbed him of his inhibition and had made him decidedly crabby.

The woman who called herself Lorelei reached into his sweat-top pocket and pulled out the Hubble-Yum. 'Have it your own way, but I find it strange that you would have bubblegum about your person if, as you say, you don't even like it.' She was turning to go, ready to let him stew for a while, admit defeat and spill the beans.

'Would you listen to me? You've got the wrong sucker here. This isn't even my gum. I found it in my sister's bicycle basket. It belongs to Ruby Red—'

Lorelei stopped, her hand on the door handle, and turned. 'You were saying?' she said.

She came over and pulled the blindfold from his eyes.

Clancy looked at her, knowing that everything had changed.

'And who is Ruby Red?' she said. 'And where can we find her?'

But Clancy said not another word.

Chapter 58.
The trail

THE ABANDONED WINDRUSH WAS NOW WAY BEHIND HER. Ruby had crossed the desert valley and was now cycling up the forest track. It was getting dark and as Ruby rode she saw tiny glow-worms light up their lights. Bug was ahead of her and nosing the route. They had travelled about a quarter-mile when Ruby checked behind to see if she was being followed. The tiny illuminators had disappeared and suddenly Ruby realised her mistake; she had forgotten all about the activator, still attached to her Bradley Baker sneaker – these were no glow-worms, these were ground glows and the only person who could have dropped them was Clancy Crew.

She rode back, collecting each glow, and slipped them into her saddlebag – her gut told her that she might need them. Looking back at the distant Twinford lights, she took her notebook from her satchel and scribbled a message to Hitch.

GO SPEAK TO MADAME SWANN, SHE WILL EXPLAIN – DON'T DELAY

Then she slipped it into the canister attached to Bug's collar and told him to head for home. The dog looked at Ruby, his eyes telling her that he thought this a bad idea – that he did not want to leave her out here in the middle of nowhere. But he also recognised that look in *Ruby's* eyes, the one that told him her mind was set.

He sniffed her face and gave her cheek a lick before turning and setting off for Twinford at surprising speed. Only when he was about to disappear down into the valley of rocks did he stop, turning just once to see where she was. The husky was silhouetted against the moon like some classic wolf image on a tacky poster. Ruby did not turn; she was concentrating hard on the trail, hopeful that the ground glows would not run out before she made it to the place where Clancy was held. How would she find him otherwise? Almost at the same moment that she thought this thought, the ground glows disappeared.

The trail was gone.

'Ah, kill him – he's no earthly good to us,' said Eduardo. 'He knows nothing. Shoot him and feed him to the wolf: two birds with one stone. One less boy, one less hungry animal.'

'Do you want to come?' asked the man with the gun.

'No,' said Eduardo, 'I can't deal with the whole chewing thing, it really puts me off my food. I'm a vegetarian.'

'Just a moment,' said Lorelei, holding up her hand. 'Before you get all carried away throwing the wretch to the wolves, don't you think we ought to consider his usefulness?'

'That scrawny kid? Useful?' said the man his hand on the gun holster like he couldn't wait to wrap his finger round the trigger.

'Shouldn't we be wondering who this girl is, this Ruby Red? She must be more than just any girl: she broke into my apartment, she was sniffing around, like she was some little detective, some little Nancy Drew. It wouldn't surprise me if she was working for Madwoman Swann. No, something smells fishy here, a little off. If I'm right, then we need to track the little spy down. Get the boy to talk. Find out where she lives.'

'How are you gonna do that?' asked Eduardo. 'Torture?'

Lorelei shook her head and laughed. 'Torture? Have you seen the little squirt? He'll be crying for his mommy in no time; he'll tell us what we want to know soon enough.'

But Lorelei von Leyden had no idea who she was dealing

with. Clancy Crew would die a thousand deaths before he gave up even one syllable of Ruby Redfort's address.

Mistake one: underestimating the resolve of a very loyal friend.

'Do you want a guard on the boy?' asked the trigger-happy fellow.

'No, no need to guard him. He's not going anywhere and some little girl will never find her way through this mountain forest; not even Hansel and Gretel themselves could make it here.'

Mistake two: underestimating the resolve of a very loyal friend.

It was while she was standing in the dark, dark forest, not knowing which way to turn, left or right, that Ruby thought of Connie Slowfoot. She could almost hear her rasping old crone laugh. *'You got brains girl, you just gotta stop relying on them, use your gut like nature intended.'*

Ruby stopped panicking and considered what she should do; she could feel the grooves in the hard-packed earth, tyre tracks. Vehicles had made great ruts in the ground from travelling this way back and forth. The other track looked used but less so; the odds were that the kidnapping wolf stealers had been up and down many times in the past month so she would opt for the well-worn track.

As Ruby rode, she made a mental note of what the air smelled of, how it changed as she moved. The overwhelming scent was of pine, so strong she could taste it, but there was also wild garlic and moss and fungus and vegetation. And something strong and animal, the dung of deer maybe; she hoped it was deer, but who knew what lurked on Wolf Paw Mountain.

She could feel the thick, soft bounce of pine needles and bark, the occasional sting of some tall plant or other. She heard sounds of night birds and insects. The bike bumped over a lump in the road, soft like a body, feathered and dead, a ground bird. Ruby stopped, took out her flashlight: this bird hadn't died of natural causes; it had been hit by a car, not so long ago either because it wasn't yet riddled with maggots.

This surely was the road that the kidnappers had taken.

She turned off the flashlight because, as Connie had so wisely told her, she could see more when she stopped trying to look with her eyes. All the flashlight did was to act as a spotlight, illuminating one small circle of blackness, thus preventing her from seeing the bigger picture and sensing what was around her.

It wasn't easy cycling a mountain path in the dark, but her bike, though beaten up and well used, was reliable and strong. Despite this, she would have to ditch it someplace soon; after all, she couldn't exactly ride on up a mountain road and pull into the kidnappers' yard. Before long she found a small turning and was able to abandon the track and her bike and make her way on foot.

Very soon the narrow track became a dirt path and minutes later the dirt path disappeared completely and Ruby looked up to see the underside of a cliff jutting out from the mountainside.

The house was built on top of this slab of rock and in order to reach it Ruby was going to have to climb up and over. On the one hand no one would spot her making her ascent as she tried to cling to the overhang, but on the other hand clinging to the underside of a rock ledge wasn't the easiest thing in the world to do. In fact, it looked like it might be more or less impossible. But then she didn't have a whole lot of choice – impossible, possible, she would have to take her chances.

RULE 20: NINETY PER CENT OF SURVIVAL IS ABOUT BELIEVING YOU WILL SURVIVE or, as Sam Colt would say: the key to survival is keeping *a positive mental attitude.*

She tied her laces very tight, pulled the dorky poppered tab across the laces just to be sure they didn't come undone, then she began to edge out along the cliff, finding footholds where she could. The rock was solid, it wasn't crumbling and it wasn't slippy, but it was a little sheer to say the least.

When Ruby was halfway along, she realised just how

hopeless the task she had set herself was. Positive mental attitude or not, one would have to be Spider-Man himself to make it up this rock face... She clung on and kicked it angrily, knowing she was going to have to climb back down. She *hated* giving up.

And that's when a very strange thing happened.

The Bradley Baker kid sneakers seemed to be actually clinging to the surface of the cliff. Somehow she had activated suckers in the soles, super strong suckers that meant she could very nearly walk upside down; all she had to do was to find handholds and it was a piece of cake. She was a human fly scaling the rock wall.

So this was the 'other benefit' Dr Harper was talking about, she thought. These shoes weren't *just* comfy after all: they made you superhuman.

Minutes later, Ruby crawled over the top of the overhang and rolled into the shadow to the side of the house. It was cabin-like in style, but not in scale. The house itself was low, large and sprawling with a good many outbuildings surrounding a good-sized yard.

Ruby reasoned that if these guys had the wolf then they would have some security. They wouldn't mess that up – these people weren't amateurs. Ruby crouched there, trying to work out just how many guards there were likely to be. She figured that there could easily be eight. There were three pickups and a couple of motorbikes. Lorelei would be there too with the young guy Ruby had seen in the department store. But where was Clancy? They weren't going to be too worried about him escaping; he was probably tied up, and where exactly was he going to run to if he did escape?

She edged round in the shadows of the buildings, but everything was quiet, no one about. No one was expecting a visit from a lone thirteen-year-old girl.

GREAT BEAR
MOUNTAIN

Cabin

WOLF PAW
MOUNTAIN

Camp
Wichitino

Emerald
Lake

WOODLAND
TRACK

Boulder
Valley

Bike Track

FIR EDGE

Chapter 59.
Better late than never

CLANCY CAME TO WHEN HE HEARD A STRANGE YET FAMILIAR SOUND. It was the call of the tawny owl, a bird not found in the United States, but yet a bird call he had heard many times in Cedarwood Drive, Twinford. It was the Ruby Redfort rescue call* – she had found him, she was outside the door. He was saved.

When Ruby heard the response call coming from the small low building on the far side of the yard, she immediately set about finding a way in. It didn't take long: as she had predicted, they weren't too concerned about the possibility of escape or rescue.

He smiled up at her weakly. 'I wasn't sure you'd come.'

'Oh, you know me Clance. I'm not always punctual, but I always show up eventually.' She took his hand and managed to gently stand him on his feet; he wobbled a bit, but he didn't fall. 'Look Clance, we're gonna have to run for it – you think you can do that?'

* HO HO HOO HOO HOO HOO.

'Sure,' he said.

She opened the door. 'Stay close to the building, OK? If you stay close, it won't trigger the security light... at least that's what I'm hoping.'

They had travelled about twenty yards when Clancy started to look decidedly unstable.

'Are you OK?' whispered Ruby.

Clancy said nothing, he just breathed all the harder.

'OK,' hissed Ruby. 'You're gonna need to keep going.'

He sort of nodded, but stood exactly where he was.

'You don't seem very OK,' Ruby said. 'Are you about to pass out on me?'

Clancy shook his head and passed out.

'Now that's what I call timing,' muttered Ruby. She caught him before he hit the deck, but there was no way she was going to be able to drag him down a mountain if he was unconscious and no way she was going to risk him fainting all over the place.

'Darn it,' she hissed.

Ruby slapped him gently and he opened his eyes.

'Am I still here?' he said.

'Yeah, and unfortunately so am I.'

'Do we have to go back?' he asked. 'I didn't like it so much there.'

'No, I don't think that's such a good idea,' she said.

She thought for a second or two. They were going to have to hide out someplace until he pulled it together; he was never going to make it down a cliff face in his condition.

'OK,' said Ruby, 'this is what we're gonna do.' She had spied a disused-looking barn; there were no lights on and for now at least no one seemed to be patrolling around there. In utter silence they edged their way slowly round the yard, hugging close to the darkness of the outbuildings, and waited for the cloud to move across the moon and, when it did, took a deep breath before they ventured from the shadows across the open space between them and the barn. They made it without the alarm being raised. The door was bolted and looped with a heavy industrial-sized padlock. Undeterred, Ruby took the barrette from her hair, inserted it into the lock and wiggled it this way and that until the padlock clicked open. A little trick Mrs Digby had taught her one rainy winter's day.

Ruby pulled the bolt and pushed Clancy inside where he slumped down onto the sawdust floor. He looked bad, eyes all droopy and unfocused.

'Sorry Rube, I haven't eaten in a while. I saw them drugging the food and I didn't want to be unconscious in case I got a chance to escape.'

'Kinda ironic, don't you think, considering you are pretty much unconscious anyway?'

Clancy smiled weakly. 'Yeah, I guess it is kinda funny.'

'Glad you can still laugh about the little things,' said Ruby. 'Would be a shame to lose your sense of humour on top of everything else.'

'You know I have a feeling they aren't too concerned about my general state of health,' said Clancy.

'Yeah, I'm guessing you're right about that,' Ruby agreed.

'You know it's a real shame Lyla turned out to be a psychopath,' said Clancy. 'She promised to get some of that Marie Antoinette perfume for my mom's birthday, made out like she could get it cut-price.'

'Well, don't feel too sore about it Clance, that perfume ain't quite as authentic as Madame Swann claims it is.'

'It's a fake?' asked Clancy.

'Kinda is,' replied Ruby.

Clancy sighed. 'I feel a whole lot better knowing that. I mean who wants fake Marie Antoinette perfume, right? Only problem is, what do I get my mom now?'

'I might be able to find you a bottle of wolf scent,' said Ruby, looking back towards the house.

'I didn't tell them about you, at least I didn't mean to,' said

Clancy, 'and when your name sorta slipped out I shut right up.'

'Don't give it a second thought,' said Ruby.

'I've been feeling kinda bad,' mumbled Clancy. 'Not about that, at least not so much about that – more about how I've been acting.'

'I don't know what you're talking about Clance,' said Ruby. He looked at her.

'I really don't,' she said, her face betraying nothing that would suggest this wasn't the whole truth.

'Anyhow,' she shrugged, 'it's me who should be grovelling for forgiveness. I nearly got you eaten by a tiger, not to mention old Madame Loup on your tail.'

'And that's the other thing,' said Clancy. 'I wanted to say thanks for passing French for me.'

'I don't know what you mean Clance, what French?'

He was staring at her now, looking up at those amazing green eyes. How could he ever have misjudged Ruby Redfort, the best friend anyone could ever have?

'By the way bozo,' she said, 'I'm not about to apologise for Wichitino Camp, since here you are all kidnapped instead of toasting marshmallows and singing "Kumbaya" with a bunch of dorks – luck musta been on your side.'

'What exactly are these guys after?' asked Clancy.

'It has something to do with a wolf,' said Ruby, 'a wolf and a vial of wolf scent.'

'Jeepers,' mumbled Clancy, 'I do seem to remember someone mentioning a wolf.'

'Where dya think they keep it?'

'I don't know,' said Clancy. 'I was hoping not to be introduced.' He shut his eyes again. 'So what dya think they're planning next?' he asked.

'They're gonna kill you for sure,' said Ruby.

'You say the nicest things Rube,' he said dreamily.

'They're gonna kill me too if that's any comfort.'

'Nah.' He looked up like he was considering the thought. 'That doesn't really help.'

'I'm just being straight with you.'

'Yeah, well, would you mind lying a little? The truth is beginning to hurt.'

'Dya think you can run, even a little bit?'

'I feel real dizzy.'

'You do look a little drugged Clance,' said Ruby.

'I'm a whole lot drugged,' said Clancy.

'Well, I guess it hasn't worn off yet.' She looked at Clancy's pupils: they were still big.

Ruby gave the situation a few seconds' thought before

coming to the inevitable conclusion that Clancy needed to eat. He probably hadn't eaten a morsel for at least twenty-four hours and that wasn't going to help the situation any.

'Stay here, OK?' said Ruby.

'Just where dya think I might go?' croaked Clancy.

'I'll go find a snack or something. Meanwhile, dya want some bubblegum – would that help?'

'That's gonna make it worse, gets the gut all bubbled up.'

'Have it your own way.' She shrugged and popped a piece in her mouth; it would help keep her focused. 'I've been up since the crack of dawn.' She yawned. 'And I'm pretty much running on empty. Wish me luck,' she said with a smile. She slipped through the doorway, pulling it tight behind her.

'Luck,' whispered Clancy Crew before his eyes shut.

Chapter 60.
The last blue wolf

RUBY SCOUTED THE CARS, looking in glove compartments and under seats, but saw nothing, not a morsel. All the buildings were locked as far as she could make out and she could see nothing lying around, no candy wrappers, no soda cans.

Bears, she thought. These guys were careful: they didn't want to attract bears so they did not leave food lying around, not even so much as a pack of mints. This left her with one option: get into the house and make for the larder.

The first thing she did was disable the vehicles, just in case. She wasn't intending to attract the attention of ruthless killers, but on the other hand better safe than sorry. She let the air out of the tyres and stabbed the spares just to be sure. She had no idea if they had other trucks hidden away – probably – but she didn't have time to check.

As she crept towards the house, she thought, *This is ridiculous; no one talks about this scenario in survival training.* Then she muttered under her breath, 'Am I really risking my life to get my pal a Twinkie?'

Somehow the foolishness of the statement made it feel more possible that she would wake up and realise she had been having an absurd dream. She found a trapdoor at the side of the house; it was a sort of vent, too small for most humans, but a mere squeeze for someone of Ruby's size.

It opened up into a basement which spanned the width of the house with a rickety wooden staircase on the far side. She moved as noiselessly as she could towards the stairs; when she reached them, she realised that she must be directly below the room that housed the kidnappers since the floor creaked heavily and sprinklings of dust fell, disturbed by the movement of their feet. She heard the scraping of chairs, loud conversation and the sound of cups being placed on a wooden surface. She guessed that there were perhaps five or even six of them all sitting at a long wooden table.

She tiptoed up the stairs, each step betraying her progress with a traitorous creak. She stopped on the very top step and waited for someone to fling open the door, but they didn't. She peeped through the keyhole, but couldn't see much, a ladder perhaps and maybe shelves. There was no sign of people, no sound of anything living.

She opened the door a crack and discovered a tall room lined with tins and packets: the pantry – she had actually got lucky. She scanned around for something that might take the edge off Clancy's dizziness. Then she saw the perfect thing, Hunger Bites, **packed with dried fruit, nuts, sugar and goodness** – *i.e. calories.*

Well, they weren't Twinkies, but they were a snack.

She stuffed them into her satchel and checked out the refrigerator. It held a lot of food and canned drinks, butter and cheese, milk, bacon, those sorts of things, but it also held some other stuff, stuff that looked like it had nothing to do with nutrition. Ruby reached in, pushing aside jars and metal containers, until her eyes rested on an item that really caught her attention. It was a small blue bottle, about two inches tall, with a label. She twisted it round and read the words *Alaskan Cyan*, the date printed next to it – it was freshly extracted.

This was the scent of Flemming Fengrove's very last Blue Alaskan. She couldn't believe her luck; here it was, the very thing she had wanted to search for, but wasn't expecting to find. She carefully removed it from its shelf and placed it in her bag.

Ruby was about to close the refrigerator door when she remembered soda; she ought to take Clancy something sugary to drink. She grabbed one of the cans, but in her haste to get going she unbalanced the whole stack, the cans toppled from the shelf and crashed to the floor, spraying soda in all directions. For a split second there was silence from the next-door room, but this was swiftly followed by shouting.

'What the Sam Hill was that?'

'I'll check it out.'

'Rats. It'll be rats.'

'I told you we shoulda laid traps.'

'I'll go check it out, see if I can't shoot a couple.'

Ruby had not waited to see what would happen next, but had practically flown up the rickety steps that led up out of the pantry to the storeroom above. There was nowhere to go from there so she hunkered down, lying flat on the bare wood floor behind a stack of boxes, her eye to the crack in the boards, and she hoped with all her might that they would not imagine these rats would climb a ladder.

The door creaked open.

'It's rats for sure,' said the rough-sounding guy. 'I'm gonna go set some traps, I can't abide vermin.'

He left the room, but Ruby stayed very, very still for she could hear the sound of breathing. Someone was directly underneath where she lay, a woman she thought. The sound of her breathing was almost imperceptible, but Ruby sensed it, the breathing of someone delicate and light of foot, someone confident, without fear. She was moving slowly, carefully, but Ruby could sense her getting nearer. Then:

'Fee-fi-fo-fum, I smell the blood of an American.' The voice like cut glass. 'Correction, I smell the *bubblegum* of an American.'

Ruby closed her eyes, and cursed herself. This must be Lorelei von Leyden.

'Now what brand of bubblegum is it...? Yum-Yum? No, too fruity. Hubble-Yum! That's it. Am I right little girl? Or should I say... Ruby Red?'

Jeepers, thought Ruby.

'I smell your shampoo; you teenagers just love Wildrose.'

Ruby had indeed washed her hair with Wildrose.

She could hear Lorelei's foot on the bottom tread. She waited, one, two, three, four, five, six. Lorelei was about halfway up before Ruby sprang from her crouch and pushed at the ladder with every ounce of her being. It was enough: Lorelei was not heavy. The ladder toppled backwards and she heard Lorelei hit the floor. Ruby jumped down through the opening and clattered down the basement stairs, clambered into the vent duct and forced her way out into the night air. She could hear the sound of running boots and voices calling in the dark.

Which way? She was a little disorientated.

Where was the moon? A cloud had momentarily obscured it; a good thing – it was dark and it gave her some cover. She stood there, heart pounding, as she watched the guards spilling into the yard, all of them shouting, the security lights from the house illuminating their faces. She was just going to have to make a dash for it.

She dodged out from the shadows and slid under a truck. No one saw, then she caterpillared her way from one vehicle to another until the only thing between her and the barn door was a few feet of empty yard. Quick as a flash, she rolled out and up and sprinted to the door.

She almost made it without being seen.

But a miss, as they say, is as good as a mile. *Bang!* The floodlights came on and the yard was lit up as bright as any baseball stadium and she was illuminated like the star attraction.

Clancy, roused by the alarms and bright lights, leapt to his feet and managed to slide the great door open just far enough so Ruby could slip inside and then they rammed the door closed and bolted it behind them. They pushed every other thing – box, crate, feedsack – they could find against the thick wooden doors. It would hold for a bit, but not more than minutes Ruby guessed.

They sank to the floor, breathing heavily.

Then Ruby reached into her pocket and pulled out the Hunger Bites.

CLANCY: *'Hunger Bites? Really? I'm not so crazy about them.'*

RUBY: *'What?'*

CLANCY: *'It's the dried cherry, it sort of sticks in my throat.'*

RUBY: *'There's gonna be a whole lot worse sticking in your throat buster; you should see the knives they got.'*

CLANCY: *'And there goes my appetite.'*

RUBY: *'Try and get it back, it might be your last chance to eat – ever I mean.'*

CLANCY: *'Do I want my last meal to be a Hunger Bite?'*

RUBY: *'You're choosing a fine time to get picky.'*

CLANCY: *'OK, OK, I'll eat it if it makes you so happy.'*

RUBY: *'Good, you start fainting and you're on your own.'*

CLANCY: *'You're planning on running?'*

RUBY: *'How else are we gonna get outta here?'*

CLANCY: *'Tunnelling?'*

RUBY: *'I'm hoping there's a back door.'*

CLANCY: *'There is. But I wouldn't use it if I were you.'*

RUBY: *'Scared of the dark?'*

CLANCY: *'No, I'm scared of the wolf.'*

Ruby stared at him. 'The wolf's here?'

Clancy nodded. 'I looked.'

Ruby scrambled to her feet and crept over to the far side of the barn, where there was a stable style door. She could hear something pacing, sense something wild and fearful lurking there. She opened the upper half of the door a crack, no more, and stared into the darkness.

The black seemed to be impenetrable, impossible to see into, but there must have been a hole in the roof, a skylight perhaps, and the moon must have found a way through the cloud because all of a sudden something appeared in the beam of light that shone down and Ruby found herself staring into the pale blue eyes of a savage-looking creature.

'The only thing to fear is the Blue Alaskan wolf.' The words of Samuel Colt echoed in her mind. She could see that he wasn't wrong: this beast did look very dangerous. He had the same indigo-ringed eyes as the wolf trapped forever in her memory, the same black-tipped ears as the wolf in Mrs Digby's photograph. This was it: this was the last Cyan wolf.

Chapter 61.
The scent

RUBY WAS THINKING HARD, her brain working fast, clicking through thoughts and ideas, possibilities and impossibilities. 'So why didn't it eat her?' she muttered.

'Eat who?' said Clancy.

'Mrs Digby,' said Ruby. 'Long ago she had her picture taken with a wolf just like this one and it didn't eat her, but why?'

'Maybe it had just eaten someone else,' mused Clancy.

But Ruby wasn't hearing him; she was hearing the voice of Connie Slowfoot. *'You meet that wolf, you better be sure you got the scent.'*

'...maybe it didn't like the smell of her,' Clancy suggested.

'Maybe it *did* like the smell of her!' said Ruby. 'Maybe there was some scent that Fengrove's people used to control it, calm it, keep it docile.'

She was thinking about the zookeeper, the handkerchief he was clutching when Clancy found him. She realised it wasn't just any handkerchief; it wasn't scented with just any fragrance.

Clancy had his eye to a crack in the stable door; he was watching the wolf. 'It doesn't look docile, that's for sure, it looks kinda mean,' he said. He was unusually laid-back. Ruby guessed he must still be suffering the effects of the sedative or he would be flapping his arms by now.

'It better be mean,' said Ruby.

'Why do we want a mean wolf in our barn?'

'It's all part of the plan.'

'What's your plan?'

'We're gonna let it out,' said Ruby.

'I knew you were gonna say that,' said Clancy.

'So you shouldn't have asked.'

'I was hoping for a different answer.'

'These guys won't dare shoot; they want it alive, but they're also gonna have to run for cover 'cause this creature is capable of ripping them limb from limb.'

'And why won't it rip us limb from limb?' asked Clancy.

'Because of this,' said Ruby, pulling the handkerchief from her pocket.

'We're going to surrender to it?' said Clancy.

'No stupid, the smell. I think the smell on this handkerchief is what the keeper used to control it with. I think the smell is from another Cyan wolf; he must have kept a little of the scent somewhere – if you've got the smell, you can control the wolf – that's what Connie Slowfoot must have meant.'

'*That wolf will rip you to shreds, soon as sniff you... Unless, of course, you got the scent.*'

'Connie who?'

'It'll work, I'm sure it'll work... probably.'

'You're saying the smell from some old handkerchief is going to stop this wild beast attacking us?'

'I'm saying I hope it will; the only thing is the scent is sorta wearing off now...'

'Oh great, so have you got a plan B if your brilliant plan A doesn't work?'

'Run for it.'

'That's it, is it? I hate to be a downer,' said Clancy, 'but I'm not sure that I'm really capable of fast movement.'

'Oh brother!' She looked at him; he was looking decidedly feeble. The Hunger Bites had perked him up, but he still wasn't his old self. Ruby kicked at the floor of the barn. 'There has to be another way out,' she said, and just then her foot struck something hard.

She knelt down, cleared the straw and found a large metal ring, the handle to a trapdoor. She shone her flashlight into the hole; it appeared to be a crawl space that ran the length of the barn and into the next.

'Clance, you're gonna have to get yourself down here and crawl along until you come out under the last building, then you gotta find my bike, OK? It's hidden in some undergrowth just off a small side track. Head as fast as you can eastwards. Just get away. I'll follow you, but just get help as fast as you can.'

'What about the guards?' he asked.

'Believe me, they'll all be outside this barn door,' said Ruby.

'So how are you gonna get away?'

'Well, I'm kinda hoping the wolf sees me as a friend on account of me having the handkerchief he likes so much, and I'm counting on the guys out there being unprepared so the wolf attacks them and I can get away.'

'And what if you're wrong, what if they *are* prepared and this wolf doesn't go crazy?'

'Then,' said Ruby, 'I'm gonna have to fall back on plan B.'

'Which is?'

'I use the handkerchief to surrender. I'm sure the wolf will be decent about it, I'm just not so sure about the murderers.'

Clancy didn't move.

'Would you get outta here!'

'No,' said Clancy.

Ruby by now had tied a rope to the stable door.

'Look Clance, I've got a plan. I don't know if it's a good one, but I got a plan.'

'How dya figure you're gonna survive?'

'I'm thinking positive.'

'That's the plan?' said Clancy. His arms were almost beginning to flap; the sedative was wearing off.

'Survival is ninety per cent attitude.'

Clancy shook his head. 'I think you're gonna fall into the remaining ten per cent category.'

'Would ya just scram before I open this stable door!' shouted Ruby. 'Or would ya prefer to be torn limb from limb?'

'OK! I'm scramming,' shouted Clancy. 'Your plan sucks, but I hope it works.'

He disappeared down the hatch and Ruby slammed the lid over him. How long would he have to reach the bike? Minutes? She hoped at least five; he needed a good head start.

Ruby climbed the ladder to the hayloft and waited up there until she heard the final crash of the barn door and the shattered wood spun through the air. Ruby tugged hard on the rope, the stable door flung open and the wolf sprang out. There were screams and cries and the toughest-looking men scattered in every direction, running for their lives, taking cover where they could. Lorelei was screaming, 'Don't shoot, don't anyone shoot! I need this creature alive!'

The wolf was standing in the barn doorway, snarling, his fur spiked along his spine. Ruby would have to take her chances, put her theory to the test. She clutched the handkerchief and carefully, very carefully so as not to alarm the creature, stepped slowly down the ladder. It sniffed the air and turned to look at her, its pale blue eyes in hers, hers in its, and for a moment they seemed to know each other's thoughts.

Run, it seemed to say, *run with me to the forest edge*. And so she did – the wolf and the girl bolted from the cover of the barn and made for the mountain road. The kidnappers, too dumbfounded to react, simply watched as Ruby and the animal ran and ran, until they reached the forest edge and then the wolf stopped, looked into her eyes one last time, before howling a sorrowful howl and, like a wisp of smoke, it disappeared into the darkness of the trees.

Chapter 62.
Run Ruby, run

RUBY RAN. She ran like a wild thing down the forest path. She ran as far and as fast as she could. She had no idea where she was headed, but she needed to get far far away, over towards Little Bear, to Camp Wichitino. As she ran, she saw tiny glows light up at her feet; Clancy must have found the ground glows in her saddlebag and left her a trail; he had not forgotten her in his haste to get away. It felt like she was running for home; she would find her way out and everything would work out fine.

In the distance she could hear the shouts and chaos of the men trying to recapture the Cyan wolf, but from what she could make out the wolf was long gone and she hoped, for his sake, would never be seen again.

There was a crack of lightning, a rumble of thunder. Ruby looked up at the sky and felt a fat drop of rain on her cheek, then the heavens opened and the rain poured down.

**Up in a small lookout cabin
high up on the mountainside
a woman was standing at
the window**

The pounding rain had woken her and she was staring out into the grey early morning.

'What are those lights?' she said, picking up a sweater and draping it over the floral dress she wore.

'What are you talking about, lights?' said the guy sitting next to the open fire. 'We're miles from anywhere.'

But the woman continued to stand there, staring out.

The man got up and walked to the window. 'Well, I'll be darned,' he said. 'I better go check it out; it might have something to do with Lorelei, the double-crossing snake.' He pulled on his rainproof coat and big hat and stepped out of the door.

'Don't forget to take this.' The woman handed him a heavy black object.

'I doubt I'll need it, but if it makes you feel better I'll take it,' he said.

'A gun always makes me feel better,' she said. 'I'll follow in the RV once the rain clears. I just need to make a house call.'

Chapter 63.
Betrayed

RUBY SAW THAT THE DARKNESS WAS LIFTING, the sun edging upwards, the rain had come to an abrupt stop and already the sky was turning blue.

She looked behind her. She had come a long way; she could actually see her path very clearly because it was dotted with little glowing lights, all the way back up the mountainside. Their mirror-like sparkle was quite something, unmissable in fact. As the glows danced their way through the forest like pixie lights, so Ruby thought about the little warning at the bottom of the gadget card.

This had to be the reason the ground glows had been taken out of service. When the ground was dry, they provided a discreet and careful trail, but when wet they told the whole world exactly where you were; these tiny turncoats were leaking her whereabouts to anyone who cared to know.

Ruby began to run faster than she ever thought she could.

She relied only on her instinct, letting go of any previous plan – she just listened to her gut, she was more animal than girl, determined to find her way home.

As she made her way out through the trees, she saw a figure standing in the clearing, his back to her. The figure of a boy, Clancy Crew. What a sight for sore eyes. He turned and smiled.

'Why did you stop?' called Ruby.

'I was waiting for you bozo.' He turned back to look at the view. 'Plus, I sorta came to the end of the road.'

Ruby looked down and saw what he meant: the mountain fell away steeply and the only way down was to climb.

'I think we should go round the other side of the mountain and then take the path down from there; you can sit on the back of the bike that way.'

Ruby agreed. It would take longer, but would be less dangerous than climbing down the rock face.

'Boy, is that ever some strange-looking storm cloud, it's huge.' Clancy was staring across the valley, towards Great Bear. The sky was clear blue but for an enormous, single, strangely-lit cloud. It mushroomed out from a dark grey mass which seemed to rise up from the forest.

'Oh no,' said Ruby in a hushed voice. 'No way.'

'What?' said Clancy.

'That's no storm cloud, that's a pyrocumulus,' gasped Ruby.

'A pyro-what?' said Clancy.

Ruby looked him right in the eye. 'Fire,' she said. 'The forest is on fire.'

**The vehicle screeched to a
halt in the middle of
the floodlit yard...**

...and Eduardo ran to meet it.

'Lorelei?' he called.

'No,' said a different voice, one he did not recognise, 'not Lorelei.' The woman stepped out into the light and the young man instantly knew who she must be.

'It's not here,' he said. 'It was, but then that kid let it go.'

The woman smiled. 'A kid you say? A kid let my client's wolf go? The one he paid for, the one he was assured would be delivered to him?'

Eduardo looked out into the forest.

'I can't help wondering what Lorelei was doing hanging onto this wolf so long. Why would she not just hand it over as planned?'

Eduardo was saying nothing.

'I can only conclude, and of course I don't know for sure so correct me if I'm wrong, but I can only conclude she was stealing some of the Alaskan Cyan from that wolf.' She cocked her head to one side. 'Is that right sweetie?'

'It was just one vial,' said Eduardo. 'She just took one vial of scent from the wolf. I mean it's not really like stealing, is it?'

The woman looked at him pityingly. 'Now there sweetheart, I have to disagree. To take such a valuable scent from such a valuable creature when it doesn't belong to you is stealing; ask anyone.' She put her hand in her purse like she was searching for a tissue. 'So where is the vial?'

'The kid took it, the girl,' said Eduardo. 'She ran into the forest – she's out there.' He gestured towards the trees. 'She's out there.'

'Looks like we're in a bit of a bind here, doesn't it sweetie?' She wasn't smiling. 'The wolf is gone, Lorelei's gone, the kid has gone, the vial is gone and it looks like I'm going to have to fix everything all on my own.'

Eduardo turned towards the house. 'Wait, I'll help you,' he said.

'And how are you going to do that sweetie?'

'How do you mean?' said Eduardo, puzzled.

'You're not going to be much use.' She pulled a gun from her purse and shot him. 'Not now you're dead.'

Chapter 64.
No time to lose

'It's a long way off,' said Clancy.

'Depends how fast you can run,' said Ruby. 'Fire moves quick and there's been a drought so the grasses are all tinder dry.'

Clancy stared at her. 'So why are we stopping here? We gotta go!' He gripped the handlebars, but Ruby stood still.

'What are you doing Ruby? We have to go! Get on!' But she didn't move a muscle or blink an eyelash. 'Now!' insisted Clancy.

'Clancy, could you just take a deep breath and keep your hair on.'

He looked at her and tried to remain calm. Ruby was thinking and if she was thinking she was sure to come up with a plan and, knowing Ruby, it would be a good one. So Clancy didn't speak; he just let go the bike and flapped his arms, a reflex action when faced with a situation beyond his control.

'Clance, if you have to flap, then could you maybe do it quietly? I'm trying to think here.'

Clancy stuffed his hands in his pockets and kicked at the dirt instead.

SURVIVAL RULE 17:

Forest fires can travel at great speed and once upon you cannot be outrun.

'Fire travels uphill a whole lot faster than it travels downhill and, if the wind's behind it, can travel at up to fourteen miles per hour.'

She checked to see which way the wind was blowing.

Clancy began to kick the earth harder. He didn't like what he was hearing; after all, they were halfway up a mountain here.

SURVIVAL RULE 18:

Look for areas of hardwoods. *Deciduous trees take longer to ignite than conifers.*

Ruby scanned the trees; all were pine trees and firs, and all made for perfect forest fire fuel.

She made a 360° turn, taking in the landscape. What she was looking for was a break in the trees: water, road, rocky escarpment. Something to put a barrier between them and the fire. She spotted a river, wide with only a few trees around it; they might make it, depending on the wind, but it was a long way off from where they were standing, and it was likely the fire would reach them first. Then Ruby had a better idea.

First they needed to aim for the ribbon of road that ran round the base of the mountain and if they were lucky they might meet a passing car, otherwise... well, otherwise, they would have to fall back on plan B.

Finally, Ruby spoke. 'OK Clance, so here's the plan: we have to get back down the mountain super fast; we need to get to that road. When we get there, we can try and find someone who'll drive us onto Little Bear, we need to warn the Wichitinos, and if the fire is too close we can all go jump in the lake.'

'What?' said Clancy.

'OK, maybe not jump, but we'll paddle out to the middle of Emerald Lake. They have canoes, I saw them; we'll be safe there, but first we need to get to that road.'

Clancy peered down. 'You mean that road as in the road at

the bottom of this sheer drop?'

'It's not sheer exactly,' countered Ruby, 'it's steep.'

'Yes, steep is a word for it, as in no footholds and no way of getting down without falling.'

But Ruby wasn't listening; she was walking towards the edge and she was determined to get down that cliff face any way she could.

'Come on Clance, it'll be OK and you know that pyrocumulus cloud might bring about something good.'

Clancy peered over the edge and didn't feel super convinced about either statement.

'Ruby, can I just remind you that I am thirteen years old and way too young to die.'

'So don't bozo. Hold on tight and get climbing.'

'You aren't exactly the most understanding person, you know that Ruby?' Grumbling helped Clancy to forget that he was on a thin ledge perched several hundred feet above a mass of sharp looking rocks.

'You know I don't like heights,' he complained.

'So don't look down,' replied Ruby.

'How does that help?' hissed Clancy.

'Because if you try to imagine you're only a foot off the ground then you won't worry about falling and if you stop worrying about falling then you most likely won't, OK? Plus, you need to hang onto me; you might not believe it, but I'm wearing Spider-Man's shoes.'

'I'll take your word for it,' said Clancy.

They began to make their descent.

'So what was the good thing you were going to tell me about these pyro-whatsit clouds?' wheezed Clancy, trying to catch his breath.

'It doesn't always happen,' said Ruby, 'but it does occasionally. Just sometimes the pyrocumulus cloud gets so heavy with moisture that it turns into torrential rain and puts the fire out, though other times...'

Clancy waited for her to finish her sentence.

'...other times it becomes a thunderstorm and the lightning created starts further forest fires.'

Chapter 65.
Twinkling eyes

THEY MADE IT DOWN THE ROCK FACE WITHOUT FALLING;
now all they had to do was get down this final section and make
it to the road.

Then, as they stumbled and slipped and skidded down the
steep mountainside, they saw what might be their salvation. A
camper van pulled into a siding off the tarmac road.

Ruby began to shout, waving like crazy, trying to get the
driver's attention. She'd lost her shoes somewhere along the
way, but she didn't care: she had her heart set on home. Clancy,
who wasn't about to leave these miracle sneakers behind, was
desperately trying to retrieve them from a nasty-looking thorn
bush, but Ruby just kept going. The last few feet she practically
rolled like tumbleweed, arriving grazed and bleeding in a heap
at the base of the mountain.

The door to the van opened and a woman clambered out;
she was perhaps in her fifties, her face weathered, friendly, she

looked concerned but unpanicked; exactly the kind of person you wanted to meet when you were in this kind of trouble.

'Hey, are you all right there sweetie?' She hurried over to where Ruby was sprawled.

'I think so,' Ruby replied. She got to her feet and made a half-hearted effort at dusting herself off.

'What happened to you?' asked the woman.

'I don't think you'd believe me if I even began to explain,' said Ruby. The woman looked at her, puzzled.

'Try me,' she said.

Ruby felt relieved looking into her twinkling eyes. The woman was reassuringly ordinary in her pretty floral dress; she looked kind of motherly, not like Ruby's mother, but sort of how a mother was meant to look.

The woman smiled. 'Don't tell me,' she said, 'you were almost captured by a band of kidnappers?'

'Kinda,' said Ruby slowly.

'But you escaped with the help of the last Cyan wolf? Is that about it?'

The woman's eyes were no longer twinkling: they were steely blue. 'Tell me sweetie, just how did you do that?'

Ruby looked back into those cold eyes and said, 'The usual way.'

The woman nodded. 'And how did you figure it out?'

'I pay attention,' said Ruby.

'I guess you do sweetie, so I hope you're paying attention now because I sort of have the upper hand, don't I?' As she said this, she pulled the gun from her purse, then she shrugged. 'You see how life turns on a dime.'

Ruby did see this. Just a minute ago she was imagining making it back, surviving.

'So how about you hand me that little blue bottle? Since you lost me my wolf, I reckon you owe me that – a lot more actually, but I'll settle for what I can get, no point being a sore loser. I can't abide a bad sport, can you?'

Ruby took the blue vial from her pocket and placed it in the woman's palm. 'All this so you can make some money out of some stupid fragrance,' said Ruby.

The woman laughed. 'Is that what you think this is about? No sweetie, this is not about some high-end perfume counter cluttered up with rich folk wanting to waste their money. This is about something important, more important than you could ever imagine.' She examined the bottle just to be sure it wasn't a fake – she was no amateur.

'No, this is not about perfume – you're getting me confused with Lorelei, not the same kettle of fish at all.' The woman smiled again as if a nice thought had just flitted through her mind.

'Lorelei is a clever girl, but silly with it. She thought that she could double-cross me by stealing some of the Cyan for herself, but a mother always knows her child, whatever the disguise. She has never fooled me and never will. I see through every lie she tells.'

'She's your daughter? Lorelei von Leyden?' said Ruby.

The woman laughed. 'Lorelei, she thinks her mother is dead, wants to believe it, but I know different.'

The woman aimed the gun at Ruby's heart and Ruby instinctively stepped back, one pace, two... and into thin air. She didn't fall far, ten feet, maybe onto a small ledge about six foot square, a sheer drop behind her, a sheer rock face in front, and the way she felt the pain shoot through her, a possible broken arm.

Now injured and without her Bradley Baker shoes, how was she ever going to climb up or indeed down? The woman peered over the cliff edge to where Ruby lay sprawled and then looked beyond to the approaching flames.

'You don't want to *be* here sweetie, don't you know? There's a forest fire heading this way, it's gonna get real dangerous real quick.' She reached into her purse and took out a box of matches. 'And you know what fires are like: once one gets going, they sorta spring up everywhere.' She struck the match and dropped it into the long grasses by her feet.

'I guess I better get going if I'm to make it out of here unscathed; there just is no predicting nature.' She smiled sweetly at Ruby. 'You don't mind if I save my bullets, do you sweetie? Ashes to ashes and all that.' She turned and Ruby watched as she disappeared; heard the engine rev and the car speed away.

Ruby looked into the flames and saw her number was up.

Chapter 66.
A real good plan B

CLANCY HAD SEEN IT ALL, the woman and Ruby, but he had watched enough thrillers to know to wait until the villain has left the stage. Ruby had a rule about it, one she'd shared with him and which he often thought about: **RULE 10: NEVER REVEAL YOUR HAND TO A PSYCHOPATH** (this rule worked for adversaries of all kinds).

He scrambled down from where he had been hiding and ran over to the cliff edge; he began stamping on the burning undergrowth, but the fire was already out of control. Ruby was stuck on a cliff ledge too far down to reach, on the wrong side of a flaming barrier with a forest fire advancing fast behind her.

'Clancy, someone's gotta warn the Wichitinos about the fire! They're up at Emerald Lake – tell them to get outta there!'

'What about you?' yelled Clancy.

Ruby shook her head. 'You gotta get out of here, you hear me?'

But Clancy didn't move.

'Run Clancy, run!'

'I'm not leaving you Ruby!' Clancy had his face set firm and his feet had become like roots in the ground. 'I can't.'

Ruby Redfort knew that face; she knew that no amount of begging, no amount of ordering would change his mind so instead she said, 'I'm gonna be fine Clancy, I gotta plan. What you gotta do is to get over to Wichitino Camp, warn them about the fire, tell them to get themselves into the middle of that lake in their canoes. You paddle out with them, OK?' She was shouting now above the roar of the flames.

Clancy didn't move.

'I'm telling you Clance, you're the only one who can save them. You're the fastest runner in Junior High, way faster than me, and you'll get there in time, I know it, and when you do you get into that lake with them. I don't care how dorky they are. And you remember, I've got a real good plan B so don't run off worrying about me.' And she smiled at him just for a split second and with the flash of that smile Clancy believed her.

'You've gotta warn the Wichitinos! OK Clance? Now scram, would ya? You're gonna mess everything up.' He turned on his heel and he ran; he ran like he was running for Twinford Junior High, he ran like Vapona Bugwart was after him, he ran like he had a forest fire at his back which of course he did.

He ran and he ran until he reached Emerald Lake and when he made it to the Wichitino camp he found the troupe leader and he made sure he understood just how fast that fire was moving.

He helped round everyone up and he got them out on their canoes and paddled out right into the middle of that Emerald Lake and only when he had organised every one of those Wichitino kids and only when he was sitting on Emerald Lake, safe in the middle of it, did Clancy Crew take a breath, and that's when he knew he had been fooled.

Ruby Redfort was not going to make it.

No one could survive a fire like that.

She might be tough, but she was no superhero, she was just a schoolgirl, a kid from Twinford Junior High. He turned and looked at the inferno blazing around him, snapping, spitting red-hot ash and flaming sparks, tongues of fire, devouring trees; he watched on as he saw the forest he had come from turn red and knew that was the last he would see of the friend he cared for more than any other living soul, the girl who was Ruby Redfort.

Chapter 67.

What to do when there is nothing to be done

RUBY RAN THROUGH THE FOREST FIRE SURVIVAL RULES and came to Survival Suggestion 11, the one that dealt with emergencies.

SURVIVAL SUGGESTION #11:

Emergencies

1. FIRE

The last resort: *when all other options have run out, dig a shallow trench in the earth, take off your coat or jacket, cover it in leaves, get into the trench face down and pull the coat over your head.*

Ruby looked at the ground: no earth to dig, it was solid rock. The fire in front of her was blazing, the fire behind was nearly with her. She had done one good thing and that good thing was worth a thousand others: she had saved Clancy Crew, the best friend a person could have, and that was a thought that made her smile.

She reached into her pocket for a cube of bubblegum and pulled out the mini locator. Not even that could save her now.

She shifted the tiles just for old times' sake; she looked down at the word HELP and thought what a tiny word it was.

Chapter 68.
HELP

RUBY REDFORT WAS NOT EXPECTING TO SEE ANY LIVING CREATURE EVER AGAIN, not an ant or a beetle: every breathing thing was dying, consumed by the fire.

She looked to the sky, gasping for one more lungful of air, and what she saw was a giant fly hovering overhead directly above where she crouched. Then the strangest thing happened: a man appeared, dangling on a silver rope.

Batman? she thought.

Her mind was giving up on her.

He spun down and down until he was beside her on the ledge, head to toe in silver.

It must be way more than 106 degrees on that ledge and the air had clearly reached the temperature of insanity.

Not Batman, she thought, *Batman wears black. So which superhero wears silver?*

The silver figure removed the mask And Ruby squinted up

through the shimmering heat.

Hitch.

Those brown eyes belonged to Hitch.

'You look like you could do with a little rescuing kid.'

She stared up at him and smiled. 'Boy, do you know how to embarrass a kid.'

'Just sometimes, Redfort, looking cool is not the number-one rule of survival.'

He pulled her up and over his shoulder, the fire cape covering them both, grabbed the cable and they rose through the dragon-like flames that were licking up towards the sky, right up to where the helicopter hovered. And then they flew through the clouds of smoke and the burning forest and up into blue, to where the air was fresh, and on home to Twinford.

A little silver key

CLANCY CAME DOWNSTAIRS IN THE MORNING, three days after the forest fire rescue, to find a card from his father sitting on the hall table. It said:

In recognition of your quick thinking in rescuing your
fellow Wichitinos. Well done son, I'm proud you survived.
Fondest regards,
your father

Wow, this was something! A *well done* from Ambassador Crew was not so easy to come by, but an *I'm proud* was rare indeed. Ambassador Crew might have been less proud had he known Clancy hadn't actually been on camp with the Wichitinos, but thankfully no one was going to enlighten him on the matter.

Next to the card was a small box. Clancy opened it and took out a bicycle bell engraved with the words *hard work will get you what you want in the end.* The words struggled to fit round the bell and in any case what good was a bell without a bike? How much hard work was it going to take if rescuing a whole bunch of kids only earned you a bicycle bell?

Clancy was just about to dip into a sort of resigned despondency when he was yanked back out of it by the buzzer; someone was obviously leaning on it. He went to the intercom and saw a blurry figure he recognised well.

'Rube?'

'Yeah, it's me. Let me in.'

'How come you're out of bed?' he asked. 'I thought Mrs Digby would keep you locked up for at least the next two months.'

'Yeah, well, I gave her the slip. Now open the gate, would ya?'

He buzzed her through and went out to meet her. She looked both terrible and wonderful, but Clancy Crew could only see the wonderful.

'You look pretty good for someone who was almost burned to a crisp.'

'Yeah, well, my hair's not the same, but it's nothing a good conditioner and six months' growing time can't fix.' Ruby was standing by the huge iron gates, her arm in plaster, her foot all bandaged up and a nasty bruise on her cheek.

'So how's your cold?' asked Clancy.

'Completely gone,' said Ruby. 'I woke up this morning and I could smell the roses... well, Wildrose shampoo anyway.'

She reached into her satchel. 'I got something for you,' she said.

'You have?' Clancy decided it was probably a donut or maybe an éclair, though most likely a donut since she had one of Marla's bags in her hand.

But what Ruby handed him was a little silver key.

'It's for my bike,' she said, nodding over to the wall where the bike was leaning. 'It's a little beaten up. Hitch picked it up in the helicopter before the fire reached it.'

It looked exactly like Ruby's bike, but for the fact that it was blue, Windrush blue. Clancy could only stare, his mouth ever so slightly open, but no words forming.

'Well?' she said.

'You painted your bike blue?'

'No, I painted your bike blue buster,' she said.

'I don't get it,' said Clancy, who really didn't get it.

'Look bozo, you need to have a really cool bike, cool, as in reliable and tough, which my bike is, right? And I know you have a thing for blue bikes and so rather than have you act all crazy again trying to get your hands on one, I thought I'd better make my bike you know, blue.'

'Jeez Rube...' He couldn't think of much else to say; this was Ruby's bike, the one she was nuts about, the one she said she would never give away, ever. He began to flap his arms. 'Rube, I can't take this.'

'Yes you can bozo because what am *I* gonna do with a blue bike? I don't even like blue bikes.'

She turned to go. 'It's nice to see you alive Clance, you know that?'

'Yeah,' said Clancy, 'nice to see you alive too Rube. You're quite the survivor.'

All as it should be

RUBY LIMPED BACK TO WHERE HITCH WAS WAITING IN THE SILVER CAR. She got in and he started the engine. A second later, a call came through. Hitch flicked the switch on the dashboard and out of the speakers came LB's gravelly voice.

'So Redfort, I hear you made it.'

'Well, some of me did – my hair doesn't look so great,' said Ruby, 'and I suppose, if you're gonna get picky about it, I broke my arm too, plus I missed taking the survival test.' Ruby was not going to whine about it – she wasn't going to give anyone the satisfaction; she would take failure fair and square on the chin. Just like someone wise had recently told her: *'The only thing you control is your reaction to what's beyond your control.'*

LB said nothing.

'So... I'm guessing that's a fail as far as Spectrum goes,' said Ruby.

'Survival doesn't sound like failure to me Redfort,' said LB.

'Sam Colt was pretty impressed with your determination and I have got to admit that your uncovering of the Cyan wolf plot deserves recognition, even though you let the wolf escape.' She paused. 'I'm putting you forward for stage three of the Field Agent Training Programme, we'll see you in September. Try to work on that smart mouth of yours Redfort.'

Ruby was about to give a smart mouth reply, but Hitch gave her an eye signal that Ruby interpreted as *quit while you're ahead*. So she did.

'Oh, Hitch, one other thing,' said LB, 'might you be able to throw any light on how my Paris paperweight went walkabout and then several weeks later made it back onto my desk?'

'Sounds like quite the mystery,' said Hitch, 'you want me to look into it?'

'I don't think that will be necessary,' said LB dryly.

Ruby glanced at him and thought she saw the faintest of smiles play on his lips, but she couldn't swear to it.

They drove home in silence. As they turned the corner into Cedarwood Drive, Ruby made to get out of the car, then stopped, turned to Hitch and said, 'By the way, thanks for rescuing me out there.'

Hitch just smiled. 'It was nothing kid. Everyone needs rescuing once in a while.'

THINGS I KNOW:
. . . .

Why Dr Harper owes Hitch — it all has to do
with a paperweight.
Which mushrooms will kill you and which ones
won't.

THINGS I DON'T KNOW:
. . . .

Who the woman in the floral dress is working for.
What she is planning to do with the Alaskan
Cyan scent.
Where Lorelei von Leyden is now.
Where the Lapis bowerbird is now.
Whether the Cyan wolf made it out of there alive.
Whether the Count has anything to do with this.

Ruby Redfort

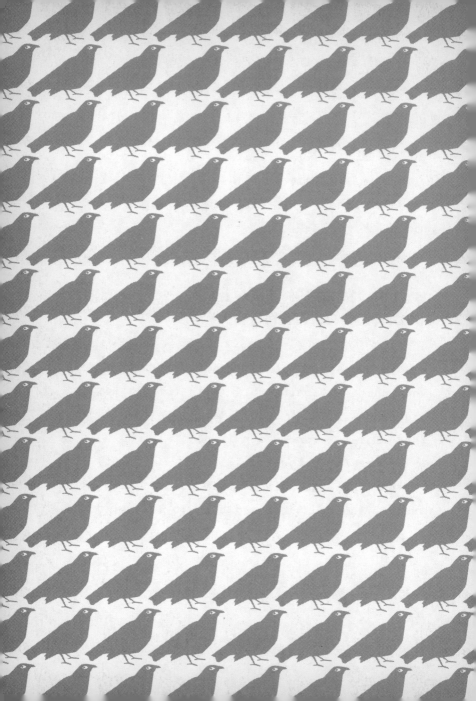

The lost perfume of Marie Antoinette

There really was a lost perfume of Marie Antoinette. A gift from Louis XVI to the young French queen, it was created by royal perfumer Jean-Louis Fargeon and contained notes of rose, jasmine, bergamot, cardamom, incense, cinnamon, sandalwood, patchouli, tonka bean and amber, as an hômage to the queen's beloved Trianon gardens.

Marie Antoinette carried the scent in a black jade vial, which she kept with her at all times – even when imprisoned in the Temple Tower during the French Revolution. Just before her execution, she handed the perfume to her closest friend and confidante, the Marquise de Tourzel, for safe-keeping. The original vial is still in the possession of the Tourzel family, locked away in their Burgundy château.

The formula for the queen's perfume was written down by the

royal perfumer's apprentice, Pierre François Lubin, under the coded name of 'jardin secret' (or 'secret garden'). Discovered two hundred years later in the archives of the Lubin perfume house, the long-lost perfume was finally released under the name 'Black Jade' in 2012.

The rare animals

The Siamese Crocodile, Pygmy Hippo, Sumatran Tiger and Black-tailed Python are all real species, and all are rare or endangered.

Siamese Crocodiles are relatively small freshwater crocodiles from South-east Asia. Adults average three metres in length but can grow to four metres. They are now virtually extinct in the wild, apart from some areas of Cambodia.

Pygmy Hippos are nocturnal, which is why Ruby never saw the one in her garden.

Sumatran Tigers are one of the smallest of all tiger subspecies, with darker, thicker stripes than those found in other parts of the world. There are fewer than 500 in the wild, living exclusively on the island of Sumatra.

Black-tailed Pythons live predominantly in the Indian subcontinent. They are endangered as a result of being hunted for their beautiful patterned skins.

Bowerbirds are also real. Native to Australia and New Guinea, they are songbirds known primarily for their extraordinary courtship behaviour. To attract a mate, the male bowerbird builds a complex nest structure called a 'bower', decorating it with sticks, acorns, leaves and shiny or brightly-coloured objects and flowers.

The extinct 'Lapis Bowerbird' was invented for the purposes of this book. However, there *is* a real bird – the Satin Bowerbird – which, like the imaginary bird in this story, almost exclusively decorates its bower with blue objects.

A note on
Lorelei von Leyden's perfume code
*by Marcus du Sautoy, supergeek
consultant to Ruby Redfort*

Our noses actually work like a code cracker. Inside them we have things called olfactory receptors. In humans there are about 1,000 different sorts of receptors. When molecules enter the nose, some of these receptors will be turned on when they react with the molecule. Once the receptors are turned on they send information via nerves to the brain. The brain then interprets the information and registers whether you are smelling a strawberry or a fish or something else.

Because the smell turns some of the receptors on and the rest remain off, this means that each smell is like a piece of binary code made out of a sequence of 0s and 1s. Because there are so many different receptors in the nose, humans can detect up to 10,000 unique smells.

Lorelei von Leyden's smell code is based on the fact that each time you register a smell your nose is using these receptors to identify the molecule that corresponds to that smell. Each molecule is made up out of a combination of atoms from the periodic table, and as Ruby learns from the book she reads within this book, often substances that smell contain benzene rings.

For example, if you smell almonds then your nose has probably detected the molecule called *benzaldehyde*. This consists of 7 carbon atoms, 6 hydrogen atoms and 1 oxygen atom. It is written C_7H_6O. But it is the shape of the molecule which is key to von Leyden's smell code.

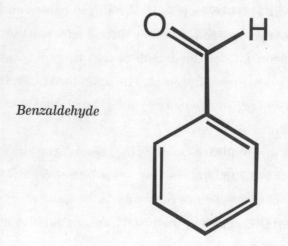

Benzaldehyde

Note that there is a carbon atom at every point where two or more lines meet and five invisible hydrogen atoms too – it's just a convention of chemical notation not to show them.

This particular molecule is arranged with 6 carbon atoms in a hexagon – the benzene ring – and then there is one interesting twig sticking out of the ring which is made up of the seventh carbon atom joined to an oxygen atom and a hydrogen atom. It is this twig that corresponds to a letter in von Leyden's code. In this case the letter T.

Benzaldehyde is a very simple molecule, but it is possible to have quite a complicated system of twigs sprouting out of these carbon rings and each molecule will have its own smell. For example five different smells (thyme, vanilla, anise, cinnamon and orange) were used to encode the message **WHY THE DELAY**.

Working backwards, you could, if you wanted to, change your name into a combination of smells that encode your name, giving you your very own personalised perfume.

If you want to play around with making molecules and seeing what they might smell like, there is a tool that allows you to do this at *www.chemspider.com*

Not every chemical has been made by chemists so the smell you come up with might not be known yet!

Marcus du Sautoy.

Acknowledgments

Thank you to Rachel Folder for some very good plotting ideas, and for writing them on big sheets of paper in very neat handwriting and sticking them up on the walls. Thank you to AD for chatting through the story and helping me sift out the not so good bits. Thank you to my editor Nick Lake for untangling a tangled book, David Mackintosh for beautiful design and illustration, Lucy Vanderbilt for her American-speak. Thank you to Le Labo for letting me sniff their delicious smells and scents and explaining how they become perfume, and thank you to Marcus du Sautoy for his brilliance in sniffing out a very tricky code.

Thank you to HarperCollins for providing me with a warm glassy office to work in when my central heating failed me.

And as always thank you to my publisher and editor Ann-Janine Murtagh, for her late-into-the-evening editing, advice and kind words.